THE WOLF
&
THE RAVEN

ALSO BY THE AUTHOR

Lady of Light
Lady of Darkness
Brisingamon
White Mare, Red Stallion
Silverhair the Wanderer
The Earthstone
The Paradise Tree
The Sea Star
The Wind Crystal
The White Raven
The Serpent's Tooth

THE WOLF
&
THE RAVEN

A Novel

·

Diana L. Paxson

WILLIAM MORROW AND COMPANY, INC.
NEW YORK

It is the policy of William Morrow and Company, Inc., and its imprints and affiliates, recognizing the importance of preserving what has been written, to print the books we publish on acid-free paper, and we exert our best efforts to that end.

Library of Congress Cataloging-in-Publication Data

Paxson, Diana L.
     The wolf and the raven / Diana L. Paxson.
         p.   cm.
     ISBN 0-688-10821-0
     1. Siegfried (Legendary character)—Fiction.   I. Title.
PS3566.A897W64   1993
813'.54—dc20   92-27416
                                                                         CIP

Printed in the United States of America

First Edition

1   2   3   4   5   6   7   8   9   10

BOOK DESIGN BY LISA STOKES

To Jim

May the wolf always run free.

Foreword

*"My forefathers to fame are known,
of myself I say the same...."*

Fafnirsmál: 4

Like the legend of King Arthur, the story of Siegfried the Volsung is known worldwide, the heritage of all who speak a Germanic language. This is due in part to Wagner's cycle of heroic operas, *The Ring of the Nibelung*, which has not only endured but seems to be increasing in popularity. Wagner's genius was to extract from the cauldron of myth and history a plot of tragic inevitability with a subtext that focused some of the nineteenth century's deepest concerns. But like all great myths, this tale has something new to say each time it is told.

For the Vikings, the form it took was the *Völsungasaga* and the poetic fragments in the *Elder Edda;* for medieval Germany, the *Nibelungenlied.* The story of the dragon-slayer is even told in *Beowulf.* Since I first studied the history of the Migrations Period in college, the story of Siegfried and Brunhilde has fascinated me, and I believe that it has something to offer us today.

In the fifth century, the Germanic tribes moved from the world of myth into that of history. The Rhineland was a country of emigrants, uprooted from their old lands and gods and seeking to connect with the new. At the century's beginning, all the world seemed to be in motion. By its end, unsettled as life remained, it had become possible to glimpse the outlines of a new age. This great movement of peoples is the foundation of the trilogy, which focuses on the moment when one tribe, the Burgundians, was caught between the chaos of the barbarian world and the decaying rigidity of Rome. It is the pressure of this historical moment, acting upon the characters, that produces the story.

It seemed appropriate, when writing about a culture for which three was a sacred number, to cast the story in the form of a trilogy, the first book dealing with the formation of the major characters; the middle volume with their tragic conflict; and the final book with the consequences of that tragedy. The first book therefore focuses on individuals, Sigfrid and Brunahild; the second on the tribe, the Burgunds; and the third on the Huns and the Romano-German world.

As the folk of the fifth century tribes were molded by their environment and history, so were their heroes. Wagner felt it necessary to add a prequel, *Das Rheingold,* to explain his characters' dilemma. Wagner also summarized and simplified a great deal of legend by making Siegfried the child of Sigmund and his sister Sieglinde, instead of the child by Sigmund's third wife Hjordis, as he is in the *Völsungasaga.* It is the latter, original version which I have followed. However, I have contented myself with a prologue.

The key is family history. Sigfrid's childhood is haunted by the feud between the Hundings and the Volsungs that began when his half-brother Helgi killed King Hunding. By the time the story opens, it has destroyed most of both families, including Sigfrid's father, Sigmund. And yet it is a second family tragedy that holds the greatest potential danger—that of the children of the Earthshaper, Hreidmaro. As in Wagner, the theft of a treasure is the source of the evil, the hoard of Andvari, which is stolen to pay the fine for the death of Ottar. This desecrated wealth eventually destroys all who desire it. The tragedy of Ragan and his brother Fafnar is only the beginning.

Acknowledgments

I would like particularly to thank the following friends for their advice and support in this endeavor—Tom Johnson, for sharing research and insights during his doctoral studies; Helmut Pesch, my German editor, for believing that an American could tackle this project, and attempting to improve my German; Hubert and Lore Strassl, my translators; Barbara Wackernagel, Bernhard Hennen and all those who helped me to better understand their country; Siegfried Kutin, for his enthusiasm and help in finding resources in this country; Jim Hrisoulas, for checking my smithcraft; Laurel Olsen and the other members of Hrafnar, who have been my companions in the search; and the Master of Huginn and Munnin, to whom this story belongs. Much that is good in the tale is due to their assistance. My mistakes are my own!

Contents

Foreword   7

Acknowledgments   9

Characters   15

Prologue: 21
    ANDVARI'S TALE

ONE: THE WELL OF FATE   25
    Salt-springs of Halle,
    Borders of the Burgund Lands
    Milk Moon, A.D. 410

TWO: WILD GEESE FLYING   39
    Hiloperic's Hall, Frankish Homeland
    Winter Moon, A.D. 410

THREE: THE HILL OF THE HIGH ONE   55
    Taunus Mountains
    Eostara Moon, A.D. 411

FOUR: TRACKING   69
    Forest of the Teutones
    A.D. 412–413

FIVE: RAVEN IN THE SNOW 84
Taunus Mountains
Yule Moon, A.D. 413

SIX: WOLFSONG 99
Forest of the Teutones,
Hiloperic's Hold
Harvest, Litha Moon, A.D. 415

SEVEN: THE MISTS OF THE RHENUS 116
Burgund Homeland
Haying Moon, A.D. 416

EIGHT: THE WALKYRJA'S ROAD 133
Land of the Huns
Blood Moon, A.D. 416

NINE: THE RUNE TREE 149
Taunus Mountains
Eggtide Moon, A.D. 417

TEN: WEREGILD 166
King Alb's Hold
Haying Moon, A.D. 417

ELEVEN: A GATHERING OF RAVENS 182
Holy Hill, Burgund Lands
Taunus Mountains
Summer, A.D. 418

TWELVE: THE SWORD SPELL 196
Forest of the Teutones
Summer, A.D. 418

THIRTEEN: THE HARVEST OF YGG 213
Plain of the Moenus
Harvest, Waxing Moon, A.D. 418

FOURTEEN: THE SHAPE OF FEAR   227
    Land of the Hermunduri, Wurm Fell
    Harvest, Full of the Moon, A.D. 418

FIFTEEN: KINDRED   244
    Wurm Fell, the Rhenus
    Harvest, Waning Moon, A.D. 418

SIXTEEN: JUDGMENT OF FIRE   257
    Taunus Mountains
    Harvest, Waning Moon, A.D. 418

SEVENTEEN: AWAKENING   272
    Taunus Mountains
    Blood Moon, A.D. 418

EIGHTEEN: WINTER STORM   289
    Taunus Mountains
    Frost Moon, A.D. 418

Background & Sources   303
Family Trees   311
Glossary of Names   312

Characters

() = characters dead before the story begins

GODS:

The Aesir:
Wodan, of the many names, lord of the Aesir, worldwalker, god of
    wordcraft and warcraft and magic, appears as Farmamann and Helm-
    bari
Fricca, the weaver of fate, wife of Wodan
Donar, the thunderer, god of storms and strength
Tiw, god of war and justice
Baldur, the Beautiful, son of Wodan and Fricca
Loki, the trickster, a Jotun allied with the gods

The Wanes (Vanir):
Fro, god of luck and fertility, brother/lover of Froja
Froja, *dis* of the Vanir, of love and fertility
Hludana, goddess of the hearth
Erda, Earth Mother

Demigods or Legendary figures:
Andvari, an earth elemental who in pike shape guarded the Nibelung
    treasure
Frodi, aspect of Fro, legendary Danish king

Ingvio, aspect of Fro, ancestor of the Ingviones (Franks)
Iscio, ancestor of the Iscaevones (Saxons)
Irmino, ancestor of the Herminones (Thuringians)
Wolse, a god of fertility in the eastern lands
Hermundurus, first-century leader of Cherusci and Hermunduri against
    the Romans
Airmanareik, third-century king of the Goths, defeated by the incom-
    ing Huns

BURGUNDS:

(Uote—ancestress of the Niflungar, people of the misty north)
Gibicho, chieftain of the Niflungar, *hendinos* of the Burgunds
Grimahild, his queen
Gundohar, his oldest son, later, king
Godomar (Godo), his middle son
Gislahar, his posthumous son
Gudrun, his daughter
Hagano, Grimahild's son by a man of the earthfolk
Ostrofrid, lawspeaker (*sinista*)
Clan chiefs:
    Heribard, a counselor
    Ordwini, Dragobald's son
    Sindald
    Unald

Attached to the household:
Father Priscus—Catholic priest
Father Severin—Arian priest

MARCOMANNI:

Heimar, husband of Bertriud and foster-father of Brunahild
Brettald, chieftain

ALBINGS:

Hiloperic, king
Hlodomar, his younger brother
Albald, his youngest son
Alb, his oldest son, later king
Hiordisa, daughter of Eylimi and Lyngheide, widow of Sigmund the
Wolsung

Albdrud and Arnegundis, daughters of Hiordisa and Alb
Geirrod, son of a clan chief
Eberwald, Ruodperch, Herimod, Werinhar—men of Alb's houseguard
Octa, called Hengest, an Anglian *"wrecce,"* follower of Hlodomar, a
survivor of the battle at Finnesburg

SONS OF HUNDING:

Heming, a follower of Hlodomar
Lyngvi
Eyolf

WOLSUNGS:

(Sigi the wolfshead, son of Wodan)
(Reri the great, son of Sigi)
(Wolse the fruitful, son of Reri)
(Sigmund the skinwalker, killed by the sons of Hunding)
(Sintarfizilo, son of Sigmund and his sister Signy)
(Helgi, son of Sigmund and Borghild, who married the Walkyrja Sig-
runa)
SIGFRID, son of Sigmund and Hiordisa

EARTHFOLK:

(Hreidmaro the Shaper)
(Lyngheide, his daughter, wife of Eylimi and mother of Hiordisa)
(Ottar, the otter)
FAFNAR, the battle-wurm, a berserker
RAGAN, the master-smith

ALAMANNI:

Liudegar
Liudegast

HUNS AND ASSOCIATES:

(Uldin, Hun chieftain who defeated Airmanareik)
Kharaton, overking of the Huns
Ruga, king of the eastern Huns
Mundzuk, his brother
Bladarda, son of Mundzuk, prince of the Acatiri Huns

Attila, son of Mundzuk, warleader of his clan
Aetius, a Roman, former Hun hostage and ally of Attila
Ragnaris, son of Kursik, a Hun/Goth warrior, one of Attila's captains
Turgun, a servant of Attila
Bertriud, Bladarda's older daughter
BRUNAHILD, Bladarda's younger daughter

THE WALKYRIUN:

Hlutgard—leader of the Walkyriun
Hadugera, the midwife
Swanborg
Thrudrun, runemistress
Hrodlind, herbmistress
Huld, wisewoman
Randgrid, warmistress
Golla, warmistress, Randgrid's lover
Raganleob

Brunahild's Nine:
Svala (the swallow) (Burgund)
Frojavigis (Burgund)
Ricihild
Liudwif
Galemburgis (Alamanni)
Adelburga
Donarhild
Eormanna
Fridigund

Students: Unna, Domfrada, Nanduhild

Rhinegold! Rhinegold!
Pure Gold!
Oh, if only thy flawless treasure
still shone in the deep!

Richard Wagner: *Das Rheingold*

Prologue  Andvari's Tale

Там is a stillness beyond time in the waters at the heart of the world. The water is Erda's blood, the life that flows through Her body. My home is in those depths. I am Andvari, Her servant, the silver pike-shape that glimmers in the darkness. The echo of all that passes in Middle Earth comes to me.

Once I watched over a deep pool below a waterfall. Tears of the sun gleamed bright beneath those waters, and bones of the moon, fashioned into things of beauty by the clever hands of humankind. As the sunwheel turned, the hoard I guarded grew. Gifts to the gods they gave, thanks to the Goddess from whom all life was born.

There came a day when a net of light cut through the waters, spun from the greed and the need of men. Folk who served new tribes had fashioned it; the might of their magic bound me. They drew me gasping into the air, and I heard their laughter.

"Canst swim in the skies, scaled one?" The voice seared like venom. "We are cold, here beside thy chill stream. Bring us that which glows so brightly beneath thy waters, and we will let thee go!" He was thin and russet of hair, and the spirit power was strong in him, to speak to me and understand my replies.

"The fire of the flood will consume you, foolish men!" I told him.

My captor looked quickly, as if for approval, at a tall man with the staff of a lore speaker in his hand.

"Tell him that the fang of a berserker will bite us if he does not help," said the tall man, but he was frowning. "We must pay the weregild for Ottar with this gold."

"Speak, wriggler!" The foxy man shook me. "Or I shall dunk thee in that river that drowns all who lie!"

"Truth, only truth, do I tell you, who say you serve the gods—" I cried. "These things were given to the Lady in return for the goods that come out of her body. Thus is the balance maintained. Take it, and though you keep the gold, your luck will leave you. Greed begets greed."

"Enough of your curses!" screamed the one who held me. I saw the bright gleam of a hook in his hand.

"I do not curse," I gasped, "and yet woeful will be the wyrd of those who keep this gold from the Goddess." And then he jabbed the hook through my gill. The spells set upon it compelled me. I could neither speak nor change shape nor resist the will of those who tossed me back into the pool.

Piece by piece I brought up the treasure: the spiraled bracelets and neck rings of twisted gold, the buckles, the brooches and the scattered beads. Axeheads of polished bronze I clamped in my strong jaws, and leaf-shaped swordblades, and a great oblong shieldskin with red enamel on the boss. I brought them cauldrons of silver and gilded bronze, and a fleshhook adorned with figures of waterbirds. I fetched up beakers and flagons and images of the gods. And still their greed grew.

I transported treasure until twilight's shadows fell across the water.

"This is the hoard," I said to them. "Now are you satisfied?"

"What is that," asked the tall man, "that still flames in the rays of the setting sun?"

I kept silent, but my captor twisted the hook cruelly.

"A round of gold," he answered, "that shines like Brisingamen . . ."

"I see a rod that glitters in the water as Gungnir glows when it flies from Wodan's hand. . . ." the lore master said then.

"Bring them, and we will set thee free," said the foxy man. I kept silent, for without those things, this place would lose its power. Then with chanted runes the loremaster bound me. Though my spirit raged, I drew up the rod from the depths of the pool.

Long ago, it had been a wand of kingship. Frodi himself had carried it when he gave good laws to his people and blessed the growing grain. But to the loremaster it seemed a spear. Runes of power he scratched into the gold with the point of his dagger; runes of wit and will, of the laws that bound the human tribes, and of justice, though he had showed little to me.

"Once, our god was a worker of magic," said the priest. "But when hunger forced us from our homeland, Wodan was the one who led us, curious as we were, to see new lands and learn new ways. Now we need a king-god to lead us against the Eagles, so we call our god All-Father and War Father. Let this be his spear!"

Once more he chanted over the rod. "Gungnir I name you," he murmured. "And with your might I will have mastery."

I struggled fiercely when they put me into the water again to retrieve the ring that was the heart of the hoard, breeding gold like the ring Draupnir as folk were drawn by its gleam to bring their own offerings. But the compulsion could not be resisted. And so the ring came forth from the womb of the waters, and the light of the dying sun turned it to a circle of fire.

"Brisingamen I name you," the loremaster said. "Runes of prosperity I grave upon your gold. With luck and love I sign you, fields heavy with harvest, wombs great with child, flocks and herds that cover the land." He held up the neck ring, turning it so the newly written runes glinted with a light of their own.

"And you I shall keep also. A priestess shall wear you." He laughed softly. "And when I lie with her, we shall renew the world!"

The treasure filled two leather sacks. But the loremaster hid the rod and the ring within the breast of his tunic. When all had been loaded, the men laughed again, and threw me back into the water like a smolt too small for the cauldron.

They did not return, nor did other men come there as once they had come at sowing and harvest, to make their offerings. The pool was barren. From the waterfall the voice of the Goddess lamented her loss. After a time I left it, moving downstream with the flow of the waters to the river men call Rhenus, the life-blood of this land.

I did not curse the treasure, and yet a curse is on it. I wait, a silver gleam in the waters, until the rod and the ring shall return to the depths once more.

Chapter 1 The Well of Fate

The Salt-springs of Halle,
Borders of the Burgund Lands
Milk Moon, A.D. 410

The sound of the people gathering for the festival was like the roar of a flooding river, but the stream below ran chuckling between reedy islets. The murmur that rose from the encampment on the broad shelf above the narrow valley came from the human tide that was growing ever greater as more of the Burgund clans came in.

Their allies the Marcomanni were already encamped on the ridge above the village on the other side of the stream. As the wind changed, their noise added a deeper note to the sound. The yellow-haired girl who was picking her way along the bank paused, listening, and shivered. It was only the voices of men and women, but from here the growing roar was like the rising of a river whose flood could carry whole peoples away.

Soon the sun would sink behind the clouds, but overhead, the sky was still clear. Did the stream that glittered so enticingly ahead of her run salt, or was it some magic of the village-folk that made the precious brine well up out of the ground?

Slowly, because her mother had commanded her to be careful of her new blue gown, Gudrun picked her way toward the stream. Here it broadened to flow between marshy islets connected by log bridges and stepping-stones. The thatched huts of the village of Halle clung to the steep slope of the far hillside. One of the islands was fenced in by a palisade of logs. That must be the spring where the people of the old race did their magic to bring the salt from the ground.

As Gudrun stepped onto a stone that jutted into the stream it tilted, and she grabbed for support. Something slick and moist and alive landed in her hand; she shrieked and sat down suddenly in the stream. As her sight cleared, she saw above her a pointed, sun-browned girl's face framed by tightly braided hair with the sheen of a raven's wing.

"Woodswife! Troll!" The words were followed by a spate of invective in a strange guttural tongue. "You made me lose him!"

"Who?" Gudrun levered herself upright, striving to meet that scornful glare.

"My frog. You had him in your hand!" The hard hands released her, and the other girl sat back, shaking her head. The stranger's eyes were as green as the stream. "Even a blindworm could tell that stone would turn."

"But not Gudrun—" a deeper voice echoed. "She has always been clumsy as a cow. You were lucky she did not land on you! Shall I compensate you for your loss by beating her?"

Gudrun felt a familiar sinking in the pit of her stomach and turned. A wide-shouldered young man whose ash-brown hair clung to his head in a mat of tight curls was watching them from across the stream. It was Hagano, already dressed for the festival in his new embroidered tunic of saffron cloth.

The other girl rose in a single supple motion that Gudrun envied all the more as her own bruises began to throb.

"You are an ox if you think I need help from you!" she spat. "Go away!"

Hagano stopped laughing when she scooped up a handful of mud. It splattered at his feet, and he stepped back as she reached for more.

"Go!" she cried. "That was just a warning. The next one will land in the middle of that fine tunic you have on."

Gudrun saw angry color rising beneath his fair skin, but Hagano was retreating. "I thank you!" she said as he disappeared beyond the willow trees that fringed the shore.

"Huh!" The other girl grinned. "So you are Gudrun? Well, I am called Brunahild, and perhaps I will beat you myself. Are you not afraid?"

"You have the right. I made you lose something, though I did not mean to. It was worth it to see Hagano run!" Gudrun rested her head on her bent knees.

"Well you are lucky, for I don't stay mad long. He *was* funny when he ran away. But why did he want to beat you?"

"He is my brother, and he hates me."

"Hmm—he does not look like you. . . ."

Gudrun looked up quickly, but there was only interest in Brunahild's bright gaze. They were the same size, for Gudrun was big-boned like all her kin, but she thought that Brunahild had probably a season or two more than her own eight winters. Suddenly she wanted to trust the other girl.

"Hagano is the son of my mother, but some say that his father was a man of the earthfolk. No one says it aloud, for she has powerful kin and is skilled in spells. But folk whisper, you see, and he feels it. I am the youngest, but everyone knows King Gibicho is my father, so Hagano hates me."

"And are you always so clumsy?" asked Brunahild.

"When Hagano is around." Gudrun colored again. "But he is clever, and never hurts me when there is anyone to see."

"I am glad to have saved you some trouble then, and caused some for *him!*"

Gudrun shrugged. "My mother will beat me anyway for spoiling my gown!"

Brunahild gave her an appraising frown. "It's not so bad. It is only your back that the mud really stained. It would be covered if we combed out your hair. Don't you think I know how? I do have a comb, and a fine one too!"

Gudrun realized that her first impression of Brunahild had been misleading. Though the other girl's gown was soaked to the knees, it was of good crimson cloth, and the belt that held in her mud-smeared wrap was studded and tipped with gold. The fibulae that pinned the wrap at the shoulders were gilded as well, and a pair of red leather slippers lay on the bank, tied together by their thongs.

"Are you Marcomanni?" Gudrun asked, trying to place the unfamiliar lilt in Brunahild's words.

"My sister's husband, Heimar, is a chieftain among them—" Brunahild shrugged. "They fostered me. But my father is Bladarda, son of Mundzuk, of the royal house of the Huns."

Gudrun blinked. She knew of the Huns, who had begun moving westward after the Burgunds came down from the shores of the northern sea. Now the lands from the Danu to the eastern plains were under their rule. No wonder the Marcomanni, their nearest western neighbors, had been happy to marry one of their great chieftains to a great-niece of the king. Gudrun had seen their warriors, broad-chested, bandy-legged men who rode as if they and their horses were a single being. It was clear that this girl was warrior-bred.

"The daughter of Gibicho, first *hendinos* of the Burgunds and chief of the Niflungar, thanks the daughter of Bladarda, khan of the Huns." She fumbled open the pouch that hung from her belt to find her own comb, carved from deer horn and ornamented across the arch with a series of concentric circles, and offered it to the other girl.

Brunahild grinned. "Is this how the daughters of princes seal alliances?" She opened her own pouch and began to unload its contents, a bone whistle, a tattered owl feather, and a smooth white stone, and finally the comb of which she had boasted, still holding a few tangles of black hair.

"My uncle Attila gave this to me. It is made from the tusk of a great grey monster that lives in southern lands!"

"Ivory . . ." Gudrun fingered the smooth tines and the carved design of leaves and flowers, accepting the fact that she had been outdone. "It is very fair."

"It works," said Brunahild, slipping the horn comb into her own pouch and tying it shut once more. Gudrun nodded. As she started to get up, the glitter of the water caught her eye once more. She scooped up some in her hand.

"It is sweet," said Brunahild. "I already tasted it. The water only comes up salt at the sacred well."

Gudrun opened her fingers and let the liquid drain away. Then, feeling rather as if her pony had decided to run away with her, she got to her feet so that Brunahild could work on her hair.

Brunahild launched herself down the steep slope below the village shrine, heedless as her sister's protests faded behind her. Everyone else had already gone down to the stream. Bertriud was like a goose that had hatched a raven, thought Brunahild as she left the Marcomanni encampment behind her. The children of the village scampered up and down the path between their huts and the river a dozen times a day without falling. Why was her sister so afraid?

The folds of her wrap billowed around her like wings. And for a moment then it was like flying, with the wind stinging her skin and the world blurring by. She glimpsed the logs that had been piled for the bonfire, the images of the gods, the brightness of streamers and spring flowers that decorated the huts. Her feet went faster and faster until she was only kept upright by her speed. She felt a flicker of fear as she realized that she could not stop, but she did not want to. Surely if she could run fast enough, her momentum would carry her into the sky!

Time ceased. Brunahild floated through a world in which each pebble shone and every straw in the thatched roofs was a separate and perfect entity. She noticed everything and nothing, for all her attention was fixed on an outstretched hand and a woman's face that rose up before her, framed by the folds of a dark shawl.

And gradually inner and outer time achieved a harmony. Her feet moved more slowly, and then she was standing still, and all things were still around her, and the woman into whose eyes she stared the most unmoving of all. Brunahild heard her own heart pounding like an echo of the festival drum as the woman lowered her hand.

"Not thus, king's daughter, shall you soar the skies."

The voice of the woman was cold and clear. There was grey in the hair that showed beneath her shawl, but her face seemed ageless. Now Brunahild could see the gleam of silver at her neck and wrists, the band of interlaced swans worked in wool around the edge of her shawl. She leaned on a knobbed staff.

"But I think that you are one of those who can learn to journey between the worlds. . . ."

Brunahild blinked, and realized that two other women had appeared behind the first, a sturdy woman in middle life, and another just out of girlhood, both dressed in breeches and short tunics like men, and wearing swords. All of them wore their hair knotted at the back of the head with the remainder falling down in a long tail behind.

Wisewomen . . . witches . . . The other name came to her then, *Walkyriun . . .* the Choosers of the Slain. She had heard that some of the wisewomen who taught the magic of the tribes might be here, but she had never seen them before.

"Go now, and go slowly. We will speak again," the wisewoman said then. The Choosers had turned away, dismissing her, and Brunahild found herself able to move once more. She continued down the curving path that led to the river, thinking.

She had heard tales about the Walkyriun. The *kams* of the Huns could walk the spirit roads, raise storms, and harm or heal, but unless she went back to live with her father, she would not learn their magic. The magic of the salt-boilers belonged to the villagers alone. But the Choosers were the Sacred Women of the Germanic tribes. Would they teach a girl of the Huns?

The sound of singing roused her. They were starting the procession! Now she hurried, pushing through the edges of the crowd.

                         *   *   *

The west wind was herding clouds across the heavens. As the
light shifted from gold to silver and back again, Gundohar blinked,
seeing the world change with it from familiar reality to something
insubstantial and strange. He fought the feeling. A prince of the Burgunds ought to be watching the warriors who stood around him. But
his eye was drawn by the glitter of water that trickled from the rocky
bank upstream from the salt well into the fountain. A bower had been
built above it, and young girls dressed in white were adorning the
framework with creamy primroses and cowslips and the late violets
that still grew in the shade beneath the trees.

Idisi . . . he named them silently, at once uncomfortable and fascinated by the grace of slender arms, and the swell of a round breast
beneath a thin gown. He thought he had seen one once when he was
lost hunting; a white glimmer beside a forest pool. But these were
singing in the Gallic tongue, welcoming the summertide. Gundohar's
fingers twitched, wanting his harp.

The Burgunds were grouped to one side of the circle and the
Marcomanni on the other, with the village-folk between them, as if
both sides feared to reawaken the conflict whose resolution they were
celebrating. The younger warriors eyed each other like dogs in a new
territory. After last night's dancing, the drinking, and the boasting,
had continued for hours as they worked themselves up for the competitions to come. Gundohar grimaced. He had tried to keep pace
with the others, but a headache was all he found at the bottom of a
drinking horn.

Amber necklaces clicked softly as his mother leaned forward,
weathered and unyielding as a goddess-image carved from the trunk
of a tree. Gundohar eyed her nervously. Queen Grimahild collected
spells as a bard collected songs. Was she after the magic of the villagers
now? He wondered why. The offerings of food and ornaments they
were making to the fountain seemed much like the sacrifices the Burgunds offered to the spirits of the land on Walburga's Day.

His sister, Gudrun, edged away from the queen's side, and reached
up to squeeze his hand. Sometimes he thought she was the only one
in the family who understood him. His father seemed to view him as
a gaming piece to be moved at his will. Godomar thought only of
fighting, and Hagano was far too familiar with their mother's secrets
for Gundohar to share his own. Only to little Gudrun did he dare
admit that he did not really want to become a king. She was the only
one who knew his fear of shaming himself and his kin on the field of

play or war. News had come that Alaric and his Visigoths were marching on Rome. Gundohar wondered whether the Burgunds would expect him to do the same when he was king.

He felt Gudrun stiffen beneath his hand. Then she tugged at his sleeve.

"I have to pee."

"You can't leave now—" He grabbed as she started to ease away.

"Do you want me to splatter your new shoes?"

Gundohar let go of Gudrun's gown, feeling the slow flush stain his fair skin.

"Tell Mother I'll be back soon!" She grinned up at him and ducked under his arm. The maidens had finished with the flowers and were beginning to dance. With a feeling of helplessness that was all too familiar, Gundohar realized that his sister had disappeared.

"I hoped you would be here," said Gudrun as she eased past two of the villagers to meet Brunahild, taking care to keep them between her and her brother's confused stare. Poor Gundohar, always so determined to do the right thing, but so easily persuaded if you knew how! She hoped he would not suffer when their mother realized that she was gone.

"Can you understand their singing?" asked Brunahild.

"They are asking the spirit of the fountain to keep the sweet waters flowing, to give life to the land." The village-folk had baked a cake as broad as a cartwheel. Now their headman broke off a piece and threw it into the stream.

"My brother-in-law Heimar says that the same families have worked the salt-springs as long as the Marcomanni have been here," Brunahild said thoughtfully. "The secret of how to get salt from the brine is passed down from father to son."

"How long?" asked Gudrun, staring at her round-eyed.

"Before my people or your people," Brunahild answered slowly, drawing her friend away down the path. "Maybe even before the Gauls came here. . . ."

Gudrun shivered, wondering who the first folk to learn the secret had been. Compared to the villagers, both Huns and Burgunds were strangers in this land. The singing behind them began again.

"And they will always be here, won't they?" she said then. "Even when no one remembers our names."

"I will not be forgotten!"

Gudrun looked at Brunahild and laughed suddenly, but the words had made her shiver, as if the other girl were casting a spell. "You boast like the warriors in my father's houseguard, who swore to win all the competitions today."

Brunahild's face reddened dangerously. "Do I? Then I challenge you! The salt-springs will be the last stop for the procession. Let us run ahead and look into the well!"

"You are mad!" said Gudrun with conviction. "They do not even let their own children see."

"The well must hold a mighty magic! The spirits will not be offended if we make our own offerings!" Brunahild held up one of her golden fibulae so that it flashed in the sun, and then, as Gudrun still hesitated, she laughed. "Well, are you afraid?"

"By the gifts we exchanged I am bound to help you," said Gudrun grimly, feeling the pony begin to run away with her again. "But I don't see what good can come of it. . . ."

The sound of singing grew fainter as they followed the path downstream. The shadows beneath the venerable willows grew ever darker as the clouds thickened above. Brunahild was frowning as she led the way, and Gudrun wondered if she was having second thoughts after all. Why had she let Brunahild persuade her to come? Was it perhaps because even danger was better than letting her mother's shadow slowly turn her to stone?

They stepped carefully, following the logs laid from stone to stone across a series of marshy islets where earth and water exchanged places each time the floods receded in the spring. Ruddy-breasted ducks and mallards paused in their feeding as the girls passed, but all the village-folk must be attending the ceremonies.

Suddenly it seemed very still. The gate to the palisade around the salt-spring was latched, but the great crossbar had not been drawn. Doubtless it had never occurred to the villagers that anyone would dare to break their taboo. Swiftly Brunahild slipped through, and Gudrun followed, sighing with relief as the gate swung shut behind her. They were on forbidden ground, but at least now they could not be seen.

From the gateposts the bleached skulls of last year's sacrifices stared at them empty-eyed. Ovens with fired-clay simmering basins set into their tops were placed at intervals around the well, which was protected by a coping of stone. But the ovens were cold, the place swept clean in preparation for its blessing. Carefully the girls crept to the edge. Two posts carved with zigzag meanders supported a crossbar from which hung the buckets that brought up the brine, and more posts held up the thatched roof that sheltered the well.

The silence intensified. The well was the height of a tall man across, the greenish water an arm's length below the edge. The dank odor came to her strongly, with a strange sharp tang. Gudrun leaned farther over the water.

"It is the same as the level of the river," said the other girl. Gudrun turned. There was an odd glitter in Brunahild's eyes.

"What's wrong? It was your idea to spy on the salt-magic. Are you afraid?" asked Gudrun.

"Of course not!" Brunahild said swiftly. "But I don't want to get you in trouble. All I swore to do was to look at the spring."

Gudrun suppressed a smile. Why was Brunahild so worried? She could hear only the faintest of whispers as the spring water lapped against the well's coping, and the sighing of the rising wind in the willow trees. From the depths the water welled upward, forever re-filling, forever becoming, forever renewed.

"It is sacred. Even if we were wrong to come here, we have to make the offerings we vowed."

Brunahild hugged herself, shivering, but Gudrun took a deep breath and looked into the water again.

"Do you think this is one of the wells that lies at the roots of the Worldtree?" she said softly.

"Wodan gave an eye for a drink from the well of memory," said Brunahild with a flash of her old spirit, "but this one will get no more than a gold brooch from me!"

"Let it be the Well of Wyrd, then, where the Norns dip up the dooms of men," said Gudrun. She took the long-handled ladle that hung from one of the posts and scooped up some of the water. At the first taste she grimaced, then sipped again, frowning.

"What is it like?" asked Brunahild.

"Salt . . . and something else, like liquid stone." Gudrun held out the ladle. "I dare you—"

Brunahild glared at her, then grabbed the dipper and drank down all the liquid left inside.

"Now we must make our offerings!"

Overhead, the sky had darkened; the silence grew heavy, as if Someone were waiting to hear what she would say. Gooseflesh pebbled Gudrun's arms as she pulled off a bracelet of gilded bronze.

"Spirit of the saltwell, forgive if we have offended and accept our sacrifice. Fair one, show me my future. Grant me good fortune!" Leaning forward, she tossed the ornament in.

Ripples rolled sluggishly through dark water. Gudrun hung over the coping, willing herself to stare without blinking though her eyes teared and stung. Slowly, the surface stilled, and a pale shape glimmered back at her.

"What do you see?" came the voice of Brunahild behind her.

"My face in the water."

Brunahild leaned closer and suddenly Gudrun saw their faces reflected together, fair and dark, distorted into a single image by the upwelling of the spring. Then it became the face of a woman with waving hair that spread out in ripples of shadow. Her eyes were wells of darkness through which Gudrun saw a great river flowing, and then a vast, heaving expanse that she somehow knew must be the sea.

By water shall all gifts come to you, and by fire be taken away. . . .

Gudrun felt herself being drawn downward as the words formed in her awareness, then the image shattered as Brunahild flung her brooch into the spring.

She sat down hard on the damp earth and stayed there, breathing in ragged gasps. Suddenly there was a blink of light and a distant mutter of thunder. Brunahild sprang back with a cry.

"What was it?" asked Gudrun. She put her arms around the other girl and felt the tremors that shook Brunahild's thin frame.

"The Eye . . . An Eye staring out of the dark. Its brightness seared my vision. When I close my own eyes I see it still," whispered Brunahild. Presently she pulled away, trying to smile. "For me, it was the Well of Mimir after all. . . ."

A wind had sprung up suddenly, and even in the protected enclosure they could feel the damp breath of the approaching storm.

"We must go." Brunahild sprang to her feet again, and this time Gudrun agreed.

As they slid through the gate, sound throbbed suddenly around them. Brunahild dragged Gudrun forward, but there was only one bridge from the island, and even as they reached it, the leaders of the procession appeared through the trees.

Brunahild stopped in her tracks, and Gudrun bumped into her. In moments the first cry had become a babble of Gallic.

"Unholy!" someone shouted in the language of the tribes. "Hold them, they have seen the shrine!"

*   *   *

The sun was going down in a great conflagration of fire and cloud. Brunahild watched it intently, fighting panic as the soft bulk of her sister Bertriud pressed against her on one side and the harder shape of Heimar held her on the other. At least her hands were not tied. On the other side of the circle Gudrun was imprisoned between her brothers. Sturdy though she was, with her fair hair in tangles and her grey eyes reddened by weeping, she seemed almost fragile standing there.

Would it be worse, Brunahild wondered, to face a mother's fury or a sister's pain? Bertriud and Heimar had made sure she understood just how she had shamed the family. But perhaps they would not have to bear it long. In the center of the slope the stacked logs of the bonfire were waiting. In years when a sacrifice was needed to avert disaster from the village, more than wood had been burned on the Beltane pyre.

Did her actions require such a compensation? Surely they had done the well no harm. Brunahild tried to remember why she had been so eager to see the salt-spring, but she understood only that yet again her passions had outrun wisdom. She drew in a deep breath of damp air. It had rained as they brought her here, and the clouds overhead promised more.

A spark caught her eye as the punkwood banked around the firedrills the men were twirling began to smolder. Deft hands thrust in tinder to feed the infant blaze. A great shout shook the shadows as fire blazed against the embers of the sky. From torch to torch sped the flame, and suddenly the faces of the people leaped into visibility once more, gilded like the faces carved on the godpoles by the light of the fire.

The tree-trunk figure of the Goddess sprang into hard relief, the firelight gilding her neck ring and shadowing the deeply carved joining of her thighs. The grain-crowned barley god was behind her, a jutting branch fashioned into his phallus. Flanked by the horse standard of the Marcomanni and the battle-wurm of the Burgunds stood a tree carved with the face of Wodan, its body his rune-carved spear.

Brunahild flinched. The eye on the right side of the god's head was a crudely carved sphere whose gaze seemed to follow the viewer, but the empty socket on his left was worse. She had seen what that shadow hid when she looked into the well.

From beneath a thatched shelter came the steady beat of a drum as the elders moved into the circle. She saw the Burgund *hendinos*, Gibicho, with his lawspeaker Ostrofrid and his chieftains around him, and Brettald of the Marcomanni, and behind them old Drostagnos, speaker for the elders of Halle.

The worst they can do is to kill me. . . . she told herself. *And the fire is a clean death. Will Bertriud weep, or will she be relieved?*

Self-pity could not change the fact that a few moments of misguided curiosity had put her kindred in jeopardy. *If the villagers do not punish me,* she thought miserably, *my own people surely will!*

And she had not even got what she was after. She had gone to the well seeking knowledge and instead had found fear.

Hers was not the only case to be judged before the festival continued. There was an accusation of cattle stealing, and compensation awarded for an arm broken in the wrestling. The wind gusted around them, whipping the torches into long streamers of flame. Brunahild shivered at the occasional spattering of rain. If the logs of the bonfire grew too wet to burn, it would be the worst of omens.

Her gut tensed as old Drostagnos stepped forward.

"Two of your women have committed sacrilege—they must be given to us to expiate their crime."

"They are girls, children!" answered the Burgund lawspeaker. "And they did no harm."

"They saw the hallows. They stole water from the well without making the necessary prayers and offerings. If the well-spirit refuses her bounty because of it, you will suffer as well as we."

"Placate the spirit with a greater offering. We will pay for the daughter of Gibicho, and the Marcomanni for their child. What weregild do you desire?"

Brunahild's father was too far away to help her, if he even cared. The tribes would pay, and never let either girl forget what she had cost them. It might be better to die!

"We are being generous—" Ostrofrid went on, stroking his flowing beard. "We offer compensation for the insult to your honor, for who can say if any evil has been done? The girls say that they made their own offerings."

"We must know more," came a new voice, a woman's. The wisewoman whom Brunahild had met that morning moved forward like an extension of the shadows. "Let the maidens be questioned."

Heimar and Bertriud released Brunahild, who stepped boldly into the circle. Someone pushed Gudrun forward. Her fair skin was blotched with past weeping. Brunahild put an arm around the younger girl and turned to face the old men of the tribes.

"Let the punishment fall on me!" Her voice wavered only a little.

"It was my idea to look at the well, and I dared Gudrun to follow me!"

"We meant no harm!" Gudrun's voice broke on the words.

Brunahild lifted her chin. "We wanted to see what our fates would be. . . ." From the west came a blink of light and a mutter of thunder. Around her, folk were making signs of warding.

"And did you?"

"I saw a Lady," said Gudrun softly.

"I saw an Eye," added Brunahild, swallowing.

"In the well?" For the first time the wisewoman's calm was shaken. Her gaze flicked to the image that frowned at them from above. Brunahild shuddered, for who else could it be but the god? She could feel him drawing near on the wings of the storm.

"Listen to the finding of Hlutgard of the Walkyriun," the wise-woman said then. "Let the Burgunds give cattle for the insult to the village. The Lady has shown herself to their daughter, and there will be no harm. As for the other, she belongs to the god." As she spoke, the other Walkyriun had appeared behind her, hands on the hilts of their swords.

"Then let him claim her!" cried Drostagnos, his face working with rage and fear. "Let your Wodan show his favor by lighting our fire!"

Once more the thunder spoke, this time closer. Brunahild flinched, then thrust Gudrun away from her.

"I will not forget you!" Gudrun dashed tears from her eyes, then ran back to her brothers. In the face of the oldest, amazement was becoming admiration, but Brunahild knew that she had never been so afraid.

"Now shall your vision be tested," hissed Hlutgard. "Look into the heavens and lend your will to our calling, for if we fail, you will surely be their sacrifice!"

The Walkyriun took position around her, but Brunahild had no defense from the power she sensed approaching. From the priestesses came a low humming that intensified until it buzzed in her bones.

A great gust of wind set the torches flaring. Thunder crashed close at hand, and Brunahild willed her body to rigidity as she felt her senses swim.

"*Wodan, Wodan, Wise One, wanderer—*" Words wove through the web of sound.

> "*Hail to the High One, Holy One, hear!*
> *Strike with Storm-Lord's lightning, spear!*
> *Fire bright, fear fight, friend's might near!*"

Hoofbeats thundered above, and in the heavens, as if a great Eye had blinked open, mortal vision was seared by a spear of light. But through that tear in perception, Brunahild saw a tumult of mounted warriors riding the skies. At their head raced a storm-grey stallion, long teeth snapping, spraying froth from his jaws. He wheeled, a whirl of legs churning the clouds, and the dark cloak of the rider whipped out upon the wind. Light leaped from the steel of helm and ringmail, but it was dimmed by the blaze of his Eye.

Now his face alone filled Brunahild's vision, and she knew that the thunder she had heard was laughter. The gaze of the god gripped the girl-child who trembled before him, and the delight in the laughter of Wodan swept her spirit away on a sudden tide of joy.

Consciousness returned with a rush of heat against Brunahild's skin. The bonfire was burning merrily. She heard Heimar speaking nearby.

"Give a bull to the village," the Walkyrja answered him. "They value our herb lore, and will not push the matter further. As for the girl, we will take her to train."

Brunahild stumbled, and someone took her arm. Rain pattered on the leaves, but none was falling in the circle. Heimar called her name, but she did not answer him.

It was the voice of the god that echoed within her, as she had seen him behind her eyelids after she looked into the well.

"Now you shall be my daughter, Brunahild. . . ."

Chapter 2 ❈ Wild Geese Flying

Hiloperic's Hall, Frankish Homeland
Winter Moon, A.D. 410

Sigfrid lay along the rooftree of the feasting hall, watching the world. The mound on which it stood was like the boss of a great hide shield whose length was dappled with reed and grassland, banded by waterways, and rimmed by the distant glitter of the sea. Far to the south folk said the earth was anchored by the solid mass of mountains, but he had never seen one. To the north lay ocean.

The mound was ringed with buildings, the longhouses for sleeping and the worksheds inside the palisade, and beyond, the oblong dwellings of the families that worked King Hiloperic's fields, pulsing now with activity as folk prepared for the feast that celebrated summer's end. On the coastal plain, even so small an eminence gave an advantage of vision. Sigfrid could see the cropped fields and moving dots of the king's cattle, sails on the northern ocean, or the smoke of the next clanhold, a half day's ride away. And he could trace the carefully tended causeway, where horsemen had startled clamoring clouds of waterfowl into the mild air. The boy suppressed a wriggle of excitement, wondering if these were the guests they were waiting for.

A light wind wafted the fragrance of roasting meat and boiling gruel across the marshes, and as the birds settled back to their feeding, the horsemen booted their ponies into a jog. The mound was buzzing like a hive with preparation, but Sigfrid lay still as the serpents carved on the ridgepoles of the hall.

"Sigfrid! Where is that boy? Sigfrid, your mother bids you come!"

Perchta stood in the yard, her fists set on her broad hips as she pitched her voice to pierce the din. Two thralls staggered past with boards to lay across the trestles in the open space before the hall. The woman swore and waddled out of their way, nearly upsetting another lad with a load of logs for the fires. More folk were coming in from the houses outside the palisade, bearing bleached linen cloths for the tables, crocks of butter and cured cheeses, balancing yokes with pannikins of milk or tubs of brown ale.

Grey eyes slitted between plump cheeks and bent brows as Perchta turned, scanning the yard in every direction but one. From his perch Sigfrid had seen her stumping through the village, questioning the gateguard and Ragan in the smithy and the cooks by the fires. She had looked in the longhouse where the family slept, and among the warriors in the king's feasting hall.

Sigfrid turned his head to follow her, his summer-bleached hair the same pale brown as the weathered reeds. She was almost below him now. Grinning with anticipation, he swung his legs sideways. The tightly packed thatch of the roof curved like a haystack. He let go, gathering speed as the slope steepened, shot off the edge of the roof an elbow's length above the ground and hit the dirt rolling, to fetch up at Perchta's feet in a cloud of dust with a triumphant grin.

For a moment she gaped, then she hauled him up by one ear and smacked him. He squirmed in her grip, dust puffing from his tunic and breeches at each blow.

"Wretched boy! You could have been killed! And look what you have done to your clothes!"

Sigfrid winced, for she was putting some muscle into the beating.

"Riders are coming, Perchta—" he said when words finally failed her. "I saw them on the causeway beyond the birch trees. Do you think it is Hlodomar at last?"

"If it is, there's just time to scrub your face and hands and pick the straws out of your hair, for your mother wants you beside her at the feasting. Lucky for you, lad, for if it were my decision, you could fight for your food among the dogs!" Perchta started in again as she hauled him along. But Sigfrid only laughed.

The rasp of metal on metal almost drowned out the noise of the people outside. Ragan puffed out his lips and bent over the axehead, the muscles knotting and easing in his long arms as he tapped along the curve. With each stroke the perfect crescent of the edge became more clear. Presently the smith paused and ran a callused finger across the smooth iron.

"Ragan, what are you doing? The king's brother is here with all of his men, and the feast is going to begin," came a shrill voice from the doorway.

The smith squinted into the bright oblong, and altered his snarl into a grunt as he recognized Sigfrid, leggy and wide-shouldered for a boy of eight winters, with the thin sunshine backlighting his hair. He seemed all a child of the tall ones, but the smith allowed him to play in the forge, watching for the moment when the boy's true breeding would be revealed. Even Hiordisa did not know all her mother's kin. Sigfrid neither called names nor did he seem to fear Ragan's magic, and he made himself useful from time to time.

"He's not *my* brother. I have food here. Why come?" Once more he caressed the axehead. There was no moment as satisfying as this, when the *rightness* of the work emerged beneath his hands.

"But all of our folk will be there—"

Ragan gave a short laugh at the bewilderment in the boy's tone, understanding what Sigfrid himself could not have put in words. The feasting table was the focus of the community. Perhaps the feast defined it, for an outcast was one who was forbidden to share in the food offered to the gods. But despite his thirty years in King Hiloperic's service, these were not Ragan's people, and he had an old quarrel with their gods.

Still, this was not the time to let them see how well he understood that although his people were earth of this earth since the beginning of the world, he would always be the alien here.

"In a little I come. This axe we need to cut more wood, after all those fires. I finish soon. You go to your mother now." He picked up the hammer and bent once more to this task, knowing by the flicker of light when the boy went away.

Heming, Hunding's son, slid off of his pony and looked at the buildings around him with interest. He had ridden with Hlodomar the Albing for three seasons, but this was the first time they had been close enough to keep the Autumn Feast with the family. The steading seemed prosperous, the houses neatly thatched, and the palisade built of stout, well-braced logs. Bright paint picked out the carvings on doorposts and rooftrees. The place would offer some good booty and a good fight to get it, Heming thought with the cold calculation of half a lifetime, if he had come as an enemy.

A fair woman with hair like new copper emerged from the crowd that had gathered to watch their entry, holding a great, silver-mounted drinking horn. She moved gracefully, though she was heavy with child. A man with the same flaring eyebrows as Hlodomar came after her, his pale hair gleaming in the afternoon sun. This must be Alb, the king's older son.

"Uncle, we nearly began without you!" he exclaimed. "Come— we have killed the bull already and poured out his blood for the landspirits in the barley field. His flesh is simmering in the cauldron, and we were about to sit down!"

Hlodomar grunted, hauled one leg over the back of his pony, and slid to the ground. "Your father's well?" He was a big, broad man with straw-colored hair escaping from beneath an iron-bound leather war-cap, much younger than his brother the king.

"Well enough to put away his share of the beer! It is only his legs that refuse to bear him these days."

Alb took his uncle's arm, rolling a little with the gait of one who spends much of his time upon the sea. He had made a name for himself in sea-fighting, while Hlodomar's warfare had been mostly on land. Heming followed the rest of the war-band toward the tables, well-worn swords banging at their sides and their necks agleam with looted gold.

At the longest of the tables Hiloperic waited with his other sons, his white beard brushed and gleaming. He was ruffling the hair of a boy dressed in a tunic of pale yellow wool bordered with tablet-woven bands whose making must have cost some woman many an hour. Clearly a favorite grandson, but one of his uncles seemed less fond. The boy had sensed it too. Curious, Heming watched them.

For a long moment the child's yellow stare held the man's inimical gaze, and it was the man who first looked away. But he was frowning, and after a moment the boy ducked under the king's arm and slipped along the table to the side of the woman who had brought out the drinking horn.

Intrigued, Heming stroked his grizzled beard, and took a seat at the end of the table where he could watch them. There had been something disturbingly familiar in the boy's stare. Above the clamor of talk and laughter, the air rang to a distant music as another flock of geese streamed south across the sky.

"A horn to Ingvio!" shouted Hiloperic as the women brought in platters of roasted pork and set them before the feasters.

"Hail Ingvi-Fro, lord and landmaster, giver of the harvest!" cried the feasters as the king blessed the horn, drank, and passed it to the man beside him. The laughter warmed as folk felt the presence of the god. Heming tore at a hunk of barley bread and held out his wooden bowl to be filled as a woman with a kettle of beans cooked with leeks and garlic went by.

From the men at the other end of Hlodomar's table came a gust of merriment as the horn came to one of their newest companions, a young man from one of the minor Anglian kingly lines who had been nicknamed the Stallion.

"Ho, Hengest—here's something to stiffen you! Be glad they don't need to make a fresh talisman, like my goodwife does when we slaughter a horse on the farm at home!"

Heming saw the young man's face redden at the reference to the horse's pizzle that was often used as a god-image at the festival, but he kept his composure. Young though he was, he was a good fighter. If luck came to him, he might go far.

"Hail to the fertile god!" The horn was passed to the table where Heming was sitting, and a woman held it high. "Strengthen my man's rod, that he may sow my field with good seed!"

The men were laughing, and the woman's husband glared.

"Grow great, Wolse," one of the older women murmured, "and be taken up, endowed with linen, supported by leeks. Let the woman be fruitful, lord, in thy embrace!"

Heming twitched. He honored the phallus-god as much as any, but a man had once borne the name men gave the god in eastern lands, and there was an old bloodfeud between his clan and Heming's.

The mead made the rounds in honor of the other gods: Tiw who gave victory in battle and justice in the Assembly, Donar the Thunderer, who sent rain to the fields, and Wodan, who was god of many things, invoked at this festival as the Welcome One, fulfiller of desires. And with each circuit, eyes grew brighter, faces fairer, as they welcomed guests whose invisible presence was as apparent as their own. Then Alb's wife, Hiordisa, got to her feet and took the great, silver-mounted horn.

"To Froja, the *disa* of the Wanes, I consecrate this horn! Froja of the Necklace, Lady of life and love, who inclines the male to the female and quickens the womb, our thanks for thy many blessings!" She held her hand over the horn to hallow it, poured out a little onto the earth, drank, and handed it to her husband.

Her son leaned against her, his yellow eyes heavy-lidded with a fatigue he was fighting with a stubbornness Heming remembered from his own childhood. He looked at the smooth curve of the boy's bent head with an odd twist of envy, for he had no child.

"Certainly the goddess has blessed *her*—" One of the older women nodded toward Hiordisa's swelling belly. "Good fortune for the mother of a strong son to make the offering!"

The sun had fled the fields of day, and the last light was draining from the sky. For a moment Heming sat at a feast of shadows. He shivered, feeling the touch of wyrd upon his soul. Then the thralls brought torches, and faces and ornaments flickered into bright relief once more.

Voices grew louder as the focus of the toasts shifted from the great gods to heroes of the past and lost friends. Frank or Angli, Hermunduri or Jute, they shared a common custom. Some of the feasters touched their lips to the rim in salutation only, but Hlodomar's men drank deep as the horn went round, and Heming deeper than any, hoping that the fire in the liquor would fight the cold that had so suddenly seized his soul.

"Godo fell in that last raid into Gaul," said the man who sat next to Heming, "so he has his share of that good rich ground, solid open country where the sea does not eat the fields, though they bless them in the name of the White Christ instead of the gods."

"And slaves in plenty to farm it," another laughed, "while the master sits at his ease. 'Tis no wonder the Roman-kind want the warriors of the tribes to do their fighting. It is folk of our blood all along the border, these days."

"And their sons grow soft with such living, and whatever profit they make from the land goes in taxes to Rome." One of the oldest spoke, a man with a long scar running from chin to brow. "I have served in their legions, and I know. Better to take the tribute they offer and come home again to the lands we understand."

Heming waited for the horn to come to him.

"If the land will have us." The next warrior poured out some ale upon the ground. "Each winter grows longer and colder. Perhaps the gods are angry at us for forsaking them! The land of the Gauls is ripe for the taking. Let us go and make our offerings there!"

"Maybe we can persuade Alb to send a keel or two of warriors with his friends the Jutes to raid Britannia," said one of the Frankish men. "Now that the Romani have pulled out the last of their legions, there should be easy pickings there!"

"Be still!" Heming took the horn. "None can escape his wyrd, not even the gods, but I for one will make my offerings on the field of spears." He tipped up the horn and in one long swallow finished it.

Someone pounded on a table, and all attention returned to the king.

"The night grows chill, and it is time to warm our blood with dancing. But before we do that, let the Albings drain a final horn in honor of the goddess who guards our kin!" An old woman, some cousin of Hiloperic, was escorted into the circle of torchlight and took the silver-mounted horn.

"Albodisa I call from the abode of the Bright Ones!" she wheezed. "White One, come riding, watch over your children! Warn them of danger, fill the wombs of their women. So shall the Albings prosper and live long in the land." She poured mead upon the earth, drank, and gave the horn to the king.

"To the Albings!" He lifted the horn. "Bravest of Frank-lords! Fairest and most free!"

There was silence from the feasters as the horn was passed. From the king to Alb it went, and then to his brothers. Down the table it moved, and the lady Hiordisa took it without drinking and started to pass it on. Then her son reached for the horn.

"No, child—" His mother's hand closed over his and lifted it away. "You are not one of Albodisa's kin."

Memory laid across the bewildered face of the boy the features of a man, contorting in surprise as he felt the bite of the spear, and Heming the Hunding knew where he had seen those yellow eyes before.

A Wolsung!

The boy jerked around as if he felt Heming's eyes upon him. He was blinking back tears, but as their eyes met, slowly the child's expression changed, and Heming felt his hackles rise as he faced Sigmund the Wolf-King's brilliant stare. For a moment he endured it, and then he too had to look away.

The child shuddered and clung to his mother, and soon his nurse came to carry him off to bed. But Heming ate no more of Hiloperic's feast, though the drinking went on until dawn. His head was throbbing, and with each pulse came the same refrain.

Sigmund had a son. A child of the Wolsungs still walks the world.

Even after Perchta had closed the door to the longhouse, Hiordisa could still hear the clamor of men at their drinking in the yard. They would go on far into the night, but she had done all that courtesy required. She leaned against one of the uprights, grateful that custom allowed her this escape into the hall. She had been on her feet too much today, and her back ached from the strain of carrying the child. But it was not the Albing babe she was carrying who brought the ache to her throat as Perchta lit the way to her own bedbox at the end of the hall, but the son she had borne to Sigmund the Wolsung eight years before.

Hiordisa let Perchta take her shawl and parted the curtains of striped wool, listening to the soft breathing within. For a moment it halted as she bent over the child, then resumed with a regularity too precise for slumber.

"Sigfrid—" She smoothed the feathery hair away from his brow. "Are you sleeping? You must listen to me."

She felt him begin to turn away, but she held him, and instead he reached out to her, his breath suddenly ragged as if he had been running, though he kept himself from making a sound. Straw rustled as she settled herself on the edge of the bedbox.

"My heartling, my little one, will you forgive me? In past years, you were always asleep before they sent round Albodisa's horn. . . ."

Once more she began to stroke his brow. She could feel the hot tears that soaked into the linen that covered his bedding, and blinked back the hot prick in her own. She had borne Alb one daughter already, and a new babe kicked in her womb, but in this moment she could admit that her firstborn had a place in her heart that could be taken by no other child.

"Who am I then, if I am not Alb's son?" he whispered hoarsely at last.

"Your father was a Wolsung," she answered, her voice fierce with memory. "A line of warriors and kings!" In the one year of their marriage, she had heard the bards sing her lord's lineage often enough to remember.

"Sigi was the first of them, the son of Wodan, who fled down from the north after he had killed an enemy. His son was Reri, who made a great kingdom to the east of here. Reri's queen had no child until the Mother sent them an apple from the orchard of the gods. She died in the bearing, but her babe was so great and strong that they called him Wolse, and he married a Walkyrja who bore him ten sons and a daughter, and the greatest of them was Sigmund."

"So Alb is not my father!"

Her hands moved down to his shoulders. His skin was so soft, so tender. In the darkness she could forget how his legs and arms had grown since the last harvest and remember the chubby child he had been so short a time ago. A surge of protectiveness tightened her grip until he squirmed.

"He has been a father to you, but it was Sigmund the Wolsung who sired you, my hero-child." The name rang in the darkness like a distant clashing of swords. "Though he was a man of my father's years, I chose Sigmund as my husband, for there was more honor in wedding a man of renown."

"That is true—" The boy spoke as soberly as one of Hiloperic's councilmen, and Hiordisa began to laugh through her tears.

It had been a coldly reasoned decision, until she saw him, until she noted the strength in his arms, and the amused understanding in his eyes. Nothing had ever seemed to surprise him, not even at the end. But her son was waiting, and with an effort Hiordisa controlled her voice once more.

"Sigmund was a great man. When his sister's husband killed all the rest of their family, he lived in the forest alone until his sister Signy came to him in secret and bore him a son who helped him to avenge their kin. That was Sintarfizilo, and when they returned to their own country he became a mighty man."

"He was my brother?" asked Sigfrid.

"He is dead now," she said flatly, "poisoned by Sigmund's first queen. But her child was a good man also, the hero Helgi who killed Hunding when he was young. He was chosen by the Walkyrja Sigruna and carried her off from among her kin. He was killed by her brother Dag, whom you must watch out for when you are grown."

Sigfrid lay silent, considering. "I suppose it is good to have famous kindred, but as they are all dead, they are not much use to me," he said finally. "And my father? Who killed him?"

Hiordisa bit her lip. It was true, the Wolsungs were not a lucky family. Already Sigfrid understood that the men of his family did not die by accident, or gasp out their lives in the straw.

"Lyngvi, the son of Hunding." She spat out the words, wishing that long-nosed, long-jawed face were before her so that she could spit on it as well. "He wanted to marry me, but I chose Sigmund, and that added fuel to the flame. So he and his brothers raided into our country, destroying everything they found, and my father and Sigmund marched out to meet them on the plains beside the sea."

Sigfrid sat up, pulling the bedfurs around him. She could feel the eagerness growing in him at the prospect of a battle tale.

"If Sigmund was so mighty, how could Lyngvi kill him?"

"They were too many—" Hiordisa's voice caught, and she shook her head, trying to control the flood of memories. It had been spring-time, and the feet of the warriors had trampled the flowers.

"From the woods Perchta and I watched the battle. I saw them kill Eylimi my father, but Sigmund slew everyone who came against him, despite his years, until his sword shattered, and then they bore him down. Lyngvi and his brothers rode off to sack our hall, but I stayed hidden until darkness fell, and then I went out onto the battlefield."

The scent of new grass had mingled with the stink of the battlefield. She remembered the raven-voices of the darkness, and the horror of treading upon a man's hand.

"And you buried my father?"

"Sigmund was still living when I found him, though there was hardly a place on his body not reddened by wounds. But he would not let me tend them." Her voice broke. Even now she could still see the dim oval of his face glimmering through the shadows, and hear his words.

"Let me be. My luck has turned. I fought battles while it was Wodan's will, but now he has broken my blade. Save the shards for our son."

"I begged him to let me help him." She could not stop her weeping, and Sigfrid tried clumsily to wipe the tears away. "I told him he would do better to live and take vengeance on Lyngvi and his brothers for the death of my father. But Sigmund said he must leave that task to the babe in my belly, for it was time for him to join his kindred who had gone before. And so I stayed by him. My father's body lay nearby; my mother, Lyngheide, had died years ago. Where was there for me to go?"

She had felt the life seeping out of him, and it was as if all the life were going out of the world. He did not speak again, though she waited until his spirit left him with the coming of dawn. And then Perchta had come running to tell her that the bay was full of ships. And Alb had appeared and carried her away.

"So. My father was a hero," the boy said flatly. "Why did you never tell me about him before?"

"Because the men who killed him still live, and if they knew of your existence, they would kill you as well."

"Why should they care about me? I have done them no harm!"

"They will look at you and see your father reborn. . . ." she said through the ache in her throat. He was only eight winters old, but already folk looked away because they could not bear the brightness of his eyes.

"Then I will kill them," came the clear voice out of the dark.

"When you are grown, my hero, not until you are a man!"

Laughing and weeping at the same time, Hiordisa gathered him against her breast and held him there, her hands memorizing the sweet child's flesh that covered the sturdy bones, the scent of hay that clung to his hair. Sigfrid was still so little, but already she could feel the strength that had made his father a giant among men.

"This morning I belonged to one kindred and tonight I have another. It is very confusing," Sigfrid said softly after a time. "And I have enemies."

"Not here, my loveling," Hiordisa murmured, rocking him. "Not now."

But it seemed to her that she could feel him leaving her as she had felt Sigmund slipping away, even though his flesh was still warm and solid beneath her hands.

Overnight a wind had come down from the north, scouring the high clouds from the heavens and the smoke of the feastfires from above the hall. It was a cold wind, and the women pinned their shawls tightly around them as they cleared away trenchers and ale mugs and swept up what spilled food the dogs had not gotten to feed to the swine. Sunlight glittered from distant waterways and sparked from helmets and harness fittings nearer at hand as the guests got under way. It was a morning to set the blood singing, and even men groggy from a night's drinking found themselves moving more briskly, once they had finished cursing the brightness of the day.

Sigfrid got out of the longhouse before Perchta could grab him, collected a piece of bread and a little cheese from one of the serving girls, and slipped through the gate of the palisade, a sheaf of arrows at his back and his bird-bow in his hand. The knowledge that had made him weep the night before excited him now. His ancestor Sigi had started out alone, and his father had been alone in the forest. If he had no living kinsmen, then he would manage without them.

But he did not have to be stupid. There was a vengeance owed, and to take it, he must live to be a man. His mother had told him he was safe, but women did not know everything. It seemed to Sigfrid that the wisest course would be to go to ground where he could watch the road and wait until he saw the man who had stared at him with such hatred at the feast ride away.

Out on the marshes, flocks of birds puffed skyward and settled back again, calling anxiously as they worked up to the moment when instinctive agreement would send them all winging toward the south once more. One by one, the families who had come in for the feasting loaded up wagons or ponies and rode out along the causeway. But Hlodomar's men showed no signs of going away.

Sigfrid frowned where he sat in the lee of a gorsebush. He had eaten up all the bread and cheese, and the wind was getting cold. It was all very well to have gotten out unnoticed, but Perchta would have raised the cry for him long since, and he refused to come scuttling back through the gate like a frightened dog.

At least he had the bow and arrows. If he brought down a goose, he might pretend that he had not realized the remains of the feast would feed them for several days more. A little stiffly he got to his feet and began the stalk toward the end of the slough where a fringe of birches would shield him until he was close enough to mark his prey.

Focused on the challenges of moving quietly through the dry grass, he did not see the flicker of motion behind him until a hard hand closed on his shoulder and spun him round.

He started to struggle, then flinched from the cold prick of steel beneath his chin.

"That is better. Be still and it will be over quickly, without pain." It was the man with the grizzled beard, the one who had been watching him the night before.

"I am the foster-son of Alb, son of Hiloperic," Sigfrid said stoutly. "You cannot kill me like some thrall."

"I know who you are," the man laughed softly. "I took care to ask the name of the lad with the wolf's eyes, last night over the mead. I am called Heming, and Hunding was my father, and you are the son of Sigmund and the brother of Helgi Hundingsbane."

"Then you know I come of noble kin—" Sigfrid fought to keep his voice from wavering. He was afraid, but most of all he was angry. It was a child's mistake to have been caught this way.

"Half the Einherior may be your kindred," said Heming, grinning through his beard. "But Wodan's hall is a little far for them to come to your assistance, though no doubt they will welcome you."

"They will call you Heming Child-Slayer. Do you think it will bring you any honor to kill a boy?"

"Are you a child? I thought all the Wolsungs came toothed and clawed from the womb! I will slay you as a hunter slays the wolf cub before it can grow."

Sigfrid jerked backward. His tunic tore in Heming's grasp as he scrambled for a foothold in the sandy soil. For a moment he was free, then an iron grip closed on his arm, and he heard a sharp crack like a snapping stick as it was wrenched round behind him. Now the knifeblade lay across his neck, but the waves of agony that pulsed upward from his broken arm held him still more effectively than the steel.

"I am sorry," Heming said softly in his ear. "I did not mean to cause you needless pain. Now, we are going to move carefully down into the shelter of these trees. I shall announce the slaying, since I have no mind to be outlawed for private murder, but I would prefer to finish this out of sight of the hill."

The world spun dizzily as the man frog-marched him toward the pond.

"I will give compensation to your mother, of course. I am sure my kinfolk will be happy to pay their share," Heming was saying now. "It is my fortune that I happened to be serving with Hlodomar, or we would never have known that a Wolsung still walked the world."

Not for long, thought the boy, for there did not seem to be anything he could do. Without Heming's grip he would have fallen, and every step sent a new wave of pain stabbing through his arm. But his forebears were not going to welcome him to the Hall of the Slain if he allowed himself to be killed like a wether, without even a cry.

They reached the birch trees. Through the screen of branches Sigfrid could see the shifting grey-brown mass of the geese, feeding in the pond.

Be you my witnesses! he thought, and then, as his captor's grip shifted so he could bring the knife into play, the boy bit down hard into the fleshy pad beneath the joint of his thumb on the man's knife-hand.

Heming yelled, and the knife wheeled glittering into the air. The geese followed it, darkening the sky as they exploded upward. Sigfrid summoned his last strength and, as Heming reached for him, dodged and threw himself into the pool.

Alb had insisted that his foster-son be taught to swim. The shock of the cold water brought the boy back to his senses, and one good arm and two strong legs sent him arrowing under water while the man was still floundering in the shallows, fending off enraged geese.

Sigfrid came up, gasping, in a clump of reeds. He could still hear Heming swearing, but the noise of the geese was lessening as they settled on the next pond. Soon he would begin to search the shoreline.

Sigfrid's strength was gone. He wondered whether it would be more valorous to stay here to have his throat cut or swim back out into the center of the pool to drown.

And then, as the war-cries of the geese subsided, he heard calling of a different kind. *Perchta has sent out searchers,* he thought in wonder. Through the reeds he could see Heming turning to face them, his empty hands open at his sides. Sigfrid took a deep breath, fighting back the darkness. Then he got a grip on a clump of sedgegrass at the edge of the water and pulled himself onto solid ground.

"Here!" He put all the power he had left into the cry. "I am here!"

Ragan the smith answered the summons to the judgment with the rest of King Hiloperic's household. He stood a little apart from the others, his corded arms and barrel chest covered by the richly bordered tunic he had worn for the feasting, his habitual scowl concealing resentment that he should have to leave his work for one of the tall people's quarrels, and anger over the cause.

The prisoner was guarded now by his own comrades, but he had been ill-used before they got him. His tunic was torn, and there was some kind of wound on his hand. Nothing could be read from his features, though, except when his dark gaze rested on the boy, who leaned against his mother on a bench below that of the king. They had splinted and bound Sigfrid's broken arm and given him something to dull the pain. Clearly it was making him sleepy, but he would not let his eyelids close.

"What shall be done here?" The king gazed at the bound man with a kind of bewildered sorrow and then turned to Hlodomar. "Brother, it is one of your warriors who has attacked our child. How shall we resolve this dreadful thing?"

"I do not defend him," Hlodomar said tightly, his hand on the hilt of his sword. "He has broken the law of the war-band as well as the sacred bonds of hospitality."

Heming tried to say something, but before he could get out the words, he was brutally wrestled down.

"He has the right to speak before we judge him," said Albald, who was Hiloperic's younger son. "Let him go. Let him be heard!"

"It is just—" came an echo from the people around them. "Let him be heard!"

A little excitement to finish off the feasting, thought Ragan dourly. *If they condemn him, do they ask me to deal the blow?*

"Let him speak," said Alb painfully, and his wife looked up apprehensively. "If there was a reason for his outrage, we must know."

Ragan frowned. For a moment he had seen his own sister's pain in Hiordisa's eyes. Lyngheide had been torn between her dying father and the beloved older brother, who killed him for the sake of Andvari's hoard. If Hiordisa had to choose between son and husband, what would she do? *No peace for your blood till Hreidmaro is avenged*, he thought grimly.

After a moment the king nodded, and the attention of the crowd shifted to the prisoner, who surveyed them with a grim smile.

"There is a reason," he said hoarsely. "I am Heming, son of Hunding, whom Helgi Sigmundson slew, and that is Helgi's brother you are fostering there."

Question and commentary whispered through the assembly like wind in the reeds, and Ragan wondered how many were only now realizing that Sigfrid was not Alb's child. Only the boy did not seem surprised. The smith moved a little closer. He had known from the beginning. It was one of the reasons he had stayed here, forging billhooks and ploughshares for a minor king. He needed a hero, doom-fated to great deeds.

"Well is it said that they who sit within hall often little know the lineage of those who come," Hiordisa burst out furiously. "Even had you named yourself kin to those who killed Sigmund, you could have claimed hospitality, but you have outraged all sacred law, attacking your host's kin."

"We were outside the enclosure and beyond Hiloperic's law," growled Heming. "It is said also that a wolf sleeps often in his son, however young. There's no safety in oaths or gold given to the child of a man you have slain. I sought only to finish what ought to have been done with nine years ago."

Alb took a step forward, his gaze sweeping the assembly. Some of the men moved as if to join him, but others were hanging back, muttering, and Alb's own two brothers were among them.

"Why should we cry bloodfeud for a line that never brought luck to anyone?" the whisper went around. *"The boy is a danger to us all!"*

The sorrow graven in King Hiloperic's face grew deeper. His brother Hlodomar still looked angry, but an element of calculation had entered his gaze.

"Compensation must be paid to the Albings for the insult and to the lady Hiordisa for the injury to her child," he growled at Heming. "You have already been cast out of our company, but we will hold you until the ransom has been paid."

"My people will pay, and gladly," spat Heming, "if only for the news."

Ragan, easing forward, saw the neat semicircle of toothmarks on his wounded hand and hid a smile.

"And then we must send the brat away!" cried Albald. Hiordisa's arms went protectively around her son.

Hiloperic sighed. "Be it so," he said heavily. "No grandchild could have been dearer, but even were the boy of our own blood, we would soon be fostering him out to some worthy man."

There was a silence, while everyone wondered where they would find a family willing to take on a bloodfeud with the Hundings along with the fostering fee. Sigfrid shook free of his mother's arm and stood upright, though his eyes were still dilated with pain.

But Ragan's smile had broadened, and folk who had never seen it before gaped as he stumped forward to stand before the king.

"I foster him," rumbled the smith, "in a place the sons of Hunding do not know. I raise him as hero. Then they may fear, for this one rights all wrongs when he is grown."

But he was looking at Sigfrid, and he blinked at the measuring clarity in the boy's gaze. It was for the king to decide, but it was Sigfrid who broke the silence.

"I will go."

Chapter 3  The Hill of the High One

Taunus Mountains
Eostara Moon, A.D. 411

Somewhere a raven was calling, one long *caark*—and then a chirrup of inquiry. Was it where the fir trees stood stark against the sky behind the hall of the Walkyriun, or in the old oak that reached over the cookshed with knotted limbs? There were many things at Fox Dance that might intrigue a raven, but it was the bird itself that interested Brunahild.

As the girl lifted her head to see, a warning cough brought her attention back to the runestaves in her hand. Six sun-flushed faces were turned toward her, avid with anticipation. So far, not one of the girls gathered for the lesson on runecasting had escaped the rough side of their teacher's tongue.

Brunahild took a deep breath and held the sticks carefully over the cloth, striving for just the right amount of pressure in her outstretched fingers and thumb. She tried to gauge the weight of the staves, but these were only practice sticks, not even carved. They felt lifeless in her hands.

"So, do you wait for them to sprout leaves?" Thrudrun asked. The tangle of amber necklaces upon her breast glowed like honey in the light of the sun. Suppressed giggles from around the circle made Brunahild's face burn, and in that moment the muscles in her hands twitched and the sticks spilled out upon the cloth.

"It is better," said their instructor, and Brunahild opened her eyes again. "There, where the two slender staves are crossed by the one, could be the Hail rune. But the other five lie stacked together like wood for a fire."

Brunahild sat back with a sigh as the seeress gathered up the sticks in her capable hands. Little Svala flushed anxiously as she took them, and Brunahild drew a deep breath, willing her friend to succeed.

The girls whom the Walkyriun took to train were more interesting than the chief's daughters who came to the Marcomanni gatherings, but they could be as vicious as boys. Galemburgis especially had been difficult. She was daughter to a chieftain among the Alamanni, red-haired as a Gaul, taller than Brunahild and just as strong. But Ricihild and Liudwif and Svala had attached themselves to Brunahild.

Svala took a deep breath and released the sticks with a jerk that sent them flying across the ground.

"Is it a snowstorm that you are forecasting, child?" asked Thrudrun. Svala's face grew pink beneath the tumble of mouse-fair hair, and Brunahild moved closer, giving the girl's arm a protective squeeze.

"Try to think about something else when you let go," she whispered.

It was a pity that Svala was so easily startled. That Burgund girl, Gudrun, had managed to retain her self-possession even when falling into the stream. But it was no use wondering how she would have fared here. Word had come that the Burgunds were trying to claw out a new holding from the Roman lands on the west bank of the Rhenus. But their king was dead in the midst of his campaigning. They had drunk his funeral ale and acclaimed his son Gundohar at Mogontiacum. While Brunahild was reading runes in the Taunus Mountains Gudrun would be learning the speech of Rome.

The mountains rose in wooded folds above the plain where the Moenus flowed toward the Rhenus, studded by outcrops of grey granite and quartz that blazed white in the sun. At this time of year, the larkspur flooded in purple splendor down the hillsides. Fox Dance lay protected from the winds where the east-west road crossed the trail that led up from the plain. There was a longhouse where the wise-women lived, and another for the girls, and a scatter of storehouses and sheds.

The Sacred Women of the Taunus came from many tribes. They usually returned to them to serve as healers, midwives, and seeresses for their people, and, at need, to perform the battle-magic of the Walkyriun. But there were always a few who stayed at Fox Dance as teachers, and others who remained in the mountains, seeking knowledge at hallows like the Hill of the High One.

Brunahild wanted to see them. She wanted to learn the swordplay

that was taught to the Choosers of the Slain. Why must she sit playing
with sticks like a child? She heard the musical clatter of falling staves
and another whisper of laughter, then jerked upright as Thrudrun
clapped her hands.

"Do you think this funny?" the runemistress exclaimed. "Do you
know how to carve the runes and use your own blood to feed them?
Do you know the spells that must be chanted so that they will tell
you their secrets?"

Brunahild saw the glitter of tears in Svala's eyes. "Wodan hung
from the Tree to learn that wisdom," she said quickly. "Why are we
tossing sticks on the ground?"

"Is that what you desire?" asked Thrudrun grimly. "Nine nights
suspended between earth and heaven, fighting for breath while your
blood waters the ground? If you survive, you may yet come to the
great testing. But a fighter practices first with a stick-sword and a hazel
wand. When we have pounded into you the knowledge of the body,
then you may dare the ordeal of the soul."

The raven called, and for an instant something fluttered in Brunahild's belly, a pulse of mingled fear and desire. She had spoken to
distract attention from Svala, but Thrudrun had challenged her now.
She swept up the sticks scattered on the cloth.

"Even a stick-spear can be sharpened! What about these? If they
will speak to me, will you let me learn something real?" She shut her
eyes tightly, thinking. There had to be a question—perhaps something
about the weather—that would be easy to see. "Let these staves be
the runes of the hailstone clan," she said softly, "let them show us what
the weather for this week will be. . . ."

Swiftly, before her nerve failed her, she let her arms sweep outward. She heard the falling music of wood on wood, and a little gasp
of surprise. But it was another moment before she could gather the
courage to open her eyes.

For the first moment all she could tell was that at least the sticks
did not look like a pile of firewood this time.

"You cast it. Now you read it," said Thrudrun.

With unmarked sticks how could she use even the little she had
learned? Then she blinked, and from the tumble of sticks the shapes
of runes sprang clear.

"There is one lying over there alone—that could be the Ice rune,"
Brunahild said softly. "And that would mean that it's not going to be
very cold." That was a safe enough prediction for Eostara's Moon.
"Those others look a little like the rune for Harvest, with the Sun rune

near it, which means good weather. It is just a guess," she added hastily.
"If the sticks were marked it would change everything."

It was late for subtlety, but helping Thrudrun to save face might
save her own hide.

"It would," the runemistress said slowly. "These are not real runestaves, as you say. But if they had been, that would be a fair interpretation. It will be interesting to see if it comes true. . . ."

Finally Brunahild got up the nerve to meet her teacher's impassive
gaze. It held neither approval nor anger. Instead, what she glimpsed
in those grey eyes was speculation, and that did make her afraid.

"So, the younger girls are shaping well," Thrudrun finished her
account of the day, "but we may have a problem with Brunahild." The
last of the daylight softened her strong features; in the hush of sunset
the shouts of the girls at play in the meadow came clearly to the hill
above the hall.

Hlutgard sighed. She had believed it was the will of Wodan that
they take the girl, but what was good for the god was not necessarily
the best thing for the Walkyriun.

"So—are you afraid she will surpass you?" Randgrid, the warmistress, laughed softly, then reached for the awl with which she was
repairing her swordbelt. "I particularly liked the comment about the
wooden spear!" Red-haired and long-limbed, Randgrid had used weapons as well as Walkyriun magic against the Romans, and now taught
her skills to the girls.

"Do you think that she is destined for your path?" Thrudrun
frowned. "She's small for her age, and who knows if she'll ever have
the weight for shield and spear? But I'll admit she surprised me."

Hrodlind looked up from the herbs she was sorting. "You've said
yourself that prophecy comes from the seeress, not from her tools—"

Of the wisewomen now resident at Fox Dance, only Golla, the
other battle priestess, and Wieldrud, the midwife, were absent. Hlutgard had heard enough from the others to get a sense of the problem;
they must decide how to deal with it now.

"Oh yes," the runemistress replied, her square white teeth showing
in a wry grin. "I've taken omens from unmarked sticks myself. I was
not surprised that it could be done, but that she should try."

"If she is one of those to whom the power comes faster than you
can train it you *will* have an interesting time," came Huld's voice from
the shadows beneath the pine tree. "Especially if, as you say, she has
become a leader among the other girls."

Hlutgard sighed. Huld was acknowledged the greatest among them, as she was the oldest, but her work lay mostly in the halls of kings. She spent spring and fall among the tribes, but came to Fox Dance in the winter, and in the summer to gather herbs and seek the counsel of the spirits in the hills. It was all very well for her to criticize, but it was Hlutgard who was responsible for the welfare of the girls they had taken to train.

"I wonder if working with the rest of them is the best way to train her?" Thrudrun sat down. "If you keep the lessons to the level of the others, she is bored, and then the trouble comes."

"Trying to teach her and Galemburgis together certainly must challenge you." Randgrid grinned. "That child would reconquer all the Alamanni territory by herself if she was allowed, and she does *not* like Brunahild!"

"We are here to serve all the tribes!" exclaimed Hlutgard.

Randgrid shrugged. "So we say. And it would be simple enough if all the tribes were fighting Rome. But when the empire stands fast, they turn on each other like penned dogs. There may come a time when we will have to choose."

"What we have to choose now is how to deal with Brunahild," said Hlutgard repressively.

"We could send her to our sisters on the Broken Mountain—" offered Hrodlind. The peak in the Heart Mountains was the oldest of the wisewomen's sanctuaries. Hlutgard shook her head. Brunahild was their responsibility.

"Well, if she's a problem to you here, why not send her up the hill with Huld?" said Randgrid, and laughed. Huld snorted, but Hlutgard began to smile.

"It might work," she said slowly. "Tell her to come to me!"

"Since you came to us, the sunwheel has almost completed a turning," Hlutgard said softly as Brunahild entered the hall. "Have you been happy here?"

The day had been warm, and there was no need for fire in the long hearth, but light glimmered from lamps fashioned from stone or bronze that hung from the crossbeams, alternately revealing and concealing the features of the girl who paused between the two central supports of the hall. Brunahild was thinner now, toasted brown from days spent in the sunshine, and there was a balance to her body that had, perhaps, not been there before. Brunahild stared back at her, and Hlutgard waited, following the flicker of expression in the girl's green eyes.

"Lady," she whispered finally, "do not send me away. I did not mean to upset Thrudrun."

"Thrudrun is not angry. But we are responsible for all the maidens who come here. The other girls look to you as a leader. That is one reason why it matters how you feel."

"Some of them hate me," said Brunahild. "And it is not my fault."

"You are the daughter of a prince. Was there ever yet a man-pack without some quarreling over who should lead?"

The flickering light of the oil lamps glowed softly on the hangings that curtained the beds between the pillars and the wall, painted hides with figures of men and gods.

"Isn't that why you called me here?" Brunahild asked.

Hlutgard sighed. "You have heard the warriors boasting around the fire. What would you say is our greatest strength in war, as compared to the Roman-kind, and what are our weaknesses?"

"The men of the tribes are brave, and they are very strong—"

" 'The men of the tribes . . .' " echoed the wisewoman. "Even looking at your black hair, I forget that we are not your people. But that should make it all the easier to answer my question."

Brunahild had stiffened, but she did not flinch from the older woman's gaze.

"Every Teuton warrior is a hero, but each clan goes its own way. In battle the Huns follow one leader, and so Airmanareik's Goths were destroyed by the khan Balimber when my father was a child. And so it is when the tribes roll up against the *limes* of Rome. They can raid, but for all their courage, when the legions stand fast against them they cannot break the border. And then the Romans let them into the empire, clan by clan and tribe by tribe, and they forget their gods and their laws, and are no longer the men of the tribes."

"I see that you paid attention, daughter of Bladarda, when you sat beside your father's fire." Divided, the Teutonic tribes could stand against neither the horde nor the empire. But they would lose all that made them Teutons if they enslaved themselves to a single authority. What wisdom could show them how to unite for defense without losing their freedom?

Brunahild shrugged, but it had been a surprisingly perceptive answer for a girl, and Hlutgard wondered if she might be marked for Randgrid's road after all.

"The Choosers of the Slain must know when to follow, and when to lead the way," said Hlutgard. "Everywhere, the peoples are moving, and even the runes cannot tell us where it will end. The tribes look to us for wisdom, but death waits for the undisciplined on the roads we tread." Hlutgard leaned forward, the decision crystallizing with her words. "And so I am sending you away from Fox Dance. . . ."

Brunahild stood with blazing eyes and lips clamped tightly, refusing to give her teacher the satisfaction of seeing her cry.

Suddenly Hlutgard smiled. "This is not a punishment. Tomorrow you will go to the holy mountain that we call the High One's Hill with Huld, who means to spend the summer there."

Huld had protested, but though the older woman had refused to bear the weight of leadership at Fox Dance, it was time she shared some of the responsibilities.

"Stay with her," she went on. "She is the greatest among us, for she possesses all our skills, and has traveled through many lands. But she grows older. She needs the strength of your young limbs, though she will not admit it. And you need her wisdom."

She watched as the light came back into Brunahild's eyes.

They left at dawn. Mother Huld rode a bad-tempered roan mare, and behind her the thralls led two more ponies with supplies packed in baskets. It was a journey that Brunahild could have made on her own two feet in the time it takes to milk a cow, but the trail had not yet been cleared of the winter's storm drift, and the thralls who had come with them must often stop to drag fallen branches from the way.

Here the mixed forest of the lower slopes gave way to thick fir wood, and though in the sky above the light was growing, beneath those branches all was shadowed and still. It made Brunahild think of the Iron Wood that folk said lay east of the Worldtree, the habitation of giantesses and wolves. It was yet another thing to depress her. Galemburgis had made sure that Brunahild was told how Huld had objected when told that Brunahild was going along.

It was unclear whether Huld was more resentful about being saddled with a keeper or being expected, as she had put it, to pluck out a chestnut that the others had let roll too far into the fire. *Let her ignore me!* Brunahild thought as she stumped along behind the packpony. *I can always run away, and how will the wisewomen explain that to my sister and Heimar?* Svala had begged her to do that very thing, and wept when she would not, and refused to say farewell.

But such thoughts disappeared, at least for the moment, when they reached the top of the mountain. Suddenly the gentle incline they had been climbing became a steep slope littered with quartz-shot granite that in places still held the shape of walls. The path led up through the old gateway into sunlight and a brisk wind that swept all her depression away.

In that first moment of emergence from the gloom of the fir wood it seemed to Brunahild that they had reached some other world, perhaps the land of the elven-kind, that was all light and air. Light glimmered from the silver trunks of birches that had rooted themselves on the stony summit and from the starry white blossoms of the rowan trees; the sky was a great bowl of blue. Once, the level crown of the mountain had been a sanctuary for the Gauls, but they had never built more than temporary shelters behind their double ramparts. Only the god-posts at one end of the enclosure and the circle that had been worn by dancing feet into the grass showed that it was a different kind of sanctuary now.

Brunahild stood still, stunned by the vastness of the world. To the south the floodplain of the Moenus lay veiled by a nacreous haze, broken by an occasional flash where the river's undulations caught the sun. North and west the Taunus stretched away in dark wooded folds. Wodan's Seat of Seeing might have shown more of the world, but Brunahild had certainly never seen so much of it before.

"The wisewoman has gone to her hut to rest," said a voice at her elbow. Brunahild turned, startled to realize that the ponies had been unloaded and the thralls were getting ready to depart. "We have put your things in the one that is next to hers, and if you need nothing more, we should be getting the beasts back home."

Brunahild blinked. What hut? The hilltop was still bare. Then she saw a wisp of smoke rising from beyond the first ringwall.

"Down there?" She pointed to a path.

"The huts are built into the lower rampart," said the man. "From some of the old stones. You'll stay warmer, out of the wind."

"And what about water?" Brunahild asked then.

"There is a cistern for rainwater around the other side, and if that runs low, a path leads downhill to the spring."

Brunahild nodded. She remembered seeing a pair of wooden buckets atop the pony's load. It would be hard work, but if the old woman had done it alone until this summer, she ought to be able to manage. She supposed that Huld could tell her anything else that she needed to know.

Huld heard a thunk as the bowl of porridge was set down outside. In a moment the child would ask her if she needed anything, already prepared for the denial she had received each day before. Pain lanced through Huld's hip as she tried to turn over. The stink of her own waste came to her, and self-disgust warred with the pain. After all the lands through which she had traveled, and the great knowledge she had gathered, it seemed ridiculous that her body should imprison her this way.

"Girl—"

A shadow fell across the doorway.

"Girl—" Huld's voice was a scrape of sound. "I need your assistance. It appears . . . we must be allies after all."

"I'll run back to Fox Dance and fetch help for you—" The dark head retreated. *The child must be afraid I'm going to die on her,* thought Huld. Was she asking too much? But even the disgust of this child would be easier to bear than the indulgent compassion in the eyes of the Walkyriun.

"If you tell Hlutgard about this, I will wither your bones!" she said strongly, and heard the girl pause. "Listen! This is no illness—only a pain in my hip that will not let me move. If I had not been a stubborn old woman I would have let you help me earlier and never come to this pass."

"Are you elf-shot?" asked Brunahild.

Huld snorted. "That's as good a description as any. But it was the riding that laid me open to it, after a winter spent huddling by the fire. It will be thrall's work to get me cleaned up. Have you the stomach for it?"

There was a silence. *Now we will see what she is made of,* thought the wisewoman, wincing again as she turned her head to hear.

"And then? You didn't want me here before."

To her own surprise, Huld laughed. "You came up here for training, did you not? I must teach you something if I ever want to move again!" *She will be thinking it would serve me right if she went running for Hrodlind after all, put perhaps I can make her understand.* "If I have to go back to Fox Dance, so will you—" she said aloud. "Are you afraid to soil your hands?"

"If you can endure the pain my clumsiness will cause you, I should be able to stand the smell," retorted Brunahild. There was only a small tremor in her tone.

Huld sighed, knowing that she had succeeded in stinging her, and during the unpleasantness that followed she used what breath she could spare to maintain the pressure. Already Huld suspected that with this one, challenge would always work better than appeal.

By the time it was done, and Huld wrapped up warmly by the

cookfire, it was almost nightfall. Between the ramparts they had shelter, but higher up the nightwind was beginning to whisper among the trees.

"I thought that a little time would take it away," said Huld when she had recovered from being moved. "But it grows worse without tending. Curse me for an old cow."

"You look more like an old crow, a little scruffy, but with a peck or two in your beak still!" Brunahild squatted beside her. "What do I do now?"

Huld eyed her speculatively. It was only natural that the forced intimacy of the nursing would erode both wariness and awe. She knew herself that all her learning had shown her only how much there was left to know, but for that very reason, it was important that this child accept her discipline. Would Brunahild obey someone whom she had bathed and tended like a babe?

"You want me to teach you a charm for elf-shot? Don't you think that if a spell were sufficient I could have spoken it myself and be done!"

"The wisewomen always do their healings with charms at home—" Brunahild replied.

"So do we all." The woman grimaced. "Let this be your first lesson, to tend your own hurts swiftly if you have the means, lest pain imprison you. We will deal with that now. Both the herbs and the spell are needful, but the mind must be free to put the power into the words. From the packet marked with the rune for Weal, take some of the willow bark, and brew me up a tea."

Brunahild's eyes brightened. Clearly this was what she had hoped for: real magic, called forth by real need.

"Put into the cauldron as much of the bark as will fill the horn spoon," Huld whispered, "and let it simmer for a while." Brunahild bent over the cauldron, whispering into it the prayer to Earth Mother that Huld taught her to say.

As the bitter scent filled the air, Huld saw the girl blink, as if it dizzied her. *In the High One's name let this work*, she thought. *Lord of all Wisdom, grant the gift of healing to her, and to me.* The wind was rising, sweeping away the silence of the mountaintop. Huld sighed, feeling the pressure of a familiar presence in the restless air.

"It needs a rune. . . ." Brunahild's voice was slurred.

Father Wodan! The girl's half-tranced already! Huld almost forgot her pain in wonder, and felt the intensity of awareness around them grow.

"Choose one. . . ." she said softly.

"I think . . . *Uruz* . . ." Brunahild named the rune of the wild ox who was also the great cow who had licked the world into shape at the beginning of this age. "Thrudrun said it is a rune to bring power into the world." Her hand moved as if without volition to trace the rune above the cauldron, and she bent forward to murmur into those bitter waters its name.

The brew was boiling furiously when Brunahild opened her eyes again. She looked around her curiously, shivered, then reached for the ladle.

"What is it?" asked Huld, taking the bronze-bound cup of horn that Brunahild had filled with tea.

"Nothing. Only for a moment I thought I heard a whispering in the wind."

"Perhaps you did—" Huld answered through lips puckered by the bitterness of the tea. Grimacing, she drank the rest of it down. "Why do you think I had myself lugged all this way like a sack of meal? *He* whispers in the spring breezes, but it is in the summer storms that rage about this mountaintop that his voice is most clear. The god—" Huld repeated when Brunahild stared at her. "Wodan. Why do you think this is called the High One's Hill?"

Another shudder shook Brunahild's body, though it was not cold. "Wodan . . ." she repeated softly. "It has been so many moons. . . . Mother Huld, I know that you did not want me here. But I beg you now to teach me. I saw the god at Halle where I met the Walkyriun. He wants something from me!"

Huld's lids lifted; a pleasant lassitude was already spreading through her body as the tea took hold, but her heartbeat quickened. Had she found the one destined to inherit her wisdom?

"Tell me," she said softly, and lay back, seeing it all behind closed lids as Brunahild told her tale.

"I begin to understand," she said when the girl had finished, "why Hlutgard sent you to me. It would be wrong to make you lair with the foxes if you were meant to den with wolves. Thrudrun threatened you with the test of the tree, but you will walk harder paths than that one if you give yourself to the god."

"Am I not already chosen?" Brunahild asked, her voice wavering between fear and desire.

"You have been asked, but you have not yet answered him. Do not hurry it, child. When the time comes, you will know!"

By the following day, the willow-bark tea had subdued Huld's pain, and the old woman announced that it was time to tackle its cause. Brunahild spent the morning learning the charms she must say when gathering the red nettles, wild garlic, and stickle-burr they would need, with feverfew and waybroad, and the afternoon ranging the woods to find them. Earth herself was the mother of all healing herbs, as Father Wodan gave folk the wit to use them, and her consent must always be asked.

On the second day Brunahild was given another verse to murmur as she seethed the herbs in butter, stirring with the wisewoman's knife, and strained the mixture through a bit of cloth. On the evening of the third day, they were ready to begin the cure.

"What have they taught you about elf-shot, child?" the wisewoman asked. Overhead, a luminous twilight still glowed, but tonight the air of evening was calm and still. With her pain controlled, Huld looked much stronger, though she still found it hard to move, and her tongue was as sharp as before.

"Hrodlind says it is a magical weapon, shot through the air by an angry spirit or a human enemy. I have seen healers extract thorns, or slivers of horn, or little arrowheads of stone—but I always wondered how a thing like that could come out of the body without leaving a wound."

"From afar off, is it easier to follow the motion of a spear or a man's hand?" Huld answered with a question of her own.

"The motion of the spear, I suppose, because it is larger—" said Brunahild.

"I will tell you a secret. The arrowhead the healer displays came from her own hand. It is a trick, and you will learn the way of it in time. But there is a reason for using it that is not trickery. It gives those with no spirit-sight something to see. They look at the arrowhead and believe, but the healer feels the evil which she has drawn from within the flesh pass into the stone, and so she cleanses it or destroys it, and it is gone."

"Then the magic is in the drawing forth? Is that what the ointment I have been boiling is for? But I have no arrowhead or thorn."

Huld nodded. "Walk sunwise round the old walls, now, in the moment between light and darkness. But it is with spirit-sight that you will be searching. Look until you see a gleam in the shadows, and bring back a small bit of white stone."

Brunahild shook her head, for the trick of unfocusing one's eyes to perceive the unseen was not something they taught the younger girls, and if she tried it, how was she to keep from tumbling down the mountainside? She would have to walk and stop to look and then walk again, hoping that she did not overshoot her goal.

By the time she found a pebble of appropriate color and size, the stars were scattering their own crystals across the sky. Brunahild could not tell if she had picked up the bit of quartz by luck or guidance, but it would have to do. The silence of the evening had deepened, as if all the world waited for what they would do.

Before the hut the fire had burned low. Swathed in the folds of the blanket, Huld's form merged into the stones. At Brunahild's step that rough shape roused, and the girl's skin prickled as she remembered tales of mountain trolls. She bit her lip and held out the stone.

"No—do not show me," snapped Huld. "Do you remember the words I taught you this afternoon?" She pulled the deerhide aside, and Brunahild saw her breasts like emptied bags, and the stretched skin of her belly, but there was still good muscle in buttock and thigh, if the joints could be made to move. "Then say them, child, before the pain grows!"

Brunahild took a deep breath, wondering if she should have gone back to Fox Dance for help despite the old woman's curses. But Huld's black glare compelled her, and though her ministrations might be painful, she supposed there was no real harm she could do. Gingerly she dipped her fingers into the pot of greasy salve and slathered it across the dry skin. It was still warm from the fire, and after a moment her fingers began to tingle. Brunahild had not anticipated that, but of course whatever virtue was in the salve she would feel too.

For a time it was enough to knead the stuff into the skin, loosening muscles made rigid by constant pain. At first Brunahild felt as if she were trying to massage the knots out of a piece of oak, but presently she heard the woman sigh and felt the flesh growing supple beneath her hands.

Her fingers felt lit from within by a gentle fire. She let out her breath and tried to allow her awareness to flow into them, and then, when Huld's eyes were closed, scooped up the bit of stone and slid it beneath her palm against the old woman's skin. Now she had only to remember the spell. . . .

> "Out, small spear, if in thou be!
> If in thou bide, bit or brand,
> Woe-wight's work, shalt wisp away. . . ."

Whose work was it, this stabbing pain? Did one of the Walkyriun hate Huld, or had the attack come from a thurs-woman or some troll of the forest angry at being disturbed? Brunahild thought of the shadows beneath the fir trees and shivered. More than beasts lived in the forest, and there were many things that did not love men.

> *"Wert shot in flesh, or shot in skin,*
> *Wert shot in blood, or shot in bone,*
> *Wert shot in limb—thy life shalt win!"*

With renewed vigor, Brunahild bent to her task, hardly aware the old woman's whisper echoed hers. Her whole body was tingling now. When she opened her eyes, her vision wavered; sometimes she saw the old woman's worn body, and sometimes the radiant flesh of a young girl. *This is the way she was . . . the way she still is, within!* The pang of realization was sharper than elf-shot, and her sight blurred with tears.

With each breath out, Brunahild pressed harder, awareness of all else falling away. As she breathed in, she eased back, trying to draw the pain into the stone, and the bit of rock grew hot beneath her hand.

> *"From shot of Aesir or of elves,*
> *Or else from hags; help I bring.*
> *Flee, evil wights, to the wild hilltop.*
> *Hip, be hale, in Wodan's name!"*

The stone stung as if she had grasped a coal. Brunahild jerked it away with a shout and flung it over her shoulder down the hill. As she turned back, for a moment she saw a wild cat huddled beside the fire. Then Huld groaned, and it was only the folds of the blanket again.

Brunahild sat blinking, listening to the whisper of the fire. Had there ever been so many stars in the sky? In a moment, surely, their patterns would merge into meaning, as the runesticks had written their will upon the cloth. She stared, and brightness blurred her vision. She forgot to breathe.

An odd sound startled her back to her body. Brunahild turned, saw Huld's face grown slack, and for a moment feared. Then the soft breasts rose and fell, and she heard the noise once more. The wise-woman had fallen asleep, and she was snoring.

Chapter 4 ✳ Tracking

Forest of the Teutones
A.D. 412–413

Sigfrid set down the armful of kindling he had been gathering and bent over the marks in the mud left from last night's rain. Ragan had taught him to read what he called the runes of the forest, and he recognized the semicircle of marks, hind feet flanking the tiny prints of the forepaws, where a squirrel had landed and leaped away. He noted the double-wedge where a deer had stepped, going down to drink in the dawn, and the feathery tracery of a field mouse crossing the path.

Two winters had passed since Ragan brought him to the forest. Sigfrid still remembered how the land had changed after they crossed the Visurgis, marsh and meadow giving way to a scrubby woodland that grew steadily more dense as they continued southward, opening out at times into wide sweeps of heathland where purple heather nodded in the breeze. And then in the distance he had seen the forest of the Teutones, rising in ridge upon ridge of green and bronze and ochre with a jeweling of red berries in the hedges, pillared by the grey trunks of trees.

Sigfrid remembered every step of the journey, but the land he had left behind him and the family who had sent him away he could not see. He had forgotten the language of the waterbirds in the salt-marshes, and the immensity of sky. He no longer feared the shadow beneath the trees. Only the woodland and its creatures had meaning for him now, and he sank into the embrace of the forest as into a green sea.

The woods were full of mysteries. Invisible spirits haunted the rocks and waterfalls. But even large animals were sometimes hard to see. He had glimpsed the humped shapes of wisent passing like brown shadows through the trees, and Ragan had said that in a hard winter even the wild ox might seek the shelter of the hills. The earthfolk knew the woods as if they had sprouted from the thin soil, and the boy had never yet found a track that the smith could not read. But the forest itself was Sigfrid's best teacher, and inscribed in the mud before him was a track he had not seen before.

His finger traced the rounded diamond shape of the pad and the five dots of the toes. He could just make out the prick of claws, but more interesting still was the webbed blurring between them. The hind foot overlapped the forepaw a little, as if the animal had been moving quickly. His own breathing quickening with interest, the boy followed.

He found more prints in a patch of sandy soil a little farther on, separated as if their maker had slowed, and then some that were half-obscured, as if swept by a narrow broom. The chuckle of running water grew loud ahead of him, and he dropped to hands and knees and crept onward. This close to the ground the scents of moist earth and green things overwhelmed the senses. Sigfrid paused, nostrils flaring at an odd fishy odor, and smiled as he saw the oily smear on a tussock of sedgegrass, glittering with half-digested scales. The animal he was following was a creature of the water-margins, and it was marking its territory. A staccato twitter and a sudden splashing ahead halted him, then he eased forward on his belly until he could see the stream.

Here, the rushing waters widened into a dark pool overhung by larch and alder. For a moment the boy saw no movement. Then his eye was caught by a widening chevron of ruffled water, peaked by a brown, whiskered head. Soundless, it moved toward a deeper shadow in the bank where a root arched into the stream. Sigfrid's lips pursed soundlessly. He had found the holt of a bitch-otter, and if the slide worn into the mud of the far bank was any indication, she had young. He pulled himself into deeper concealment behind a rock and stilled, becoming one with the stones and the trees.

Ragan heard the boy's footsteps on the flagstones of the smithy, but he did not turn. The iron in the forge was glowing dully already. He took another pull at the bellows, and the charcoal pulsed with pale fire. He watched intently while the metal it cradled brightened, listening to the sounds behind him as the boy stacked the kindling neatly

in the bin. The iron paled from cherry to the color of flame. Ragan
clamped the tongs around the ploughshare and swung it over to the
anvil.

"You're late," he rumbled as he reached for his hammer. Flakes of
burning iron spat from beneath his strokes as he shaped the point of
the share. In a few moments the color faded, and the iron began to
resist his blows. Grunting, he heaved the piece back into the charcoal
and began to pull on the bellows once more.

As the coals flared, he turned, blinking away brightness, and saw
the boy silhouetted against the shifting radiance of a late summer
afternoon. The log-and-turf roof sloped down to the ground the length
of the smithy with deep porches at either end, and shrines to the smith-
god Wolund and the Earth Mother beneath the eaves. In the winter
they fastened boards across the broad doors in the end walls, wide
enough to drive a wagon through, but in the warm season they needed
only wicker hurdles that could be moved as the wind changed. All the
green glory of the forest beckoned from beyond those doors, if the
smith had cared to see.

"Ragan!" Sigfrid took a step toward him, his eyes aglow with
excitement beneath the dark feathering of his brows. "There is an otter
living down the beck, and she has three pups. I got close enough to
touch them, nearly. Their bodies were just the length of my hand.
How old do you think they would be?"

"Three moons, maybe, if they're swimming. First two, they stay
in the holt."

Otters . . . Once, Ragan had known a great deal about them. He
closed his eyes, remembering a sleek head cleaving dark water, a body
twice as long as that of the otter the boy had seen.

"The mother brought them fish to eat. Her paws are like hands.
But they played with the food. They were playing like children—"
The boy's voice faltered a little on the last words.

"You miss playfellows?" The smith frowned from beneath bushy
brows. "Have to be alive to be lonely."

Sigfrid shrugged, and some of the light went out of his eyes.
"There were no children my age at Hiloperic's hall either. I hoped that
my mother would bear a boy to play with me."

"Maybe . . ." In that place behind his eyes, Ragan was seeing an
otter slide belly-down over the slick stones of a waterfall, turn a flip
into the pool, and emerge grinning. Then the shape of the long body
shifted. Ragan saw pale man-flesh glimmering through the water,
lightly furred with brown hair, and the emptied otterskin was laid

on a rock by the shore. With the same supple grace as before, the young man began to clamber back up the falls, daring a small boy to follow him.

"I had two brothers. One was an otter and the other a battle-wurm." Ragan saw Sigfrid's eyes widen and gave a short bark of laughter. "One was kind, and died. The other killed our father, tried to kill me." He turned back to the forge where the metal was brightening with each moment that passed.

Sigfrid was still staring. Ragan felt the old anger heating within him as the metal took the heat of the fire, and saw the boy's gaze grow wary, but he clamped down upon the words that would have driven the child from the forge. Two turns of the seasons had lengthened Sigfrid's legs, and forgework had sheathed shoulders and arms with hard muscle. It was a boy's body still, but the promise of power was already present: power of the tall folk . . . Ragan searched in vain for traces of the other blood he knew was there. Still, perhaps the time had come to share the rage, to begin preparing Sigfrid for the deed that Ragan had brought him here to do.

"Once I had family," he said somberly. "In these hills, we were the last of our tribe. Long ago, my people guide the Romani, the eagle-soldiers, into these hills and lead them astray so Hermundurus and the Cherusci kill them all. Hermundurus pledged protection, but tall folk increase and forest people dwindle." Ragan moved heavily across the stone floor and dipped up water from the barrel in a little cup of bronze.

"Hreidmaro my father was last spirit singer of my people. Folk came to him for magics, even tall folk, your folk, when they find the way. He was skinstrong, had many shapes and allies, but first son Ottar had only the otter shape, and Fafnar became a great wurm—a serpent—when he went to war."

"And you?" asked Sigfrid softly.

"Hreidmaro taught each son part of his magic—" Ragan frowned, remembering. "Ottar knew all ways of the woods and every living thing. He spent days in forest in otter skin, fishing in the stream. Fafnar learned battle-magic and served kings. To me Hreidmaro give the secret of where iron and gold grow under earth, and how to shape them to my will." The smith lifted his massive arms, knotted with muscle and furred with wiry dark hair. "I have only man's shape, but earth-power is in these hands."

He stood as if part of the stone, legs slightly bowed and short in proportion to his arms and torso, braced against an invisible enemy. And as he drew breath, he felt the earth energy rising within him, drawn from deep beneath the soil to feed the flame of his wrath. For Ottar the earth-power had flowed with the waters. Fafnar had become animate earth itself, deadly to all that lived. The fire at the heart of the earth was the core of Ragan's power.

"What happened to them?" asked Sigfrid.

"What is it to you?" The anger boiled over suddenly. "You are of the race that began the evil!" He rounded on the boy, his scarred smith's hands groping for something on which to avenge his grief, and Sigfrid ran.

The boy dreamed, sometimes, that he was back in Hiloperic's hall. In those dreams someone would be holding him. He felt vividly the softness of her arms, but when he looked up, her face was a blur. Sigfrid would wake from such dreams weeping in his corner of the sleeping hut beside the forge. Often, after those nights, he would make his way up the stream to watch the otters play, and he knew that the reason he kept returning was that they were a family. He did not speak of them to Ragan again. And one day, near the end of the summer, he came to the stream and found that the pups had gone.

The next time Ragan sent him out hunting, Sigfrid took the other way, following the traders' road that led past the Pillar Stones. He had never seen a stone building, but he had heard tales of the Romani and their mighty walls. He thought that the Pillar Stones in the forest must be the remains of a barrier built by giants to guard the pass through the hills. Once, a great rampart of sandstone had blocked the ravine, but time had broken it into a series of uneven columns that rose like houseposts above the trees. At certain times of the year the earth-power pulsed in the stones.

If you were determined and active, they could be climbed. Sigfrid was not the only one to manage it, for shortly after Midsummer he had found atop one of the middle stones, beneath a carved sun-cross, the blackened remains of a fire. But when he asked Ragan who went there, the smith had roughly ordered him to stay away. He did not obey. More and more, he kept his own counsel about what he did when he ranged the woods alone. But though he scouted the stones carefully whenever he was near, he never saw any other humans there.

By early afternoon Sigfrid had brought down four grouse with his light bow. He thought of climbing one of the stones just for the pleasure of seeing out over the trees. But it was too hot to try. As he passed the stones his steps began to lag, for Ragan had been in a bad temper lately, and the boy was not eager to go home.

Here the headwaters of the beck trickled between marshy banks and the soft ground made a good surface for tracking even when the weather was dry. Sigfrid's gaze noted the marks where the deer had come down, and a badger, and all the small tracings of mouse and mole, without surprise. Then he stopped short, the dead birds dangling. Before him was a clearly defined impression of a triangular pad and four oval toes with prominent claws. He knelt and pressed his palm into the soft soil—the print was nearly the size of his hand.

Sigfrid had heard the local wolf-pack howling on the hills, but he had never seen them. And he had never found so fresh a track. Grinning, he began to follow the trail.

It led into the oakwood. The prints were fainter on the dry ground, but Sigfrid knew what to look for now. He saw the marks of the scuffle where the wolf had pounced on a squirrel and gulped it down. He found the spot, still wet and pungent, where the wolf had pissed against a thornbush. The animal had charged suddenly at an oak gall, picked it up, and and carried it a dozen paces into the shade of a rowan tree before losing interest and dropping it again. He had stopped to roll in something smeared on a patch of dry grass. The marks were so fresh that the boy slowed, half convinced they were being made by an invisible wolf just ahead of him.

Then, just as he was rounding an outcropping of sandstone, he heard an odd squeaking sound. Sigfrid stopped with one foot in the air, holding his breath, then, very carefully, set it down. Moving like a leaf on the breeze, he slipped behind the rock and pulled himself up so that he could see.

The wolf he had been following was below him, a fawn-colored male brindled with black guard-hairs, prancing towards a lighter female, ears pricked and tail high. They danced around each other, in a flurry of poking snouts and twining necks, bowing and leaping, greeting each other with soft squeals and whines, then stood for a moment with heads resting on each other's backs in pure content.

Sigfrid must have made some sound then, for the male wolf's ears flicked and he whirled. For a long moment two pairs of amber eyes met and held, those of the boy widening in wonder, those of the wolf rounded in sheer astonishment to find a human there. One stiff-legged leap had already carried the female a few yards away. Her yip of warning broke the spell. The male blinked, and then he was off, tail level and ears flattening, forehead still wrinkled in confusion as he ran.

Sigfrid slid back down the rock, laughing, but when he finally was able to stop he found that his eyes were full of tears. Were they tears of laughter, or had he been crying because he could not go too? He did not know, but he was glad that no one had seen.

If I were skinstrong, he thought, *that is the shape I would choose.*

But he did not tell Ragan about the wolves.

From time to time travelers would turn off from the road that led along the beck toward the Visurgis, seeking the forge. It had taken a few moons for the word to get about that a smith of Wolund's race was there again, but after that, Ragan did a steady trade. Sigfrid quickly learned to smudge his face and act the part of a forge thrall when they had visitors. Usually he thought it a good game, but occasionally there would be a child or a woman with the travelers, and he would grow silent, remembering.

He would slip away from the forge then, and seek out the wolves. It had been a fat season, and undoubtedly a hard winter was coming, but for now the pack did not need to range far to feed. Each night Sigfrid could hear them howling as they quartered their territory. Gradually he traced the network of paths they followed, and learned to understand the calling of the ravens that told him where they had killed. He thought that the two he had seen first were brother and sister. The leaders of the pack were older, a big male with a tattered ear, and a grey female to whom they all deferred. There were three others, a female and two males that sometimes ranged off on their own. At first, when Sigfrid's scent reached them, they would run, but after a time they seemed to accept him as a strange but harmless part of their world.

Autumn winds were stripping the trees when a trader rode in from the west with an order for spearheads, to be ready in the spring. Sigfrid came back from watering the tired pony and paused in the doorway, trying to remember the man's name.

"It is for the Burgunds that I'm buying," came the amused, burred voice of the stranger. He was a lean, sandy-haired man in a stained cloak and floppy hat with a face weathered like sandstone from his seasons on the road. "Still aiming to get a toehold in the empire. They chose the wrong side this year, though, and when Jovin the usurper surrendered, the war-band the Burgunds sent to help him had to give up their arms."

He was called Farmamann, Sigfrid remembered, and he had wandered from the Scythian Sea to Ultima Thule, where there was no night in the summer and in the winter, no day. Ragan had greeted him as if they had met before.

"Anyone can sell spearheads," snapped the smith. "They make them by dozens in Colonia and Mogontiacum."

Ragan would put an iron sheath on a plow or rivets in a cauldron for the folk that lived nearby in exchange for what food his three goats or the forest did not provide, but Sigfrid knew that it was only the special commissions, the fine swords and the ornamented spangen-helms, that were worthy of the smith's craft.

"Indeed," Farmamann laughed, "they can make them, and tell the Romani how many, and who they made them for! Quite a nice little welcome the Legions will have waiting when next the Burgunds break the border, if that word gets around. Come now, man, do you have so much work to keep you busy this winter?" he went on. "And it is not so many—if I had asked you to arm the Visigoths you might have cause to complain, but they are snug in Tolosa by now, and I doubt they will trouble you here!"

Ragan snorted and bent to his bellows again. It was only a pair of firedogs he was making this time, heating the iron bars section by section and drawing them out with the tongs, no challenge to his skill.

"Why?" said the smith. "Better for all if all stay home!" He beat down on the bar with a sudden clangor that left the ears ringing even when the hammer fell still.

The trader leaned back against one of the houseposts, arms crossed and head bent so that half his face was in shadow beneath his hat's tattered brim. Sigfrid frowned and moved closer, for it seemed to him that something about the man had changed. He looked at the relaxed lines of the trader's body, wondering why it seemed balanced, and the hewn upright somehow out of true.

"Why do they come?" their guest asked softly. "I walked the misty shores of the northern sea where the Burgunds began their wanderings, and I rode the eastern plains with the Goths. Why did they leave their homelands? They would say it was sickness or bad harvests or worse enemies, but in truth even they do not know why. . . ."

"Do you know?" asked Sigfrid, taking a step closer.

The man's head turned. The boy felt himself being measured by the hidden gaze beneath the hat's slanted brim, but he held his ground.

"They changed, boy. It is the way of the world." And then, more softly: "All things change, even I."

The bellows wheezed as Ragan began to pump once more, scowl-ing into the flames.

"You will change too, master of the old magics, or you will die," said their visitor.

"The old ways better," muttered the smith, "before you tall folk came."

"You cannot turn back the summer." Farmamann waved his hand as if tracing a sign in the air and smiled. "I know no way but by surviving the winter to see the spring. And that is true for everyone, even the holy gods."

Ragan shrugged and picked up the tongs. "I honor Earth and what she holds. That does not change."

A soft, rich clinking came from the leather bag the trader was holding as he tossed it from hand to hand. As the smith turned, his eyes caught the glow of the forge.

"Like gold?" Once more Farmamann laughed. "This, now, is Roman coin, that the prefect gave Gundohar to stay on his own side of the Rhenus. They have plenty of treasure, these Burgund lords, and plenty of children as well. With the Huns breathing down their backbones, they want land, and will buy it with blood if need be."

"Their *hendinos* goes to battle too?" Ragan asked.

"Wet-nursed by warriors from his father's comitatus like a sickly babe," said Farmamann, "but yes, he goes."

"Give me enough more to make him a king-spear, and I do the other." Ragan's cavernous laughter rumbled through the forge.

"Inlaid with silver?" The trader raised one eyebrow. "No doubt it will please him. I will not haggle, after having come so far. But I think that for you also, there is something more important than gold. Is it the chance to exercise your skill? Perhaps the prince will order a helm from you, with a charging boar on the crest and plates of gold ornamented with figures of gods. Can you craft a helm to make a man a hero—an armor to make a man shapestrong for war?"

Ragan's eyes flashed. "What do you know of the skinwalker's craft?" He took a step toward the stranger, his hammer uplifted in his hand.

But Farmamann only laughed. "A wanderer must change his soul as he moves from land to land, and learn to see the truth of things. I see, for instance, that this child bears the blood of warriors, despite the straw in his hair!"

Once more the shadowed gaze was turned on Sigfrid, and the boy remembered Heming with a shiver of alarm.

"He has wolf's eyes," said the stranger, and smiled.

"He is lazy," barked Ragan, stepping swiftly between them. "He should bring water now."

Released, Sigfrid took his cue and darted toward the door.

"If Gundohar likes the spear, maybe he orders more. That would please me," said the smith quickly. "And you will come again also, and bring more news. . . ."

"With a little off the top for me here, and a little at the other end as well?" Farmamann straightened, and tossed the bag of gold onto the worktable. "Or perhaps just to gratify my own curiosity? Well, perhaps I will. And as for you, I think you should consider making a helm."

The next morning, Sigfrid made a point of peering beneath the trader's hat as he mounted and met the man's puzzled grin. It was a perfectly ordinary face, the grey eyes still a little bleary, as if he had not slept well. As Farmamann's back dwindled down the road, Sigfrid wondered why the night before he had thought the man had only one eye.

As soon as the trader disappeared, Ragan set Sigfrid to packing their own two ponies. They had enough raw iron, but to forge so many spears would take more hardwood charcoal than they had ready, and winter was fast coming on. There was not much time left before snowfall, but the year before, a windstorm had laid waste the beech-wood on the western crest of the hills. They would find fallen trees in plenty, already seasoned there.

"The trader?" Ragan answered the boy's question as they got under way. "I know him from before, and he does no harm, but he does sell news. You disappear if he comes again."

Sigfrid nodded, but he felt an odd disappointment. The stranger had frightened him, but there had also been an odd excitement in facing him—the same feeling he'd had when he heard the howling of the wolves.

Their trail was an old hollow way that paralleled the line of the ridge to the southeast. Sigfrid's new woodcraft enabled him to follow it easily, but several times they had to stop to clear deadfalls, and it was clear that since the previous winter, the only hoofed beasts to pass this way had been the deer.

"Very old, yes. My people make it long ago." Ragan chuckled suddenly, and Sigfrid felt his tension ease. "Many paths like these in the heart of the hills. Even men of the tribes do not know them. But we showed Rome-folk once, not far away." He laughed again but said no more.

There followed several days of hard labor, chopping the dead-wood and building it into tight, interlocking stacks, then digging enough sod to cover them. The late autumn sky was a clear, pale blue, and when they fired the stacks, the acrid smoke rose in wraiths through the branches to hang in the still air. The fires required constant attention, but they burned steadily even when frost covered the ground.

But presently the smoke ceased, and there was another period of furious activity while they pulled the sods away to let the brittle, iridescent charcoal cool. The labor seemed to have freed Ragan from the dark mood that had haunted him at the forge.

"No need to watch now. Come—we wash at the stream, then there is a thing I will show you, quite near. . . ."

When they were clean, the smith led Sigfrid downhill through the trees where the bones of the mountain poked through the soil. He stopped at a place like the gap in a broken wall and pointed. The boy could just see an opening half-hidden by bushes, and he looked around in surprise.

"It is a cave! Does anything live there?" It looked like the sort of place where one might find a troll.

The smith snorted. "Not anything alive." He pulled a slab of rock away. Sigfrid could see now that one would have to bend double to get in. He watched in amazement as the smith crawled into the passage and presently backed out again. He was pulling something swathed in rotting leather after him.

"Huh, time to make a new wrapping. Open"—Ragan answered the boy's unspoken question— "and see."

Sigfrid pulled the fragments aside and blinked as a blaze of gold met the sun. The objects were worked in a style he had never seen before, but they were unmistakably bronze eagles, covered in gold and made with sockets so they could be carried on poles.

"Did the Rome-folk lose these?" he asked, beginning to understand.

Ragan gave his bark of laughter. "The Cherusci took them, when the soldiers all dead and the officers hanging from the sacred trees. These two a reward to the fathers of my fathers, who brought the Romani to where the warriors of the tribes could slay. I hear the Legions look for them still."

"But surely an even greater reward would be given for returning them."

But Ragan shook his head. "Those who come into our land, we bury. What we have, we hold." And then his face darkened, and he would say no more.

                              *   *   *

They had scarcely returned to the forge when the hard winter
that Ragan had foretold closed in. As storm after storm battered the
mountains and the woodpile diminished, Sigfrid began to fear they
would have to use the charcoal for fuel. It made sense, then, to sleep
in the smithy, for storm or shine, the smith's labors continued, and
the pile of dully gleaming spearheads in the corner grew higher as the
season drew on.

Sigfrid plied the bellows until he thought his arms would drop
off, and learned to tell from the color of the metal when it was ready.
Countless repetitions showed him the subtleties of angle and energy
in the hammering that drove out the impurities and shaped the steel,
and presently the smith began to give the boy a share in the work,
and his muscles learned the meaning of what his eyes had seen. The
boy forged a spear for himself that winter, all his own work from
picking the rough-cast iron bar to fixing it to a well-seasoned length
of mountain ash, and was well pleased.

Yuletide passed, and the outmonths waxed and waned, but the
cold showed no signs of giving way. Sigfrid heard the distant music
of the wolf-pack and wondered how they were faring. Even at the
smithy, supplies of meat and meal were getting low. The boy thought
of the rich savor of fresh flesh, and his belly cramped with desire, but
Ragan worked without seeming to care whether he ate or not.

And then the last of the soldiers' spears was finished. The smith
began work now on the king-spear, and for a time he had no need of
his fosterling's assistance. At the next break in the storms, Sigfrid bound
on all his furs and took his new spear from beside the door. Ragan
hardly looked up from the design he was working out on a piece of
bone to see him go.

The blaze of sunlight on the snow was blinding after the shadow
of the smithy, and Sigfrid's face burned in the icy air. He pulled down
his hood to shade his eyes, but even through the fringing of fur the
light made them sting. He wiped them with the back of a mittened
hand and started across the meadow, using his spear for a staff. The
going was not easy, but the surface had hardened, and he did not sink
in far. As movement warmed him, he began to step out more strongly,
exulting in the energy that pumped through his limbs.

Closer to the buildings than he had ever seen them, he came
across the line of wolf tracks in the snow. One animal, probably the
big male leader, had broken trail for the others. The tracks led toward

the grey tangle of the forest, where a hungry deer or wisent might go
to strip the bark from the young trees. Grinning, Sigfrid followed, for
surely the wolves knew more about hunting the winter woods than he
did, and where they found prey perhaps a human hunter could as well.

A long bowshot from the edge of the forest the single line of wolf
prints split suddenly into five rapid trails, and after a moment the boy
found the reason: a trampled area where something very large had
been trying to paw away the snow to reach the buried grass. The tracks
that led away were cloven—they were cattle tracks, but larger than
those of any cow Sigfrid had ever seen. From their depth, the beast
was heavy; it had lumbered along as the wolves closed in on it, heading
for the protection of the trees.

From somewhere near, he heard the rasping call of a raven, and
as he looked up, another bird flapped above the branches, answering.
The boy threaded his way among the tree trunks. The sounds of battle
came clearly, the panting of the wolves and a yelp as one was caught,
and the furious bellowing of the prey.

Sigfrid crept forward. He saw the swing of a heavy-bearded head
beneath an impossible curve of horn. This was no strayed heifer, but
the great bull-aurochs of the deep forest, an immense dark bulk against
the whiteness, covered with coarse rusty-black hair. But for the aurochs, the woods were as much a trap as a shelter. In the drifted snow
he floundered, and if he retreated too far he would catch his horns
upon the trees. There was blood on the bull's horns, and one of his
attackers lay half-buried in a drift between the trees. The wolves flowed
around him like grey shadows, taking turns to dart at his nose and
haunches, attacking in eerie harmony.

For a time Sigfrid watched the battle, scarcely daring to breathe.
Then he thought he saw a twitch from the wolf that had been knocked
into the snowdrift and leaned forward. Whether it was his own movement or a shift in the air, suddenly the others whirled away from their
prey and stopped, staring, waiting to see what he would do. In the
silence he could hear them panting, and the deep, groaning wheeze
of the bull.

The boy stood frozen, but his mind raced furiously.

If he tried to run, the wolves might decide to chase him, and he
would be far easier prey than the aurochs, even with the spear.

The aurochs was gaunted by winter, but so were the wolves.
Already the pack was smaller than it had been; even through the thick
winter fur he could see how lean the survivors had become. The bull
was old, but still vital, like a lightning-blasted oak that stood against

the storm. Perhaps he could beat off this attack, but with the wounds the wolves had already inflicted, could he survive for long?

The flesh of this bull will feed the pack for several weeks, Sigfrid thought soberly, *but my carcass would last barely a few days.* And it would be a poor end to be torn apart by wolves.

Without shifting his eyes from the wolves, the boy pulled the mittens from his hands. Then, getting a good grip on the shaft of his new spear, he started toward the bull.

The wolves eddied away before him, ears pricked in amazement. But the bull's head lowered, and Sigfrid wondered if he had faced human hunters before. Close up, he looked even bigger, the height of a man at the shoulder. Each horn seemed as long as the boy was tall. He moved sideways, trying to figure out how to get past the bull's guard.

His point would penetrate hair and hide, but even muscles hardened by hours at the forge could not thrust it through bone. A lot depended on choosing the right spot, but he did not have to deliver a killing blow. If he could cripple the animal, then surely the wolves would finish him.

Sigfrid crouched, balancing, and without knowing, his lips drew back from his teeth in a wolf's snarling grin.

To his left, the big male wolf padded forward, head lowering, ears pricked sharply. The aurochs turned a little to see, and in that moment, the boy's body clenched and released, sending the spear with all his strength toward the bull's throat.

As the shaft left his hand, Sigfrid slipped and went down in the snow. He crouched on hands and knees as the aurochs's bellow of outrage shook the air, bracing for a return stroke from those lethal horns. He glimpsed blurred movement as the wolves leaped past him and looked up, trying to make sense of the tumult of blood and grey fur and tossing horns. Then the spear, shaken loose by the bull's plunging, wheeled past him. He rolled and grabbed for it, rolled again, and came upright still holding on.

The bull had stopped bellowing. What came from his throat now was a horrid liquid gurgle as he choked on his own blood. He still fought, but the wolves were mobbing him. Sigfrid scrambled back as the great black body heaved skyward. Then everything disintegrated into a tangle of thrashing legs and snarling wolves.

Sigfrid's head was pounding. They had already begun to tear at the beast's belly. Through a fiery haze he saw the bull's head arch back in agony, and shrieking, leaped in past the horns. The spear flashed, and he thrust the sharp point through the unprotected softness under the cheekbones and up into the animal's brain. There was a jerk, then he dragged it out as the aurochs collapsed.

Snarling, the boy beat the wolves back with the spearshaft, and for a moment they were astonished enough to obey. The aurochs lay sprawled and bleeding. It was dead meat, thought the boy as the fires in his head began to fade, and why should he try to delay what he had risked his life to do?

But that was his meat too! A swift gash with the spear opened the bull's belly, and as the guts cascaded steaming onto the snow, Sigfrid plunged his hand into the abdominal cavity and wrenched out the liver. Starved of nutrients by the preserved fare of winter, the boy's body knew better than his mind what it required. He tore at the bloody mass, and it was better than anything he had ever tasted, and as he devoured it, the wolves slipped past him and began to feed.

Awareness returned by degrees, but the wolves, tearing at the great carcass, paid little heed to Sigfrid even when the rage left him and he started to feel the cold once more. They growled when he began to hack off a haunch to take to Ragan, but he snarled back at them and they let him be.

His mittens and hood had been trampled into the snow, but as he looked around, he saw one of the horns of the aurochs, broken off when the beast crashed into the tree. Carefully he picked it out of the snow. Then, with the horn thrust through his belt and leaning heavily on his blooded spear, Sigfrid started back to the forge.

Chapter 5 ✳ Raven in the Snow

Taunus Mountains
Yule Moon, A.D 413.

The feast of Yule was past, but if the sun had begun her long journey back from the south, there was no sign of it in the lands of men. Ever since the solstice it had been snowing, and when for a moment the air cleared, the sky was still covered by unbroken cloud. Even beside the hearth that ran the length of the Walkyriun hall it was cold.

Galemburgis jabbed the awl through the tough leather of her shoe sole and winced as the sharp tip scored her thumb, then began to poke the sinew through. The other girls were busy with similar tasks. They spent the nights in their own longhouse, well wrapped against the cold, but everyone gathered during the daytime to save fuel. Across the firepit she saw Brunahild hold up the arrow shaft she was smoothing as if admiring it.

Very pretty, Galemburgis thought sourly, *but Randgrid hasn't invited you to go hunting with her, and she has asked me!*

Melting tallow stank and hissed in the stone lamps that hung from the crossbeams, and from time to time an oak log would crack in the firepit, sending up a spurt of flame. Then one saw the haze of smoke beneath the thatch, the jumble of gear hanging from pegs on the uprights, and the hides and hangings that curtained the bedboxes. Leaping firelight lent a rosy flush to faces paled by weeks spent indoors and picked out the designs painted on the pillars of the high seat in the midst of the hall. Then the flames would die, and there were only dim woman-shapes huddled above the dull glow of the fire.

A few benches down, Frojavigis was brushing out her long hair, golden as a cornfield at harvest time. It glinted with light even when the flames were low.

"It is past my waist," she said to Svala, who had been admiring it from her seat beside Brunahild. "I shall have to cut it soon."

Burgund bitches—Galemburgis sighed. What were they doing here? When she looked at them, she could not help remembering the lands their tribe had taken from hers in the name of Rome.

"Not too short—" said Raganleob, one of the older girls. "The hair of a Walkyrja must be long enough to strangle her if there is need. . . ."

Conversation came to an abrupt halt.

"Don't you believe me?" Raganleob grinned. "You haven't yet learned our history! When the Rome-folk overcame the Teutones and the Cimbri, who were the first of our people to try to settle in Roman lands, they captured the priestesses who had taken refuge in the lager of wagons. When the women asked if they would be allowed to serve the goddesses of Rome, the soldiers laughed. And so, rather than be slaves, our women strangled each other, one by one, with their long hair."

Still laughing herself, she twisted her own long braid around her neck, and let her head flop sickeningly. Frojavigis stared, her brush poised in midstroke above the golden hair.

"A very proper death for a priestess of the hanged god," Galemburgis said into the silence. She saw Brunahild fingering her own black braid surreptitiously; others were doing the same.

"I suppose it would be better to die so than to live as a slave in Rome," Frojavigis said finally, and began, with short, vicious strokes, to brush once more. But Svala still sat with wide, shocked gaze.

"Not all have thought so," said Ricihild. "I hear there are plenty of crop-headed Teuton slave girls in the empire. The Romans make wigs for wealthy women out of their hair."

"What a people!" Galemburgis replied. "Why are we so intent on settling in their lands? We should all go back to the north again!"

"The Roman lands are warm. . . ." said Ricihild succinctly, holding out her hands to the fire. Svala shivered and picked up her spindle. Even in the winter, there was always something to be done, and one could spin without being able to see.

"Those who want them are welcome," Galemburgis replied. "Let the Burgunds kill Romans or die, so long as they stay out of Alamanni lands."

"Borbetomagus was a Roman town, not Alamanni, before the Burgunds came!" exclaimed Frojavigis.

"The whole valley of the upper Rhenus is Alamanni land—" Galemburgis began.

"You gabble like geese!" Thrudrun's voice silenced them. "Have you no work to do?"

Galemburgis bit her lip. Politics was specifically the province of their elders, who decided which side the Walkyriun would favor in a combat, if they took sides at all. Each tribe trained its own wisewomen on the sacred mountains, but the Walkyriun of the Taunus had been established in the time of Hermundurus to serve in the greater conflict against Rome, and girls came to them from many peoples.

After a moment Raganleob laughed once more and began to talk about her consecration to the Walkyriun, which was due to take place that spring.

"If she cannot learn not to make the wrong joke to the wrong priestess before then, she will not last that long," Brunahild whispered, and for once, Galemburgis agreed.

Svala gave a shuddering sigh. "Nor will I—" she said softly. "When the snows melt, I am going home. . . . Do not look at me as if I were betraying you!" Svala exclaimed. "My father has already arranged a marriage for me with a man of King Gundohar's war-band."

Since Galemburgis had come to Fox Dance two groups had made their dedication, but six girls had gone home, and now Svala was leaving too. The child was a weakling who did not belong here, but the Walkyriun were supposed to go about in groups of nine. Would nine be left to be initiated?

"I thought we were going to finish our training together," said Brunahild, and Galemburgis wondered why she sounded so disturbed. "Surely you can refuse—"

Svala shook her head violently. "It is all very well for you, off every summer with Mother Huld. Even Galemburgis has to respect your skills. You don't understand what it has been like for me when you were gone. I know what I am doing. Don't try to make me sorry for you."

Galemburgis raised an eyebrow. What *did* she think of Brunahild? The Hun girl was not a tribal enemy, but she went her own way always. There was no doubting her skills, but Galemburgis felt less easy with her than she did with the Burgunds, whom at least she could understand.

"Why should I want your pity?" Brunahild said tightly. "As you say, you have made your choice, and I shall make mine."

"I thought you would take it that way! You are stubborn and proud," said the other girl, "but I think that in the end my weapon will prove more powerful than yours!" She tapped the arrow with the spindle in her hand, then gathered up the cloud of wool she had been working on and stalked away.

Proud? thought Galemburgis. *Was that why Brunahild was so hard to understand?* The Hun girl did not speak, and she did not move, and after a time, she picked up the arrow and began to work on it again.

"That is good," said a new voice. "We will need it. Our meat is going fast."

Randgrid was looking down at Brunahild's arrow, her grey-brindled hair glinting red in the glow of the coals. Even here, she wore the breeches of a warrior. Old scars gleamed from arms corded with lean muscle by years of work with sword and spear.

"I can go out with the hunters?" Brunahild asked. Her voice betrayed nothing.

Randgrid, can't you see she does not care? Galemburgis glared at the Walkyrja's back. *Don't let her come!*

"You are ready. Gather your gear for tomorrow's morn."

Brunahild nodded. "My thanks to you," she said quietly. "It has been hard to stay penned like a sick heifer inside."

Randgrid laughed and squeezed Brunahild's shoulder with her strong hand. "It is your shooting that has earned you a place in the hunting party, not my pity. I am never kind."

Brunahild bit her lip. Randgrid bent suddenly and plucked the arrow from her hand. Galemburgis watched hopefully as the Walkyrja ran her fingers along the shaft, remembering times when her tongue had been less than kind indeed.

"Do you mean to sand it to a splinter? It is ready for the point and fletching now." Brunahild nodded, and Randgrid dropped the shaft back into her hands. "Get your gear together. We will leave at dawn."

Galemburgis shook her head in admiration as the warmistress moved along the hearth, forgiving even her approval of Brunahild. She would have recognized that easy stride even if she had not known who it was. Randgrid was a true Walkyrja. Galemburgis sighed, her imagination fired by visions of the old days and the old ways, when warrior priestesses like Sigruna had led heroes to glory. Did Brunahild dream the same dreams?

The other girl was running her fingers back and forth along the arrowshaft, staring blindly into the fire. Then she reached into her bag for her knife and began to scratch in the runes to speed it to its goal.

"Look, I have finished it!"

Huld looked up from the cloak she was mending as Brunahild pushed aside the bearskin that curtained her bed-place and held out the arrow.

"And tomorrow I am going hunting," she added brightly. "It will be *so* good to get outside. Will you put a blessing on it, please?"

Huld frowned, catching an odd undertone of bitterness in words that should have been exultant. What was wrong with the child?

"I am sorry—" A momentary flush darkened Brunahild's sallow skin. "I know that even the thought of going outside must make you feel colder."

Huld grimaced agreement. She had spent most of the past month huddled next to the fire not because she liked it there, but because her bones ached in the cold. The wisewoman's bed-place was at the lower end of the hall where the outbuildings broke the force of the wind and the thickness of the thatched roof sloped nearly to the ground. There she had her sleeping furs, a carved oaken chest for her tools and robes, and a worktable. Bags of magical gear and bunches of herbs hung from the uprights and eaves. To insulate it further, they had stretched hides along the wall and stuffed the space between with straw, and coals burned in a brazier of Roman bronze, but when the wind changed, chill air still got in.

"Have I not taught you charms enough, child? Paint a spear rune upon it to make it fly true." Huld forced a smile and turned to her work again, weaving the grey wool in and out of the cloth to make the tear in the fabric disappear.

"I have done that already," answered Brunahild bracingly, though the embarrassment in her face remained. "But if you charm it for me, I will bring you a fat doe. Fresh meat will warm your bones."

Huld grunted. "Can you hunt down the sun and hurry her northward?" She tempered her words with a smile, remembering how easily girls were hurt at that age. "I have promised to be in the land of the Franks for the Spring Feasting, and at this rate I will freeze my bones."

"If you can think about traveling, then surely you have the strength to magic one arrow for me! You do nothing but sit all day!"

Huld snorted derisively, but she could see Brunahild's eyes regaining their brightness. "Now I see what comes of letting you run wild. You have no respect for me."

"How can you say it? Have I not brought you the very first arrow Randgrid said was good enough to use? Bless it, mother," the girl's voice faltered suddenly, "and your wisdom will walk with me!"

Huld gave her a sharp look and picked up the arrow. "It is well made. Have you decided then to follow the warrior's path?"

Brunahild rested her head against the housepost. "I don't know . . . I don't know," she whispered. She blinked as if her eyes were burning from too much close work in the smoky air, or perhaps it was from unshed tears.

Huld peered up at her. "Who has hurt you, child?"

"Hurt?" Suddenly Brunahild was sobbing, "Svala is going home. . . ."

Huld sighed. "So, the swallow flies to her nest. She is wise. She would not have lasted here."

"She said I was proud. She said I did not care!" Brunahild burst out suddenly, and sat down on the three-legged stool at the wise-woman's feet.

"And you, I suppose, sat there with a face like stone and said not a word?"

The girl buried her face in her hands.

"Who can I love? My father has forgotten he has a second daughter, and my sister is busy with her own family. I thought that here I would find sisters, but even you call them vixens—perhaps Svala is right. Maybe I should go home too!"

"Ah, I am a silly she-goat to let you think so. Surely there is love among the Walkyriun. Randgrid and Golla have been closer than sisters these many years, and the others form alliances also, once all the testing is done. Only there are some of us for whom no love of man or woman is enough. It is I who have left them behind, seeking the gods. But you see how they care for me—" She gestured at the brazier, and the furs. "And I love you, my child. . . ." Heart aching, lightly she touched Brunahild's hair. It had been a long time since she had been shaken by such passions and such uncertainties, but she remembered. For a moment she could not tell if it was Brunahild's pain she was feeling, or her own.

Have I learned to love her too much? Her road will be so hard, and she must be strong!

Brunahild turned so that her forehead rested against the older

woman's thigh. Huld continued to stroke her hair, sensing when her
pain began to ease.

"Then bless my arrow, old she-goat—" Brunahild's sob turned into
a hiccup, and she laughed.

"It is much warmer today!" exclaimed Raganleob, pushing back
her fox-fur hood. "Thanks to the gods! I was beginning to wonder if
Ragnarok had been fought while we were all sleeping, and the Ice-
giants had reconquered the world!"

Brunahild nodded. She had already loosened the overlapping folds
of her sheepskin coat as well.

The clouds had parted at last. There was a heady hint of spring
in the moist air that touched their faces, but this thaw was no friend
to hunters. Brunahild told herself that was why the delight she had
expected to find in the day had disappeared, not the fact that Randgrid
had also asked Galemburgis along. The snow was growing mushy
already, and any tracks left from the night before would blur at the
first touch of the sun.

Brunahild squinted across the whiteness that swathed the familiar
contours of the Taunus and was suddenly very glad that she had not
boasted about her woodcraft. Two summers spent on the mountains
with Mother Huld had given her a knowledge of this land that few of
the others could match, though she had learned not to tell them so.
She knew the names of the healing herbs and when to pick them, and
the charms to be chanted when doing so. She knew where the red
deer lay up in the heat of the day and how they raised their young,
and where the tender shoots they liked best grew. But this winter
landscape was a new world, and it was all she could do to make out
the underlying shape of the land.

Still, Randgrid seemed to know where she was going. Brunahild
trudged along after the others, trying not to mind when snowmelt
worked its way through the seams of her calfskin shoes and the layers
that padded them. In all that bright landscape, the crunch of shoe-
leather on snow, their harsh breathing, and an occasional thud as a
branch released its load of snow were the only sounds.

But against this whiteness, any movement showed clear. A little
before noon they glimpsed two dark shapes crossing a slope, and within
the hour Randgrid's arrow brought down the first deer of the day.

After that, though, their luck seemed to turn. The second deer
had bounced away in a spray of white while Brunahild was still nocking
her arrow, and every other beast in the mountains seemed to have

gone to ground. When she found herself pulling her coat closed she realized that the temperature was falling once more. High clouds were gathering overhead, leaching all the light from the day. Beneath the sun, the blazing whiteness had been beautiful. Now there was only a featureless pallor.

But while they were clambering through the snowdrifts something in her awareness had awakened, linking memories of summer wanderings with the contours of the land, and even in the dimming light she knew where they were now.

She paused to tighten the straps that held her leg-wrappings, wondering when Randgrid would give the word to head home. Anyone could see that it was going to snow soon. Galemburgis and Raganleob, the tallest, were carrying the deer, while Randgrid scouted the trail. Brunahild felt the wet kiss of a snowflake on her forehead and increased her pace up the slope, using her bow as a staff. And it was at that moment, just as they reached the brow of the hill, she heard a sound like a breaking stick and saw Randgrid fall.

In moments they were all gathered around her.

"Perhaps it is only a sprain," said Raganleob hopefully. "And if you lean on somebody's shoulder—"

But Randgrid was shaking her head. "It is broken. I did not look where I was putting my feet and stepped through the crust of the snow into a hole!" She bit back a gasp of pain.

"We'll need to bring a horse then, to get you out of here," said Galemburgis a little desperately. She turned to look back up the path.

But the path had disappeared. Even in those few moments, the scattered flakes had become a flurry of white that wiped out the world.

"Get her into the shelter of the trees," said Brunahild. "We can cut branches to lay her on."

"Do you think the snow will let up soon?" asked Raganleob when they were done. Randgrid was sweating despite the cold, and it took her a few moments to reply.

"I think . . . this is only the beginning of the storm. Build up the snow over these branches to shelter me, and cut wood . . . if you can find any dry . . . for a fire." Between clenched teeth, Randgrid got out the words. "Then you must go . . . while you can."

"And leave you here?" Raganleob exclaimed. "A pity that the deer is so small! I have heard of a man surviving a storm by cutting open the belly of his horse and crawling in. But we have the wood for shelter, and we can eat the deer!"

But Brunahild saw in Randgrid's eyes the bleak recognition that she would not be able to survive both the cold and the shock of the broken bone.

"What the Norns have woven will be," said the warmistress. "You must leave me."

"I will go for help," said Brunahild.

"Not alone—" Randgrid began, but Brunahild shook her head.

"I hunted herbs here last summer for Mother Huld, and I recognize where we are. Hrodlind knows the hills too. She will be able to find this place from my direction, even in the snow."

"Then I'll come with you—" Galemburgis began, and Brunahild found herself almost liking the Alamanni girl. But Raganleob was having no luck at all with her flint and steel.

"If you cannot start a fire, it will take the two of you to keep Randgrid warm, and my chances will be no worse alone. . . ."

Randgrid tried to protest, but to Brunahild it all seemed perfectly clear. Without waiting for an answer, she turned, and in moments the others were hidden by the falling snow.

Vigorous motion warmed her. Brunahild tightened the strings of her hood around her face so that the fox fur that lined it would catch some of the snow, and forged forward, head into the wind. The wisewomen would certainly want her if she could save one of their own. She tried to imagine Hlutgard's smile of approval, and the wonder that would fill Svala's face when she learned of Brunahild's deed.

After a time she ceased to feel the cold in her toes. This was not a good sign, but she could not afford concern. With the springy yew bow for a staff she could compensate for the numbness and keep on. She squinted into the flurrying whiteness, trying to recognize familiar outlines of tree-shapes beneath new humps of snow. Surely that stand of firs marked the path to the meadow where she had picked waybroad last spring. If she turned to the right, the land should slope upward, and then she would strike the trader's road that led toward Fox Dance.

But when Brunahild rounded the trees, she found herself at the edge of the forest. There was no path here. Perhaps she should have been turning left all along. She retraced her steps and found a way through the trees, but this path, if it was a trail and not a natural gap in the forest, gave her no sense of the familiar. Still, it led upward. If she could reach the ridge, she might still find the road home.

At the crown of the hill the wind struck her with a bone-chilling force that drove her back among the trees. Pale forms thickened and swirled from the summit as the wind rose. Brunahild clung to a fir trunk, staring, for a moment certain that she had seen a gaping maw and reaching arms. Then another gust swept the shape away. She blinked. Had it been only a trick of the storm? Here came another, more than man-high. Howling, it rolled toward her.

She fled back into the forest, and tried to continue parallel to the ridge, but she could not be sure in which direction she was following it.

Randgrid was a fool not to watch her footing, but perhaps I have been a greater one. . . . Brunahild thought numbly. Without clouds to hide the horizon, she might have managed to see her way if there had been no snow to cushion the contours of the land. But now both sight and shape were failing her. As snow filled the hollows, it was even becoming hard to distinguish up from down. Only the granite bones of the mountains still retained some identity. She came to an outcrop she thought she remembered and marked it. If she kept on in the same direction she was going, perhaps she would come to something she knew.

Exhaustion slowed her more than fear. It would be so easy to simply lie down and let the cold take her, and it seemed to her that her death would be small loss to the world. But then Randgrid might die too, so she had to keep on. It was harder to keep moving when she thought about it, and the snow clung to her shoes and tried to drag her down. Brunahild tried to distract herself by listing the names and uses of herbs that Huld had taught her, or the lineages of kings, but there was no longer any meaning in the words.

Perhaps she could distract her mind with puzzles, with the kennings that were a singer's way to uncover the truth of the world. *Snowfields . . .* she thought muzzily, *the gardens of Skadi.* And the trees in the forest might be called the bones of houses. But better not think about bones, for her own were too close to being frozen. *Think about something warmer*—Brunahild told herself. *What cooks the food that feeds its food?* She tried to visualize the leaping flames of a funeral pyre, but a white fire stung her skin.

Ice, whispered a treacherous voice within her, *is the body of Orgelmir from which the world was made, and to which it will return. . . .*

Brunahild paused as something loomed up before her. It looked familiar, but it took her several moments to realize that it was the same outcropping of granite that she had noted before. Thought moved as slowly as the blood in her veins, arriving at last at the awareness that there was no point in exhausting herself, only to end up where she had begun.

She wondered dimly if Raganleob and Galemburgis would be able to keep Randgrid warm. If the warmistress died, the other Walkyriun would mourn her. Would Svala weep when Brunahild did not return?

Would Mother Huld, whose spirit had walked in Hella's halls and back again, weep too? The wisewoman had said that she loved her. It seemed hard that all her training would be wasted now. Brunahild had never even used the arrow that her teacher had blessed for her. Somehow that seemed the saddest thing of all.

I will shoot her a spirit deer, she thought muzzily. Swaying as the storm wind shook her, she struggled to string her bow. The arrow kept slipping from the wet cord, but all of Brunahild's awareness had narrowed to the simple determination to do this one last thing. She gripped it, gritting her teeth, and aimed the arrow toward the sky. As it slipped from her fingers, the wind roared down around her and whirled it away.

The bow slid from strengthless fingers. Brunahild lurched toward the rocks, wishing they were high enough to offer more shelter. But at least they would serve as a marker for her bones. Would Froja accept her, or would she have to find her way to Hella's cold halls? She leaned gratefully against the stone, unwilling, even now, to lie down in the snow.

The roar of the wind was like singing. . . . Brunahild jerked upright, wondering how long her eyes had been closed. She could not feel her feet, the air seemed oddly warmer around her. Snow swirled in dancing shapes, but she did not fear them now.

Brunahild watched as the snow-sprites leaped and whirled away. Then she frowned. Beyond them a cloaked figure seemed to be approaching, its lashing tail beating back the chaos of the snow.

"Brunahild, Brunahild, you must keep moving—"

The words were far too distinct to have been shouted through the storm. The girl blinked, trying to see. Through a flurry of white the figure of a woman came walking, wearing the face she had seen when she worked to heal Mother Huld, and mantled in a wildcat's hide.

If this was the wisewoman's fetch, and not a product of her own disordered imaginings, the one message that mattered must get through. Brunahild struggled to form words.

"Randgrid lies with a broken leg among the trees where we found the falcon's nest last year. If you send Hrodlind with horses they might reach her and the others in time. But I do not know where I am."

"I do," came the calm answer. *"Shelter is near. Follow me. . . ."*

This is madness, thought Brunahild. But Mother Huld was beckoning, and it seemed easier to obey.

She stumbled through a world without landmarks, floundering as her feet sank deeply into drifted snow. There was no distance, as there was no time, only the ache of exhaustion and the cold. She did not see the rocks until she bumped into them.

"To your left, there is an opening. . . ." The calm voice distilled in her awareness. Brunahild was already on her knees. She crawled forward into darkness, chill, but dry, and out of the wind.

Brunahild wandered in a world of mist, weeping. There was someone she wanted, someone who loved her. Not her mother, who had died when she was born. Was it her father? She tried to summon his black-browed face in memory, but it was turned away. Why should she want him? He had never troubled himself about her.

There had been someone who did care—memory trembled to the touch of dark wings.

Had she died after all and found her way to the Underworld? Surely the caverns at the roots of the world were darker, and where were the bloody rivers those who sought Hella's halls must pass? Misty though this place might be, she had the sense that it was somewhere much higher. A raven called, and she saw a shadow shape fluttering between the hard, humped shapes of stones. With effort she found she could see through the mists. She felt her way forward, following the bird.

Grit crunched beneath her feet as she passed between weathered stone pillars like houseposts, though this place was open to the sky. Upon her cheek she felt the moist breath of moving mist, then it thinned, and a shimmer of rainbow ignited the air. In the next moment the light was gone, but Brunahild moved forward more boldly. The passageway opened out before her; dimly she sensed that she was at the entrance to a larger space surrounded by more stones.

In the center great slabs of rock formed a high seat. Someone was seated upon it, swathed in a cloak whose blue-black folds flowed into the shadows. The raven who was guiding her called harshly, and from the pillars above the high seat another bird-shape replied. The air was brightening. Brunahild took another step and stopped short, a cold deeper than that of the storm congealing in her veins as she saw who was sitting there.

"Daughter, why are you afraid?"

Her feet carried her nearer, but she could find no words. She had seen that face exulting as he rode the thunder, but in the past two years she had learned too much about him not to fear.

"Did I not claim you? It is you who have avoided me!" Beneath the black broad-brimmed hat the left eye of the god was in shadow, but the other seemed to pierce her soul. "Well, perhaps you have reason—"

He laughed softly, and the sound set her to trembling once more, for she could not tell whether it was at himself or at her that this dry and not altogether kindly amusement was aimed.

She planted her feet firmly and gave him stare for stare.

"I am not afraid of you. . . ."

"Are you afraid to die?" His good eye considered her curiously. "That is what waits for the body you left below. You have come to a time of decision, child. That is why you are here."

"If I die, will I dwell with Hella?"

"You will dwell with the other maidens of Gefion in Froja's many-seated hall."

"And if I live?" Brunahild took another step toward him, and her heart stopped at the light that transformed his face as he began to smile. Amber glints still showed in his greying hair, and he did not seem old to her now.

"Then one day you will bear mead to the heroes who serve me. . . ."

Brunahild shook her head, aware of her danger. She could feel the force in him, as if she stood too close to a fire, but she could not draw away.

"I do not want to serve your heroes. You called me your daughter. What did that mean?"

"My daughters dwell in the deep places of my soul. Through them I know the heart of woman as my mind knows man. My daughters carry me to the place where no male can go."

"Then you only want to use me?" she asked.

"Do you expect me to love you?" His eye gleamed maliciously, and he reached out to the long spear that leaned against the stone. "To those I love, I am most dangerous of all. . . ."

"I understand," she said quietly.

His single gaze turned inward, and Brunahild winced, seeing his pain. "Do you understand that I may not spare you, that you will feel all that I feel? My children must serve the same fate as I."

"But will you love me?" She met his stare with her own. All existence had narrowed to the point of brilliance that was Wodan's eye.

"The world is changing. But though peoples and empires fall to dust, my love endures." His voice resonated through the stones, through her bones, throughout all the worlds.

"Then I will belong to you. . . ."

He got to his feet. The garment beneath his blue cloak glimmered like netted starlight. In some dim distance she heard ravens crying, but he was speaking once more.

"They must pass through death, who live for me. Is that your will?"

The voice was very gentle now. As Wodan lifted the spear, light glowed in the runes etched in its shaft and glittered balefully along the blade.

Brunahild nodded.

The point swung round, and she felt the cold prick of steel beneath her heart. Then the spear stabbed inward, and the world exploded in light. Rainbow shards shattered into a thousand visions as agony pulsed through her. She gasped, spitted upon a lance of ice and fire, feeling what he felt—his pain, and his ecstasy. And then she sensed the healing sweetness of the god's lips upon her brow.

"My beloved . . . my child. . . ."

A blessed darkness whirled consciousness away.

Raven voices tore at the calm air. Women's voices clashed and called, muted by snow. Huld took a breath, winced as the bitter air stabbed her breast and forced feet to carry her up the last bit of slope below the stones.

"Madness for you to come," said Thrudrun, reaching out to steady her. "With Randgrid down we'll have enough nursing without having to tend you too! If the girl is still alive, you'll do her no good if you catch the chest-fever here!"

"We will find Brunahild alive—" muttered Huld. "And I'm not as fragile as you think. I've just gotten lazy, huddling by the fire."

Thrudrun grunted skeptically and pointed at the ravens who flapped heavily up from the rocks as they neared. Huld shook her head. Surely the force of will that had arrowed through her awareness the afternoon before would have kept the girl going. The desperation in that mental cry had alarmed Huld enough to send her own spirit winging outward, and in that outfaring she had found Brunahild and led her to safety in the cave.

Unless it had all been a delusion, born from her own need to save the child. They had found Randgrid and the other two girls where

Brunahild had told her to seek them. That part of it was proven. But had she survived the night in the cave? The wisewoman looked at the circling ravens and scrambled the rest of the way up the hill.

"Look there—at the back of the crevasse between those two stones," Huld grunted, panting. Thrudrun peered into the darkness as the thrall wriggled into the opening.

"I see something! He has her!" The runemistress reached down to help the man pull what looked like a draggled tumble of rags into the open air, and Huld knelt, feeling for the flutter of pulse at the throat. Brunahild was alive, but burning with fever.

"Brunahild, child, can you hear me?"

The girl's eyelids fluttered, and she moaned at the brightness, then her eyes opened, widening as she saw her teacher bending over her.

"You are in your body again—" the girl whispered. "But you came to me across the snow. . . ."

"Hush, child," Huld answered. "Do not speak of that now." Brunahild drew breath, coughed, and clutched at her chest as if she had been speared. Her face was flushed, but the skin of her neck was sallow, her dark hair draggled into mare's tails with the damp.

"How did you find me?"

"How could we miss you," Thrudrun pushed in beside the older woman, "with a cloud of ravens whirling up from here like smoke from a pyre? And that's what I thought we should be needing, but you are alive after all!"

"He stabbed me," she whispered, hugging her chest above the pain, "but I shall not die."

Thrudrun felt her forehead and frowned, looking up at Huld, but that did not matter now. The wisewoman bent over the girl she had trained. Her own heart began to thump heavily as she read the truth in those glittering eyes.

"Wodan! You saw the god?"

It was not delirium, despite the fever. Brunahild's hand moved weakly to her forehead, and it seemed to Huld that the mark of a kiss still burned on her brow.

She will be a Walkyrja, and a great one! The wisewoman needed no runes to read that destiny. Brunahild's gaze grew unfocused as consciousness receded, and Huld sensed, rather than heard, her words.

"I belong to him now. . . ."

Chapter 6 ✳ Wolfsong

Forest of the Teutones
Hiloperic's Hold
Harvest, Litha Moon, A.D. 415

On a morning at the end of Eggtide Moon the wolf cubs emerged from the den in the sandy bank below the rowan trees into the light of day. Sigfrid's breath caught as the first black nose poked out of the darknesss, mouth opening in an almost inaudible howl. The bitch-wolf lay by the entrance, whining encouragement, and presently two more brindled heads appeared, blinking amazement at the light. Sigfrid grinned as they wobbled toward their mother, sitting down abruptly at every other step. With a sigh she stretched out to let them suckle, and they clamped onto her teats, the one familiar thing in this alien daylight world.

In the two winters since he had discovered the wolf-pack, Sigfrid had observed them whenever he could get away from the forge. He had watched their matings in the blustery days at the end of winter; he had seen how the grown wolves worked together to feed and teach the young. Once, he had actually squirmed into the empty den, curious to see what a wolf considered a snug home. The burrow led downward into the hill the length of a grown man, then angled up again to an irregular chamber whose earth floor had been worn smooth by years of use, and he had curled himself into the secret darkness, imagining himself a cub in the womb of earthmother, waiting to be born. All these things he had known, but until now, he had never managed to be present at the moment when the cubs emerged into the unimaginable blaze of day.

After a time, the boy rolled over onto his back, gazing up at the luminous flicker of sunlight sifting through new leaves. His flesh shook to the deep heartbeat that pulsed through the world around him, or perhaps the tumult was within him; he was growing so fast these days, his body scarcely seemed his own. Close to the ground, the rich scents of decomposing bracken and new grass came clearly, and some kind of wild mint was growing nearby.

Sensation throbbed through him in a spasm of pleasure. For a moment Sigfrid *was* the world. Then he took a deep, shuddering breath and relaxed again. Like the wolves, he lay upon the breast of Erda, but who was there to care for him as the pack cared for its young? He had only a teacher, and Ragan seemed to grow more exacting with each moon that passed.

I am not like him. . . . thought the boy. *I will never be like him, no matter how hard I try.* He knew that he had become competent in the daily work of the forge. Although there were still some tasks beyond his strength, he could band a bucket or mend a cauldron or hammer a raw piece of iron into a serviceable knife or spear. But he did not hear the secret singing in a piece of iron, or caress wrought gold with a lover's hand.

Thought drifted in a bright haze. Wolves ran through that radiance, each hair of their pelt tipped with a spark of light. He blinked, and the light became a glittering stream of spearheads spilling across a grassy plain. Was that what he wanted? He blinked again, and saw only flames.

When he came back to common awareness, Sigrid was cold despite the mild air. He propped himself on his elbows, looking down at the den. From the tumble of dark fur at the bitch-wolf's side came the faintest of growlings. One of the cubs had got another's paw between its teeth and was worrying at it, but even as he watched, the attacker fell into sleep, and after a moment's confusion, so did his prey.

Sigfrid laughed, and the bitch's head came up, ears flicking toward his hiding place. She could not see him, but his laughter died. Though the wolves had become used to him, he knew that their forbearance ended here, at the den in which each spring their link with the future was forged. Individual wolves were born and died; the pack lived on.

Even the wolves have kindred, he thought, frowning. *But my own kin have cast me out.* This was what he was missing, and his pleasure in the wolves, which had been intended as comfort, had only intensified his need. He wanted a mother to love him; he wanted brothers to try his stength and stand at his side.

But what he had was Ragan, who would surely beat him if he did not return soon.

Ragan stared at the messenger, the image of the sword he had been working on fading as the man's words sank in.

"Th' lady Hiordisa says to come, master, and bring the boy—" the fellow went on. The smith remembered him vaguely; he was one of Alb's people, more at home on a ship than a steed. "And we'll need to hurry. Of the kindred, the two of ye have the farthest to go."

"You can catch horse?" asked the smith. At the man's nod he motioned toward the door. "Take ropes from the peg and follow path. Ponies are feeding in meadow. Save time if you bring them in."

Ragan frowned in irritation as the sound of the fellow's footsteps faded. It would save even more time if Sigfrid came back soon. The boy had been off before the dawn again, roaming the woods like a wild thing, and only the wood trolls knew when he would decide to return.

The smith shook his head and began to sort through his gear. The big anvil and bellows would still be in the smithy at Hiloperic's hall, but he had better take tools for fine work. Someone was sure to have broken a piece he had made and want him to set it right.

Where was that boy? Listening now for Sigfrid's return, he hauled out a leather sack. But it was a change in the air that told him someone stood in the doorway. Ragan jerked around, glaring. He had forgotten how silently the child had learned to move.

"What is it?" The boy shifted the carcass of a young deer from his shoulders to his arms. "There is a strange pony in the pen."

Ragan grunted. "Hiloperic's dead." He rolled a chisel in soft leather and dropped it into the bag. "From your mother the messenger came."

Sigfrid let the deer slide to the floor. "It's a week of riding. He'll be burned by the time we could arrive." There was no emotion in his tone.

"We be in time for the funeral ale—" said Ragan. "They gather all the kin." It had been five winters since he had brought the boy away. And the old man had loved him. One would think Sigfrid would at least show some curiosity.

"What does that have to do with me? If I were of their blood they would not have sent me away with you." Sigfrid leaned his hunting spear against the wall.

Ragan grimaced. So, the child had understood the talk at that last family council of the Albings, and it rankled still.

He looked at the boy who stood before him, all legs and arms and shaggy brown hair, and wondered what the Albings would make of him. In this fine weather Sigfrid wore only a pair of stained leather breeches, hacked off at the knees, and a laced goatskin vest. There was a smear of blood on his brow. Before his relatives saw him, they would have to do something about his clothes. The boy could have the good sagum cape that someone had given Ragan in trade, and one of the smith's gold brooches to pin it with. Sigfrid might still be all unkempt angles, but at least then no one would take him for a thrall.

"That does not matter now," Ragan said repressively. "When king-ship passes, it is more than family concerned. All those sworn to the chieftain must be heard in choosing a new one. All agreements must be remade, all alliances. Oathed to Hiloperic was I for your fostering. We go not for love or blood, but loyalty." He went to a chest and rummaged within it for the piece of wool.

Sigfrid's yellow eyes rounded within their fringing of dark lashes. "Is it they who would break the bond if we do not come, or you?"

Something in Ragan resonated to the quaver beneath the boy's control as it did when he heard the ring of the metal change beneath his hammering. He set down the cloak and turned.

"Ragan, son of Hreidmaro, breaks no oath!" His deep voice rumbled through the flagstones. "I swore to raise Sigfrid as worthy son of Sigmund. Swore to Hiloperic, and swore to *you*. You choose to come with me!" He leaned forward, gripping the stone rim of the raised hearth, willing the child to understand.

"But I will never make a smith, and you know that." The boy had regained his composure, but now Ragan knew what burned within. "You want me to be Sigmund's son, not yours. Why? What do you need from me?" Sigfrid met Ragan's gaze across the cold ashes, and from the fire of the boy's need, something long-smothered within the smith took flame.

"Weeping because you have no kindred?" he asked hoarsely. "I have no kin. *I* am alone. I know better than you think, boy, what you feel. No need for a son. I need . . . a hero. . . ." The words came slowly, like wrought iron drawn out above the flame.

From beneath bent brows the boy returned his stare. "What for?"

"I tell you . . . when you are a man."

From outside they heard the hollow ring of hooves and the messenger's pony whickering a welcome.

"Very well," said Sigfrid gravely. "I owe you more than can be covered by Hiloperic's fostering fee. You will tell me when it is time."

The words hung between them like a memory of the dead fire. Ragan took a step toward the boy. Then the messenger shouldered through the door.

"Well, here's your ponies, and here, I see, is the boy. He *is* going to be a big one, isn't he? You almost ready to go?" He looked from one to the other, blinking after the brightness of the day.

It was Sigfrid who spoke, as if continuing a conversation that had been going on before.

"And what should I do with the deer?"

Ragan drew in a shuddering breath. "Cut off some to cook tonight. Take the rest to your wolves! You think I did not know?" He saw the boy's expression, and suddenly he found himself laughing, a sound that seemed to rumble up from the depths of the earth. "There are cubs now, not so? Give them the food!"

Sigfrid squirmed on the hard bench and tried not to think about how much his new wool tunic itched across his shoulder blades. Perchta had had it waiting when he got here, but it was really too small, and over Ragan's second-best breeches, which flapped around his long legs, he knew it looked ridiculous. All he could do was to keep the cloak wrapped around him no matter how warm it got in the hall.

"Hiloperic hammered Jutes as Donar hammered etins!" sang the bard, and half a hundred drinking horns swung high in salutation. "Heruli he harried, Saxons he smote with sword!"

Hiloperic was nine days dead, and his ashes cold in the mound, but his funeral feast was just getting under way. In a long lifetime the old man had done many deeds, each of which had to be celebrated separately. Ragan had told Sigfrid to watch who sat together, who roared approval, and who stayed silent, to listen for the meaning behind the words. But it meant less to the boy than the gabbling of the geese on the marsh.

The warrior to his right was deep in conversation with his neighbor. The man on his other side seemed most interested in getting his share of the mead. Sigfrid picked at the piece of roast pig before him, wishing he could flee the smoky shelter of the hall.

"Will you follow Hlodomar now that the old man is gone?"

"He has many fair words, but can he back them?"

Sigfrid's attention focused on the speakers behind him. They were behind the pillars, and no doubt thought themselves safe from being overheard. Was this the sort of thing Ragan had told him to listen for?

"They say he is become a great lord on the Rhenus now that

Ulpia Traiana lies within his ward," said the first man. "A ring giver and a land giver he is now, generous to those who swear to him."

"By what oaths, and what gods?" came the reply. "There is venom in that Roman gold. The chieftains who take it want to be like the emperor, who owns men's bodies, and his god, who owns their souls. I will stay with a king who knows he owes his high seat to the folk who set him there."

Alb sat between the carven pillars of the high seat now, with Sigfrid's mother beside him. His bright hair had faded, his face grown heavier with the years, and lines of care had replaced the weather wrinkles carved by peering across the open sea. The boy understood enough to know that Hlodomar might have been a serious competitor for the leadership of the clan in Germania, but it appeared that Hiloperic's brother had changed the rules. He wondered how many would follow him.

"Have it as you will, but our cousins of the Saltwater clan are well into Belgica Secunda. I think all the Franks will dwell beyond the river one day, and it is those who crossed earliest who will fare best in the new land." The voice of the first man faded as if he was moving away.

Sigfrid frowned. Should he tell somebody what he had heard? But surely all this was no secret. The meat on his trencher had congealed, and his head was aching. His mother could not see him, and no one else seemed to even know he was there.

One of the older warriors had taken the horn and was beginning an interminable story about a raid against some tribe that had left the north before Sigfrid was born. Unobtrusive as a wild thing in the wood, he folded his legs against his chest, swiveled on the bench, and eased into the shadows beyond.

Sigfrid came out into the yard just as the sun was setting, and tugged off the embroidered band with which Perchta had attempted to control his hair, grateful to feel it ruffled by the breeze. To the west, ragged streamers of cloud blazed as if Hiloperic's pyre still burned. The boy took a deep breath, wondering how he could have forgotten how immense the sky was here, or the salt tang of the sea.

Cheering resounded hollowly from the hall, but the clamor was not less in the yard. For all comers there was food in plenty to honor Hiloperic's memory. Children chased each other, shrieking. Thralls lay at their ease on heaped straw. In the open space before the gate, some of the younger warriors were practicing their swordplay with yew staves and shields. Sigfrid knew all about spearwork, but the technique of sword and shield was new.

The meaning of the praise singing in the hall had been clear. *If I am to be a hero like Hiloperic,* Sigfrid thought sourly, *I must learn to kill men.* He moved closer to see.

Clearly there were rules to human combat, just as there were for wolves, but instead of the snarling tangles of pack fighting, he noted a curious deliberation in the confrontations of the warriors. The blows, when they came, were swift and hard, but the men took turns to deliver them. The suspense was in where the wood stave would be aimed, and when it would fall. Pairs of fighters circled, eyeing each other over the battered rims of their shield. It was a battle of wills that was going on here, the boy decided, each man strengthening his own spirit and attempting to break the other's before he struck his blow. And that too was like the wolves.

"Do you suppose he's one of the duergar? They do good smith-work, I understand."

As the words penetrated Sigfrid's concentration, he realized that for some time there had been whispering behind him.

"No—he's too spindly, but he's shaggy as a bilwisse—" another replied.

"A wild man!" came a third, with a snort of laughter. "He is a wild man out of the woods who has stolen the dwarf-smith's clothes!"

Sigfrid had hoped to meet other boys, but these did not sound friendly. They were a new pack, and he was the stranger here. And they were right about his clothes. He felt the flush of embarrassment heating his neck and waited for it to fade. Then he turned.

Five boys of varying ages stood by the weaving shed, all of them richly dressed in colored tunics banded with gold-woven braid. They were watching him with an avid glee that he had never seen in the eyes of any animal. The old hurt began to ache within him, but living with Ragan, he had learned not to let his feelings show.

"Were you speaking to me?"

"Donar defend us, it talks!" The largest of the boys laughed. He looked a year or two older, and had begun to grow into his bones, but to Sigfrid, who had spent five years learning to move like the beasts of the wood, he seemed awkward and constrained.

"It fights too," said Sigfrid calmly. "Is that what you want to do?"

"Why, what a troll it is," said one of the others, "not to know we'd be fined for breaking the peace that way. Did you think they were fighting?" He nodded toward the warriors. "They are oathed house-guards, and they are practicing their skill. . . ."

"Yes," said Sigfrid, but his eyes still held those of the big lad. Clearly this one led the boy-pack, and if Sigfrid defeated him, perhaps the others would accept him as well. "Do you want to practice with me?"

"It is forbidden," said the leader, but a note of uncertainty had crept into his tone. Sigfrid was not reacting the way they had expected.

"We weren't forbidden to wager!" exclaimed the boy who had been doing the talking. "Geirrod, you could wager your new dagger against that fine hunting horn he bears!"

Sigfrid's hand moved protectively to the aurochs horn that hung at his side, which he had banded and rimmed with silver under Ragan's direction after he had brought it home two winters before. Geirrod was older than he, and heavier, but Sigfrid was tall for thirteen, and life in the forest had made him strong. What challenge could these house-bred boys offer that would test him?

"You could dare him to climb the roof of the hall—" The talker was like Loki, always ready to lead someone else astray.

"I did that when I was five years old. . . ." Sigfrid interrupted them. The speaker blinked, and another boy poked his head forward.

"Let them both sit out the night on King Hiloperic's grave mound!"

From the others came a murmur of uneasy approval. Sigfrid shrugged. Physical danger he could understand, but why should the dead cause fear? Yet he could see that Geirrod was afraid.

"Very well," he answered, and for the first time he smiled.

The long sweet dusk of late spring was fading into a misty darkness when the boys reached the mound. The Albings had burned their chieftain's body in the traditional way and filled a pot with his ashes, but instead of burying it in the urnfield with the others, it had been laid with a store of food and the old man's arms and armor in the ancient barrow south of the hold where the land began to rise, because Hiloperic had been a king.

For fear of being seen and stopped, they had brought no torches, but Sigfrid thought that more than fear of discovery kept the others silent as they made their way up the path.

"Was that a wolf?" whispered someone ahead of him, moving closer.

"Only a hunting owl," Sigfrid answered.

"But there are wolves in the heathland. Last winter they got two of my father's best cows."

Sigfrid sighed. The singing of a wolf-pack would have made him feel more at home, but he had the sense not to say that aloud. A long shape bulked before them, and he saw a great stone like a fallen sentinel. Beyond it he could just make out a rectangular enclosure of upright stones. The boys moved forward, and now he saw the hump of the mound, with the rock that supported it sticking out here and there like bones.

The entrance to the barrow was black even against the shadows; a doorway to darkness, or perhaps to the Underworld.

"All you have to do is to climb the mound and stay there," said the one who had suggested the dare. "And in the morning we'll come to see who's still alive!"

Behind them someone snickered, and Geirrod turned angrily.

"Perhaps a great slimy wurm will come up from the marshes and devour them," came another whisper. "Or a hag drowned in the peat bog for her evil spells. They pin their bodies down with withies, you know, but sometimes the stakes come loose and the woman walks, wanting revenge. . . ."

"Be still!" Geirrod exclaimed. "Or they will eat you on your way home!"

Geirrod strode to the mound and clambered up it, and more slowly, because he was listening to the night sounds around them, Sigfrid followed him. It was not really fair, he thought as he settled himself on the grassy slope and wrapped his *sagum* around him. For him the night held no terrors, but he could smell the other boy's fear.

"Are you too scared to talk?" asked Geirrod loudly. The rest of the boy-pack must be well on their way back to the hold by now. Geirrod had not spoken before, and Sigfrid had seen no need to.

"What would you like me to say?" He supposed he ought to thank the other boy for this chance to escape the crowded confines of the sleeping hall. He had not realized how uneasy the presence of so many people made him until he came out beneath the open sky.

"Well, don't all those ghosts we're sitting on frighten you?" asked Geirrod. "Sometimes the ancient ones set barrow wights to guard their tombs."

"The forest where I live is full of bones," said Sigfrid. "Long ago the Romani sent their legions there, and the tribes killed the soldiers and hanged their bodies on the sacred trees. The Romani recovered some of them, but there are still trees whose bark has grown around bones. I have walked at midnight beneath those trees and never felt any danger, and those men had reason to hate our kind."

"The more recent dead may not be so accepting. What if Hiloperic comes, wanting new flesh to cover his bones?"

"I would be happy. I would have liked to say good-bye to the old man. He was kind to me when I was a child."

Geirrod made an odd sound halfway between anger and exasperation.

"I don't know if you are brave or too stupid to understand the danger, but you are a strange one. Perhaps I should have fought you. Have you started learning swordplay?" Once started, Geirrod chattered determinedly, using words to fill the darkness, and it did not seem to matter whether or not Sigfrid replied.

It must have been near midnight, and Geirrod, who had at last fallen silent, was huddled in his cloak, shivering, when from one of the stones of the enclosure came a sneeze. The waning moon had finally lifted above the trees, and the uncertain light made new mysteries from shapes grown familiar in the darkness, but Sigrid could see that there was one stone that had not been there before.

"Who's there?" he called softly.

"Simpleton, be still!" hissed Geirrod, flattening himself against the mound.

"Why, who should be here, at night's noontide, save one who seeks those herbs that flower only in the light of the moon?"

Geirrod gave a convulsive start. "Run! It is the ghost of the witchwoman they drowned in the bog last year when the fever came, and she will steal our souls!"

"I don't think so," Sigfrid began, "unless ghosts smell of goat cheese—" but Geirrod was already sliding down the other side of the mound.

"And who are you," came the voice from the darkness, "to disturb the peace of those who sleep in the ground?"

Sigfrid heard the whisper of grass as the speaker approached him, and the snapping of branches as Geirrod scrambled away through the trees.

"I am Sigfrid the Wolsung, and it would take more than Geirrod's tramplings to wake those who are sleeping here."

"So you do not fear the dead?" The woman, who was certainly old enough to be a hag from the way she moved, sat down on one of the stones. "Or the living? But it is wise to be afraid of the things that can hurt us. I suppose you do not fear wild beasts either—but what about hunger, or pain?"

Sigfrid shrugged. With Ragan, he had learned not to complain.

"I wonder what the folk who built this barrow were afraid of?" she continued more softly. "What they tried to wall away with such mighty stones? The winds have blown away their bones with the dust of the years, and the world no longer knows their names. Is not that something to fear?"

"The stones are still here," said Sigfrid stoutly, but something in her voice sent a shiver down his spine. Back in the hall men were still singing Hiloperic's praises, but even the bards could not preserve a man's fame into a new age of the world. When everyone who had known him was gone, would anything of Hiloperic remain?

Sigfrid looked up, but the moon had moved, and he could no longer make out the old woman's shape among the shadows. He listened, hearing only an echo of her laughter. She had left him alone, and that did disturb him, although not for the reasons that Geirrod had been afraid.

By the time dawn came, the boy understood one thing that could touch him. And that was the fear that it would always be so—that he would never have any kindred or anyone to love.

Hiordisa heard the growling first, and then the laughter. She stopped and waited for the pounding of her heart to slow. Her two little daughters were shrieking ecstatically, and so the sound that she could hear beneath their noise could not be coming from one of the big war-dogs as she had feared. Then the growling was replaced by a series of odd whimperings that reminded her of a bitch with pups. Alarm changing to curiosity, she straightened her headwrap and pushed aside the hide curtain into the main part of the sleeping hall.

Arnegundis was tugging enthusiastically at one end of a belt whose other end was clenched in the jaws of a boy who crouched on his hands and knees, shaking his head and growling. Albdrud danced around them, yipping joyfully, and darted in to smack the boy on the behind. He dropped the belt and whirled with a snarl that made the hairs rise on Hiordisa's neck and, still on all fours, launched himself after her.

"Don't eat me, wolf! Please don't!"

"I only eat naughty girls—" It was still a growl, but at least those were human words. "And I am going to eat Albdrud . . . now!" He uncoiled from his crouch and brought her down, twisting so she fell on top of him.

"Then I'll tickle you!" Albdrud locked her legs around the boy's ribs, and her sister joined her, tickling the captive until his growls became howls of very human laughter.

"Arnegundis . . . Albdrud!" The tangle on the floor stilled suddenly as first one child, then the other, realized that their mother was in the room. They struggled to their feet, fair hair flying like dandelion fluff around faces pink with excitement. The boy sucked in air with a snort and then contracted, rolled and gained his feet in a single smooth movement that made her blink.

Hiordisa saw a face whose sun-browned skin glowed just a little from the exercise. But his eyes, outlined in dark lashes that would make a woman sigh, blazed like twin suns. For a moment her heart paused. Sigmund had looked like that, when he roared approval at the warriors' games. Then the light went out as if someone had closed a shutter behind the boy's eyes, and he was only a child, at that awkward stage when none of the limbs seem quite to belong. But there had been no awkwardness in the way he moved.

"My mother—" Sigfrid bobbed his head apologetically. "I meant no harm. I do not know how to play with little girls. . . ."

"No? Well, they seem to have taken no harm." Her daughters ran to her side, and she held them against her, still looking at the boy. "They can be terrors. I am surprised to see you whole!" Arnegundis was giggling into her skirts, and Albdrud clung tightly to her hand. Carefully Hiordisa detached the plump fingers and ruffled the child's hair. "Run along now, my loves. Perchta is waiting, and I need to talk to your brother awhile."

With lagging steps and smothered laughter the two girls edged toward the door. Then they slipped through, and Sigfrid and his mother were alone.

Hiordisa could not speak. She held out her arms, and hesitant as some creature of the forest, Sigfrid moved forward. *Like some wild thing,* she thought as he came to her and she felt the angular boy's body and caught the wild-hay scent of his tangled hair. *Oh, my child, what have you become?*

"Albdrud is four now?" he asked when at last she let him go. "And Arnegundis seven? I am glad I have sisters. They are nicer than boys. I never knew whether the new baby was a boy or a girl."

"I wish—" Hiordisa began, then shut her lips upon the words.

But she saw understanding flicker in Sigfrid's eyes. "You have grown too," she said briskly. "What has Ragan been teaching you?"

"Smithcraft—" He shrugged. "I put the banding on this horn." He patted the hunting horn. She ran her fingers along the smooth surface admiringly. A golden-hilted dagger was sheathed next to it. Hiordisa suppressed a smile, remembering that she was not supposed to know about the wager in which it had been won. If Mother Huld had not come to her in the hour after midnight with word of Sigfrid's safety, she wondered if she would have slept at all.

"And what did you trade for the horn?"

There was a little silence.

"I killed an aurochs two winters ago," Sigfrid said finally. "I and the wolves. . . ."

Hiordisa's breath caught. How foolish she had been to worry about his safety here! No use now to say he could have been killed, or that slaying an aurochs was a challenge that many a young warrior had sought to prove himself a man. What mattered was the other thing her son had told her. All the clues fell into place now—the growling, and the smoothness with which he moved.

"Sigfrid, are you shapestrong?" She turned him to face her.

"Like Ragan's kin?" Sigfrid asked, his dark brows bending. "I wish I were, but all I can do is imitate the wolves."

Hiordisa bit her lip. Perhaps, indeed, imitation accounted for it. But if the boy was fated, then she had to warn him.

"What do you know of Sigi, the first of your line?"

"He was an outlaw who fled from Scandzia in the northern sea," the boy replied.

"Not only a wolfshead, but a wolf in truth, according to the tales," said Hiordisa. "He was shapestrong. So was your father. If you have inherited the magic, it will come to you now, when your body is becoming that of a man."

She looked at him and her heart sank, for his eyes were shining.

"How will I know?"

"Has your body hair begun to grow?" she asked. He flushed, and she guessed that his body had begun to do other things as well, to show him what it was to be a man. "Take off your tunic—"

"Gladly!" He grimaced. "It is too tight, and the other boys laugh." He stood up and pulled it over his head, and as he turned she saw on his back a fuzz of brown that grew like a cape across the long muscles of the shoulders. On Sigmund it had been wiry, grizzled as his hair, but the pattern was the same.

"On your back the hair grows in a way they call the wolfpelt," she said softly. "And they say that those who bear it are shapestrong. It could be. . . ."

"But how?" he exclaimed. "If thinking like a wolf were enough, I would be able to do it already! How did my father make the change?"

"I do not know," Hiordisa answered him. "He never did it while I knew him. And I do not think he had used the skin since he was young. I tell you this only so that you will understand if the change comes upon you. But do not seek it, and tell no one. Folk fear the skinwise, and sometimes the shape becomes too strong, as it did for Ragan's brother, and the wearer forgets what it is to be a man."

"What skin?" Sigfrid asked, and Hiordisa's heart sank as she realized that he had not understood her at all. "Did he have a wolfhide like Ottar's skin? Did he give it to you?" His voice squeaked with excitement, but his golden eyes held hers—his father's eyes.

Slowly Hiordisa went to a great carved chest that stood by the wall. It had held her bride-gear, and her best robes were still stored inside. And one or two things more, at the bottom, beneath the gowns. She felt beneath the folds of fabric and drew out something softer, hidden in a linen bag brown with age.

But the pelt inside was unharmed. She saw how Sigfrid held his breath as he unrolled the rich black and tawny fur. It had been a big beast, weighing perhaps as much as the boy did now, and the hide was tanned intact, so that the mask might be drawn over the head and the forepaws looped across the chest to hold it on. Sigfrid lifted the fur, and she snatched at his arm.

"No! If that thing still has magic, I do not want you changing here, with Alb scarcely seated in his power! I should never have told you it existed!" she said fiercely. "But you had the right to know. Hear me, Sigfrid—if you are wise, you will never put it on. But if you must, promise me that you will never wear it to fight against men!"

"That would indeed be unholy," he said somberly. "I would not insult a noble kindred by using it so. When I war against humans, I will use the teeth and claws we craft in Ragan's forge."

Hiordisa managed a smile, though she was not at all sure he had been joking. But it was not until the wolfskin had been wrapped up again that she could put her arms around him once more and pretend that he was only her child.

When Sigfrid returned to the forest with Ragan, the wolfskin went with him, but the spring days lengthened into summer, and still he did not put it on. At first it was because there was too much work waiting for them, and he was kept busy at the bellows or preparing the rough iron for Ragan's finishing. And then, lying in his hiding place and watching the cubs grow from balls of dark fur to leggy youngsters as awkward as he was, he thought that perhaps this should be enough for him. After all, he was not a wolf, but a man.

Then autumn came, with a crisp wind that blew the leaves into flame. The deer were fat that year, and it seemed to Sigfrid that the wolves howled for the sheer joy of being alive. He would lie awake and listen, pressing his nose against the hole he had poked in the wattle and daub of the sleeping hut to sniff the night air.

And then came a night when a harvest moon golden as a wolf's eye lifted over the treetops, and the world was changed. The day had been golden too, with the mellow warmth that came sometimes just before the beginning of winter, as if the earth were basking like a sated beast, fat with the produce of the year.

Inside the sleeping hut it was stifling, but a little wind had sprung up with sunset. Through his peephole Sigfrid could smell the rich scents it was releasing from the forest, and suddenly he could not bear the stink of human bodies in the hut anymore. Ragan breathed like a bellows in his bed beside the other wall. Sigfrid stiffened as he stirred; then the smith turned over and began to snore.

The boy smiled and sat up. He was naked atop his sleeping furs already, and the night was not cold enough to require clothes, but as he started to rise, he heard the wolves howling in the distance, and his heart began to pound. The night was magic, and he could no longer deny his hunger. Very quietly, he felt behind the clothing that hung on the peg in the wall and unhooked the linen bag that he had hidden there.

He went first to the stream and scrubbed away the scents of sweat and cooked food and woodsmoke with handfuls of sweet herbs. Then he moved off along the trail the deer used, letting the air dry his skin. He felt the hair that grew across his shoulders rising as the wind's cool fingers touched him, but he did not think it was from cold. He came out into a clearing and stood bathed in the light of the moon, and a trembling came upon him. He unrolled the wolfskin with shaking fingers and slung it across his pack, pulling the mask up over his head and hooking the forepaws across his chest with the thong.

Nothing happened. The old leather was soft against his back, the long guard-hairs tickled his skin. Perhaps to become a wolf, one must move like one. Sigfrid glanced around him, but nothing was watching but a dark bird that was roosting in one of the trees. He dropped to a crouch and moved forward, letting his limbs loosen in the bouncing wolf-trot he had so often seen. Whatever else might happen, there was pleasure in the movement that he had not expected. The black bird stirred as he passed beneath its tree and flapped heavily skyward. Sigfrid started to laugh, then turned the sound to a wolf's whine. Now he was going faster. If he was not a wolf, at least he could run like one.

Limbs moved more easily as his blood warmed. There was no self now, only the act of running. He sensed rather than saw the wolf trail and turned to follow it, plunging into a world of new sensations. His eyes distinguished easily between a hundred shades of light and darkness. Above the faint brush of bare feet on leaf mold or grass he heard the scurry of a foraging mouse, the slower rustle as a badger pushed through the bracken. But more remarkable still were the smells. His nostrils flared at the rich earthen scent where the badger was digging for acorns in fallen leaves still damp from yesterday's rain. A hint of musk told him that a fox had crossed the path, and then he smelled the old stump, richly pungent, where the wolves of the pack had scent-marked their trail.

It was then that he sensed the two wolf-shaped shadows paralleling his path. As if his awareness had forced them to take on substance, first one, then the other, flowed out of the undergrowth and lolloped ahead of him down the trail. Grey as mist and larger than any wolves he had ever seen, they did not belong to the pack that laired by the Pillar Stones. Their fur glistened in the moonlight; in the shadows their eyes glowed.

Then they burst into a clearing, and he saw the pack waiting. He slowed, expecting a challenge, but the two grey wolves melted into the tangle of snapping muzzles and wagging tails like brothers, and before he could retreat, he was engulfed by rank breath and rough fur, the poke of a cold nose and the warm lick of a tongue, and the chorus of whines and yips and squeals. Those sounds were coming from his own throat too, and when the black leader gave a final bark and bounded off on the scent of a young doe, the creature that had been Sigfrid leaped after him with the others, the two grey wolves running at his side.

They killed a league to the north, and started back, more slowly, toward the old den. The moon was sinking westward when they found themselves at the Pillar Stones. The older wolves flopped down on the grass by the stream while the cubs began to play tag among the Pillars. But it seemed to Sigfrid that the two mist wolves were climbing the stones. He started after them, and paws that were remembering they had fingers pulled him upward. Panting, he scrambled to the top of one of the middle pillars and crouched on hands and knees on the cold stone, sucking in great gulps of night air.

Around him the world fell away in insubstantial swathes of hill and forest. Sigfrid stared into the heavens, seeking the wolves. Power pulsed from the depths of the earth through the core of the stone and the mortal creature that clung to it. Blinded by moonlight, he thought he saw figures in the radiance; two wolves trailing a man on a great horse who hunted across the skies.

Sigfrid felt his back arching, his head tipped back, and his throat opened wide. And as the pack below burst into song, all his pain and passion burst free in an ecstatic howl.

Chapter 7 ✻ The Mists of the Rhenus

Burgund Homeland
Haying Moon, A.D. 416

It was only just past the first daymark, but Midsummer heat gripped the land as if it were noon. Even in the hills of the Taunus the air shimmered with heat-haze. The hall of the Walkyriun was stifling, but the dark needles of the fir grove above Fox Dance glittered as they caught a stray current of the upper air. In the summer, the wisewomen held their deliberations here. Sighing, Huld let the voices of her sisters drone on and turned her face toward that illusory coolness. If she had wanted wind, there was always a breeze at the High One's Hill, and there she would not have had to pay for it by sitting through this meeting. She sighed again as the ordinary accounting of their lives rolled onward: tallies of stored grain, the output of milk and cheese calculated in terms of mouths to be fed.

If I had waited a little longer to return from my visiting, I would have missed this, Huld reflected. She was welcome at any of a hundred holds, and she had hoped to get back to King Alb's place this year. The child Sigfrid was growing interesting, and he might need more counsel than Ragan could provide to cope with his inheritance.

But today the Walkyriun had more important matters to consider than whether they needed to trade for additional grain before fall. Huld lifted the damp cloth of her robe away from her breast and forced herself to focus on the conversation once more.

"They say that new Burgund clans are moving into Germania Prima with every moon," said Hrodlind. "Their warriors could be driven from occupied lands, but if their families are taking root there, I think they will stay."

"Perhaps," Randgrid answered her. "But now that Wallia has pacified Iberia, the Visigoths are settling quietly down in southern Gaul. With Singereik dead and that Roman princess that Adolfus married gone back to her kin in Ravenna, the legions will have more leisure to think about the Rhenus. They may regret making the Burgunds *feoderatis*, and take back the lands they gave away."

"That would suit the Alamanni," Hlutgard observed. "They have never given up their claim to the valley, and ever since the salt wars in my father's time, they and the Burgunds have been bitter enemies."

"Since when has our purpose been to support the Alamanni?" Randgrid sat up, frowning.

"We support whoever will keep the Romani from this land," the leader of the Walkyriun answered sternly. "Let the greedy tribes push westward and leave the rest of us in peace behind them. If strengthening the Burgund hold on the Rhenus will accomplish that goal, we will support them. If they falter, then the Alamanni will have our aid."

Huld snorted. "The greedy ones go westward," she echoed, "and there they learn the Roman ways. One day they will run out of lands to conquer and come flooding back upon us with the strength of our people still in their arms and the speech of the White Christ on their tongues. What price then the old ways?"

"Who—" Randgrid began.

Huld shrugged. "Perhaps the Goths, if they fail in Italia. Or the Franks who have moved into northern Gaul. I have been among them and seen the changes. They bury their chieftains now, instead of sending them to Wodan with fire."

"They grow fearful as the Romani, hiding their dead in boxes of stone," said Hlutgard scornfully. "Wodan does not need such warriors! We will preserve the magic that serves the gods as long as the chieftains send us their daughters to train!"

"Let us discuss the girls, then," said Hrodlind impatiently, "and stop speculating about armies we may never see!" Golla laughed, and a murmur of approval came from the others. From the tree above them a raven jeered as if in agreement. Huld looked up, eyes narrowing.

"So, Hidden One, is your messenger here to make sure we decide correctly?"

She glared at the raven, and it seemed to her that laughter whispered through the trees in answer. When she looked back at the others, Hlutgard was regarding her suspiciously, and she shrugged. Ravens were common enough on these heights; not every sighting was an omen, and she could have imagined the laughter. Then, although the sky seemed cloudless, she heard the low rumble of thunder.

"I hear you!" She closed her eyes, gooseflesh pebbling her arms despite the heat in the air. *"But the decision is not mine alone. You must tell your other daughters what you desire!"*

"It is time to consider whether the Nine we have currently in training are ready for initiation. Frojavigis, Donarhild, Fridigund, Galemburgis, Ricihild, Liudwif, Eormanna, and Brunahild have all completed their training here," said Hlutgard.

"But it takes more than training to make a wisewoman, and as you all know, the learning is never really done. Before a girl binds herself to life among us, we must be certain of her commitment, and we must believe that she has the spirit of a Walkyrja, that she will be accepted by the gods. Raganleob, you are the youngest among us and have trained with them. What do you say?"

Raganleob, who had lost a great deal of her brashness at her own initiation, flushed to the hairline as the other Walkyriun all looked at her. The rest of her Nine were already scattered to other duties, some taking further training in their specialties, others in service to their own tribes. Of her group, she was the only one who had stayed at Fox Dance to assist in the training of the girls who came after.

"I think that Frojavigis is as ready as she will ever be," she began. "She is steady; the others all like her."

"I agree." Hrodlind took pity on her confusion. "As you know, I have been training Frojavigis in herb lore. Her skill is not remarkable, but her knowledge is adequate, and she is very careful. But I think she will be called to serve as wisewoman at some thorp or steading. She needs the life of a village around her—I do not see her staying here."

"Well enough, when she is ready—" said Hlutgard. "Are we agreed?" The other women were nodding. "Very well. Hrodlind, tell the girl and help her to prepare."

As the afternoon wore on, the Walkyriun haggled their way through the strengths and weaknesses of the other candidates. The ideal was for a group of nine to finish together, though often enough sickness or family politics or failure to pass the testing diminished the number. This group had already lost Svala, and all agreed that Fridigund was not yet ready. Huld said little, knowing that Brunahild was being kept for last because Hlutgard expected a heated discussion, but she could not help tensing when the leader finally turned to face her.

"Now we must consider your student, Brunahild, who has been

with us for six winters. Is she ready for initiation? Is she worthy to be a Walkyrja?" There was a silence as she looked around the circle. "Raganleob, what do you say?"

The younger woman shook her head, smiling. "What can be said? You all know that Brunahild is the best of them at everything."

"Her knowledge of herbs does credit to your teaching, Huld," said Hrodlind a little reluctantly.

"She has a good instinct for the spells to use with them too." Huld smiled sweetly.

"Her swordwork would be more effective if she had more weight to put behind her blows," said Golla, "but she knows enough to protect herself on a battlefield. She can ride anything with four legs and a tail, but that is no credit to us—the Huns put their children on horses as soon as their legs are long enough to straddle a pony's back."

"And she is wonderful with a lance or bow—with anything requiring a good eye," Randgrid added.

"She understands my lore well enough, though I don't think it really interests her," commented Wieldrud the midwife.

"But the runes do." Thrudrun laughed a little ruefully. "They speak to her. When she casts the staves the patterns are always clear."

"We all know that she works hard and without complaining," said Hrodlind. "As far as knowledge goes, she could have been initiated two years ago. But that is not the point, is it? Can we trust her? Can we work with her? If we initiate Brunahild, where is all that energy going to go?"

"That is what I wonder—" said Hrodlind. "She is almost too good. She goes her own way."

"She takes after her teacher—" Randgrid began, not unkindly, but Hrodlind shook her head.

"I do not blame Huld! But what is admirable in a priestess of proven wisdom could be dangerous in a girl."

"She has the power to draw others to her," said Raganleob. "She used to be very popular with some of the younger girls. But she seemed to withdraw after Svala went away."

"How can she function in a Nine if she doesn't get along with the others?"

"It is only Galemburgis who really dislikes her, and they have been keeping their tempers at least as well as we do, these days!" Golla laughed.

"It was after she was lost in the snow that she seemed to change. . . ." observed Randgrid. They all looked at Huld.

"After Wodan claimed her," Huld said flatly, and laughed. "You are chattering like magpies, sisters, as if the decision were yours! If you do not initiate her, *he* will do it himself. If the god wants Brunahild, a raven priestess she will be, whatever you do. Better cooperate, and keep some control!" There was a heavy silence, and Huld listened, waiting for thunder.

"The god may want her, but what about the goddesses?" asked Wieldrud. "If she does not also have their aid he will devour her."

"About her preparation there is no doubt," Hlutgard said slowly at last. "Nor about her commitment. But we must live among men, and she is Bladarda's daughter. For six years he has ignored her, but the Huns grow steadily more powerful. When she came to us, no word of her future was spoken. Do we dare to claim a royal daughter of the Huns' royal line?"

"A fine turn-up it would be if we initiated the girl and then found her father had betrothed her to some chieftain of the Goths!" exclaimed Raganleob.

"If Wodan wants her, let him handle the Huns," said Thrudrun, grinning. "I'll vote for making Brunahild a Walkyrja, but before we do it, she must be released from her father's authority."

"To send a message and get word back again will take until winterfall," objected Raganleob. "It is not fair to the other girls."

"Let Brunahild seek her own freedom," said Hlutgard. "A visit to her people will test her desire, and the will of the god."

"Why not send the others with her as their final testing?" suggested Huld. "If they are still all speaking to each other when they return we will know they are a Nine indeed!"

"I like that! Send them all off together, and initiate the ones who return!" Thrudrun's large white teeth gleamed as she laughed, and as if in echo, the raven cawed from the tree.

> *"One is for the Worldtree,*
> *Standing straight and tall,*
> *One is Earth our mother*
> *Who giveth food to all—*
> *Nine worlds upon the Tree abide,*
> *Nine by nine the Choosers ride—"*

The voices of the other girls echoed sweetly along the trail as Brunahild drew rein. Before her, the great river rumbled to itself like some gigantic serpent as it cut through the rising ground where the

Taunus came down to the plain. The grey-green wrinkles changed shape constantly, glittering as they caught the sun. Her young bay mare, sensing its rider's distraction, stopped and began to nibble at a low-hanging branch of alder that shaded the trail. Clearly nothing would stop this water until it reached the northern sea. Why was she riding south when even the river was rushing the other way?

> *"Three is for the High One,*
> *The Highest and the Third;*
> *Three the holy Norns who*
> *ward the Well of Wyrd.*
> *Nine worlds upon the Tree abide,"*
> *Nine by nine the Choosers ride—"*

came the words of the song.

"Brunahild!" Galemburgis's laughter startled her back to awareness. "Move that beast along! One would think you had never seen a river before!"

"Not this river—" she answered, but her heels drummed against the mare's sides, and the animal snorted and bounced forward, raven feathers fluttering from the bridle. "I came to Fox Dance from the east, through the hills. Is it like this all the way?" She squinted to see the shining mass through the summer haze.

"It is calmer to the south, where the valley broadens," said Galemburgis, "and when it reaches the great plain to the north they say it turns westward and hardly seems to move at all. It is only here that it is so dangerous, because of the gorge."

That was not what Brunahild had meant, but she nodded. Now she could see upriver, where the western hills fled away in long slopes from the river meadows, but she thought that even among those reedy flats the river could show its strength. In their lands along the Danu her people preserved the reverence for water they had learned in the arid steppes from which their fathers came. This river, the greatest in Germania, was clearly a being of great power.

Wanderer, she asked silently, *which way should I go?* But this time the voice she heard so often said no word.

"Father Rhenus!" Galemburgis lifted a hand in salute, only half-mocking. "I am sorry our way lies away from you!"

"Does it have to?" asked Frojavigis. "Why not follow the river south for a while and turn east along the Nicer instead of following the Moenus now?"

Galemburgis opened her mouth, and then, with visible restraint, shut it again. Of course the Alamanni girl would not want to venture into Burgund lands. But Galemburgis knew as well as any of them that initiation depended on their completing this journey in harmony.

"Along the Moenus lies the shortest way to my father's lands," said Brunahild reluctantly. The mare laid her ears back, and the girl jerked at the rein before she could aim a kick at Galemburgis's grey.

> *"Eight are the airts of heaven*
> *from which the winds do blow,*
> *Eight legs on the stallion,*
> *whereon Wodan doth go.*
> *Nine worlds upon the Tree abide,*
> *Nine by nine the Choosers ride—"*

The others were still singing.

"Well, we must follow it for a time to reach the ford no matter what we decide," said Ricihild.

Brunahild nodded. The others, even Galemburgis, seemed to be looking to her as leader, although no one had precisely appointed her, and she was glad not to have her authority tested for yet a while. Together now, the riders lifted their voices to finish the song.

> *"Nine days and nights All-Father*
> *did hang upon the tree;*
> *Nine nights Fro waited, longing,*
> *his etin-bride to see.*
> *Nine worlds upon the tree abide,*
> *Nine by nine the Choosers ride—"*

Brunahild was still undecided the next day when they saw the brown gleam of the Moenus in the distance and came to the fork that led down to the ford. But it was foolish to want to take that way— the sooner she settled things with her father, the faster she could return. And she did want to return—she had built her life on that assumption; she could not question it now. She kicked the bay mare firmly in the ribs and led the way at a smart trot down the road.

It was as they started to pass the turnoff that Brunahild's pony shied. She yanked on the reins and turned the mare in a tight circle, looking over her shoulder. *A body* she thought as she glimpsed a heap of rags in the road with the largest raven she had ever seen perched upon it. Then the bird flapped heavily upward, and the bundle quivered and unfolded itself into a human shape, wrapped in a ragged cloak with a tattered broad-brimmed hat pulled down over its eyes.

Not dead, only dead drunk! she thought as her pony reared again, snorting. It was a young horse, and Brunahild had counted on this journey to complete its schooling. The other girls, with more warning, had pulled up, snickering as they watched her struggle with the mare.

"Out of my way, fool, before I trample you!" She added a few well-chosen epithets in her father's tongue.

For a moment he blinked at her with a vacant, rheumy eye. Then awakening intelligence suddenly transformed what she could see of his features, and he began to laugh.

"You be a greater fool than me, if you go that way!"

"What do you mean?" Brunahild got her mare under control finally and held her in as the beggar shuffled forward, leaning on his staff.

"Hermunduri and Goths are fighting. Goths got a Hunnish sub-chief, but the Hermunduri are between ye. You'd make a fine hostage, a maiden of the royal Huns—"

Brunahild bit her lip, frowning. *But I'm not!* her spirit cried. *I am Walkyriun!* and then, *How did he know?*

"They would not dare!" Frojavigis booted her mount forward. "We are Sacred Women, under the protection of the gods!"

But would the Hermunduri respect that, wondered Brunahild, especially since she and her companions were not yet sworn?

"Would we be any safer among the Burgunds?" she asked then.

"Burgunds don't dare offend Huns now, with their best men away trying to hold the western lands. You go, get a good welcome."

"This is ridiculous," exclaimed Brunahild, as a babble of debate erupted behind her. The old man's rags fluttered as the mare danced around him, but he stood without moving. A second raven had joined the first in the beech tree, jeering mockingly.

"How would we get across the Moenus?"

The old man grinned wolfishly. "River's low. You only get a little wet, you take the ford. Go south, daughter—meet an old friend. . . ."

Daughter. . . . Brunahild felt the hair prickle on the back of her neck, and the bay, sensing her disquiet, began to sidle once more. If only the wretched beast would stand still so she could see—

But the other girls, relieved to have the argument settled, were already reining their ponies past her, and the mare wanted to follow.

"I am Bladarda's daughter," she hissed, wrestling the animal down.

"Are you?" He straightened, suddenly taller. The droop of his hat hid his left eye, but the one she could see held hers so that she could not look away, and even the mare stood still, trembling. "Brunahild, south lies your way. Go!" He lifted the staff.

Brunahild felt the bay mare's muscles bunch beneath her; then they were bolting after the others.

Masked god ... Many-shaped ... Wanderer.... The pony's hoofbeats drummed out names as they shot down the road. It could be. Huld said that the gods spoke sometimes through the mouths of men. But she of all people should have recognized Wodan! Brunahild told herself that she would have known him if she had met him in a vision, but the shock of seeing him clothed in mortal flesh still had her shaking.

Why must she take the southern road, and what friend waited there? Would her father let her join the Walkyriun? *Did he still love her?* Her visions had always come at the god's will, not hers, and she had so many questions! When Wodan spoke to her, doubting was impossible. It was when he was silent that she began to wonder if her own loneliness had made her imagine it. Why should she have been chosen, after all, who had forsaken her own people and her father's gods?

She twisted in the saddle as the pony slowed and saw the old man staring after her. He was leaning on his stick now, but his head was tipped back, and she could see very clearly that he had two eyes. The ravens were dwindling black specks in the summer sky. But the brown waters of the Moenus gleamed ahead and the others were already splashing in the shallows.

They called to her, beckoning, and she let the mare go. In the tumult of getting all the animals safely across the ford, they did not notice how silent she had grown, and how thoughtful.

The east bank of the Rhenus was rich land, long cultivated and bearing rich crops of emmer wheat and barley. In some places men had already started to harvest, and the gold of the grainfields deepened with each day. The girl rode between field and wood and waving reedbeds that parted to show the flat green of the deep-flowing river that was the heart of the land.

At night they camped among the alders near the river's edge. The harvesters were glad enough to give them newly cut grain in exchange for a blessing or a cast of the runes, and Brunahild shot waterfowl with her bow. It was a smiling season, in a smiling land, and Brunahild's companions rode with laughter. By day she laughed with them. But at night, despite her longing, she slept without dreams.

For four days they traveled, until they saw the blue waters of the

Nicer flowing down from the dense wall of forested hills on their left, and turned eastward at last.

Through the high window Gudrun could see swallows, flickering in and out of vision as they darted in and out of their nests beneath the eaves. The swallows had been here since the Romans built this fort they called Rufiniana. Now only two walls of the old stone hall remained. Her father had rebuilt the rest with braced timbers and put on a thick thatched roof to replace the scattered Roman tiles. Now they called the place Holy Hill after the sacred mountain across the river, but the swallows remained. The girl's gaze followed the swift, swooping flight, and she thought that even if the Burgunds should leave this land, the swallows would be here still.

"Gudrun?" Footsteps rang on worn marble. "Gudrun!"

For a moment her awareness, still aloft with the swallows, fluttered helplessly. Then consciousness plummeted back into her body, and she knew the familiar clutter of the women's rooms, and the massive shape of the woman sitting across from her, and her own name.

Godomar skidded to a halt in the doorway as he saw their mother and lifted a hand in formal greeting, still breathing hard.

"Yes, my son?" Queen Grimahild's heavy-lidded eyes lifted from the embroidery in her lap as she surveyed him.

"People are coming!" he muttered. "Walkyriun—that Hun girl that Gudrun met at Halle. . . ." His words trailed off, and he shot a glance at his sister; clearly he was remembering how Gudrun had disgraced them all. But that, she thought indignantly, had been six years ago! She jammed her embroidery needle into the cloth.

"Father Priscus is muttering, and the men want to know if we should let them in. . . ." Godo went on.

The queen's green eyes opened a little wider. "But of course. We are not yet so Christian as to refuse any traveler hospitality in this hall . . . even heathen priestesses." Her lips thinned. "Particularly when one of them is the khan Bladarda's child."

Gudrun suppressed a smile. Father Priscus squabbled with the Arian priest Severin at dinner each evening, but both of them retired to their huts babbling prayers, when the Burgunds feasted the old gods. And even men of the ancient faith might be startled into a warding gesture when they met her mother returning from the rites that she celebrated in the forest from time to time. Carefully Gudrun began to fold the linen she had been embroidering.

"Go, child. What do you wait for?" The queen's sharp gaze fixed her daughter. "The Walkyriun shall have no cause to complain of their welcome here!"

Released, Gudrun sprang to her feet and followed her brother out the door.

By the time Brunahild and the others had ridden through the tumble of huts and houses that huddled below the old fortress, all of Gibicho's offspring were gathered, even little Gisalhar, the old king's posthumous child. Godo was frowning critically at these girls who rode like young warriors with lance and war-cap and linden shield, but as Brunahild reined in her dancing mare and slid in one supple motion to the ground, Gudrun heard a choked sound behind her. In one moment, it seemed, all the self-conscious assumption of kingliness that her brother Gundohar had been cultivating since they proclaimed him had disappeared.

Why were they all staring? The Walkyriun wore breeches and tunics of darkest blue, but Brunahild's cloak was held by a jeweled pin. Riding in the sun had given her skin a golden glow, and her hair was its shadow. One could not call her beautiful, not with that pointed face and the odd slant to her eyes—and yet she moved with the same vivid grace as her mare. Gudrun, who had pulled on a gown of yellow linen with red and blue braiding around the neck and hem, felt like a heifer with her horns garlanded for a festival.

"The little water rat has improved since you met her at Halle. . . ." came Hagano's voice from behind her.

Gudrun glared. Things had changed indeed when Gundohar stared like a stunned ox and even Hagano looked at Brunahild with a thoughtful frown. She, at least, must greet this glowing girl like the child of a king.

Then Brunahild recognized her and began to grin, and Gudrun remembered only that here was the only human being who had ever really been her friend.

"Today, perhaps, you might like to take the girls up the Holy Mountain to the sacred spring," said the queen. She wore a gathered skirt with a tunic over it, keeping to the old style to honor their visitors. Gold plaques gleamed from her belt; golden fibulae held the tunic closed, and around her neck her amber necklaces glowed in the morning sun.

Gudrun looked up from her gruel, her glance moving quickly from her mother to Brunahild. No one had yet discussed how long the Walkyriun were going to stay with them, but after a week on the road, the girls seemed grateful for the chance to sleep in soft beds and get their clothes clean. Only they were not really girls, thought Gudrun. To her they seemed women grown, though she was already as tall as Brunahild, and none of them was more than two or three years older than she.

It is because they have chosen their own fates, she thought morosely, *while my every move is at my mother's beck and call.* Gudrun understood now why her mother had made her wear the old sleeveless gown that could be kilted up for walking.

"Of course," she said quietly. "If they desire to go, I should be delighted to show them the way. . . ."

Brunahild looked at the queen, frowning. "An old shrine?"

"The holy women of the Gauls worshipped there," said Grimahild. "The Romani desecrated it by building a signal tower on the summit, but a tremor of the earth shook it down. Now it is the Burgund women who take the nixie of the well her offerings. I think you will find it interesting."

Brunahild met her measuring stare squarely, then turned to Gudrun.

"Will you show me? It sounds safer than the last time we looked into a well!"

Gudrun knew that she was blushing, but she could not help joining in the other girl's laughter.

But it was not until the Walkyriun passed through the council hall on their way out of the fortress that she understood just why her mother had arranged for them to climb the mountain today.

The benches were empty now, and only a pale wisp of smoke twining lazily through a shaft of morning light at one end of the long hearth bore witness to last night's blaze. At the table below the window she could see Father Priscus's white robe and the darker shapes of her brother and the lawspeaker, Ostrofrid.

"When the legions guarded Germania, they were supported by a third of the produce of the country, taken in taxes," Priscus's voice came clearly. "This is the food in the state storehouses that has fed your warriors. If now you are moving their families in, you must take no more than the third of the lands that grew that food for them to settle on."

"Do you mean that a single man will take over part of each estate with its bondsmen and collect its produce directly?" asked Gundohar.

"That is not the way of our people," Ostrofrid objected. "Let them settle the land clan by clan, a man and his grown sons and their families together, with common land for grazing the herds—"

"The old ways are over," the priest shouted. "Now you have to live by Roman law—"

The draft from the opening door twisted the smoke and rattled the scrolls spread out on the table as Gudrun led the Walkyriun into the hall. Father Priscus turned, glaring. But Gundohar unfolded his weedy length and stood, the big hands that were still more deft with a harp than a sword dangling at his sides.

"May the eye of the Day shine brightly for you, Burgund lord," Brunahild said politely.

"It is your eyes, maiden, that light this hall. . . ." Gundohar answered her. But his voice cracked, and Gudrun could see him coloring, even in the the gloom. One of the other girls giggled, and Brunahild blinked.

"We go now to climb the Holy Mountain. Forgive us for disturbing your councils." Brunahild nudged the girl ahead of her forward.

No wonder her mother wanted to get their guests out of the way, thought Gudrun as she shepherded them toward the far door. It was clear that her fool of a brother thought he was in love with Brunahild!

"Froja's blessing on your path!" Gundohar said hoarsely. Light flooded in as Gudrun pulled the door open, and showed them all too clearly his eyes, like those of a good dog whose master is leaving him, and Father Priscus's outraged glare.

The Walkyriun were already beginning to giggle as Gudrun slammed the door shut behind them, and as they started down the road through the huddle of huts that had grown up around the hall their laughter pealed into the bright air. Surely they could hear it in the hall, thought Gudrun. Suddenly she pitied Gundohar.

"Your brother is how old?" asked the one they called Frojavigis as they turned down the path to the river.

"He has eighteen winters," answered Gudrun.

"And they have not yet found a wife for him?"

"They have found any number—" Gudrun shook her head and guided the other girl around a pen full of swine. "But none on whom the whole Council can agree!"

"What a pity that Brunahild is about to be sworn to the Walkyriun!" said Frojavigis, and laughed.

It was true, thought Gudrun as they went down to the water. A Hun alliance would be extremely useful, pinned as they were between the expanding Hun confederation and the Romans on the western bank of the Rhenus. The Council was bound to seek such a marriage for one of Gibicho's children.

Before them the waters of the Nicer ran deep and strong, sparkling in the sun. Brunahild already stood poised in the bow of the flatboat that would ferry them over, black hair blowing and arms extended as if she were about to take wing. Gudrun tried to imagine that shining spirit bound to the duties of a Burgund queen and suppressed a sigh. It was too bad. When they were children they had sworn to be allies, but it would have been so glorious if Brunahild could have really been her sister.

And then they were at the ferry, and the other Walkyriun were clambering into the boat, laughing as it dipped and swung. Seeing them so, Gudrun was struck anew by how alike they were. Perhaps it was the way they moved, strong and graceful as young mares running wild in a field.

They are Brunahild's sisters, she thought, blinking back tears that did not come from the wind. *And I am alone.*

"I should like to come this way after harvest when those chestnuts are fruiting," said Brunahild, pausing in the path.

They had caught their breath after the first steep climb up from the river. Here, sunlight came dappled through the broad, toothed leaves, and the spiky green husks of the unripe nuts trembled in the breeze. The figures of the other girls, strung out along the path behind them, shimmered in that changing light, and even Gudrun's bright hair had a greenish glow. The Burgund girl stopped beside her, gazing upward.

"I wish you could," she said softly. "Just you and me alone. We would walk without speaking, and listen to the patter as the trees rained nuts upon the ground. Or we could lie beneath the branches with cloaks outspread and let the mountain feed us. The fresh nutmeats here have a sweetness I have not found in any other forest."

Brunahild looked at her curiously, trying to understand the undertones of longing beneath Gudrun's words. Something was wrong here—Mother Huld would have known in a moment, but Brunahild did not yet have that skill. *Will even this journey make me ready for initiation?* she wondered. *I still have so much to learn!*

If she had been talking to Frojavigis, that tone would have meant the girl had been too busy, and needed time to let her spirit catch up again. Liudwif's longing would have come from pure greed, and Ricihild's from a natural indolence. Galemburgis would have added a comment about how much sweeter the nuts were in the Alamanni lands. Only now did Brunahild realize how well she had come to know them. It seemed to her that she understood even Galemburgis, who had always been her rival, better than this Burgund princess who had been her first friend.

It was traveling together, she thought then, seeing just how their shared training had separated them from those who stayed at home, that had made them all aware of the bond. Was this why the Walkyriun had sent them off together? Had the wisewomen known how it would be?

Brunahild sighed and strode out again, realizing only now, when exercise had loosened her muscles, how she had chafed at even a few days spent indoors. When she was initiated—if she was initiated—she would have to stay in the Taunus. Even the freer life of a Hun woman would be too confining now. More than ever she pitied Gudrun, condemned to life as a princess in a royal hall.

My father must give his permission. She shook her head in self-mockery. *I will run away and live alone in the forest if I am not allowed to join the Walkyriun!*

They left the chestnuts and passed into a mixed forest of beech and oakwood as the trail swung westward in a long spiral around the mountain.

"Look—" Gudrun caught her arm suddenly. Between the stout trunks of the beech trees silver gleamed suddenly. Brunahild's breath caught.

"The Rhenus?"

Gudrun nodded. "The Holy Mountain guards the gateway to the valley. From here you can glimpse the plain that slopes down to the river, but mist hides the lands on the other side."

"It is as if the world ended there," said Brunahild. "And Elvenhome began on the farther shore."

"Nothing so fair, but maybe as dangerous," answered Gudrun. "Those are the lands the Romans call Germania Prima. Two years ago my brother swore oaths to the emperor Honorius as a *feoderati* prince, and was given them to hold against all other tribes."

Brunahild nodded. Galemburgis had made the Alamanni view of that development quite clear.

"We have the right to live there, but we cannot shed blood to take the land. That is why you saw my brother caught between those two greybeards like Wodan between the fires, trying to decide how the land law of the Romans and our own can be made one."

"And when they succeed?"

"I suppose the rest of us will have to move across the river," answered Gudrun. "They say the soil is rich, but I don't want to live trapped among the flat farmed lands!"

Brunahild frowned. She had heard this question debated endlessly among the Walkyriun, but now, listening to this girl who was caught in the midst of the changes, it was suddenly real.

"Will the spirits of the land accept you?" she asked. "What gods dwell there?"

"The priest Priscus says that among the Romans, only the Christos and his father rule." Gudrun laughed nervously. "I think they have frightened all their land wights away!"

Brunahild shivered and turned abruptly back to the friendly green shade of the trees.

Now the path angled back and upward again. Soon she saw a scattering of rough blocks and knew they must be the tumbled walls of the old Gallic hill-fort, for they were very like the stones that ringed the High One's Hill. She could hear the voices of the others coming up behind them, and lengthened her stride.

"We are almost to the top, now," said Gudrun. "Come this way."

The inner ring of stones enclosed an area the size of a small village. To the north and eastward the forest stretched away in endless swales of green. Southward the mountain sloped steeply toward the great cleft that the Nicer had cut through the hills. And to the west— Brunahild shook her head—she had already looked that way.

Frowning, she reached out to touch a block that lay on the ground. *What foes threatened the men who built you,* she wondered suddenly, *that they had to flee to the mountaintops and hide behind such walls as these must have been?*

Her vision blurred, and for a moment she could see them, tall and bright-haired . . . then that vision was replaced by another, of a broad-built folk with earth-colored hair . . . of a lean, pale people with black hair . . . of others, shaggy of hair and dressed in furs. So many, so many! Each race in turn had held this mountain, and now they all were gone. *Does it even matter who claims the land?* she wondered then. *In the end it belongs to the trees and the stones!* Dizzied, she pulled her hand away.

"Brunahild, are you all right?"

She blinked at Gudrun. "There is power here!"

"There is, though the Romani do not seem to have known it!" She pointed to the crumbling walls of a small tower. "They used this for beacon fires."

Even the Romans have left this land, though they claimed all the world! Brunahild began to smile. But the power remained whether or not they could feel it. She could sense it now, a slow welling of energy that tingled around her as moisture weighted the air near a stream. Perhaps the landspirits would outlast them after all.

Shouting, the other girls came through the gap in the wall and ran toward them. Brunahild held Gudrun's blue gaze, and in that moment of shared understanding, it was they who were kindred.

"I am thirsty," she said, smiling. "I will pledge you our sisterhood a second time, Gudrun, if you will show me your sacred spring."

Chapter 8  The Walkyrja's Road

Land of the Huns
Blood Moon, A.D. 416

Autumn came, with sharpening winds and the first hint of color in the trees, and Brunahild and her sisters took the road south through the gorge cut by the swift-flowing waters of the Nicer, escorted by Gundohar's men. They turned eastward into a land of hilly woods, and ate apples gone wild beside tumbled walls where once Roman guardposts had been. With every league the tilled fields grew fewer, but sometimes they met lowing herds of cattle being driven down from the high pastures to their homes.

Presently they came to a land that seemed empty of men. Fields were sprouting with young trees, and charred beams poked through the tangled vines. There had been too much raiding, said the warriors who rode with them. Sometimes it was Goths, sometimes Huns, and sometimes mixed tagends of forgotten tribes that had no name. The farm folk had all sought safer homes in the new lands to the west.

The travelers had come now to the end of the Burgund territories. But though they had met no one for some days, the woods held watchers they had not seen. As they pushed up the far bank of the Hunter's River they felt the earth before them trembling beneath the feet of many horses. The Burgunds shifted their shields from back to arm and got a better grip on their spears, but Brunahild straightened in her saddle, her blood stirring to a beat she had almost forgotten.

The branches before them shivered, and suddenly the road was blocked by broad-chested, wiry men who clung to their ponies' backs as if they had grown there. For a moment there was silence. But their leader was tall and lean, with straw-colored moustaches beneath the noseguard of his helm. His grey gaze dismissed the Burgunds and flicked from one to another of the girls. Then his mount took a few steps forward, though the rider had made no visible sign.

"*Tänri khatun*—" He bent before Brunahild until the rim of his war-cap touched his pony's stiff mane, the horn plates of his scale armor creaking softly.

Heavenly lady . . . She struggled to translate the words. His face might be that of a Goth, but in bearing he was more a Hun than she. And then with an almost physical shift the cadences of her own language came back to her, and she understood his next words.

"I am Ragnaris son of Kursik. You will ride with us now. The khan your uncle has commanded me."

"I will come with you, *su tzur.*" She nodded to the commander. For better or worse, she was among her own people once more.

Brunahild licked mutton fat from her fingers and contemplated the fluffy boiled millet on the platter before her, wondering whether she could hold any more. A few fragments of meat remained, but she had done well enough to satisfy the demands of hospitality. Most of the feasters had finished, and the other girls, given a less prominent place near the door of the *ger*, were already slipping away to the longhouse that had been assigned to them. She set the small table aside and leaned back against the embroidered felt pillows, watching thoughtfully as the warriors on the men's side of the round tent emptied their beakers of Roman wine.

A moon had passed since her uncle's riders had brought Brunahild and her friends to this camp in the hills above Castra Batava on the Danu. Her father was far to the eastward, serving with Ruga Khan in the lands around the Maeotis Sea. A message had been sent to him, but if some decision was not made soon, Brunahild and the other girls might have to spend the winter here. It was her uncle who would have to give her permission to return to the Walkyriun. She watched him beneath lowered eyelids, wondering how she could convince him to let her go.

Physically the khan was not so different from the others; powerfully built with most of his height in his torso, a skin deeply tanned by constant riding in all weathers, a face that seemed flat next to the axe-hewn profiles of the Goths among his men, dark hair with a hint of red and a thin beard. But the black eyes set so deeply beneath Attila's strong brows missed nothing, and even now, with his companions

around him and a cup of unwatered wine in his hand, he moved with
a poised tension, as if at any moment he might spring to his feet and
away. He was not unkindly—the folk who served him had called him
"little father" for so long now that no one ever used his Hunnish name.
But when Attila commanded, no one disobeyed.

He would not be swayed by old affection, though Brunahild could
dimly remember how he had played with her when she was a little
child and he a young man just freed from his time as a royal hostage
in Rome. Certainly, even if she could have produced them, he would
not be swayed by tears.

Every man who served him was "lochagos," notable for his skill with
the bow or spear, as a linguist or songmaker or a leader of men, and
Attila kept no man with him who had not proved his worth in peace
and war. But what were women good for? Hun girls learned warfare,
but, as everywhere, the primary value of a female of the royal line was
to seal alliances between princes and to breed more. Her own mother
had been a Tervingi princess married off to Bladarda for that purpose,
though she had only produced two daughters and died bearing the
second.

If Brunahild had been raised at home, she would have been given
to some up-and-coming warrior like that half-blood, Ragnaris tzur, who
had escorted her here. He sat near Attila's side now, and she had seen
how often he looked at her over the rim of his drinking horn. The
golden ornaments on Brunahild's headdress tinkled as she shifted on
the pillows, wondering what it would feel like to lie in his arms. Then
she shook her head. She wanted to ride with him, inspiring his deeds
as Sigruna had done for Helgi, not warm his bed! Bladarda had many
other children—let Ragnaris marry one of them. Somehow, Brunahild
must convince her uncle that she would be more use to him as one of
the Walkyriun.

A burst of laughter from the men's side recalled her attention to
Attila, who was raising his silver-lined drinking bowl, made from the
cranium of the first man he had killed, to the stranger who sat beside
him. The other man was a prince of the Romans who had come to
buy Hun troops because he could not trust his own. His name was
Aetius, a big man with the blond coloring of his Gothic mother and
a nose like the beak of the Romans' totem bird.

Aetius can give Attila gold, and with gold, he can buy allies, she thought,
watching them. To the Burgunds, the Huns might seem a single,
overwhelming horde, but Brunahild knew their clans moved even more
freely than the German tribes, for they had always been wanderers.

Only a strong leader who gave his followers gold could unite them, and then, even the Roman legions could not match them for devotion and discipline. Her great-grandfather Uldin had commanded such loyalty. Now Kharaton's clan was the greatest, and Uldin's kindred waited, making alliances, gathering wealth, and earning renown. The word was that Kharaton was failing. When he fell, Attila would help his surviving uncles, Oktar and Ruga, to seize the power.

He knows how to wait for what he wants, she told herself. *Do I?* Abruptly the heated air of the feasting *ger* was stifling. Brunahild uncrossed her legs and rose from among the pillows, bowing to the shrine opposite the door and picking her way across the sheepskin rugs that cushioned the floor to the entrance. She had been home long enough that it took no conscious thought to slip through without touching the threshold.

Brunahild straightened gratefully as she stepped out onto the mat before the door. The last light of the autumn evening lay soft along the dark swales of forest that sloped down to the Danu. The scatter of round felt *gers* and wooden longhouses made a pleasing jumble of silhouettes against the fading glow of the sky. This land could be fierce when winter came, but tonight the air, weighted with the familiar odors of horse and woodsmoke and roasting mutton, seemed warm.

The Pannonian slave girl Attila had given her was waiting to exchange her indoor half-boots for stout boots of leather. Brunahild pulled off the heavy headdress, with its fringe of beads and golden diadem, and the open caftan of embroidered silk sewn with triangles of gold foil that she wore over her tunic, her fingers lingering on the smooth cloth. It startled her to realize that they were already beginning to feel less stifling.

But I don't want to stay here! she told herself. *Or do I?* The waiting stillness forced her to honesty. If Attila refused to let her go back to the Taunus, would it be so bad? She realized suddenly that the inner tension that was always with her among the Walkyriun had begun to ease. Constricting though the life might be, here she was *tänri khatun*. Her place was secure, and for once it was the other girls who were the outsiders, their status depending on her friendship as hers had depended on their tolerance before.

Will they ever really accept me? Have I been deluded all along? She thrust the garments into the slave girl's arms and started toward the horsepens. She had to think. For certain she had better know her own mind before she tried to talk to Attila!

But she was only a few paces from the *ger* when she heard a step behind her. Unmistakable even in the half-light, the tall Roman was following.

"*Salve*..." She wondered what to say next, for that was almost all the Latin she knew. Aetius laughed.

"That is not needful, *khatun*. I was hostage with Ruga four years, and swore brotherhood with Attila. I remember your tongue well enough to speak with you."

"Maybe better than I do—" She found herself returning his grin. "I have talked only the speech of the Alamanni and Burgunds since I was ten winters old."

"Let us see if I remember that language then," Aetius switched to the oddly accented Germanic of the Visigoths. "I lived a year with King Alaric before I was sent to the Huns."

"You have traveled widely," Brunahild answered in a dialect close enough for him to understand.

"And you—" he replied. "You are the niece, are you not, who has been training with Walkyriun."

Brunahild stared. "What do you know of them? Are not the Tervingi—the West Goths—all Christians now?"

"Arian heretics—" he corrected. "But it is true, there are no priestesses among them anymore. I have read the works of Tacitus, though, and heard that east of the Rhenus there were sibyls like those he described. Do they still train them as in the old days?"

"We have women who serve the gods—" Brunahild said slowly, feeling a prickle of apprehension along her nerves. This was no proud patrician who despised everything outside the gates of Rome. Aetius was intelligent enough to keep pace with her uncle, and one assumed that like Attila, he learned from everything he came across. Why did he want to know?

"Are there no wisewomen in Rome?"

"Sometimes I think that in Rome there are no wise *men!*" Aetius exclaimed, and there was little amusement in his laughter.

"That is because you have forgotten your gods—" said Brunahild soberly.

"The bishops would say it is because we suffer Arian heretics to survive," came the swift reply.

"Is your Christos so small a god that he can be worshipped in only one way?" There was a moment's silence as they moved down the path.

"I will not argue with the priests," Aetius said carefully, "who say that a single faith is necessary for a united empire."

"Why not go back to your old gods then, if the new one causes such dissension?" Brunahild said practically.

"The emperor Julian tried that, but Jupiter did not save him. The gods of Rome are dead, lady. Would they not have punished Stilicho's lady for wearing Vesta's necklace, and the general himself for burning the Sibylline scrolls, if they still had power? Perhaps it is better to follow the philosophy of Marcus Aurelius, and depend on no gods at all."

Brunahild stopped short. "How can you say it?" Even believing in the Christos must be better than walking alone through a world from which all holiness had gone.

"Listen, Brunahild, *khatun*—" Aetius turned to face her, and suddenly she realized that he was scarcely older than Gudrun's brother Gundohar. "Like me, you are a child of many peoples, all of whom swear by their own gods. Have you not seen how much the gods of each race resemble its men? Do you really think the Thunderer lives in the skies? I have seen many a Gothic warrior who could double for Donar. Perhaps what the priests have called *divinitas* is that quality we display when we are being most truly men."

"You could just as well say that men and women are the eyes and ears through which the Shining Ones know the world!" Brunahild snapped back at him. "I have *seen*—" She stopped herself. She had not even told the other girls, who would have believed her, how Wodan himself had set her on the road to the Burgund lands. She must not belittle that memory by sharing it with this godless man.

"People see what they need to see, *domina*," Aetius said gently, as if she had been a child. "Remember that when your god abandons you, and seek your strength within."

"People are blind to what they fear, noble-born," she answered tartly. "Remember that when your philosophy fails you, and open your eyes to what is all around!"

They faced each other, the tall Roman a more solid shadow against the dim sky. From the royal *ger* came a great shout of laughter; in the pen before them a pony stamped, but the land beyond lay in a deepening stillness. What did he hear, this young warrior of a people who had been easy prey to a new religion because they had lost their gods? Did he think the forest was only trees?

Brunahild let her awareness expand until the pressure of the life that pulsed in wood and field was almost too great to bear. This was where she belonged—where she could feel that mystery. Mother Erda

was not empty, She was waiting, as the girl was, for the night wind
to speak to the treetops with the voice of the god.

Galemburgis yipped as Brunahild's stick whacked her shoulder.
This was the second time the Hun girl's swiftness had scored. She felt
the shock as her own stick struck Brunahild's lifted shield, swung again,
and laughed as she grazed the other girl's thigh.

"Good blow!" called Ricihild. Galemburgis stepped back, blowing,
and after a moment Brunahild straightened from her fighting crouch,
and the fire began to fade from her eyes.

"Finally— With all the lying about and feasting we have done
lately, I was beginning to think I had lost all my skill!"

A dull color rose in Brunahild's sallow cheeks. "I am sorry. I want
to go home as much as you do."

Galemburgis raised one eyebrow. *She doesn't call this her home, where
everyone treats her like a queen? Perhaps she belongs with the Walkyriun after all.*

"Then we had better be on our way. The Blood Moon is waxing,
and snow will fall soon," Liudwif commented.

"I know," whispered Brunahild. "But my uncle gives no answer
when I beg him to let me go!" Attacking, she had been a fury. She
looked smaller now, tense and fragile, and Galemburgis felt an unaccustomed pity. She and Brunahild would never love each other, but
in these past moons they had become friends.

Suddenly Brunahild straightened. Galemburgis heard the hoofbeats and turned as a lathered pony burst into view and slid to a halt
before the *ger* of the khan. In another moment the yard was full of
clamoring people. As the messenger kicked off his boots and bent to
enter, Brunahild ran toward the *ger*, and the other girls followed her.

Presently a babble of rumor began to buzz through the crowd.
A band of Alanic warriors, rebels from their old alliance with the Huns
who had not gone west with the rest of the tribe, had raided cattle
and horses from the pastures of a Gepid clanstead to the north. Most
of the Gepid warriors had been hired out as Roman auxiliaries, and to
punish the raiders they had called upon the khan.

The bodyguards who always accompanied Attila were already
arming; stocky Huns, legs permanently bowed to the backs of their
ponies, long-limbed younger sons from the noble families of the Goths,
and men of every combination of races that the Huns had swept up
with them as they rolled along. But they all wore good scale armor,
and they all bore the powerful Hun bow, and every one of them moved

with the assurance of experience and hard training. The likeness among them became even more apparent when Attila emerged from the *ger* with the messenger and they saluted him.

The khan paused in the doorway, looking at the crowd, and everyone immediately became still.

"You have grown soft from lying about in camp—is that it?—and you want something to do."

There was a murmur from his warriors, half a growl at the insult, and half amusement as they realized he was teasing them.

"Very well, my children, in a moment we shall go," said Attila. "Supplies for a week, Turgun—" He gestured toward one of the men. As the khan stepped into the sunshine, the Roman, Aetius, emerged from the *ger* behind him. "So, little brother, will you join us on this hunting? It has been too long since we rode to war side by side!"

While Aetius, grinning like a boy, was getting his gear, and slaves were loading the pack ponies, Galemburgis worked her way through the tumult to Brunahild's side.

"Ask him to take us with them. Maybe if we can prove our value he'll let us go!"

Brunahild frowned, then turned to her uncle. Galemburgis tried not to flinch as the khan's piercing gaze moved from their faces to the hazel sticks in their hands.

"Would you let a sword rust in the sheath?" Brunahild stammered. "We have arms and are trained to use them, and we have been taught the battle-magic of the Walkyriun. We will not slow you. Uncle, let us come!"

For a moment his attention seemed to go inward, and Galemburgis wondered what else they might say to move him. Folk said there was always more than one reason for Attila's deeds.

"Come then—" he said at last. "And show me the magic of the Walkyriun. . . ."

The white horsetails on the khan's standard stirred gently as the dawn wind fingered the treetops, but the riders stared into the valley with the same fixity as the empty eyes of the stag skull on the pole. The wind's breath was bringing life to the grey landscape, awakening patches of auburn and amber in the masses of surrounding trees. On the slopes below, the stolen animals grazed on dew-soaked grass. The rude camp beyond seemed equally peaceful. Two women were stirring porridge in a cookshed, and as they watched, a man emerged from one of the tents and began to urinate against a tree. Brunahild's mount tossed its head; she tightened the rein to keep the bits from jingling, and the animal, a hammerheaded Hun pony trained for battle, stilled.

The young oak tree beside them quivered, and the two scouts Attila had sent out materialized from among the bronze leaves.

"No guards. They sleep after their drinking—"

Attila snorted. "Did they think we could not follow them? Very well, we attack now, as planned—"

The warriors to his left and right began to move. Brunahild felt the tension in the girls behind her. Despite her boasts, they had never fought before. She had a sinking feeling that the wisewomen would have forbidden this, but they all knew there was no pulling back now.

"And you"—the khan turned to her— "stay behind me! Until we are among the tents, make no sound."

Brunahild flushed. Did he think that she, any more than the others, needed to be reminded? She saw his lips twitch and colored again. The Walkyriun battle-shriek was meant to unnerve the enemy, not your own side.

They gathered speed as they burst through the trees. The men on the flanks led, curving out and around. Ragnaris *tzur* led one of the wings. Cattle lumbered away lowing; dogs set up a shrill yammering. A woman screamed, and a warrior, still crouched as he burst past a doorflap, began to shout in the Alanic tongue.

It would not be a simple slaughter, thought Brunahild, and found in the knowledge both relief and terror. She let her reins drop, guiding the pony with her knees, and readied lance and shield.

"*Tiwaz . . . Uruz . . . Hagalaz . . . Thurisaz . . .*" she whispered the battle runes. "*Tiw . . . urs . . . hagal . . . thurs . . .*" The names slid into a sequence of pure sound. She thought that thunder echoed from the heavens as if a great horse were racing ahead of them, though the sky was clear.

Wodan . . . Victory Father . . . be with me now!

Awareness expanded. She was both attacker and foe, the excited ponies and the barking dogs and the men. Gasping, Brunahild fought for control. Then they were among the tents. Sound burst from the throats of the girls behind her. Unbidden, her own throat was opening. Exultation and fear released in a sustained ululation. Shadow swirled around her like a flurry of dark wings, and Brunahild's spirit shuddered as she sensed a presence at once familiar and strange.

A man's shape appeared before her, naked chest very white in the gloom. Instinctively she thrust and jerked back and saw red flower behind the point of her spear.

"You are the Chooser. . . ." said a still voice within. *"Bring me heroes, Brunahild. . . ."*

Abruptly, her vision cleared. Before her, a tall Alan was holding off a Hun horseman, lance against longspear. Light seemed to play around him; Brunahild sped toward him, her lance point touched his shoulder, and in that moment his guard went wide, and the Hun's lance thrust him through.

Galemburgis kicked her pony closer, shouting. A sword swung toward her; Brunahild thrust and the man fell. The other girl mouthed her thanks, but the battle swirled them apart before she could answer.

Brunahild sped on, and where her spear pointed, men died. Not all of them were Alani. Brunahild knew only that the men she touched *shone* before they went down. Once she saw Attila before her, but the glow that blazed from him was not the eerie flicker that marked her prey. A woman rushed from one of the sheds, brandishing an axe; the shaft of Brunahild's spear swung outward and took her on the side of the head, and the axe spun away into an Alan's side.

Her pony bore her onward. Ahead, a huge man with a black beard stood at bay, holding off the Huns with great strokes of a long and heavy sword. The captain, Ragnaris, was in the forefront, his pale eyes blazing. As the Alan hewed he dodged backward, saw Brunahild and grinned, then leaped to the attack with an exuberance that had not been there before.

Showing off for me— Brunahild shifted her weight farther back in the saddle, and her pony slowed. The other men were giving him room, and there seemed to be less movement around her. The rest of the enemy must be beaten, and they could afford to let this last encounter become a fight between champions.

The Alan blade was longer than the man's arm, slightly curved. Ragnaris was using a straight blade like a Roman *spatha*, and he still had his round, leather-covered shield. Metal clanged as the Alan knocked Ragnaris's sword aside; the Hun captain let the momentum spin him around, bringing up his shield to take the next blow. Brunahild stared as the battle-light began to flow between them, flickering forward and back as one or the other combatant took the offensive. The Alan chieftain was taller and heavier, but she thought he was tiring, while Ragnaris, though lighter, had armor, and was just as fast.

Ragnaris jabbed, and a line of red opened across his foe's torso. Brunahild nudged her mount closer. The others had formed a ring around them, Attila in the middle, watching with narrowed gaze. Ragnaris moved like a leaf on the wind, and Brunahild was suddenly

sure that he had never fought so well. But despite his wound, the
Alan's blows still fell heavily. Smashed wicker poked like dry bones
through the leather of the captain's shield, and he flung it away,
thrusting up his lighter blade to block his enemy's strokes and rocking
at each blow.

The radiance around them blazed brighter. But suddenly she realized that the Alan's was deepening to a dull glow, while that of
Ragnaris became a silvery glitter as if she were seeing him through a
mist of light.

Not this one! Not Ragnaris! I won't give him to you! Brunahild tried to
turn her pony away, but only her arm would move, and it was lifting,
pointing the spear.

Ragnaris opened another gash in his enemy's gut; the Alan's left
arm already hung useless at his side. He stood like a bear at bay,
swaying, and the Huns were already cheering their comrade's victory.
Ragnaris danced in, grinning; then his foot slipped. As he struggled
for balance the Alan's great sword crashed down at the joining of neck
and shoulder, smashing flesh and bone.

The Huns howled as Ragnaris fell backward, and suddenly the
brightness was darkened by flying spears. The compulsion that held
Brunahild released her. Her own lance fell from nerveless fingers, her
heels dug into the pony's sides.

Men scattered, shouting; trees and horses seemed to rush by. And
then, abruptly, there was nothing before her. Her pony stumbled to
a halt. Her sight darkened; then the weight of her own body dragged
her into human consciousness once more.

"Brunahild? Brunahild! Are you hurt?"

Brunahild pulled herself upright in the saddle, and Galemburgis
let go of her arm. Her pony was unconcernedly cropping grass. She
felt as if she had been beaten with sticks, and just below awareness
lay a dark shadow of memory. How long had she been sitting here?

"Tired—" she whispered. "Just tired. And you?" A great splash of
blood reddened the other girl's side.

"Not mine. We won—" She did not sound very jubilant, not at
all the way they had thought winning a fight would feel.

Brunahild looked around her. Most of the leather tents had been
flattened, and the cookshed was in flames. Dead men lay where they
had fallen. The carrion crows were already gathering. Some of the
khan's men were carrying the wounded into the shade of the trees,
while others picked through the debris. Shouts from the hillside told
her that someone was rounding up the stolen animals.

"We should help," Galemburgis said then. Liudwif and the others were busy among the wounded. Brunahild nodded wearily, relieved that none of her friends had been slain, and kicked her pony toward the horse lines.

Coming back, she tripped on an oak root and grabbed at the tree to keep from falling. For a moment she clung to it, wondering why she was still so tired. It seemed as if a day had passed, but the young sun had barely cleared the trees. The fight had been shorter than most practice sessions. She took a deep breath, and felt the strength in the wood beneath her hands.

Help me, brother! Give me a little of that life I feel flowing so strongly through your trunk. . . . She leaned against the rough back, embracing the tree. The oak was solidly rooted, but it seemed to her that she could feel the faintest of vibrations through the tree trunk. The tree exchanged the powers of earth and heaven, and as she clasped it some of that strength flowed into her, and the world grew clear at last.

Now she could remember the rune-chant, and the fighting, and how she had chosen warriors for the god. She had Chosen Ragnaris. . . . *That* was what had taken the strength from her. Resentment flared at the way the god had used her to destroy a young man whom she might have loved. Then she sighed. She had invoked Wodan as she rode into battle. What clearer invitation did he need?

No doubt the older Walkyriun had ways to prevent the exhaustion. For certain they would have something to say about the danger into which she had led the other girls. But at the time it had been the only way she could see to get them all back home. And now Ragnaris was dead, and she still did not know if Attila would let her go.

Feeling almost herself again, Brunahild picked up the healer's kit she had taken from her saddle pack and continued toward the men lying under the trees. Some had needed only a rough bandaging, and were up already, grimacing as movement jarred their wounds. The other girls were all busy, but there were more waiting. It had been a bloody little battle, for all that it had not taken long.

As she reached the trees, Liudwif called her name.

"Hurry, Brunahild. This one is still alive, and he is asking for you."

For a moment she did not recognize him without his helm. He looked so young, lying there. But his eyes brightened as they focused on her, and her own filled with tears.

"Ragnaris—" She knelt by his side.

"*Tänri . . . khatun . . .*" He drew breath carefully, grimacing, but when he breathed out, more blood bubbled from between his lips.

The horn scales of his corselet had turned the edge of the Alan's blade, but the weight of the blow had crushed both collarbone and shoulder, driving fragments into the lung and likely into the membranes around the heart. No doubt he was bleeding inside as well. She had heard of healers cutting into a man to remove an arrow lodged there, but there was so much damage that even if Ragnaris lived, he would never fight again.

"*Su tzur,* I am here." She tried to smile.

"My mother told me . . . of the Walkyriun." Ragnaris was speaking the Gothic he must have learned at her knee. "Taught me to worship Wodan . . . told me . . . about his hall." He fought for breath once more. "I have served the khan . . . I will serve Wodan now. Walkyrja . . . guide me where I must go."

Her lips parted to protest—she was not yet hallowed; without one of the wisewomen to guide her she was forbidden to take that road. But the hand she held was so cold, and Ragnaris was gazing at her with such hope in his eyes.

Does he know it is because of me that he lies here? she wondered then. Even if it cost her own life, surely the least she could do was to show him his way.

"I will come with you," she said softly. She settled herself cross-legged by his side. "The god has claimed you already. Now I mark you with His sign." She touched her finger to the red ruin of his shoulder, and drew the Deathknot in his own blood on his brow.

A shudder ran through him at her touch; then the last tension seemed to go out of him. His face was bloodless beneath the crimson sign on his forehead. He tried to answer her, but could only cough. Brunahild bent to kiss him, flinching at the iron tang of blood on his lips. Vision contracted to a tunnel in which his face was all she could see. The warrior's eyelids fluttered closed, but she could still hear the tortured wheeze as he forced air into his lungs.

"Listen to me, Ragnaris. See what I see, and together we will walk this road. . . ." It seemed to her that she felt an answering pressure from his fingers. Disciplining her breathing, Brunahild let her own eyes close. She could still feel the nearness of the man beside her; she let her own senses flow toward him, following the thread of his name. She touched his pain and confusion, and deliberately let all other awareness fall away.

"A cool mist surrounds you, Ragnaris. Let the mist soothe the pain. You must leave the pain behind you. Think of a pathway, the road through the forest where you met me. Feel yourself as you were then—" As she spoke, Brunahild found the image of the path forming behind her eyelids, and there was Ragnaris, but this time they were alone.

"Let's follow the road now. Soon we will come to a turning—" And as she spoke, she saw it, and now they were moving into woods that grew ever deeper as they went on. These were trees of earth, but they grew in another reality, in the true Midgard that lay within.

Guided, Brunahild had walked this way before, but never had the trees made such a tunnel of darkness. It was sucking them in; dimly she was aware that she was being drawn into Ragnaris's dying. She had to control it if both of them were not to be lost.

"The way is dark and perilous." She formed the words, though she no longer was speaking aloud. "We are passing through the Underworld. Here is Iron Wood, where the wild wolves roam. Here is the River of Swords. . . ."

Words brought images, and the darkness took shape around them. One by one she named the hazards; the rivers, the bridges by which they were crossed. Great tree roots plunged from the shadows above to chasms. The path led ever deeper, until a roar like thunder assaulted the silence, and an iridescent glitter began to drive the darkness away.

Mist swirled around them as a great cataract plunged down from on high. Great rocks edged it. Beyond them dark water gleamed beneath the arching roots of the great tree.

"Where are we?" Ragnaris spoke at last.

"This is the Thunderflood, that flows past the well where the Norns ward the Worldtree. Here the high gods sit in council, riding down from heaven on a bridge that is a rainbow. Here lies our way."

"I do not see it—"

For a moment panic shook her as she strained to bestow some shape upon that swirl of color in the mists. *Wodan! Help us! I cannot abandon him here!*

"See light!" she said desperately, staring at the flicker of rainbow. They said that Bifrost glimmered. Perhaps her vision was simply too slow to perceive its shimmering. She tried to focus on a single trembling droplet, felt an odd shift as awareness of all else fled away. Suddenly her companion was haloed in the same glittering light that had doomed him on the battlefield.

"I see the brightness. . . ." said Ragnaris, and now she saw it too; a radiance that grew to the point of pain and passed it, comprised of all colors, identifiable as none. The warrior let go of her hand and stepped

forward, a pale silhouette against the light. Approaching them was another figure that was more radiant still. Ever more swiftly, Ragnaris began to move toward it. And now Brunahild made out, as if through a mist, the Other's features, and it was the face that had shone on her when she was lost in the snow. Now she saw what had cast the shadow of Wodan she had seen on the battlefield.

Father! Brunahild began to run toward them. But before she could touch him, a bar of searing light speared across her path.

"Go back, my child!" She knew the Voice, as well. *"It is not time for you to come to Me!"*

Brunahild caught her breath, staring. Both figures were receding now; the rainbow was carrying them away. She ached with longing to follow. It was so beautiful, beyond the pain and fear. Behind her lay only shadow. She did not even know if she could find the path.

Then two ravens swooped out of the mist, each feather fringed with brightness, and as the gloom closed around her, the glimmer from their wings showed her the way.

Brunahild opened her eyes and blinked at a world grown colorless in the plain light of day. Something within her was still wailing for the glory she had seen. Why had Wodan forced her to return? She sighed and looked down at the warrior, every muscle protesting her long stillness, but Ragnaris would never move again. Then something stirred behind her. Attila was standing there. It seemed to her that he must have been waiting, watching her, for a very long time. But she could not read the expression in the khan's eyes.

She tried to get up and staggered, and suddenly his hand was under her elbow, steel beneath the rough wool. He continued to steady her as she stood, and without a word she found herself walking with him away from the others down the hill.

"So," Attila said finally, "that is what the Walkyriun do."

Brunahild opened her mouth to answer and closed it again. Did he mean walking the spirit road, or the heal-craft, or had he somehow understood what happened when she pointed at men with her spear?

"Did your god accept him?"

Mute, she nodded.

"That is well. Ragnaris was a true warrior. I honor his spirit."

Brunahild licked her lips, still unable to tell whether Attila was admiring or angry. He could kill her, and none of his men would even question him. Abruptly her sight cleared, and she saw the beauty of the world around her. This was not the glory of the Otherworld, but suddenly she wanted to live. A fine sheen of perspiration moistened her brow as they walked on.

"I will send you back to the Walkyriun. Their magic is strong. It is good that one of our people should learn what they know."

Brunahild stopped short, trying to read his gaze. If they left now and rode fast, they could get back to the Taunus before snow closed the roads. This was what she had been striving for—why did she feel as if he had condemned her instead of setting her free?

"This Wodan of yours is powerful," Attila added thoughtfully. "I prefer him to the god of the Christians, but they take only the weaklings. Your god likes warriors, and he is greedy. I think it better that you raise your spear in the lands along the Rhenus, Brunahild. My warriors must fear only me."

The khan's grip tightened painfully on Brunahild's shoulder as she digested the fact that he had understood better than she did exactly what she had done, and what it might mean.

"There are people whom the gods use to work their will in the world." Very softly, he went on. "God-driven, dangerous to themselves as to their foes. I hope you follow your god willingly, Brunahild. He gives you little choice, that I see. You are my blood-kin and I would like to protect you, but I am also the khan. I owe my people more.

"Go back to the west, little one. Let Wodan use you there."

Attila lifted his hand from her shoulder, and she shivered, feeling suddenly very much alone.

Chapter 9 ❋ The Rune Tree

Taunus Mountains
Eggtide Moon, A.D. 417

"I spin the skeins with skill;
I weave with wit and will;
The road I go, the need, I know.
My fate I shall fulfill. . . ."

Brunahild's thin body flexed and swayed as she thrust the knot of thread between the front and back warp threads and shifted the heddle rod to reverse the threads and make a space to draw it back again. From one moon to the next she had been at this weaving, making the cloth for her ritual gown. It was her last task before the rites that would dedicate her to the Walkyriun.

"Strong are the threads that bind;
And strongly are they twined;
The warp and weft that life has left,
The ways that wyrd doth wind. . . ."

When Brunahild and the other girls had at last won back to the Taunus, the waiting had seemed endless. All that winter they had spun the linen thread from which they would weave the robes, and while they sat at their spinning they were questioned, hour after hour of detailed interrogation that covered every rune and spell, every god-name and king-list, every herb of power. Not until the full moon after the feast of Eostara could they begin to weave the cloth.

> *"Many the threads I weave,*
> *And many powers perceive,*
> *The web of fate holds small and great*
> *And gods, as I believe. . . ."*

The song had come to her, verse by verse, through the long days of working in the hut she had built in the forest. During that month no one spoke to her but the wisewomen who brought her food.

Brunahild paused, measuring how the day's work had grown upon the frame, and the melody of her weaving song faded to silence. It was time now for the other magic.

"O . . . tha . . . laz . . ." she whispered as she pulled the thread tight and beat it up with the weaving rod. For twenty-three days the runes had been chanted into the weaving, one for each day of labor, and now the work was almost at an end. She tried to summon up the images that would give her the meaning of the rune. But she had never really understood *Othalaz*, the sign of home and kinship, the sacred odal ground.

Wind stirred in the pines, bringing the scent of woodsmoke and cooking food, the smells that meant Fox Dance and the Walkyriun. *Is this my home?* The question severed the thread of her chant. Brunahild clung to the loom, hand stopping in midsweep as darkness swept over her. Home was with one's family, and Wodan was her father . . . or was he? They had been kept so busy all winter there had been no time for visions of the god. When she rode with Attila, she had seen both Wodan's darkness and his light. Was it time that had kept her from seeking him, or something deeper? Attila had asked if she served her god willingly. During these past weeks, when she had been forced to face her own fears as never before, she had realized that she did not know. But if she was not his daughter, she was no one, and Ragnaris's death without meaning.

In five days would come the ritual, when the moon was once more full. In the ordeal, she would have to face the god. Brunahild forced stiff fingers to slide the hank of thread the rest of the way between the warp threads and pulled it out the other side.

"All-Father," she whispered, "help me. I do not want to be afraid of you. . . ."

*   *   *

At the moment between sunset and moonrise, they brought the maidens from the spring where they had been taken for their cleansing to the summit of the High One's Hill. Huld stood with Hlutgard and Hrodlind by the harrow of heaped stones, listening to the wind whisper among the trees and the crackling of the fires. She had assisted many times at the making of a witchwoman, but it had been a long while since she had waited like this, strung tight as a hunting bow. She took a deep breath, drawing in the pungence of growing things released as the air cooled with the ending of the day.

"Be patient," said Hlutgard. "They will be coming soon."

"I am not used to standing in all this regalia—" Huld ran a finger beneath the ropes of amber beads around her neck. Her cap was sewn from the skin of a wild cat, and her dark blue cloak was trimmed with its fur and ornamented around the edge with jangling bits of metal and cast-bronze bells. As she shifted her weight, the polished stones set into her carved staff glimmered in the last rays of the sun.

Hrodlind, standing on her other side, gave a grunt of agreement. Her cloak and staff were like Huld's, but her headdress was made from the back and wings of a grey goose. Hlutgard wore a diadem of golden plaques from whose crown the pelts of pine martens hung down. But beneath their cloaks their gowns were of linen, white as the robes of the priestesses who had sacrificed Roman prisoners long ago, white as the garments the girls they awaited had been weaving all this past moon.

"I will be glad when this is done," said Hlutgard. "It was time to bring up our numbers. I think our new priestesses will be needed soon."

"Because of the Burgunds?" asked Hrodlind.

"If they are allowed to establish themselves on both sides of the river, the Alamanni fear they will become too strong."

"One tribe grows powerful and another declines," said Huld sharply. "Why should we be involved?"

"The Alamanni have already sent gifts to us. I told them that the decision to form such an alliance could only be made in full assembly."

Hrodlind grunted disgustedly. "Huld's right—better stay out of it."

"This may be more than just a struggle between tribes," Hlutgard replied. "Remember the oaths that we have sworn. . . ."

The Walkyriun of the Taunus were pledged to defend the old gods and the old ways of their people, and even as the power of Rome's legions faltered, the influence of her manners and her religion seemed to have grown. In the end, it was the side most likely to serve their oath that the magic of the wisewomen would defend.

Huld stiffened as the pulse-beat of the drum came drifting up on the wind. Something glittered in the darkness of the fir trees on the far side of the flat hilltop. Then the first two priestesses emerged over the rim, carrying torches whose pale fire flared against the sunset sky. The maidens were following them, blindfolded, their linen robes very white against the trees.

Huld felt a little flutter beneath her breastbone as Golla and Randgrid led the girls into a line just beyond the two fires. She could remember very clearly the day, forty winters past, when she had been one of them. If they had been confident before, now they would begin to fear.

"Daughters of the tribes, why have you come here?" Hlutgard's voice rang out across the grass.

"I seek to serve my people and my gods." The first answer came raggedly.

"Will you bind yourselves to this wyrd in the presence of our assembly?"

"I will—" This time they spoke in unison. Hlutgard moved forward.

"Since the Great Cow first licked away the ice and revealed the body of earth to the sun; since the time when the high gods breathed life into humankind, women have learned the ancient wisdom. From Wodan Runewinner they learned, as he learned from them, and from Froja, Mistress of Magic. Norns and *idisi* taught them. Bird and beast and plant shared their wisdom; they were instructed by Earth Herself, the Mother of us all."

Huld found her eyes returning to Brunahild. The girl's skin was sallow from long hours spent indoors, but her thin face was set in lines of determination. *That is well*, thought Huld. *You will need to be strong.*

"From sister to sister the knowlege has been passed since the ancient days. All that we can give is yours. Now it is for you to give yourselves to the gods."

Golla stepped behind Liudwif and looped the long pale hair around the girl's throat, yanking it tight while Randgrid lifted her spear and pricked her beneath the breastbone. Liudwif started to defend herself, then slowly forced her hand to drop. Golla grinned and nudged her forward until she stood between the two fires, then removed the blindfold.

"What oath will you offer, Liudwif daughter of Gundfrid, as you lay your life in our hands? Swear truly, for if you break faith, know that it is to rope and steel and fire that your life belongs."

Liudwif, already perspiring from the heat of the flames, coughed. Then she found her voice and began to repeat the ancient words.

After her, Frojavigis and Ricihild and then Galemburgis were sworn and led away. Then it was Brunahild whose shining dark hair was being looped about her neck before she was led between the fires. Her gaze was unfocused, and she spoke with the intensity of someone pronouncing a spell, proclaiming not what was, but what she willed to be.

"I renounce all ties of birth and blood, and declare myself kin-bonded to all the people of this land, to teach, to heal, and to defend. From this hour forward, as Wyrd shall lead me, I shall obey only the gods, my own immortal soul, and the will of the Walkyriun."

That should be easier for Brunahild than for the others, thought Huld, for her own people had already rejected her.

"I honor the spirits of bright day and of shadowed night." The girl's voice grew stronger. "To landspirits I give worship, to wights of wind and water; to the elves and *idisi*, and to Mother Earth. I offer my life to the goddesses and the holy gods. Shining Ones, hear me now!"

"Offer, then—" said Hlutgard gently. "The harrow stands before you."

Randgrid's spear swung up, and Brunahild grasped it. Above, the first stars were pricking through the afterglow; the trees were a solid mass of darkness surrounding the mountaintop, but firelight gilded the girl's white robe. Huld looked around, seeking an omen, but even the wind had stilled. And yet she felt a pressure, as if in that stillness something was listening.

"Grant me healing hands and words of power," Brunahild whispered harshly. "To the one who stands here before you, give victory." She drew the spearhead across the underside of her arm, holding it out steadily to let the bright blood drip onto the stones, and her voice rang out with the same sudden sharpness as the blade. "Thus do I make my offering. . . ."

Abruptly the pressure in the air became a tingling that lifted the hairs on Huld's arms. Wind gusted suddenly; the firelight flared and faded, and a dark wing of shadow rushed in. Huld moved to Brunahild's side with a strip of bandaging to tie around the wound. At the touch, the girl shuddered, and for the first time met Huld's gaze.

"What was it?" she whispered.

Huld shook her head, smiling. She must remain silent now, but she let her hand remain upon the girl's arm in reassurance a few moments more than was required.

"Your oath has been accepted," Hlutgard's voice came clearly. "Go now to your testing."

"Nine days and nine nights the High One hung upon the World-tree." Huld's voice was like the whisper of wind in the trees. "We only ask of you nine hours. Are you still determined to make this offering?"

They stood with Randgrid at the edge of the yew wood, a place gloomy even in daylight. Now the darkness beneath the branches was almost total, like some forest in the Underworld. Brunahild forced her gaze back from the shadows beyond the torchlight to the features of her teacher, seamed and shadowed till they seemed the face of a stranger.

"I am ready—" she answered steadily.

"Neither meat nor drink was given to the god, nor shall they be given to you. As he was wounded with the spear, so shall you be wounded—"

Brunahild looked at her teacher. "I have been stabbed with that spear already," she said flatly. "Why should I fear?" Huld knew all that—why must they go through every step of this ritual?

"For nine days and nine nights he hung upon the Tree, laboring to bring into being the runes. No doubt you feel you know them. Are you ready to root them in your very soul?"

"For this have I come here," said Brunahild. She knew that the wisewomen were frightening her so that the tension would push her toward illumination. But she had been waiting for this moment too long. All she wanted was to get on with it now.

Huld looked at her with exasperating understanding, and Randgrid laughed.

"Then it is time to ascend the Tree. . . ."

The darkness closed around them as they moved down the faint trail beneath the trees. The air still held some of the warmth of the day, and Brunahild let her cloak hang open. The yew wood was ancient. Here only mature trees grew, their dense dark green foliage shutting out the light so that no other plant could survive. It was dry beneath the canopy, the ground covered with a dusty litter of fallen needles and dry branches brought down by last winter's storms. With no undergrowth, there was no cover for animals. They were alone with the trees.

Soon Huld slowed, lifting the torch so that Brunahild could see the notched log ladder leaning against the trunk of the largest of the trees. At its top the trunk split into three, which divided again into a

tangle of branches. Where the limbs forked, the dusty bark seemed
unusually smooth.

"It is a natural high seat," said Huld. "This is not the first time
this tree has served us this way." She nodded to Randgrid, who took
Brunahild's arm and led her toward the yew.

When they reached it, Brunahild embraced as much of the lower
trunk as her arms would cover. *Mother, will you stand for the Worldtree?*
For one night will you cradle me?

At first she felt nothing. This tree was ancient; already well established when the Romans first saw the Rhenus. Its life ran deep
beneath the bark. But presently it seemed to her that the wood warmed,
and she had a sense that something very old and very patient had
turned its attention her way.

Brunahild let go of the tree and set her foot in the first notch of
the log. When she had got up it and settled herself in the fork, Randgrid
followed. There were ropes already draped around the middle limb.
Swiftly the Walkyrja wrapped the girl's cloak around her body and
bound her at waist and breast, immobilizing her upper arms. Another
rope dangled from above with a noose at its end. Brunahild held her
breath as Randgrid slipped it over her head. If she leaned her head
back against the tree there was no pressure, but she knew that the
rope would tighten if she tried to lean forward to undo her bonds.
Then the Walkyrja brought a final line around the trunk to tie her
legs, descended the ladder, and took it away.

"This is the first ordeal, to be silent and alone. . . ." said Huld.
"Remember the offering of Wodan, and follow him."

She turned, and led Randgrid swiftly back the way they had come.
Their shadows lengthened as they departed, distorting as the torchlight
dwindled. Brunahild watched the spark flicker through the branches
until it disappeared.

The division of the trunk gave only partial support to Brunahild's
body. Without the ropes, she could not have held her position long.
Cocooned in her cloak and bound to the tree trunk, she was suspended
in the dark. Brunahild let out her breath in a long sigh and leaned
back against the tree.

Something dug into her shoulder, and she shifted. The first step
was to relax, to let all tension flow from her muscles so that the mind
could float free. A muscle in her leg began to cramp, and she straightened it. There seemed to be enough slack in the ropes for her to make
such small adjustments. It occurred to her that this must be intentional,

or else she would learn nothing tonight but how uncomfortable it was to be tied in a tree.

A tree . . . the Worldtree. . . . Wodan had sought the greatest of all trees for his own testing. Some said that Yggdrasil was an ash tree, straight and tall. But others believed it was a yew, sometimes called the needle-ash, longer-lived and more enduring even than the oak of Donar. Certainly its spreading branches were more suitable than those of an ash tree for hatching Walkyriun. The needles of the yew were not pungent like those of other evergreens, but it was not only the dust that made her nostrils tingle. The leaves of the yew could poison animals. What would breathing the air around them do?

A muscle in Brunahild's back began to ache, and she shifted her weight against the ropes until it eased.

Wodan had gone, then, to the center of the world. Was it north, in Scandzia, cradle of the tribes? Too far north, said the traders, neither yew nor ash would grow. It would have to be a birch tree there. Perhaps the center was south and eastward, for some said that Wodan had come originally from Mundberg, the city of the imperator Constantine. But from the Huns she knew that the steppes were grassland. The Worldtree could not be growing there.

And yet, if she closed her eyes, she could see it, as she had seen the hollow among the rocks where she had encountered the god. Did the nine worlds lie in any of the directions by which men found their way about Midgard, or must the journey be made by turning the spirit in a direction that was different from any of them?

Brunahild felt the first flutter of deepening consciousness, took a careful breath, and let it out slowly, allowing awareness to ease out from her body like a fallen leaf being drawn into the stream. She knew that her back hurt, but it no longer seemed so important. This was the way that she had been trained to follow. She could see the Worldtree, deep in the center of the wildest woods of all. There was an open space around it. Its spreading branches mingled with the forest canopy, but its trunk rose beyond, and from above, flickers of blinding radiance sifted through the leaves.

As she squinted upward, a large grey squirrel scurried down the tree trunk, considered her for a moment with a suspicious eye, then disappeared through an opening where one of the tree's three great roots plunged into the ground. It was more than an opening. As Brunahild drew closer, she saw that it was large enough for a human to slip through, the underside of the root and the rock beneath it smooth and shiny as if many had passed that way.

With the ears of her body Brunahild heard the distant hoot of a hunting owl. There was pain in her knee; she bent it, and the physical movement became part of her first step into the passageway.

The air here was dank with the smell of earth. Rock jutted from the sides of the passage, cold and slippery where water seeped down from above. But somehow her eyes had adjusted to the darkness, or else the rocks themselves were producing the cold, pale glimmer that outlined them. Carefully she picked her way past. Chill wind rushed up the passageway from unknown depths. Back in the world she had left, a wind was rustling the treetops; the two became one in her awareness, and she went on.

Now the passage forked in three. From one branch curled a chill fog and the sound of roaring waters. That was the path by which she had led Ragnaris. She must not take that way. From the second fork came faintly the sound of hammering. That way the goddess Froja must have gone when she sought the dwarves who fashioned her necklace, Brisingamen. But the tree root seemed to curve to the right. Though the third passage was narrow, Brunahild followed it, spiraling sunwise around the roots of the Tree.

Presently she saw a radiance that did not come from the stones. The air here was moist with mist, and the thunder of the flood that made it pulsed in the air. Droplets glittered with rainbow light—no, the light was a rainbow, the bridge that bore the brightness of heaven to the roots of the Tree. On the bank were twelve seats of stone beside a well. Her nostrils flared to the dank scent of brine, like the saltwell she and Gudrun had seen so long ago. She realized in surprise that she had found a shorter way to Bifrost and the Council Plain of the gods.

For a moment she stared at the rainbow shimmer with fear and longing, remembering how the god had descended it to take Ragnaris away. But she had not been called to follow him. The path before her forked again, and one branch curved down to the well. The other ran up along part of the tree root, and she could see that notches had been cut into the wood, leading up the trunk of the Tree.

But she had been descending. How could she climb the Worldtree from here? For that matter, how could Bifrost plunge through the surface of Middle Earth to link Asgard with the Well of Wyrd below? The paradox shook her; her eyelids flickered, and for a moment she saw the multilayered darkness of the yew wood and felt the hard surface of the tree. Then she seemed to hear Huld.

"Even the distance around the Worldtree is not so great as the area contained inside. . . ."

Though Brunahild had been from the land of the Huns to the Rhenus, even the distance she had traveled was not so great as the leagues she could journey when she turned in that other direction that led within. The Worldtree was only another step in that spiraling, and she saw now that the closer she got to the center, the greater it grew. As she had climbed the notched ladder into the yew branches, Brunahild began to climb the Tree.

Gusting wind whipped out her hair in long, stinging strands. In the yew wood, the wind was rising, murmuring through the trees. Brunahild felt her way upward; a hanging rope brushed her hand, and she pulled herself into a crotch in the tree. There were more ropes here, as there had been in the yew tree. One by one she tied them until she was securely bound. The Tree swayed, groaning softly in tune with the wind's music.

"I am here—" she said into the darkness. "Is this what you wanted me to do?" She waited, then wondered if she had really expected anyone to answer. Perhaps it was enough to simply be here in the windy darkness, supported by the Tree.

For the first time she was able to consider the strength of the yew tree that held her body and the greater Tree to which her spirit was bound. But the wood that had seemed unyielding and cold had somehow warmed and adjusted its harsh contours to cradle her. Sighing, Brunahild released the last of her tension, reaching out with her awareness to the spirit of the yew.

It seemed to her then that she could feel the life in the great Tree pulsing back and forth through its trunk, energy drawn downward from the light above and moisture from the depths. But she had become part of it. The power in the Tree flowed through her as well, up and down her spine. It occured to her that she was the fruit that the Tree was bearing . . . and then, suddenly, it was her own mother who held her, and the wind that stirred the branches was murmuring her name.

Sense told her that she could not possibly remember. Her mother had died before she was a year old. But this was not memory. A grief suppressed before she had possessed the words to name it welled through her in a long moan.

"Why did you leave me? Why did you leave me alone?" her spirit cried.

"Be still, my child," came the answer. *"I am here. I have been waiting for you. . . ."*

Time passed. When Brunahild became aware of herself once more, a cold wind was drying her tears. Her throat muscles ached, and the branches of the yew tree groaned as they swayed, echoing her moaning. Or perhaps the sound came from the Worldtree. She could no longer tell the difference, and when a glitter of light appeared between the trees before her, she did not know whether it belonged to the world outside or the one within.

The light bobbed and blinked among the tree trunks. Slowly it grew into a torch carried by a cloaked figure. At the edge of the clearing, it paused.

"Runes you will win; well will you read them," said a voice she ought to know. "Of wondrous weight, of mighty magic, which by the wisest god are given. Perceive them, receive them, make them your own!"

The figure stepped forward and swung the torch up, and then upward again in two strokes to the side. "Feeeee . . . uuu . . . " The name reverberated through all the worlds.

Brunahild blinked. She was seeing with her body's eyes, but the figure seemed to stand on the other side of a great gulf. Only the fiery shape of the rune existed in the same dimension as she did, glowing in the darkness even after the cloaked figure had turned away.

Fehu . . . The first of the runes had been almost the first thing they taught her. In a cast it might foretell wealth or fertility for the questioner. But what did it *mean?* The question sent awareness spiraling inward. She hung in the Worldtree, and the Rune flickered mockingly. *Gain . . . grasp . . . make them your own. . . .* She remembered the wisewoman's words. But how?

She knew what the rune meant for others, but what was its significance for her? Not fertility of body. If she became a Walkyrja, she would bear no child. Nor did she want wealth; the tribes would see to her needs. She had to seek a deeper meaning now.

Fehu was a rune of the Wanes, the gods of the land. Fro and Froja, Lord and Lady, ruled its powers. Froja was mistress of the most ancient magics, but that was not the face she showed to those who drew this rune. Brunahild blinked, for the lines of light were re-forming, and now a woman's features shimmered there.

"*Who are you?*"

"*Do you not know? Look around you, child of two lands, rooted in none, and see. . . .*"

The image shivered again, and Brunahild saw the yew wood, but now each branch was outlined in light. Her vision expanded; below her the jagged heights of the Taunus lay sleeping beneath the stars, but still awareness was widening. Now she perceived the shining coils of the Rhenus, the folds of hill and valley, forest and field, and the tiny twinkling lights that marked the homes of men.

"You must serve all of these, though none may claim you. You have pledged yourself to the High One, but to fulfill that oath you must first serve Me. . . ." The image reformed into the face of a woman, but now the face was far more ancient, the eyes deep as forest pools, the features seamed and wrinkled as the face of the land.

"Erda . . . " she cried, and instantly was answered.

"That is one of my names."

For a moment she saw the shape of the Rune shining through the face of the Goddess, then the radiance was rushing toward her. Brunahild cried out as its fire struck her, then fell into darkness.

She did not know how much time had passed when she became aware once more. She was still hanging in the tree, and in the distance she saw the flicker of a torch approaching.

"Uuur . . . oooz . . . " The second Rune blazed in the air, and once more Brunahild set herself to understand it.

Thurisaz came next—the rune of the primal forces of the world and the power that masters them—and with it the vision. Brunahild waited, awareness sharpening to the point of pain as the fourth rune was drawn in the air.

"Aaan . . . soooz . . . "

Ansuz meant a god . . . the god. . . .

The rune shape hung in the air as the Walkyrja departed. Brunahild let out her breath in a long sigh.

"All-Father, where are you?" The impact of the other runes had been overwhelming. Where was the one power she knew already? Where was the god who had already claimed her soul?

"Where I have always been . . . "

The answer whispered from somewhere deep within. Brunahild trembled, for suddenly she was feeling everything with new perception—the damp night air, her bindings, the hard surface of the tree. She let her head drop forward, and the pressure of the rope against her throat sent awareness whirling dizzily inward.

"No . . . " came the voice within. *"Not that way."*

But when she opened her eyes again she could not tell if she was perceiving through his senses or her own.

"What do you mean? Are you in my head?"

"Always," came the answer, *"as I am always on the Tree, and on my High Seat, and watching from the Well. You will receive the Runes once only, but I*

am taking them up now and always and continually releasing them into the world."

The runes that Brunahild had seen already flared in her vision, and with them the others that were to come, rotating in an unending cycle that was like the circling of the stars in the heavens or the dancing of the witches at their festivals. In that rhythm all things were encompassed, if only her perception had been great enough to take it in, but no sooner did she reach for one image than it sped on.

"Stop! I do not understand!"

Instantly the motion ceased, and there was only the rune *Ansuz*, glowing in the darkness.

"It does not matter. You will know when you have need."

Gradually the runeshape faded, and then she saw the torchlight returning. But she could still feel that other presence sharing her body, waiting patiently for the next rune. She understood then that he had been with her from the beginning. Not this rune only but all of them were the words in which he spoke to her and to the world.

Night's horses sped onward, and the runes appeared, their order as precise and inexorable as the wheeling of the distant stars. Brunahild's awareness adjusted itself to the pattern, bringing her out of each vision in time to receive the next rune.

Gebo . . . Wunjo . . . Wodan's joy flowered through her, and Brunahild realized with a vague wonder that the first eight of the runes were done. She had spent many hours in spirit journeying, but never with this dual perception of outer and inner worlds, never with such focus, or for so long. She did not even notice the small movements by which her body kept itself from stiffening.

Naudhiz. . . . The spindle of Wyrd whirled into Brunahild's vision. She tried to hold it steady, so that she could see whence the thread had come. Images flickered in and out of awareness; Hun horsemen thundering across a dusty plain, Gudrun bending over the sacred well. She saw Huld's face warmed by firelight, the face of Ragnaris as he died. Memory of all that had brought her to this moment swirled through her vision.

"This I have been . . . " she spoke to the presence of the god within her, *"but what will I be?"*

"It is Fricca who knows all fates. She counsels Me," with a hint of laughter, the answer came. *"I do not wind your wyrd, little one. Follow the thread yourself, and see where it leads!"*

For a moment nothing moved. Then she seemed to be watching the thread unwind from the other end of the spindle, spinning out into a starry darkness that resolved itself into a loom that spanned the sky, and whose warp threads were spun of ice and fire. Her life thread was being drawn into the weaving along with many others, whose source she could not see. The threads seemed to weave themselves into the web, but some greater power was moving the heddle back and forth to receive them. Her vision sharpened, and now she could see the giant shape of the Mighty Weaver working the loom.

The Norns spin our threads, she thought then, *but we twine ourselves into the weft, and the Powers that have been from the Beginning weave all into a single whole.*

As she watched, Brunahild's own muscles tensed with the memory of the days of weaving that had gone into her gown; she swayed to the melody of her own weaving song. But new words echoed in her ears.

> *"A mighty weaver I—*
> *Strung between earth and sky—*
> *I sing the spell and weave it well,*
> *My life the thread I ply."*

She followed the glimmer of her own thread through the weaving, wondering about the others with which it was twined. For a moment she knew that it was her own need that compelled her, and if she could only understand it, she could indeed weave her own wyrd at will.

Then loom, thread, and song all faded, and she readied herself for the next of the runes.

Eiwaz, the Yew Tree, the thirteenth rune . . .

This was the time of greatest darkness. They had passed the midpoint now. Silently Brunhild named the rune and found herself once more aware of the yew tree. Its solid strength was unchanged, but now her body was angled to the curve of its trunk as if she had grown there. She waited for visions but there was only the tree—the Tree—existing simultaneously in all the worlds.

Perhaps that was the vision, she thought suddenly. *Eiwaz* was a rune of connection, linking the Underworld into which its roots plunged with the heavens. She sought downward, and heard the deep, sweet song of Earth's dreaming. Upward she cast, and once more she heard the voice of Wodan, whispering in the leaves.

The Tree connected them, and she was part of the Tree. . . .

For a moment, then, Brunahild understood herself and the runes and all that she had seen in her visions as parts of a continuing conversation between the god above and the goddess below.

*   *   *

Rune by rune, the bright images marched through the night. In the still hour before the dawn a grey ground mist came creeping through the trees. The Walkyrja's torch was surrounded by a halo of shimmering droplets as it scribed the Day rune in the damp air. Brunahild blinked, unsure whether the fog came from damp earth or the Thunderflood's rush, wondering if the dim shapes that were emerging were roots of the Worldtree. Some part of her knew that her body was tired, but in her dream of power she did not feel it.

A last time the torch came bobbing through the gloom. She recognized the trees of the yew wood; she moved with the mist back toward the waking world.

"Ob . . . tha . . . laz . . ." The sung syllables hung in the air.

Home, thought Brunahild, remembering how she had worried about its meaning when she was weaving. *My home is the tree.*

And the tree was at home in Middle Earth, and she and Huld were at home, and the Burgunds and the Huns, and even the Romans. Once she had seen a hall that had made use of a living oak tree for a housepost. This Tree was the pillar that upheld the world, and all who sheltered beneath its branches were one kindred.

"*Do you understand now?*" came the Voice from within, and a glimmer of vision showed her the god upon his high seat, but its posts were the branches of Yggdrasil, and the world was his hall. As long as she remembered that, she could never be forgotten by this father, or lose this home and family.

With a sigh Brunahild relaxed against her bonds, and the outlines of the Otherworld merged finally into those of the forest. She felt no need to move, but two figures were approaching through the veils of mist that swathed the tree. The sense of Presence that had overshadowed her began to withdraw.

Remember, came the Voice within her, *and carry this wisdom into the world. . . .*

Already the details of her visions were dimming, leaving her only fragments of images like the coals of last night's fire. Suddenly her body's weariness overwhelmed her. Brunahild blinked as Randgrid replaced the log ladder and came up it, bearing a drinking horn. Steam rose from its mouth like the mist in the trees.

What, indeed, had happened? When she had need, would she really remember it all? She suspected that her whole life might be scarcely long enough to bring into conscious awareness all that she had learned. She knew only that she was safe now, and all things had been brought to balance in her world.

Then the bronze-banded rim was set to her lip. Instinctively she swallowed, and as the hot spiced ale flowed down her throat, awareness of her body flowed back into every limb, and time began.

Once more the first of sunset had kindled the sky, and Huld stood with the other Walkyriun, weighted by cloak and headdress and beads. But now the open expanse that crowned the Hill of the High One was ringed by torches, and rich scents of roasting meat drifted from the firepits below. Brunahild and the others stood before them, blinking like young owls as they finished waking from the day of recovery and breathed in the good smells that weighted the air. While they slept their white gowns had been washed. In rosy light they seemed to glow.

"It is always such a relief when this is over," said Hrodlind. "But now we are up to strength again."

Seven more priestesses for the Walkyriun, thought Huld. All of the girls had completed their testing. It was not always so. There had been times when girls screamed to be released from the tree, or when that long night of vision revealed that despite the approval of their elders and their own desires they were fated for another path. But these had all endured till dawn, and if for some of them the night had been no more than a long waking dream, at least they had awakened still devoted to the gods and the Walkyriun.

What had the god shown Brunahild? Tonight Huld remembered her own ordeal with painful clarity. In the beginning of her own vision the goddess she served had appeared, and that, she had expected. She had not expected that the god who had been Froja's lover would come to her also, and that in his embrace she would find joy.

She lifted her eyes to the fir trees, upper branches stark against the blazing sky. Black birdshapes balanced on those branches, waiting for the scraps from the feast whose rich scent was filling the air.

"Beloved, did you come to Brunahild? Did you comfort her?"

Hrodlind grunted beside her, wincing as she turned. "I grow too old for this. Let the young ones do the runegiving next time!"

Huld nodded. The girls looked well rested, but she could feel the ache of the long night's watching in every bone. She looked back at the ravens. *It has been a long road, my lord, and you have been good to me,* she thought, remembering how she had served the Lady and the land and lain with kings as well as counseled them. *But now I am tired. Will Brunahild continue the task you gave to me, and will you be kind to her?*

"I wish they would get on with it," whispered Hrodlind. "My old belly growls for a taste of that food!"

Huld smiled. Once she had thought that age would temper such appetites, but she too was hungry. Her body knew that she had a road or two left to travel, and it wanted fuel.

Randgrid strode toward them, her features half-hidden by the wolfskin that formed her headdress and mantled her shoulders. Those who had been finishing the preparations fell into place beside her so that a crescent of blue-cloaked figures faced the maidens.

"Hear me, all you hallowed beings!" Hlutgard lifted her arms in invocation. "Elves and Aesir and Powers Above and Below—here be maidens sworn to your service. They have learned your lore, they have woven their wyrd, they have been tested by the Tree. Stand witness, Mighty Ones, as we receive them into our company!"

One by one, the girls were called forward and named and embraced by the Walkyriun. They were draped with new cloaks of dark blue wool and crowned with the headpieces of their totems and as they took their places among them, the circle grew. Brunahild stood behind the others, watching the ravens. She would be the last to be called. It seemed to the wisewoman that there was a centered stillness in her waiting that had never been there before.

What is she thinking? wondered Huld.

Soon, I will feed you, Brunahild told the ravens, or perhaps it was the god within her. The tracery of branches against the sky seemed almost painfully beautiful. Was this the way Wodan perceived the world? Ever since she had awakened she had felt his presence echoing in her awareness. She wondered if it would go on.

Frojavigis was receiving her headdress now, fashioned from the fur of a winter hare. Happiness blazed from her like the heat of a fire.

And then it was Brunahild's turn. She moved forward. Faces floated around her. She knew them all, but she had never seen them so clearly. The blue cloak settled around her shoulders, warm as an embrace. Huld lifted the headdress, shining black feathers glistening in the ruddy light, and as she placed it upon Brunahild's head the birds rose in triumphant clamor from the fir trees.

"Raven-priestess . . ." Huld smiled at her. "When you are among us, what name will you choose to bear?"

"I am Sigdrifa, Bringer of Victory," she answered steadily. "Through me may the god make his purpose manifest in the world!"

Chapter 10 ✲ Weregild

Ragan and Sigfrid rode down from their forests into a country ripening with harvest gold. The previous winter had been hard and the sowing delayed by floods in the spring, but the hay had been cut already, and in such fields as had sprouted the emmer wheat stood stiff in the late summer sun. It seemed a land of peace and plenty, but Ragan frowned as they rode, remembering when fields cut this year for hay had been planted with grain, and stretches that now were saltmarsh had grown sweet hay, and a tumble of beams and rotting reeds beside the path had been a home.

"Did the storms get them, or they go west with Hlodomar?" wondered the smith. He had always cared more for the gold that lay buried in the earth than the kind that sprouted from the soil, but he felt oddly troubled by this subtle erosion of men's presence in the land.

Sigfrid, sitting slouched on his pony, appeared not to have heard.

"You sleeping?" growled Ragan, booting his mount alongside. "Or blind? There was good fields and fat cows here, last time we come this way."

"I saw where the sea-eagle is nesting. I saw a wading heron catch a fat frog. . . ." said Sigfrid. "If my mother dies, why should I care for the fate of other men?"

Ragan noted the hard planes beneath the curves of the boy's face and fell silent. He supposed Sigfrid had a right to be bitter. They would not even have known Hiordisa had miscarried of another child and was still ailing if a wandering trader had not babbled it. If Ragan had not agreed to come with him, Sigfrid would have run off alone. His mother was the only kin the boy knew.

The smith considered the unyielding line of Sigfrid's back, and an unaccustomed stab of pity made him frown. He had thought he was raising the boy as he had been raised, but he had a father and brothers when he was young. Why would he be surprised that except for Hiordisa, the lad cared more for the wild beasts than he did for humankind?

"Do you think she will be glad to see me?" Sigfrid said suddenly. "They said we should come more often, that five winters without a visit was too long."

"Fast as you're growing, two winters seem like five," Ragan answered him. "She will be pleased."

At fifteen, the boy was six feet already, and though he had not a man's weight yet, there was good hard muscle on those long bones. The mop of hair had darkened, and a fuzz of brown shadowed cheeks and chin. Sigfrid had reached the age when a boy might ride with the warriors, and it was time to show the Albings what Ragan and the forest had made of their fosterling.

"You're almost a man," he added carefully. "Time to claim your inheritance."

Sigfrid reined in, the straight brows lifting in inquiry.

"Your father was a *rich* hero." Ragan smiled grimly. "Sons of Hunding search for his treasure after the battle, but could only burn his hall. Sigmund hid his woman and his wealth in woods, an arrow-shot from the battlefield. King Alb took the gold with him too, when he carry your mother away."

They were crossing a piece of marshland, and the hooves of their ponies echoed hollowly on the causeway of split logs.

"Are you sure?" asked the boy. "I never heard anything about a treasure before."

"Sons of Hunding want the gold almost as much as they want you." Ragan gave a short laugh. "But gold's easier to hide. I saw it when I came to serve the king. Ancient work, some of it, and they wanted it valued. Helped to hide it too. Alb took part for your mother's dower. Rest of it's waiting for you."

"I don't want it!" said Sigfrid, his mood shifting suddenly. Purple heather trembled to either side as the road wound toward a hump of higher ground crowned with pines.

"A man of the tribes needs armor, clothes, arm rings, to show his standing. You need gold for gifts, support retainers, make alliances."

"I like the wolves' way better," the boy answered sullenly. "What do I want with retainers and allies?"

"To avenge your father . . ." Ragan grimaced, remembering how the red blood had stained his own father's white hair.

Sigfrid was watching him curiously. "But why? My brother killed King Lyngvi's father, and Lyngvi and his brothers killed mine. We are even now. Why not let the old feud die?"

"Does that bump where Heming broke your arm ache when it rains?" Ragan asked. "The pain answers. Man's kin pay for his deeds or are paid for his dying. To keep the balance it must be so. Death wants weregild, in blood or gold. Blood is better," he added painfully. "Gold breeds more killing, sometimes."

From above came a rasp of demented laughter. Ragan looked up, snarling—Fafnar had laughed that way, when their father died. But it was only a black stork, startled from her nest in the top of the pine tree. She settled once more, clattering her bill angrily, as they passed by.

"I need neither—" Sigfrid began, but Ragan shook his head.

"No choice. Heming's blood burned, knowing you lived."

"I don't believe you," the boy said stubbornly. "No one troubled me when we came back before—"

"Whole Albing clan was gathered when Hiloperic died," growled Ragan. "Even the Hundings not that strong! But one day they come after you. You have to win. You made a promise to me!"

The boy's gaze rested on Ragan's face. "Do you still need a hero? I thought you were fostering me for the sake of my gold!"

"Gold? Remember the eagles of Rome? If I was greedy, you think I let them lie?" He stopped, realizing that Sigfrid was laughing at him. "Only gold I want is my share of the weregild for Ottar."

"And you want me to win it for you?" The boy's amusement faded. "Why?"

Ragan squinted at him beneath bent brows, then he sighed. There was no female left of his own blood to bear him a child. When he was younger he had tried women of the new races, but it seemed that none had quickened to his seed. If his line was to be remembered, to whom could he tell the tale but this boy, the hidden inheritor of Hreidmaro's doom, whom he was forging into the weapon for his revenge?

The sun was high now, and they had been on the road since dawn. Ahead he saw the gleam of open water, and a line of willows that promised shade. "We eat now, and I tell you about Ottar," Ragan said heavily, reining his pony toward the trees.

"My brother had a holt by the riverside," the smith began when they had watered the ponies and tied them where they could graze. The willows grew above one of the rivulets that trickled through the marshes and spread into a brown pool. A fly lit, and the surface shattered in rolling rings as something rose to take it from below, then the ripples smoothed and all was still once more.

"He caught fish," said Ragan, looking back at the boy. "We sold some, but he ate many, like otters, because they need food always, like the forgefire. One day he's eating a salmon, so hungry he heard nothing. Travelers come walking, a loremaster of the tall ones and his men. They see only big otter, and one of the men speared him." He fought to keep his voice steady. The time for anger would come when the story was done.

"Dead, the magic left him," he rumbled. "They knew him a man, but the skin was good, so they throw the human body into the stream. And they go on, come to the next hall at nightfall asking shelter. But it was Hreidmaro's house, and when they boast of their hunting, he smell the blood of his son on the skin."

Sigfrid paused with the hard bread half-eaten in his hand, waiting until Ragan could go on.

"We should have killed them. Fafnar wanted to. But they were wily, those thieves who stole Ottar's life, like Wodan, their thieving god. They tempt my father with talk of treasure, and the earth-magic in him wanted the gold. Their god show them the sacred pool beneath the falls where the spirit Andvari guarded the offerings. He looked like a great pike, but they were spellmasters. They wove a magic net to catch him; they took the gold."

A little breeze scattered sparks of sunfire across the pool, but Ragan's vision was fixed on another kind of treasure now.

"The servants of Wodan cover the otterskin with gold to the last whisker. They put the rune rod that was there into the pile, and the neck ring, though they wanted them for their magic. My father took the weregild. Then the gold-lust came on my brother Fafnar. He killed Hreidmaro and took the treasure. Now he guards it in shape of the great wurm."

Ragan pulled the stopper from the bronze flask that hung at his side. It held strong mead, and he needed it now.

"Fafnar killed your father, but he is your brother. . . ." said Sigfrid slowly, his features darkening and brightening with the movement of the leaves. "To whom is the weregild owed when the strife is among kin?"

Ragan shook his head back and forth as if that would dislodge the pain. "Kin-strife is unholy, but Fafnar must pay! You kill him for me!"

"A berserker who is serpent-wise, and your brother?" Sigfrid's eyebrows quirked upward. "I am well grown for my years, but I have no battle-craft for such a foe! You must give me a little time yet, foster-father."

"Time!" Ragan laughed harshly. "More than twenty winters pass already. Can wait a little more."

Sigfrid moved like a shadow through the reedbeds, setting one foot where the other had rested, timing his movements so that the rustle of his passing had no more rhythm than the wind in the reeds. As men grew fewer the deer were coming farther into the lowlands, feeding on the rich grass of the water-margins and the isles. The Albings had milk and cheese in plenty, but until the winter slaughtering, flesh would be scarce, and his mother needed red meat to build up her strength again.

The bending reedheads told him that the wind was still in his favor. A wading heron stiffened, and he froze until it decided that he was only some odd kind of tree.

Good hunting, brother, thought Sigfrid, *for you and for me. . . .*

The wedge-shaped tracks of the deer led toward a bank where the grass came down to the edge of the water. He glimpsed movement among the willows and stilled, scarcely daring to breathe. Infinite care and infinite patience were the way of the hunter. He waited, becoming part of the pattern of earth and wind and water, of life and death and the slow descent of the sun.

And they came, a young buck of four points and a doe with two half-grown fawns, and then another doe, barren this year though she looked fat and healthy. Sigfrid slid an arrow into position, and then, with a slow, sure movement like the bending of the willows in the breeze, bent the bow.

It was of stout yew and almost as tall as he was, but his arms stayed rock-steady as he turned, following the doe's hesitant progress across the grass. He had made no sound, but her head lifted, and the world stopped as she stared into his eyes.

We are one, said that clear gaze. *In death or life we are Earth's children. I give myself to you.*

Then time began again as the doe turned, foreleg lifting, and in the moment when the space behind the elbow showed clear, Sigfrid set the arrow free.

He was so close that before her leg came down again the arrow had crossed the space between them. It struck, drilling through to the heart beyond. Deer leaped in graceful arcs in all directions; all but one, who lifted upward, then fell back in her tracks and lay still. The doe's eyes were dulling already when the hunter reached her side.

Sigfrid came home through the fields with the deer across his shoulders, following the track of the harvesters. Dark shapes still labored against the sunset, cutting and binding the stiff sheaves while others built them into smooth humped shocks that would shed the rain. Alb worked among them, the heavy muscles of his back sliding smoothly beneath the sunburned skin as he cast handfuls aside for the binders who came after him, stepped forward and slashed again. Sigfrid waited at the edge of the field.

As he reached it, the king straightened, glancing at the clouds gathering to the northward. Then he saw Sigfrid standing there and waved.

"You have had good hunting!"

"Yes, but my kill will not feed so many as yours—" said the boy.

Alb's smile became a grin, and he turned back to his fields. The reapers were almost finished; only a single section still stood, but instead of cutting it, the harvesters were binding the stems together with a chain of cornflowers. One of the girls smiled at Sigfrid, then whispered something to her companion. He thought she was the same one who had rubbed herself against him the night before when he passed her going into the hall. That night he had dreamed he was consumed by brightness and wakened to find a wet spot in his sleeping furs.

"Well, we have finished ahead of the rain, and the Old Woman has her share!" Alb handed his sickle to one of the thralls and slung his tunic across his shoulder. "Mother Earth has shown us some favor at last, and we will get through another winter. But I think that your mother will be happier to see that deer. . . ."

For a moment Sigfrid could not answer him. Singing, the harvesters started down the cart-track toward the dinner that awaited them at the hold, and they turned to follow. The two girls had contrived to be last. It seemed to him that the movement of their hips had become more pronounced. They glanced back at him often, laughing.

Trying to ignore the oddly pleasant tightening in his groin, Sigfrid turned back to the king. "Perhaps flesh-meat will strengthen her. . . ."

"They say the beasts grow fat in the fields of Gaul," said Alb, "where so many of our folk have gone. . . . The Riverbank clan as well as the Salt-folk, and some of our own people too. Hlodomar has no heir, and wants me to bring the rest of our clan to help him hold his new lands, but your mother does not wish to leave her home."

"She will get well here. We will make her well!" Sigfrid exclaimed.

"You are a good lad," said the king, sighing, as if that were an answer.

Sigfrid gave him a quick look. He had just been thinking that his mother's second choice was worthy of her first, whether or not Alb was the warrior that Sigmund had been.

"I was wrong," the king added suddenly. "I should not have let my brother argue me into sending you away. If I had adopted you, your mother might not have risked her health trying to give me a son!"

Sigfrid stopped in his tracks, staring. He wanted to strike the man down for saying the thing that he had been trying not to think since he first saw his mother when they had arrived a week ago. Hiordisa had lost flesh and color, and grew tired from any exertion at all. *If she dies,* cried his heart, *Alb's pride killed her!* But even in his grief he could hear the man's pain. The king loved Hiordisa, and in a sense, Sigfrid had lost her seven winters ago.

The gates of the hold were swinging open ahead of them. Old Eberwald, who headed Alb's household guard, pushed past, shouting a greeting as the women came out with horns of ale. Someone saw the deer, and they began to praise Sigfrid along with the harvesters. Suddenly he and Alb were surrounded by cheering warriors, and the moment for accusation or blame was gone.

"There are two more fields to harvest, but the weather is holding," said Alb, easing back in the high seat and holding out his horn to Arnegundis to refill. "I think we will get all the grain in!"

Hiordisa smiled at the self-conscious gravity with which her daughter tipped the jug of ale. Alb thanked her, and she moved along the hearth to Sigfrid, frowning impatiently as she waited for him to put down the bone he was gnawing and pick up his horn. His lips twitched a little as he held it out to her, as if he could not quite believe that this leggy maiden with the long tail of golden hair was the little sister with whom he had played wolf two winters ago.

But his mother had seen the girls changing day by day. To Hiordisa, it was Sigfrid who was the wonder. He was growing into his height, and she had yet to see him make an awkward move. She had known only one man with that kind of grace. In the uncertain light of the torches it was easy for imagination to add the muscle that manhood would bring, and to see not Sigfrid, but Sigmund as he must have looked before she knew him. Hiordisa sighed and, with her horn spoon, stirred the pieces of venison and herbs that Perchta had simmered for her, wondering if she could make it appear that she had eaten more than a bite or two. She had dreamed of Sigmund the night before, standing with his hand raised in warning and the wounds that had killed him gaping red, but the vision had faded before she could question him.

"Is the meat not good?" Sigfrid's voice recalled her. "Perhaps tomorrow I can bring you a tender duck or a young swan—"

Hiordisa looked up, and the flinching in his face told her how much he found *her* changed. *Is it my own death that Sigmund is warning me of?* she wondered then. Sometimes she felt fear, but she told herself she was being foolish, for she had no pain, only this weakness, and a sense that she stood still while the rest of the world was flowing away.

"It is very good, but Perchta fed me a dish of curds and honey just before you returned," she lied, "and I had not much room for more."

His gaze slid away, and she could see how much he wanted to believe her. *My poor child,* she thought, *I have been able to do so little for you.*

"The men are merry!" Sigfrid said brightly.

The level of sound in the feasting hall was rising as the ale went round. One could measure men's anxiety about the harvest by their relief at getting it in. The farm-folk had gone home to their houses outside the palisade, but the extra workers Alb had taken on to help with the reaping were drinking deep at the other end of the hall. They were men without kin, survivors of shattered clans washed up upon this land in the marshes as the westward flood swept on. And they were a rough lot; she was glad that they were quartered in the feasting hall, and not in the smaller building with the family.

"Eberwald used to let me help him polish his helm when I was a little boy." Sigfrid gestured toward the grizzled warrior who was lifting his horn in a toast to the reapers. "But some of the others are strange to me."

Many of the others were strange to Hiordisa as well, but she knew the men of Alb's household guard better than she knew this tall boy with the yellow eyes who was her son.

"Do you not remember Ruodpercht? He has served the kin since Alb was your age. He was with him when they rescued me."

"The man with the white hair?" Sigfrid peered through the fire-light. "I did not recognize him."

"If he were not a clever warrior, he would not have lived to grow those silver hairs!" Hiordisa hid a smile. "Herimod, the one with the scars, took his oath six winters ago. He was here at the kingmaking, but you might not have noticed him in the crowd."

"And the redheaded lad next to him?"

"That is Werinhar, who came to us last year from Juteland. He is reckless, but he fights well." She continued to describe the warriors, glad of a topic that would distract him. As men finished eating and tossed the bones to the dogs, the conversation had turned to another kind of harvesting.

"Do you remember how we battled the men of Gotland?" cried Ruodpercht. "Came at them from the sea and caught 'em napping. We brought home a shipload of gold that season!"

"The pickings are better in the Roman lands," said Werinhar. "Embroidered hangings and jeweled dishes, and gold coin that can be melted down to make arm rings!" The conversation became general as men recalled prizes won in a dozen raids. Hiordisa let her eyes close, wondering how soon she could seek her bed without alarming her family.

"And what of Sigmund's treasure?" a deep voice rumbled close by. Hiordisa sat upright, blinking, and saw that Ragan had joined them. But the smith had pitched his voice so that only she and Alb could hear him—and Sigfrid, who had flushed a dull crimson.

"Ragan, I told you—" muttered the boy, but Alb was frowning.

"Do you doubt my honor, smith? I can see that the boy is ready to receive arms. He shall have all he is entitled to, never fear!"

Hiordisa watched the muscles leap out on Sigfrid's lean arms as his grip tightened on his drinking horn. Sigmund had won wagers by shattering swords. What weapons would be stout enough to serve his son? She shivered, remembering the glimmer of moonlight on the last blade to break in Sigmund's hand.

It is time. . . . she thought then. *It is Wyrd that has brought Sigfrid here.
Tomorrow I will give him the pieces of his father's sword.*

*Sigfrid was bringing wood to the forgefire. The blaze leaped high as he laid
on the logs, but Ragan was yelling at him to bring more. Another log and another
fed the flame. Sweat rolled down the boy's back, but the skin of his face grew tight
at the hot breath of the fire. He threw another branch into the fiery maw, and sparks
whirled toward the thatch. Tongues of flame leaped out above, but Ragan was still
calling for fuel. Sigfrid backed away as sparks began to shower down. Then a
breath of cool darkness swirled around him; he saw black wings fluttering between
him and the fire, and heard the raven's cry. . . .*

"Sigfrid, Sigfrid! Danger—wake now!"

Sigfrid woke, coughing, the words still echoing in his ears. But
the scent of smoke was real. He wrenched free of the bedclothes,
rolled onto the floor, and came up in the same motion, hearing others
coughing around him, sleepy grunts of protest and dawning alarm as
men fought their way to consciousness. An inner time sense told him
it was the chill hour before dawn. The hearthfire was dead, but the
smell of smoke was growing stronger, and through a chink in the wall
came a red glow.

"Fire! There's a fire!" His voice cracked, and others took up the
cry. Someone staggered to the door and flung it open, then screamed
as firelight flared from steel.

"Albings, fire and the sons of Hunding surround you!" came a
shout from outside. "But with you we have no quarrel. Send out your
women and children now; and the men, one by one, unarmed. It is
the Wolsung brat we are after—leave him inside to roast or give him
to our spears!"

Sigfrid could hear Arnegundis whimpering and Albtrud's outraged
wail as Perchta dragged them toward the door. The oblong flickered
bright and dark as the women went through. Voices rose in a babble
of arguments as Alb ordered his men out after them.

"Lord, it galls me to give up a good blade!" came Eberwald's growl,
"But I'll follow your lead—"

"Then get out now, and take your woman," came Alb's reply.
"The boy and I will come out fighting, or not at all."

Sigfrid's skin grew cold as he realized his mother had not gone
with the others. He heard a chorus of protest from the house-
guards.

"Albald was right," muttered someone, "the Wolsungs bring ill
luck to everyone—"

"Wyrd has cast us an ill fate," came the answer, "but Alb has my oath, and I will not leave my lord!"

Hiordisa's voice rose above them all. "I stay as well. Do you think my life will mean anything if they kill you and my child?"

My fault! Sigfrid thought desperately. *I came to help her, and I have brought disaster upon them all!* Now he recognized that voice outside, and a terror seven seasons old chilled his veins. Ragan had been right. Heming still wanted revenge.

"Mother, leave now—" He found his voice at last. "Or I will go out to them unarmed. You cannot die for me!"

"Lad, all men die in the end. It is Wyrd, not you, that decides when it is to be," Alb said gently, but something twisted in Sigfrid's solar plexus as he saw his stepfather's smile. "Wodan would laugh at me if I allowed any man under my protection to be butchered, and Hella will have me for certain if I can be frightened into giving up a man of my kin!"

The exultation that had swept the boy as Alb claimed him chilled as his mother spoke again.

"I have lived with you too long to survive you, my lord. I will not go from this place until you are free."

"Then in Wodan's name let us break out fighting," cried the boy, "or she will burn!"

There was a roar of agreement from the others, and Alb began to grin. They reached for helms already warm from the fire, swords scraped from their sheaths, and Alb thrust a heavy war-spear into Sigfrid's hands. Someone soaked a blanket in the water barrel and draped it around Hiordisa, then they all moved forward, Eberwald and the other men first, with Alb and Sigfrid following. The boy blinked as smoke billowed inward, but it was no worse than the heat of the forge.

"Now!" cried Alb, and they burst out into the ring of enemy steel.

Sigfrid glimpsed Ruodpercht falling with a spear through him as he passed the doorway, dodged the blade that stabbed toward his own guts as he had evaded the horns of the aurochs, and thrust. There was a yell and a sudden weight bore down his spear; Sigfrid wrenched it free as another dark form came at him, slashed this time, parried another spear-shaft, jabbed and whirled, seeking another foe.

Metal cracked on wood as two swordsmen came at Alb, and Sigfrid saw splinters fly from his shield. Werinhar and Herimod were battling back to back; Eberwald hewed at his foes as if he were scything grain. Some of the masterless men hired for the harvest were among the attackers. Sigfrid stabbed at one of them and, breathless, jerked his spear out again, looking for the next foe. There were so many! He had hunted dangerous game, but never more than one beast at a time. The boy gulped raw night air, saw a spear flying toward Alb's back, and batted it aside.

The rest of Alb's men had been in the feasting hall. Had the traitors surprised and bound them before they let in the enemy? Had they killed Ragan as well? The gate to the palisade had been barred again, though he could hear angry cries from beyond it and the thunk of axes. Sigfrid wondered if the village-folk would break through in time to avenge them. Werinhar collapsed, blood spurting from his thigh, and Herimod straddled him, trying to cover both of them with his shield.

Sigfrid leaped foward to catch up with Alb. A spearman came at him; he lifted his shaft to guard, and wood jarred on wood as it met that of his enemy. He shoved, the man fell back, then came in again. Once more the spear-shafts shocked together. Sigfrid pushed again, and as his opponent gave way, twisted, binding the other's shaft, and thrusting onward to the shoulder of the spearman, ripping the iron point through flesh and out again.

Beyond the tossing spears Sigfrid glimpsed Heming's dark beard. Another man stood beside him, older, but very like him, with gold gleaming from his helm. Could he reach them? He sprang sideways, thrusting, and ducked as a swordblade whipped by, felt the wind as it missed his head and then the jolt as it struck full upon the shaft of his spear.

Sigfrid staggered as the wood, weakened by the previous battering, broke beneath the blow. He was still turning, momentum whipping the dangling spearhead into the face of his attacker, then the last fragments parted, and the boy was left with a stick no longer than a practice sword.

Muscles trained to wield a smith's hammer swung mightily, but shieldless, there was little he could do against spears. Still forms dotted the yard; perhaps one of them had dropped a serviceable weapon. He turned, searching, and saw an explosion of sparks as the thatched roof of the sleeping hall began to fall in. A woman's figure was silhouetted against the flame.

On the other side of the yard he could see more of the Albing men pouring out of the feasting hall with Ragan in the midst of them, laying about him with his hammer and roaring like a bear. But all their foes lay between them. A scream ripped from the boy's throat, and he leaped toward the burning building, the useless stick spinning from his hand. Heat blasted him as he grabbed, then his hands closed on flesh and he yanked his mother forward into the yard. He was burning in a forge of fire and darkness; fury and the will to defend her were all he knew.

Hiordisa screamed as steel flared, and fire flashed through him, burning all human awareness away.

Snarling, he drove upward past the blade. There was a crack of breaking bone, a sword struck from behind him, he ducked and felt hot blood spurt across him as it struck his foe. He turned inside the second foe's guard, sprang, and his strong hands closed. Someone was screaming, but the sound that rasped from his own throat was louder. His enemies were fast, but he moved with more than human speed. He left his man with a broken neck and, half-crouched, whirled toward the next, dodging his blow.

And then there was only the blaze of light and the taste of blood and the howling of the wolf within.

"Sigfrid— Wake up, my dear, it is over. . . ."

The wolf shivered and tried to burrow back into the darkness. He knew the voice, but it was part of a nightmare. Cool hands stroked his forehead, but his mind was still blinded by the fire. Something cold touched his lips, washing the foul taste in his mouth away. Instinctively he swallowed.

"There is no head wound; what is wrong with him?"

"Exhaustion." A second voice seemed to rumble up from the earth below. "Same with my brother after battle. Spirit needs time to come home."

He knew this voice too. His hearing seemed painfully sharpened. A little farther off, people were whispering; he heard wood being dragged outside, the distant cry of an osprey, the wind sighing around the eaves. His sense of smell was working too. He smelled spilled ale and thought he must be in the feasting hall, but the sour reek of charred wood came to him from outside. He whimpered, fighting awareness, but as he stirred, he felt a damp cloth being drawn across his forehead. . . . Why did it seem so strange to feel the touch of cloth on skin?

"Sigfrid, can you hear me? Open your eyes and see, we are all safe now."

He was Sigfrid. Groaning, he reached out and his fingers closed on cloth. He had hands . . . he was human then, why was he so surprised? Carefully, he opened his eyes. His head lay in his mother's lap. Hiordisa's face was bloodless, her hair singed; he could see the skull beneath the skin. But she was still alive. He took a deep breath, images of the fight beginning to return.

"Is Heming gone?"

"Gone, yes—he run!" Ragan answered. "But Lyngvi's dead, and Eyolf, and most of their warriors. You remember when our men broke down the gate?"

Sigfrid shook his head. Now that he could feel his limbs again, every muscle in his body was beginning to scream.

"No matter," said Ragan. "Maybe better so. Rest now." Gratefully, the boy let his eyes close.

"*He* may have forgotten, but *I* can't," someone said in a low voice. No doubt they thought he could not hear. "He was a wolf! I saw it, and I saw him tear out the throats of two men! No wonder the Hundings went running! If he stays here, I might run too!"

Sigfrid remembered the rotten taste in his mouth, and his gorge rose. Strong hands held him as he retched into the straw, then laid him back down. He turned his face against his mother's thigh, trying to sink into unconsciousness again.

He did not know what he had done, but behind his closed eyelids, an afterimage of light danced through his brain, and Sigfrid shuddered, remembering the ecstasy.

When they rode out through the gates of Hiloperic's hold two days later, the smell of burning still lay heavy on the air. Sigfrid would stay no longer. He had saved his mother, but he could not forget that she would not have been in danger if he had not been there. All the folk of the holding were there to see them depart, showering them with provisions and praise. But Sigfrid heard the relief in their congratulations. The girls who had flirted with him ran away now, and he had noticed how men's glances flickered when he tried to meet their eyes. Only Hiordisa's smile had not changed. But she had been married to the wolf-king. Even his sisters flinched when he looked at them, and that was the hardest thing of all to bear. Better by far to return to his woods and the wolves.

"Alb make good on his promise!" Ragan patted the sack that held the more portable items from Sigmund's hoard. He had promised to redeem the rest with arms and clothing when Sigfrid was ready for them. "A princely inheritance!"

Sigfrid glanced back one last time as they reached the ridge where the pine trees grew, then nudged his pony down the slope through the heather. Larks were trilling in the heavens, but the boy scarcely heard them. All his awareness was focused within.

"They were buying me off," he said shortly. "They would have given me gold whether I had a right to it or no, just to get rid of me."

"Fafnar did not complain, but I think he like folk to fear him," said Ragan with a growl of laughter. "Men fear when they don't understand. Is better for berserker to serve kings."

Berserker . . . Sigfrid tasted the word for the thing he had somehow become. Some kings had whole companies of warriors who fought as wolves or bears, dedicating themselves to Wodan. And then there was Fafnar, whose favored form was the great Wurm that the Romani called Dragon.

"I thought you had to wear the beast-skin to change, or at least a bit of its fur. . . ."

"It helps," answered Ragan, "but fear, danger, can bring it on."

Sigfrid shivered, remembering those moments of waking when he had thought he had paws, and fur instead of skin. Had he really changed into a wolf? Certainly he had killed like one, and there were plenty of folk to swear they had seen a half-grown wolf with brown-brindled fur tearing at the foe. How could he have done that? He had lost himself sometimes, running with the wolves, but he had always killed in his own form.

Was it better, he wondered, to kill men as a wolf, or as a man? In saving his mother's life, Sigfrid had lost her more surely than if they had both died in the fire. He would not see her again. As soon as he regained his senses, Hiordisa had allowed them to put her to bed at last and had not left it. But if the days of her life were numbered, at least he had not shortened them.

He glanced at the bundle behind his own saddle, where he had stowed his mother's last gift to him—the fragments of Sigmund's sword. The sleeping hall and its contents had been a mass of charred wood and ashes when he and Perchta went to search for it. Hiordisa's dower chest had burned, and the scorched fragments of the sword's original wrappings fell to bits as he lifted it. But the shining pieces of metal had not even been discolored by the blaze.

"*Wodan gave Sigmund the blade, and Wodan broke it, when his time was done. . . .*" Hiordisa had told him. "*Your father told me to save the pieces till you were grown. Reforge the sword, Sigfrid. It is a hero's blade!*"

Such a sword would not fail him unless the god broke it as he had before, Sigfrid thought bitterly, provided, of course, that it could be reforged at all. He wondered if Ragan's bellows could build a blaze hotter than the fires that had destroyed the hall. He had not told the smith that he had the shards of the sword. He was not even sure that he wanted it remade.

The gifts of Wodan were double-edged. The wolf-blood of his ancestor Sigi had saved his life, but it seemed to Sigfrid that the price had been his humanity.

"So, we go home now," said Ragan cheerfully. "You take vengeance for your father already. Soon you do the same for mine. . . ." He looked sidelong at Sigfrid, questioning.

"Oh yes, I will kill Fafnar for you," Sigfrid said bitterly. "I'm a berserker myself, now. You forge me a sword that will kill him, and I'l be off to do the deed. It should be no trouble at all."

Chapter 11  A Gathering of Ravens

Holy Hill, Burgund Lands
Taunus Mountains
Summer, A.D. 418

The flames of the great bonfire flared across the field of assembly and fell in a flutter of shadow like ravens' wings. *The field full of folk*, thought Gudrun, watching the warriors whom that light revealed. She shivered, though her face felt fevered by the heat of the fire, wondering how many of the Burgund warriors who had come to this Midsummer Thing-meet would soon be feasting in Froja's hall. They sat grouped by district around the fire and the king's high seat, balanced on log benches or cross-legged on the grass, debating the Alamanni war.

"We know that the Alamanni want the valley of the Rhenus, but do they really think they can enforce their claim?" asked one of the older men who had been settled on the new lands.

"There is no doubt that they're preparing to try, if that is what you mean," said Ostrofrid the lawspeaker. "And that we are going to have to face them alone."

"But the Romans are our allies—" Gundohar began, his golden arm rings glinting as he leaned forward. Ostrofrid turned on him, scowling.

"No, my king, we are theirs! There will be no help from the Legions. The whole point of making us *feoderati* was so they wouldn't have to defend those lands!"

Through the smoky air Gudrun saw men stroking their moustaches to hide grins, and Gundohar was blushing again. She sighed. Her brother did not lack courage—sometimes she thought it took more bravery for him to face all these warriors than it did for them to face their foes—but he had nightmares, and now she was having them too.

"I do not doubt the valor of our warriors," Gundohar said sharply, and gold glittered from baldrics and arm rings as the warriors of his comitatus, ranged at attention around the high seat, stiffened like hunting dogs. "A warrior who fights only for honor gains glory from facing overwhelming odds, but we moved into the Valley of the Rhenus so that our people could survive. We owe it to our women and children to seize whatever advantage we can."

Some of the younger men scowled at this, and Gudrun sighed. Gundohar was right, of course, but the warriors wanted a king who would feed their dreams of glory. He would have done better to appear a hothead who had to be argued into reason by his counselors.

"Are the odds so overwhelming?" came a question from the far side of the field. "The Alamanni are only a single tribe."

"Who knows what they are!" exclaimed Heribard, one of the elders. "All the Men—that's what they call themselves, tag ends of a dozen peoples, with neither king nor lineage to bind them. Gauls and escaped slaves and the gods only know what rabble fill their army. How can you count their strength when they take in every landless man who can shake a spear?"

"Our latest word gives them twenty hundreds," said Hagano. "And the talk among them is that they are gathering to take back the lands along the Rhenus again."

There was a little murmur of comment, for though the Burgund people were many, their holdings were scattered, and it would be hard to gather that number to oppose the enemy.

"This word is sure?" asked young Unald, a friend of Godomar's.

Hagano smiled. "I trust the messenger as myself."

Gudrun coughed. Hagano had gone himself in a charcoal burner's guise—not a thing that these proud warriors could even imagine. He had broadened out as he grew. In royal gear he fitted well enough among the children of Gibicho, but in a woodburner's leathers he could be told from the earthfolk only by the color of his hair. Was it his unknown father's blood or their mother's training that had given Hagano his talent for subterfuge?

"It will be a good fight, then!" said Unald happily, and his companions slapped their thighs, bare beneath the short trews and tunics they wore.

Gudrun shifted uncomfortably on the hard bench. If only there were something she could *do!* But it was too late to become a warrior-maid like Brunahild. Peace was not a natural condition for any of the tribes, but neither was the kind of full-scale warfare that the Alamanni were threatening. During the long migration of the Burgunds south and westward there had been battles and raids like the one that had convinced the Romans to give them the valley of the Rhenus. But when faced by too determined a foe, the folk had always moved on. Now there was nowhere left to go, and the Alamanni, seasoned by generations of conflict with the Romans, were driven by the same need.

"Can we buy allies?" Ordwini Dragobald's son was the youngest of the chieftains, but known already as a man of sense.

Ostrofrid stood with folded arms. "Our lord has shared out what gold he had freely, as befits a noble king," he answered. "The treasure of the Burgunds is the land we hold."

"Then let us cease this arguing and prepare to defend it!" exclaimed Ordwini. The fire billowed upward as if the chorus of agreement had fueled the flame. The warriors, the younger men especially, leaped to their feet, banging on their shields.

"Victory to the Burgunds! Let the battle-wurm awaken! Victory to the Niflungar!" they cried.

They want this war, thought Gudrun. *Of them all, perhaps only my brother can imagine what it will mean.* It occurred to her that if Gundohar were less intelligent he might find it easier to survive both as a man and as a king. He got to his feet, still as an image in his long gown with the heavy folds of the crimson cloak falling around him, waiting until the clamor had died down and they were all watching him.

"It is war, then." Gundohar's voice was thin, but his eyes were beginning to burn with a desperate resolution. "And may the Father of Victory speed our spears!"

The cheering faded to an echo behind them as the royal kindred walked back up the hill to the king's hall. It was only when the house-guard had left them in the friendlier warmth of the women's quarters that Hagano spoke again.

"There was another thing I heard among the Alamanni that you should know. They have sent gifts to the Walkyriun. If they win them as allies we will have battle-magic to face as well as spears."

The queen stopped, eyes narrowing, and Gudrun felt a chill in her belly at the thought of Brunahild as an enemy. Gundohar stopped in the act of pouring wine, and she knew he was thinking of it too. Gudrun gave him a quick pat as she sat down beside the brazier, and saw him sigh.

"What would move them?" he said painfully. "I have no more gold."

"You do not," Grimahild agreed, "but for their help I would give my own ornaments." She resumed her pacing.

"What, and scandalize Father Priscus?" Godo began to laugh.

"Father Priscus be damned!" said the queen, quelling her second son with a look. "And Father Severin too. I place more faith in the battle-magic of the Walkyriun than in any prayers they know."

"Will you go to them?" Hagano eyed her curiously. Gundohar's eyes were burning in his thin face. He gulped the wine he had poured, stared at his cup for a moment, then splashed in more.

"No, not I—" Grimahild's lips twisted. "The wisewomen have never trusted me, and my going would cause too much talk. Nor would they listen kindly to you. But that girl who guested with us, Bladarda's daughter, has become one of their sisterhood, and she always had a kindness for Gudrun."

"Send her, then," said Hagano. Gudrun got to her feet, pulse pounding, as the others turned to stare. "Will you go, sister mine?" asked Hagano, still with that infuriating smile. "Will you seek out the Walkyriun? Think of it, with one journey you can save your people and have a good gossip with your friend."

She glared at him, aware that once more he was taunting her.

"Do not mind Hagano," said Gundohar, and the wine cup trembled in his hand. "Go to Brunahild," he said. "Ask her to help us. Ask her to help *me*. . . ."

"Brunahild, when you go to the battle, will you really ride wolves, and gallop through the stormclouds?" piped Unna.

Her friend Domfrada giggled. "Galemburgis, what will you do if the weather is clear?"

Galemburgis stifled her own smile, remembering the days when she and Brunahild had questioned their teachers as eagerly as this child. It was hard indeed to imagine the battle storm on a day like this one, when every needle on the fir trees glittered in the light of the sun. The two young women had brought the little ones to the hilltop in hopes of catching a bit of breeze, but the air remained warm and still.

She eyed the other Walkyrja curiously, remembering how they had fought when they were girls, both of them prickly as a gorse bloom. Brunahild stood now sleek and shining as a well-honed spear, and almost as invulnerable.

"The storm that the battle-hag rides rages within, little one, when the Walkyriun make their magic. Even though the sky is cloudless, the enemy will feel their presence there," Brunahild answered, and Galemburgis shivered, remembering the rush of that wild wind.

"But we ride horses, not wolves," Galemburgis added repressively. "We summon the wolf-riders from the Hall of the Slain to come to our aid." And sometimes, she thought then, remembering a frosty morning in the land of the Huns, they came without summoning. She wiped perspiration from her brow and considered the four girls. Unna was frowning thoughtfully, but Domfrada's eyes were on a butterfly, and the other two seemed to be half-asleep.

"Domfrada, tell us how the Walkyriun of Fox Dance do battle," she said sharply. The child blushed and pushed fair hair back from her forehead, but she answered steadily.

"The Walkyrja is the shield of the hero. She frees the warrior she is protecting and fetters his foe. She gives him courage, but unmans the enemy; she blunts swords and breaks spears."

"That is good," said Brunahild. "Nanduhild, how is this done?"

For a moment the child looked panicked, and Unna jabbed her in the ribs, whispering.

"She yells. . . ." The answer was scarcely audible, and Galemburgis's lips twitched.

"She *shrieks*—" said Brunahild, and something in her tone stilled the laughter. "And that is a thing we cannot teach you. Already you are learning how to control your breath and pitch your voice for the uttering of spells. By the time you finish your training, you will have the ability to make the battleshout, but the knowledge of how and when to use it is the gift of god. It is battle-madness that the Walkyrja's cry summons; it echoes between the worlds."

They sat wide-eyed as Brunahild took a deep breath, obviously shaken. Galemburgis watched her curiously. The younger Walkyriun were expected to set an example for the girls. She herself had hardened since her initiation. But she knew also that beneath that shell there was still love for her people, and hatred for their enemies. Her younger brother, whom she had tended as if he were her child, would be fighting in this battle. She had no choice but to care.

In the year since they had taken their war-names there had been something inhuman in Brunahild's self-control. Galemburgis watched as the winged brows straightened, the flutter of pulse in the other girl's throat eased. When Brunahild spoke again, the tension that had sharpened her voice was gone.

"That is why you must practice, so that when the need comes to you, the power will be there." There was a short silence.

"I understand how we protect our own side, but why are we called the Choosers of the Slain?" Unna, always the boldest, spoke then.

Brunahild closed her eyes, and Galemburgis answered for her.

"Wodan's Walkyriun know which warriors are fated to fall in battle, and bear the spirits of those the god wants for his war-band to the Hall of the Slain."

"But you know sometimes too, don't you?" the child continued relentlessly. "I heard that when you point your spear at a man, he dies."

"I know all . . . I remember all . . . but I am moved by nothing. . . ." whispered Brunahild. Did she realize she had spoken aloud? She opened her eyes.

"The god chooses," she said harshly. "The Walkyrja only points out what is fated to be."

From farther down the hill came the calling of a horn.

"Be off with you now," said Galemburgis briskly. "Hrodlind wants your help in the garden. Tomorrow we will begin to learn the fettering spells."

The children were already in motion, leaping down the path like puppies released for a run. Galemburgis shook her head.

"I don't know where they get the energy. In this weather all I want to do is pant in the shade," she said, eyeing the other girl curiously. Since their initiation, they had managed to leave the old quarrels behind, and Galemburgis did not forget how Brunahild had shielded her from the Alan's sword when they fought beside the Huns. What was wrong with her today?

"I don't know where they get their questions!" Brunahild said bitterly, and Galemburgis laughed.

"Didn't you realize that our adventures in the land of the Huns have become one of the legends of Fox Dance?" she answered. "And you can be sure they have lost nothing in the telling. The girls all dream of going home and astonishing their fathers, and their brothers, with their powers."

"But it wasn't like that—" said Brunahild, with a look almost of alarm.

"Of course not, as they'll find out when they face real fighting. So will we, for that matter," Galemburgis said as they began to make their way down the hill. "I don't suppose a full-scale battle will be much like that skirmish between your uncle's folk and those Alan renegades." She shook her head, remembering how they had ridden side by side against the enemy. "I wish the old vixens would make up their minds who we'll be fighting for soon!"

Brunahild shrugged, and Galemburgis stared at her. Did she truly care for nothing? It had seemed, when they guested with the Burgunds, that Brunahild and the king's young sister had been friends. But in a way, Galemburgis thought then, Brunahild was without kindred. Perhaps it was easier for her to wait upon the will of the Walkyriun. But if such cold detachment was the mark of the perfect Walkyrja, Galemburgis was content to remember her humanity.

"Those little ones look at us as if we were Norns, but when it comes to using the lore we've learned, we really don't know much more than they! And waiting is the hardest of all!" she said brightly, probing. "Do we understand what we're doing? What about you—I saw you point your spear at men, and their enemies killed them. How did you choose?"

"It wasn't me. . . ." whispered Brunahild, and Galemburgis's gaze grew more intent as she realized there was some emotion behind those green eyes after all. "I saw the death-light on them, and my spear moved."

"Then how can you be sure your choice and that of the Walkyriun will be the same?"

"It was not *my* choice!" Brunahild repeated. "It was the god who moved the spear. And if his ideas about who should live and who should die are different from ours, I don't know what I will do!"

Abruptly she quickened her pace and darted down the trail, but Galemburgis stood staring, feeling as if she had just seen the first crack in the perfect surface of a spear. Perhaps it was only a discoloration, a natural uncertainty that battle would scour away. But if it was not . . . Was this something that their elders ought to know? Slowly she followed, but Brunahild had disappeared.

Soon I will see her . . . soon . . . soon. . . . Gudrun nodded to the motion of the pony beneath her and wondered if the dark fir woods through which they were climbing had an end. She had never made so long an uninterrupted journey, and she ached in every bone. But Hugomar, who commanded her escort, said that they should reach Fox Dance before noon. And then she would get off this damned horse and see Brunahild. At the moment she was not entirely sure which she wanted more.

The road wound around the curve of the hill and emerged from beneath the close, resin-scented shadow of the trees. The sun was just reaching the midpoint of the sky when the ground leveled, and she saw the scatter of deeply thatched longhouses at the meeting of the roads. Dark-clad girls were casting staves through a rolling hoop, laughing at their game. One of the horses whinnied, and they turned, shouting. Older women emerged from the buildings, peering at the newcomers from beneath their hands. Gudrun's gaze passed over fair heads and grey, seeking the raven hair of her friend. Surely Brunahild would come running as soon as she heard. She kicked her pony ahead, ignoring her escort's frown.

"Tell Brunahild that Gudrun daughter of Gibicho has come to guest with her."

Gudrun stared at the young woman before her, seeking for words. The raven hair had not changed, nor the vivid, angular face. But as she met that calm smile it seemed to Gudrun that she did not know her at all.

She thought that perhaps it was the stillness. . . . The Brunahild she had known was always in motion, responding to everything that passed with eager curiosity. This woman sat like an image. She had welcomed Gudrun to Fox Dance, but she had not even asked why the Burgund princess had come. She started as a group of girls burst around the side of the building, gabbling. They stopped short as they saw Gudrun. Brunahild scowled at them, and they scurried off, giggling behind their hands.

"They let the younger priestesses teach the girls," Brunahild sighed. "I suppose they think we can keep up with the little trolls. I am glad that I will never marry. I do not think I was meant to raise children!"

They sat on a bench in the shade of one of the buildings, but the air was close and still. The flurry of excitement that had attended Gudrun's arrival had not lasted long. The sound of men's laughter came faintly from down the slope, where the warriors of her escort were setting up their camp. A pony nickered, then was still. Closer, she heard women's voices; two girls were winding yarn into skeins in the shade of one of the other longhouses, and older women sat talking beneath the pines.

"Surely we were just as bad," said Gudrun. "Do you remember the trouble we got into when we stole a look at the saltwell at Halle?"

Brunahild nodded, her lips curving in a secret smile. "How could I forget, when the result was to bring me here?"

Gudrun sighed. The woman she faced now would never dare her to sneak into a holy place. Brunahild *was* the well: dark, still, her smooth, reflective surface hiding unknown depths of mystery.

"The god has strange ways of enforcing his will sometimes," Brunahild went on. "But surely he was leading me that day!"

Gudrun stared at her, casting back through her own recollections. *The god?* It seemed to her that Brunahild had been impelled by defiance and sheer curiosity, but if her friend wanted to believe it had been Wodan's doing, she knew better than to disagree. It occurred to her suddenly that living with her mother had prepared her to deal with people who lived in a world of their own. Only she had not expected to have to do so with Brunahild.

Why are you so surprised? she asked herself then. *For seven years she has trained to become just such a one as Grimahild. The only difference is that my mother walks her path alone!*

Gudrun wiped perspiration from her forehead and took another drink of the barley-water her friend had brought to her.

"It *is* hot, isn't it!" Brunahild agreed. Gudrun glowered at her, for the other girl, clad in loose braes and a short, sleeveless tunic like a boy's, showed no signs of feeling it. "In winter our hills shelter us from the storms, but in a summer like this one, a little wind would be welcome." Her gaze brightened suddenly. "Do you have the strength to go just a bit farther? There is a place I would like to show you, and there will surely be a breeze up there—"

"What do you mean?" Gudrun was still seeking the courage to mention her errand. The Walkyriun leader, Hlutgard, was away and not expected back for several days. She could not speak to the wise-women until then, and she did not want her private plea to Brunahild to be overheard by the other Walkyriun.

"The Hill of the High One, where Huld used to teach me. She is off with the other elders now, but there is no reason we could not go there. I made it to the top of your holy hill—can you climb mine?"

Gudrun grinned, for that had sounded almost like the Brunahild she used to know. "So long as I do not have to get back onto that pony. If I can go on my own two feet I will follow you anywhere!"

Brunahild leaped the last few paces up the trail and burst over the rim of the hill. Gudrun, puffing along behind her, gulped air. Only a little farther now. She glared at the other girl's straight back. The Walkyrja had not just finished a long journey, and even at its beginning Gudrun had not been in the hard condition expected of the Walkyriun, but she refused to complain. She pushed herself to take the last steps. Then the top was before her; she gasped with relief as she felt the first breath of breeze and dropped to her hands and knees.

"Look—" After a time she realized that Brunahild was talking to her. "From here you can see the whole world!"

Gudrun's head had almost stopped spinning. She glimpsed brightness before her and moved toward it. The slope of the hill fell away sharply before her. Below, the Moenus coiled away into the distance until both land and river were lost in a golden summer haze. She blinked back tears.

"Not the whole world," she said softly, "but my world. I see the Burgund land. Soon it will be spearpoints that glitter like the scales of a serpent upon the plain. When the battle-wurm awakens, the river will run red. The warriors chant of glory, but I am afraid. Whoever wins this battle, things will never be the same for us again."

There had been a kind of liberation in her journeying, away from her mother's shadow and her brothers' hopes and fears. But the sight of the plain reminded her painfully of her purpose here.

"Tell me—" Brunahild said softly. She stood with her back to the sun, a shape of shadow against the brilliance of the day.

She shivered. "How? You are different. I don't know how to talk to you anymore."

"Perhaps I can make it easier," said Brunahild. "Your family sent you to ask the help of the Walkyriun in the Alamanni war. I cannot tell you how they will decide. Hlutgard and Huld are even now speaking to the chieftains. We will debate the decision when they return." She seated herself on a boulder, and Gudrun found herself able to meet those shadowed eyes once more.

"You speak truth. That is my message for the Walkyriun," she said slowly, "but I have something to say to you as well. My brother Gundohar asked me to beg for your help, whatever the others do.

"He is trying so very hard to be a king!" Gudrun went on hurriedly. "The Burgunds are good folk, but the time is past for Gundohar to be a king like our father. And yet they are not ready for him to rule in the way of Rome. He wants a safe place for his people, where cattle can graze and the crop that is planted in the spring will grow untrampled till harvest-tide. He will fight because he has to, but he prefers the singing of the harpstrings to the clatter of spear on shield. Can you understand that, warrior-maid?" she burst out suddenly. "Have they taught you to despise everything but war?"

"They have taught me obedience. . . ." Brunahild said, frowning. "I will fight as my sisters decide, and they obey the will of the god. I am sorry for you, and for Gundohar. But you must see that I can give you no answer. You would not desert your tribe if I appealed to you—do not ask me to betray the Walkyriun."

For love I might. . . . thought Gudrun. *But what does a Chooser of the Slain know of such things?* There had been friendship between them once, but nothing, she saw now, to weigh against the training of the past seven years. *Brunahild, Brunahild,* she thought sorrowfully, *I did love you.*

She turned her gaze back to the glittering plain and saw it suddenly through a haze of crimson, as if the blood that would be shed there soon already soaked the ground.

Brunahild settled her ravenwing headdress more securely and checked the fastenings of the blue cloak. Though night had fallen, the air was still warm. She felt the trickle of perspiration beneath her white gown, but she did not move. Since she had taken her initiation, this was the first Great Council of the Walkyriun. It would have been unthinkable to show herself less disciplined than the oldest of her sisters.

Torchlight blazed in the shadows ahead and flared down the line in bursts of brightness with the lighting of the torches. Brunahild lifted her own brand, and Randgrid held her flame close until it caught. Then she was turning to pass the fire to Galemburgis. Before the flame had reached the end of the line they were moving, and the line of torches became a fiery serpent winding through the dark trees. From the head of the column came the bitter harmony of women's voices:

> "*We walk the Way to Wisdom, the way between the worlds,*
> *We walk the warded way,*
> *The way that leads to dawning, the doorway into dusk*
> *from darkness into day.*"

At the Hill of the High One their seats awaited them; rounds of sawed wood set in a circle like the judgment seats of the gods. As the Walkyriun assumed their places, it became a circle of flame. Bobbing lights danced on headdresses of fur and feathers, not goddesses but landspirits—she-wolf and raven, grey goose and osprey, bear and otter and wild cat of the hills. For a moment the round of lights hung suspended. Then the torches were flung into the piled wood in the center, and the bonfire blazed up and revealed the woman shapes beneath the masks.

> *"We walk the way of doom, we walk the way of Death,*
> *The shadowpath of strife,*
> *We walk the way of birth, we walk the way of growth,*
> *We walk the way of Life."*

When she was a child—it seemed very long ago—the girls had made up their own words to that chant, giggling in the darkness after the teachers had gone back to their longhouse. But here in this firelit circle, it seemed to vibrate in her bones. It was only then that Brunahild realized there were others on the hill. In the shelter of the birch trees she saw a dim blur of faces—Gudrun and two of her brother's men, and the envoy who had come from the Alamanni. On the other side of the circle the girls who were yet unpledged watched in silence with shining eyes. But they were outside the circle of firelight and the circle of the Walkyriun. Outside. . . .

> *"We walk the way of wonder, we walk the way of power,*
> *We walk the way of fear,*
> *We walk the way of valor, we walk the way of peace,*
> *The way that brings us here. . . .*

The women ceased from singing. But the bonfire was crackling loudly, and somewhere in the woods below, an owl called. Randgrid stood forward, leaning on her spear.

"Who comes to the Council of the Walkyriun?"

"I do—"

Brunahild saw Galemburgis straighten proudly as Liudegar, the Alamanni spokesman, limped into the circle.

"I speak for the men who defend the old ways of this land. War looms upon our borders like a storm—a storm from the west, for our foes come with Roman swords in their hands, for all they number themselves among the tribes. Our Council of Chieftains has sent me to entreat alliance. Join us, Women of Wisdom! Support us in our battle! And in turn we will keep the ancient faith of Hermundurus, and you will have honor in the land."

He stared around the circle with a mixture of pride and calculation.

At least he had had the decency not to mention the gifts that had been offered, and yet, although the Walkyriun swore that such things made no difference, Brunahild had heard in considerable detail just what they were.

Gudrun moved forward, and even though her escort stood behind her, she seemed very young with her fair hair falling down her back, and very alone. Brunahild remembered how she had tried to protect her at Halle, and felt an odd twinge of pity. What were her family about, to send a child on an errand of such importance? Had they sent her because they hoped she would make Brunahild her advocate, or because they knew already that their plea was hopeless, and would subject no one of greater worth to the humiliation of being refused? Or was it that they had already turned Christian, and did not dare admit that they sought the favor of the Walkyriun?

Brunahild had heard all of these speculations when they debated the offers. But she had disdained to ask Gudrun. It was enough that the child had braved the journey, and was standing forth now to face them, refusing to give way to her fear.

"I speak to you in the name of Gundohar, my brother, the Burgunds' king." Her voice quavered only a little. "Long ago tribes now scattered held the banks of the Rhenus. But they passed over the border to serve Rome, and it has been almost four hundred years since folk who spoke our tongue ruled in that land. Now my brother is king there, and the Romani are content to have it so. Would you rather see the watchtowers of the *limes* rebuilt, and the Eagles flash in the sun? If we are driven out, it may well be, and so we ask your prayers for our battle, or if you cannot aid us, at least do not lend your strength to our foes!"

She finished on a gasp and stepped back, her color going from red to white and red once more as she became aware of the watchful scrutiny of the Walkyriun.

"My sisters, you have heard the words of those who seek our assistance. In the stillness of your hearts, seek now the will of the gods," said Hlutgard into the silence that followed.

Brunahild fingered the lots in her belt pouch—a birch stave for the Alamanni, apple for the Burgunds, and thorn for a decision to favor neither one. Randgrid was moving around the circle with the covered basket. The applewood stick had a knot at one end; thumb and forefinger closed upon it, and when the basket came to her, she slid it beneath the cloth.

Randgrid returned to Hlutgard, who knelt and overturned the basket, lifting it so that the sticks were revealed upon the cloth.

"Birch . . . apple . . . birch . . . birch . . ." The calm voice droned on as sticks were separated into piles. Even from across the circle Brunahild could see that they were uneven. She suppressed a suspicion that the others had marked their tokens. Whether it was the will of the gods or of her sisters, Hlutgard's interpretation would bind them all.

"The lot falls to the Alamanni—" The older woman lifted her head, and the envoy tried to suppress his grin. "Tell your chieftains that it is to their aid we will ride."

Some of the older women nodded. From Galemburgis came a small, stifled sound of triumph, but Gudrun's anguished gaze sought Brunahild, and the Walkyrja was glad her headdress kept the other girl from meeting her eyes. *Does she think me unfeeling?* she wondered. *I could weep with her, but the word has been given, and there is nothing I can do.*

The bonfire leaped and crackled, and raven-shapes of shadow fluttered avidly across the grass.

Chapter 12 ❄ The Sword Spell

Forest of the Teutones
Summer, A.D. 418

"**M**ore Burgund spearheads?"

Ragan straightened, arching his back and flexing the knotted muscles so that bones popped in his spine. Sigfrid stood in the doorway with the golden light of summer blazing behind him and the raw skin of a pine marten slung over his shoulder.

"Alamanni—" he grunted, changing his grip on the light hammer with which he was compacting the edge of a spearpoint.

"For the fight that all the traders say is coming as soon as the harvest is done." Sigfrid nodded. "Well, at least you serve both sides equally. Do your spearheads refuse to bite when they encounter each other in battle, I wonder, or is that beyond your magic?"

The boy picked up the pegs he would need to stretch the fur for tanning, moving with the tense grace he had grown into since their return from the fight at Alb's hall. He was never clumsy, but on the other hand, neither in rest nor in motion was he ever wholly at ease.

"I make them hard and sharp. They kill." Ragan shrugged, and steel chimed softly as he tapped along the edge of the blade. "If tall folk wish to slay each other, what is it to me?"

Sigfrid laughed. "How hard and sharp you are . . . like your spears! And what about swords? Have you found the craft yet to make one for me?"

Ragan glared at him. In a corner of the smithy lay a pile of broken swordblades. After they had returned from the north, the forest had rung with the clangor of forging, harvest moons chilling to winter and warming to summer again as Ragan beat out one sword after another upon the anvil, laid it upon the coals to draw strength from the charcoal, and hammered it out once more. The first two he had filed and ground and polished. The others were still rough, glimmering with the rainbow colors of their tempering.

Rough or smooth, they had all fared the same. Each time Sigfrid smacked the newest blade against the age-hardened oak that held the anvil, it would shatter, and Ragan would roar with fury and search through his store of scraps and ingots for metal noble enough to make the sword his champion required. And Sigfrid would laugh, and take up his bow and spear and disappear into the forest again.

"I need new iron," Ragan said with an effort. He must not antagonize the boy. Sigfrid had grown over the winter, and filled out as well. Sigmund himself would be pleased with what Ragan had made of his son. "We sell the spearheads, go to hills by the river where they fire the ore. Some men of my people still live there. Maybe they find something special for me."

"That will take us into winter," observed Sigfrid, moving restlessly around the forge. "By the time we search out your brother another season will be gone. It does not matter to me, of course. I am only a sheathed sword, waiting to be drawn on my foe!" He grinned mirthlessly.

Metal sang out suddenly beneath Ragan's blows, and with an effort he forced himself to go more gently; Sigfrid had this effect upon him too often lately. It was inevitable. The boy was growing up, and the young were always angry. And he was anxious about Hiordisa.

"I do not complain," he said between his teeth. "You are a hero. Your father the same—broke all swords but one. And that one"—clang!—"was broken"—clang!—"by the god!" Steel screamed beneath his blows and shattered suddenly, the socket-piece falling while the joint drove itself into one of the beams.

"Yes, that's what my mother told me," Sigfrid said reflectively into the silence. "When she gave me the shards of my father's blade. . . ."

The stillness became profound. Ragan could hear the hiss of the flames, the fall of a leaf, the pounding of his own heart. He saw the boy's form waver with dreamlike deceptiveness through the heated air.

"*You have the sword?*" His own voice echoed in his ears like the rumbling of distant thunder. "For how many moons I sweat over mortal metal, and all the time you have god-blade? You waste my time and yours! *Why?!*"

He stepped toward Sigfrid, gnarled fingers clenching and un-closing, but the boy stood his ground.

"Do I know the limits of your skill?" His gaze met Ragan's and then returned to the fire. "I hoped that *you* could make me a blade. My father's wolfhide has cost me enough already. I do not want his sword—I am surprised that you do! Or have you forgotten that it is spell-steel, forged by your enemy."

"Give it to me! I unmask its magic, make god-sword take payment for Wodan-priest's crime!"

He waited while Sigfrid fetched the fragments, the great drum of his chest vibrating to the battering of his heart. Spell-steel! He had only seen one such sword. Such a blade blazed like lightning, and even by the strongest hero it could not be shattered. But each weapon was different; lust woke within him to wrest its secrets from this one.

And then he heard Sigfrid's footstep, and as he entered, the last sunlight, slanting over his shoulder, turned the shards of steel he was carrying to bars of fire.

Sigfrid loped along the path at a steady wolf-trot, trailing his spear. The day was warm, and he wore only a pair of leather breeches that he kept for hunting, away from the smoke of the forge. He had washed himself as well, to get the stink of smoke and man-sweat off him. After a week spent plying the bellows, he was glad to get away.

He had pumped till the shards of the sword glowed like a sunset in the forge. But the heat only seemed to make the metal harder, and though the clatter of Ragan's hammer echoed like the hoofbeats of Wodan's war-steed, even his great strength could not force the severed segments of Sigmund's sword to join.

Perhaps I am not destined to become a hero. Sigfrid's lips curved silently. *I could live in the forest, trading a little smithwork for what the woods do not provide. It would be a good life, away from the tumults of men.* The thought was forgotten as he sighted a line of fresh wolf prints crossing the trail and turned off to follow them.

He had expected to find the pack taking its ease around the half-stripped carcass of its last kill, gnawing bones, or playing, or drowsing in the warmth of the autumn sun. They were where he had expected, but when he emerged from beneath the beeches most were already standing, ears pricked and tails curled. For a moment he thought they had scented him, but these wolves had grown up accepting him as a sort of odd adjunct to the Pillars pack, and they were looking the other way.

The stronger members of the pack were gathering behind their chieftain. A ripple of tension ran through stiffened back fur. Tails wagged tentatively, then went still. But the mother wolf stayed behind the others, keeping the cubs in line with the assistance of the oldest male. Their sense of smell and hearing were superior, but from where he sat he could see farther. He peered down the slope—the hazel branches were moving. Then he glimpsed a black-tipped tail. A strange wolf on Pillars pack territory! Frowning, he hunkered down to see what they would do.

In a moment the stranger's head poked through the leaves, ears flattened and head low, closed lips drawn up in an ingratiating grin. Whining gently, he stepped forward, while the tension in the wolves who waited grew. The wolves were always challenging one another; the present pack chief had come to power only last winter, when his father had been weakened by an encounter with an elk. The old wolf was still with them, but he helped guard the cubs now. Would this stranger succeed in winning a place as well?

Suddenly the Pillars wolves were prancing on stiff legs all around the newcomer; tension lifted their fur as they nosed at his head and rear. Sigfrid saw a few tails wag. What was happening? Once more he wondered at the mysterious communication that decided such things. It was not strength only that made the difference. He had seen smaller animals achieve dominance or single beasts face down a pack. It was some invisible quality of spirit that made a hero among the wolves.

The low growling in the pack leader's throat swelled to a snarl. The stranger went down, rolling over on his back with throat exposed in an agony of submission. It was not enough. The tension that had held the group snapped suddenly. The boy was on his feet again, forgetting to breathe. Furry backs heaved; the growling grew like the roar of an approaching storm. Whines thinned to a yelp of pain. He glimpsed crimson—they were tearing at the stranger—and in another instant the wanderer was trying to break free.

For a moment it was touch and go, for the pack was mobbing him. When at last the strange wolf fought his way out of the tumble, his hindquarters were red with new blood. Tail tucked tightly between his legs, the interloper scuttled for the hazels and disappeared.

One wolf nosed at the bloodspots that stained the leaves. The others were still staring after their victim. It took a long time for the rigidity to leave their bodies, and even when the others had gone back to gnawing their bones or scratching for fleas, the chieftain remained vigilant.

At Alb's hall I was the stranger. . . . thought Sigfrid, turning homeward. *If I had not gone away, would they have torn me to pieces one day?* Suddenly the wind felt colder. He found himself hurrying as he headed back to the forge.

Sigfrid could hear the sound of Ragan's hammer as he came down the hill. More spearpoints, from the sound of it. The magic metal of the sword had a clearer ring. He stopped at the sleeping hut, changed his breeches for the sleeveless tunic he wore in the forge, and went to bring more water from the stream.

Ragan grunted as he entered. The water splashed into the quenching vat, and Sigfrid straightened. The smith had been busy. Two more rough spearheads lay in the row, and a third was taking shape with each skillful blow.

"Do you want me to start grinding these?" asked the boy.

"Now he wants to help," muttered the smith as the hammer clanged down again. "No beasts left in forest? Nothing better to do?"

"You said the Alamanni will be sending for their spearheads at the beginning of the Harvest Moon. There's not much time."

"You think because I can't forge that troll-sword I lose all my skill?" Ragan lifted the spearhead with the tongs and glared at Sigfrid over the weapon's edge. The boy felt the hair on his back tingle. He stilled.

"I think," said Sigfrid evenly, "that you have only two arms."

"When I'm working on sword you're off in forest, but now you want to help? I think you don't want me to forge that blade." The bushy brows bent. "Will you be oath-breaker? Is Sigmund's son afraid?"

"I swore I would kill Fafnar if you would make me a sword," snapped Sigfrid. He could feel the spirit surge within him, and suddenly he understood the wolves. "I do not care if your brother lives or dies, old man, but before you call me craven, fulfill your side of the bargain!" He straightened to his new height, glaring down at the smith. "If you can!"

The rumbling in Ragan's throat became a roar. The boy saw his arm blur, and a predator's reflexes spun him aside as the spearhead flashed past his head and embedded itself in the wall. He came to a halt, laughing, and Ragan lumbered toward him.

"I am no forge-thrall for you to thrash, old one! You can't even catch me!" He danced aside.

"I kill you," cried the smith, reaching for the hammer.

"And who will bring you red meat or pump the bellows if you do?" the boy replied.

Sigfrid could feel Ragan's rage, like the fury of a brown bear whose sleep he had once disturbed. But for the past two winters that bearskin had kept the boy's sleeping place warm. The smith's shape seemed to waver, and Sigfrid's laughter faded. Anger he could deal with, but now what he sensed was pain.

He is a wounded bear, he thought, watching the forgelight kindle red sparks in the smith's eyes. *Bleeding where no one can see. One of us will be hurt if this goes on.* Best be gone, he thought then, until the old man calmed.

He edged toward the open door, and stopped short as an angular shadow extended suddenly across the threshhold.

"If a man ye need t' ply the bellows," came a rough voice from outside, "give me my food and a place to sleep, and I'll serve ye well!"

Ragan looked around, blinking in confusion. Sigfrid peered through the door. An old man was standing there, leaning on a spear.

"Who comes?" growled the smith. Sigfrid sighed with relief, seeing the fury leaving him.

"Helmbari they hail me," came the answer, "a warrior too lame for the wars. But there be strength in these arms yet—" He straightened, and Sigfrid saw that he was not so ancient as he had seemed, only battered like an old helmet, with a scar half closing one eye and running down into his long beard, "an' sense in this skull. I could serve ye well."

"Come in, where I see you." Ragan transferred his baleful stare from Sigfrid to the newcomer as the old warrior limped over the threshold, using his spear as a staff. His cloak was ragged, fastened by a thorn, but at his side hung a sword.

"You will need me to do the grinding and him to pump the bellows, if we are going to finish those spears. . . ." Sigfrid said quietly. The wolf-pack had no use for another member, but he and Ragan needed help, if only to keep them from each other's throats.

Ragan's shoulders sagged suddenly. "It is so. A little while you stay, help me, help the boy, until this task done."

"Until the task is done—" Helmbari echoed, leaning his spear against the wall. But suddenly Sigfrid was not sure he liked the old warrior's smile.

*   *   *

Ragan squatted on the bare earth behind the smithy, staring at the sword. In the morning sunlight the pieces winked back at him, only a little battered by the beating he'd given them, and still bright. *God-metal* . . . He ran a callused finger along the smooth steel as if the touch could reveal its secret. He had expected the sword to be unusual, but he was a master of earth-magic. All that came from Earth's womb—stone and ore and the metal it contained—spoke to him. That this thing the priests of his enemy had made could so defy his skill challenged all that he was.

It had gone beyond his desire to forge a weapon Sigfrid could use on Fafnar. He had to understand the sword. He set one palm against the earth and the other on the pieces of the blade, and then, closing his eyes and reaching with other senses, sought for the earth-song. Gradually his heartbeat slowed to match that stately rhythm, but there was only the faintest resonance in the steel.

Where are you? What are you? Why do you run from me?

"The lad says we're getting low on charcoal," came a voice from behind him. "Do ye want him to send to the burners in the hills?"

Dazed, Ragan looked up and saw a radiant figure bending over him. Then he blinked, and realized that it was only Helmbari. Swiftly he flipped the leather wrappings over the fragments to hide them from the old man's gaze.

"Do ye think I would want it? I prefer to have my weapon in one piece, even if it's only common steel. But that's a fair thing. It reminds me of King Sigmund's sword, that I saw so long ago."

Ragan tucked in the flaps of hide and struggled with the ties.

"When the spear points are done will you be fixing it?" the man asked guilelessly. "Now that would be a marvel to see!"

"You have no work to do?" Ragan surged to his feet. "We don't feed you to stand here—"

"Such wrath, and for so little! If you live as long as I have, you'll learn to save your strength for more important things. . . ." He shook his head in amusement. "But we do need that charcoal—" He blinked at the smith with suddenly uncertain eyes.

"Trolls take the charcoal, and you as well." Ragan exclaimed and stalked away.

"What's it like, in a battle?" said Sigfrid, opening the rough wooden chest to lay the latest row of completed spearpoints upon the layer of dry grass.

Helmbari grunted. "Blood, dust, being so tired ye don't care who spits ye—and the moment of glory when ye get beyond the pain and become a god!"

Or a beast . . . thought Sigfrid, remembering. But the wolf had overwhelmed his spirit because he had not the skill to win that fight as a man. *I will not let it happen again!*

"Why? D'ye want to be a warrior? Smithwork pays better!" He handed the boy two more spearheads.

"Since you came here you've been talking of how the tribes have had to fight their way across the land. In such times even a maker of weapons might need to know how to use them. I kill beasts with my bow or spear, but I know nothing of the weapons men use against men." Chances were Ragan would never get that broken blade put back together, but if he did— During the past moons it had occurred to Sigfrid that even a hero born needed to know more than which end of the sword to grasp.

The old man gave him a keen look. "The shield . . . and the sword? Ye think I c'n teach ye?"

"I think you did not wear down that blade you carry chopping trees!" Sigfrid snapped back, and saw on Helmbari's scarred face the beginnings of that unsettling grin.

In the days that followed, Sigfrid sometimes wondered if he had been mad to ask Helmbari to be his teacher. Once persuaded, the old warrior proved as hard a taskmaster as Ragan, all the worse since he was trying to cram several seasons' worth of training into so short a time. It helped that hunting had honed the boy's reflexes, and he had endurance from running with the wolves. Working at the forge had built him an upper body few men had at any age. The strength was there already, but he had much to learn.

The first lesson was to stand with legs braced and body balanced, right shoulder back, left forward, as he defended himself with a shield boss while Helmbari swung at him with a piece of wood. When the first set of bruises began to heal and he was able to block most of the old man's blows, his teacher had him make a linden-wood shield. It covered more of him, but it was awkward. He collected more bruises learning to maneuver it, and then Helmbari put him back to working with the boss alone once more.

"Ye go into battle, all the shields shine bright in the sun. But soon enough they be cut to pieces, 'n the boss is all ye have. Learn to fight with a whole shield, or part of one, or none."

He gave the boy an axe and set him to cutting firewood with swordcuts, overhand, backhand, circling, and up from below.

"A man stabs down with a spear, but a sword goes every way. The balance is different, but motion's the same. Ye see that branch, now—that's a spear, coming at ye—" said Helmbari suddenly as they walked through the woods, and without thinking, Sigfrid brought the axe up, powering his overhand swing with the odd twist of the hips that the warrior had taught him. He hardly felt the shock as the blade bit, the continuing motion bringing the weapon back and ready as the lopped branch fell.

Sigfrid laughed. "Next time, old one, I'll lop you!"

Helmbari only grunted, but the next day at practice he handed Sigfrid the piece of oakwood with a bit of iron bound on for a guard, and stood facing him with the shield boss in his hand.

"So, slayer-of-beech-trees, see if you can hit me now!"

For such an old man, Helmbari was fast. He appeared to be making no effort, but those small, efficient movements always seemed to put the shield boss in front of Sigfrid's wooden sword. The boy was breathless and sweating before he finally managed to graze his teacher's arm.

Helmbari blinked, then grinned. "Ye might learn something yet, youngling, if ye keep on." And Sigfrid felt his skin go hot with sudden joy.

Two days later, they were both working with wooden sword and shield, and the sequenced moves in which the warrior had drilled him were beginning to meld into a flowing pattern in which attack and response were one. He was good enough, now, to sense that with a proper blade the clumsiness with which the wood swished through the air would become the keen whistle of a bird of prey. He was beginning to dream of such a sword.

"Now d'ye see?" said Helmbari, putting up his weapon. For once he was sweating too. "Ye stop t' plan yer moves, yer head will be off before yer done figuring. Learn t' take advantage of openings without thinking, like yer feet choose the good ground when ye run. A man's got to move his shield t'swing at ye, an' then ye slice at his sword-shoulder, or strike if he's got mail or Roman armor there. An' don't forget, yer sword's got a sharp point too."

Sigfrid nodded. "And what if the sword breaks?" Helmbari had lowered himself to a sitting position against the birch tree that stood in the yard, and the boy hunkered down beside him. The old man looked at him narrowly, and it seemed to Sigfrid that something changed in his expression, though he could not have said just how.

"Like that blade yon smith is trying to reforge?" the warrior asked dryly. "You dodge, or you use your shield, or you die. Like Sigmund." He sighed. "Ragan is right though. If that sword is remade, it will not break in your hand."

Sigfrid stared. Ragan must have been talking, and that amazed him even more than Helmbari's words.

"Unless a god breaks it!" The words flooded forth, now that he did not have to keep the secret anymore. "Sigmund was Wodan's chosen hero—why did the god let him die?"

There was a long silence. Helmbari's scarred eye drooped closed.

"Sigmund lived long—very long for a hero. Do not mourn him," he said, but there was sorrow in his tone. "He experienced much and won wisdom for the god. As he desired, he dwells now with the Einherior, awaiting the great battle that will end the age. He was a man of his time, but that time is ended. The world needs new heroes now."

"The world, or Wodan?" asked Sigfrid bitterly.

"Don't you want to be a hero?" The mockery had returned. "To earn eternal glory, do great deeds?"

"Do I have a choice? That's what Ragan wants me to do."

"There is always a choice. . . ." Something in the deep tones made Sigfrid shiver. "But most men let chance choose for them. The hero chooses because he knows his need. He walks with his wyrd instead of fighting it, and so he is strong."

"I don't need to be a hero, only a man—" *Instead of an animal.* Sigfrid looked at the gleam of fine hairs on the backs of his hands.

"Men fear the shapestrong, but they admire heroes," said Helmbari, as if the boy had finished his thought aloud. "Sigmund the wolf-king won renown with his sword."

"Sigmund's sword is broken," Sigfrid said flatly.

"For now . . . for now. If yer rested, lad, help me to stand"—the old man's voice brightened suddenly—"an' let's try that shoulder cut once more."

Ragan hunched over the anvil and let the white river sand sift through his fingers across the glowing metal, watching as the fine grains bubbled and fused. The spearheads were finished and paid for, and the inlaid spangenhelm for the Burgund king, and now, as darkness spread its wings above the forest, he was free once more to challenge the sword.

Perhaps this time . . . His hand was trembling; he forced it to stillness.

So . . . so . . . Swiftly he grasped the tongs, lifted the other half of the sword from the coals and laid it upon its twin, clamped the vise to hold the pieces together, and reached for his hammer.

Now! steel shrieked as the hammer crashed down, *and now!*

He heaved up the hammer, and in the moment of held breath before he struck once more heard something that rocked him back, staring. It was such a small sound—no more than the crack of a breaking twig beneath the foot of a hunter. But no branch ever snapped with so sweet a chime. He bent over the blade, blew gently, and saw the finest of hairline fractures angling across the steel.

Ragan shook his head and stepped back from the anvil, trying to deny what he had seen. Before this steel fused it would shatter; so brittle had it grown that Sigfrid could have snapped it when he was a child. The anguish that had tightened his throat tore free. He swung up the hammer.

"Break, then, break, you hag-spawned steel!" The hammer hit, and a fragment of steel went flying with a whine of almost human pain. "I smash, I shatter. I am your master or no one!" More pieces split off as he brought down the hammer again.

"Have you tried annealing?" came a voice from behind him.

"I try everything! Everything the earthfolk know!" Ragan screamed, swinging round. "God-cursed steel!" Helmbari ducked as the hammer whistled through the spot where his head had been.

"God-forged, more likely," said the old man. "Maybe you should ask the Aesir what to do—"

"I—will—never—take—help—from—Wodan's—kin!" The words forced their way between clenched teeth. Ragan's head was ringing. In another moment he would shatter, like the sword. The tongs slipped from his grasp. As if from a great distance, he heard the other continue.

"Then Wodan's kin will be your bane. . . ."

But the smith was already staggering into the darkness beyond the door.

"What happened?" asked Sigfrid. He peered into the darkness of the smithy and saw Helmbari bending painfully to pick up something that gleamed from the ground. "Is Ragan hurt?"

"Only in spirit," said the old warrior. "He could not forge the sword."

Sigfrid's throat tightened as he realized what those bright bits were. He poked up the fire into a blaze and began to search for the others, fingering the smooth steel. There were nine pieces now.

"Then I am afraid the spear must be my weapon after all, despite your teaching," he said, saying farewell, with a pang whose keenness surprised him, to his dream. Those girls who had run from him at Alb's hall might smile once more, if he was a hero with a sword. He dreamed of them sometimes, and woke aching with a need for which he had no name.

"Even when I was no swordsman, I broke all the blades he made." He nodded toward the pile of metal fragments by the wall.

Helmbari laughed dryly. "If the sword is yours, wolf-child, then by you it must be reforged."

Sigfrid stared at him. "The son of Hreidmaro is the greatest smith living," he said, choosing his words. "Wolund's heir. Iron speaks to him. Much he has taught me, but the earth-magic must be born in the blood. At least I know enough not to attempt a deed that has defied his craft!"

"The power of earth Ragan has indeed, but this steel came from the sky. . . ." The old warrior had not moved, but in the shadows he seemed taller.

"Then a smith who has the sky-power must remake it." He tried to answer steadily.

"That power belongs to Wodan's kin," said the quiet voice. "Son of Sigi Wolfshead I name you, son of Reri, son of Wolse who was father to Sigmund. Kin of Wodan were you born!"

Sigfrid felt the hair lifting on the nape of his neck as it had ridged the backs of the wolves when the stranger appeared. The old man with whom he had eaten and worked and fought for the past moon was nothing to fear, but suddenly he was not entirely sure who was standing there.

"Who are you?" His voice was a thread of sound.

"I am called Helm-bearer. I told you."

"And other things?"

The laughter that came from that hidden face was the rattle of the first dry leaves plucked by the wind that heralds the storm.

"Lay the shards in the forge, Sigmund's child, and I will pull the bellows rope until the task is done. . . ."

Sigfrid sensed his ordinary self slipping away as it did when he put on the wolfskin, and yet his body had never felt so strong, his head so clear. With dreamlike deliberation he shoveled more charcoal into the forge, selecting it from the basket where they kept the hardest pieces, the oak and ash. Carefully he nestled the first gleaming fragment into its dark bed.

"Pull then, whoever you may be—" An answering laughter rose in him as the leather sides of the bellows began to wheeze in reply.

Smoke swirled in creamy billows toward the smokehole as the blast of air stirred the smoldering coals to flame. In a moment the new pieces caught. Sigfrid coughed as the smoke grew thicker, striving to see. The cold steel began to brighten, first a glimmer of color that bloomed beneath the silvery surface like a blush on the cheek of a girl, then a rosier glow. He poked with the tongs, adjusting the coals so that they would heat the length of metal evenly.

Tension built as he watched the colors change, waiting for he knew not what transformation. Now the steel blazed like the coals that cradled it. But the fire could go hotter. He heard the bellows sigh and turned to urge his helper on, but Helmbari was letting the rope go.

"Wait," he said softly, "let it cool." He watched the forge, whispering, and Sigfrid observed the changes in his face as he had watched the brightness bloom in the steel. Then, suddenly, Helmbari grabbed for the bellows.

Once more the steel blazed, but not quite so brightly as it had before. In a few moments Helmbari let the bellows rest and looked at Sigfrid from beneath bent brows as the metal began to cool. Firelight gilded the right side of his face like a mask, but the left was in shadow. Sigfrid forced his gaze away, saw the hot steel fading to a deep cherry glow.

"Try it now—" came the command.

Sigfrid's heart pounded in his chest. With tongs he lifted the glowing shard to the anvil and picked up the middle-weight hammer, reminding himself how many times he had done this before.

Muscles remembered their old skill despite his mind's distraction. The hammer chimed, but the steel did not shatter. Sigfrid stared, and struck again. Sparks scattered, but the metal had been dented. Whimpering with excitement, he began to beat up and down the fragment, lengthening and compacting it into a rod.

As it thinned, he saw that his companion had placed the next piece of steel upon the coals. Sigfrid took a deep breath and began to strike with his heart in the hammer, seeing in his mind the moment when nine rods of sky-steel would lie ready to be welded into a single blade.

It was dawn before they were done with the annealing. Sigfrid sank down to rest against the stones of the forge, and in another moment sleep leaped upon him. The sun was high when he awakened, aching from the night's labors and the contorted position in which he had slept. For a moment he could not imagine how he came there; then memory began to return to him. He leaped up, wincing, certain it had been a dream. But there on the stone rim of the forge-bed he saw the nine bright rods.

Now Ragan could forge them, he thought, looking around him. But of the smith he heard nothing. There was only the singing of birds in the oak trees, and a toneless whistling he recognized as Helmbari's. *Surely,* he thought, *that part of it was a dream!* Then the old man was in the doorway, outlined in light. Sigfrid stiffened, but the scent of food teased his nostrils. The old man had brought bread and dried meat and cheese on a platter, and two wooden beakers of ale.

"Thought ye might be a bit hungry." He grinned as the boy wolfed down the food.

In daylight he did not look so mysterious, and his speech was the old warrior's again, but lack of sleep must be blurring his vision, thought Sigfrid, for he still saw an edge of brightness around him, as he did around the pieces of steel.

"Will ye forge the sword?" came the question when he had done.

"I should wait for Ragan. . . ."

Helmbari snorted. "He's the better smith, maybe, but of all men living, only you have the secret of this steel!" He eyed the bellows like a familiar foe. "Are you too weak to finish the task?"

Sigfrid swallowed. The old man's speech had changed, and Sigfrid knew that the power that had filled him the day before was possessing him once more. *Wodan . . . ,* he thought then, accepting it. *Does he want me to be a hero too?* It could explain why the god was helping him to remake the blade that he himself had broken. But the thought was not exactly comforting.

But sunlight, slanting through the doorway, was dancing along the rods, sparking hope to life again. *Truly, it would be a great thing to make that metal into a sword,* the boy thought then. *If I do that, I will have earned my father's heritage. He was a king among men. Perhaps I can make a place for myself as well.*

"If you can heave at the bellows, old man, I suppose I have strength enough to hit the steel," he said, challenging, but the only answer he got was the glint of a grin.

He bound the cleaned rods in groups of three with wire and laid the open end of the first bunch in the coals. *Nine for the nine worlds and three for the Norns,* he thought as the bellows began to blow. *But the thread I spin is steel. . . .* When the end was an even cherry red, he strewed the flux across it and laid it in the forge once more.

Presently the rods began to spark and sing. Sigfrid seized them with the tongs and began tapping and twisting, grinning as they hissed back at him. Section by section he repeated the process, until he had a thing like a length of rope, but this cord gleamed silver. He picked up the second group of rods.

"One for what has been, one for what is becoming, and one for what Wyrd may decide. . . ." said Helmbari softly as the third was finished. "You have done well." Somehow the day had faded. The setting sun was kindling the forgefires of the sky.

Sigfrid heard without quite comprehending. The dream had hold of him again. Forgetting who assisted him, he knew only the next task, the next blow, the next turn of the steel. Ragan had taught him more of his craft than he knew. Without answering, he bound all three rods together and thrust them into the forge. He heated and beat them, heated and hammered, willing the separate strands to become one, and sparks scattered like angry bees.

Steel rang and rippled. Beneath his blows the bound rods became a lumpy length of steel. He chose smaller hammers then, taking care to strike evenly and not too hard, coaxing the metal into the shape that shimmered in his soul.

Before he broke them, Sigfrid had gotten a feeling for the weight and balance of Ragan's blades. Playing at wooden foils with Helmbari had shown him what he needed: a sword long as a Roman *spatha*, but heavier, its tip pointed, its tang just the right width for his hand. And it was taking shape—now he could see it— A song surged through him, and the hammer beat out the tune.

> *"Beat, beat, beat—*
> *and beat, beat, beat—*
> *the sword is forged by force and fire,*
> *by weight and will and my desire!"*

He tapped along the edge of the blade and sensed its structure aligning. He beat out complex patterns across the midsection and felt its balanced tensions like the cross-play of muscle beneath his own hide.

"Ring, ring, ring—
I sing, sing, sing—
the sword is shaped by song and spell,
by breath and body, crafted well!"

He dragged the rasp across the dimpled surface, leveling the irregularities. Later he would polish it, but this would finish the shaping and give it edge enough not to slow a swing.

"Bright, bright, bright,
its might, might, might—
the sword is sharpened by its pain,
from grief reborn to blaze again!"

Once more Sigfrid tapped the blade and heard it sing back to him as the wolves sang over the hills. He looked up, and met the gaze of Helmbari's good eye across the fire. Now, with this miracle that he had made glittering before him, he could face that keen glance without fear.

"Now"—had the other spoken aloud?—*"you must temper it. . . ."*

Tenderly Sigfrid cleansed the blade and held the shining steel above the coals. Once more Helmbari bent to the bellows. They brought the sword to a brown sheen this time. Sigfrid took it from the fire and turned toward the quenching trough, but the old man held up one hand.

"This is sky-steel. It will harden in air alone. . . ." He flung open the door to the smithy, and wind blasted suddenly. Sigfrid swung the blade high and felt it come to life in his hand.

Somehow it had got to be midnight again. When the strange wind had passed, the stillness was absolute. Sigfrid heard the sound of his own breathing and an occasional pop where charcoal still burned. But the ashes were grey at the edge of the forge-bed. Trembling, the boy touched his blade.

There was still a faint warmth in the metal, as if some living spirit now dwelt within. But he could hold it well enough to rivet on the gold-wrought guard and pommel it had borne in Sigmund's day, and bind the ivory slats of the hilt around the tang.

"My wolf son . . . you have done well indeed. . . ."

Sigfrid smiled, his gaze still savoring the blade. The dim shape of the anvil loomed before him. As if of its own will, the sword sang upward. His hand knew now how to grip it, his body how to balance the weight, uncoiling behind it as it slashed back down.

He felt the shock of connection all the way along his spine. There was a crack like the slam of Hella's gate, but the full mass of the blade still weighted his arm. He looked down. It was the anvil stone that had cracked, and the oak block beneath it, not the sword.

He was still staring when he heard a sound at the door.

"Helmbari—" he began, but the words died. Where had the old man gone? The shape he saw was too short for the warrior, the shoulders too broad.

"A hero," said Ragan hoarsely, "with a hero's sword . . ." He moved heavily forward, and in the fitful light Sigfrid saw his face gaunted with exhaustion. As the smith reached out to touch the bright steel, envy and exaltation warred in his dark eyes.

"It is called Gram—" Sigfrid whispered the name that had come to him out of the music of hammer on steel. It was a name for a god's doom, or a god.

"It is Fafnar's bane," said Ragan, and Sigfrid understood that somehow during that day and night of striving, he had made his choice, and set his own feet upon the hero's path.

Chapter 13   The Harvest of Ygg

Plain of the Moenus
Harvest, Waxing Moon, A.D. 418

When the first thin sickle of the Harvest Moon swung through the sky, the Burgunds began to sharpen their spears. Stubbled fields and pastures grazed close by the herds made for easy marching. In the northern hills the Alamanni were rallying to their chieftains' standards, and in the south warriors from both sides of the Rhenus were summoned to the hosting below the Holy Hill.

By day, the banks of the Nicer echoed to the sound of hammering as shields were banded and spearheads socketed into stout shafts of oak and ash. Blades were honed, new rivets set into battered spangenhelms. For those with the wealth to buy them, there were pieces of Roman armor or sarks of overlapping scales made from the hooves of mares, and sometimes bits of butted mail. At night, the chieftains shared out the vats of beer, and the darkness grew clamorous with boasting and song.

More than once Gudrun, tossing on her narrow bed in the fortress, wondered if they were already fighting their battle. But when at last the mustering was ended and the Burgund host marched northward, the stillness that they left behind them seemed absolute, like the silence of the grave.

Four days later an exhausted rider on a staggering horse clattered in through the gateway. The Alamanni had been sighted, and the Burgunds were choosing their ground. The next day, or perhaps the one after, the battle would come.

*   *   *

"The first weapon of the Walkyriun is terror—" Randgrid looked at the women who had come with her from Fox Dance. "Tonight, before ever a blow is struck, we must carry evil dreams to the enemy."

"The Burgunds hardly need our help for that, knowing what they will face come the morn," came a low whisper, and someone laughed, Galemburgis, perhaps, or Ragenleob.

Of the older Walkyriun, Golla and Hadugera had also come with them, and three others of those who had been initiated with Brunahild. *Nine by nine the Choosers ride. . . .* She thought of the old song.

Brunahild did not turn. This was the moment that she had trained for. It must be met with detachment and integrity, as if she were indeed one of the Choosers who served in Wodan's hall.

They had made their camp on a small rise among a stand of linden trees. The Alamanni army was encamped on the slope beyond them, each clan and district around its own campfire. Earlier in the evening they had sung and shouted, but now things were growing quieter. Occasionally she could hear a cry from the Burgunds, spread out along the higher ground beyond the marsh. The air was close and still, but overhead thin clouds were hurrying to hide the stars. Weather was coming in. Tomorrow might bring more than one kind of storm.

"You understand what you are doing, yes? Then I wish you good journeying!" Randgrid traced a bindrune in the air, linking the horse rune and the rune of riding. The flames leaped, then the glowing logs fell into a heap of coals.

The priestess seated herself with her back to a tree, gripping the flat drum by its crosspieces, the beater ready in her other hand. One by one the others wrapped their cloaks around them and arranged themselves beside the dying fire. Soon an observer would have thought them sleeping; but as the drum began its soft rhythm, the cloaks rose and fell with the regular breathing of trance.

"So, my daughters, now we shall journey. Now we shall ride the wind!" The drum carried the cadence of her words. "The lovely lich that Lodhurr gave, in Earth's protection safely lie. The holy gods shall guard your guise till safely home again you fly!"

Brunahild took a deep breath and let it slowly out again, then another, willing taut limbs to relax until her breathing was the only thing she knew. "I am Sigdrifa. . . ." she whispered, and as she claimed that identity she felt the power begin to flow.

"Hold now in mind the holy hide, strength of spirit set you free! Put on a shape to soar the skies, prepare with spirit-sight to see!"

With a sigh, she extended her awareness. Despite the folds of the cloak, she could feel warmth pulsing a hand's span around her. Something that was not physical relaxed, and she sensed her body as an amorphous glowing shape stretched out upon the ground. As always, then, there was the moment of surprise when she felt her spirit shoot out through the crown of her head. Dizzied, she hovered beside her body. Then the discipline she had learned drew her upward. She looked around her, seeing the blurred outlines of cloaked bodies, the dull flicker of the fire. Far more vivid were the glowing forms that swayed above them.

"Battle-hags, to war I call ye! Put on your helms, take up the spear! Wild wargs summon, serpent bridled, steeds more fit your shapes to bear!"

At the words, Brunahild felt her semblance shifting. She was gaunt, misshapen, with pendulous breasts and tangled hair. But she was strong, and the spear she plucked from the darkness to be her weapon shimmered balefully. Around them the dim air was stirring. Beside the hags, shaggy wolf-shapes appeared, but no wolves of the forest ever had such gleaming fangs or glowing eyes. She whistled, and an icy nose pushed against her palm.

With a cry, she swung one leg across the bony back, and then they were moving, all of them, led by a figure from nightmare who glared with Randgrid's eyes. Like dry leaves swept up in a sudden blast the battle-hags were swirled aloft. Tattered locks streamed out behind them as they raced the icy wind. In the wake of their passage air currents, swept into sudden disorder, whirled upward and fell back in stinging showers of hail. Cloud curdled behind them, blotting out the stars.

"*I am the Woman of Battle, my mouth is bloody!*" cried Randgrid.

"*In my hands I hold the serpents of strife!*" Another brandished her spears.

"*I am the wings of the raven; I am the wolf-rider; I am the Chooser of Fate, the changer of fortune,*" a third sang out then.

"*He who fears the fray I fetter. His sword I blunt, his spears are broken, his guts I gather for the wyrd-weavers' loom,*" Golla cried.

"*I am the wife who welcomes the warrior, I hail the hero in the hour of victory; when defeat is doomed, death is the dowry I offer the fated, for I am ever-faithful.*" Harsh laughter echoed across the skies.

"*My embrace is madness, my embrace is ecstasy. I brew the mead of battle, and the brave grow drunken. . . .*" They raced the wind above the plain, and the Burgund campfires blinked like frightened eyes below.

"I am the swan who sings among the spears," Brunahild shouted, *"I am the chosen virgin; I am victory. My thighs are bloody. I am the battle-bride!"*

Her cry thinned to a shriek. They were all shrieking, like ravens, like wolves, like men in their final agony. The wind slashed downward, and they swooped over the Burgund camp, howling. Fires flared and tents tore free; horses screamed in terror.

Where the battle-hags passed, men started up from their blankets, swearing, but there were no masters of magic among them to make the nightmare flee. And then they were gone in a last gust of wind and a memory of mindless laughter. The Burgunds tied down their tents, calmed their horses and made up their fires. But when they lay down to sleep once more, their dreams were haunted by contorted faces and spectral hands that seized them in a parody of a lover's embrace.

From the earth that the night's storm had soaked, a dank mist rose in the dawning. Men saw each other as ghostly silhouettes; clan standards were distorted shapes dissolving into the upper air. The chieftains of the Alamanni laughed and thanked the Walkyriun for confusing their enemies, but it was none of the wisewomen's doing.

"They should be using the mist to move forward, not sit here boasting," said Randgrid tartly. "We are here to help heroes, not wet-nurse a pack of fools."

But by the time the sun began to burn the mist away, the two armies were in position, and the vapor pulsed to the booming beat of spearshafts on shields. Brunahild shivered, and kicked her mare to a trot after the others. She felt as if her body as well as her spirit had been rampaging through the heavens the night before, and she could only hope that their enemies had had a worse night than she.

She rode with two spears and a short sword, but her only armor was her blue cloak and raven headdress, over a short tunic and trousers of the same dark hue. There were silver plaques on her belt and scabbard, and ornaments of silvered bronze jingled from her pony's breastband. Instead of a saddlecloth, she sat on the skin of a grey wolf she had killed the winter before.

Brunahild pulled up beside the others. At that moment the sun broke through the fog, and suddenly the air blazed with brightness as spearpoint and shield boss, buckles and helms and harness fittings all caught the light. She blinked, dazzled. When she could see again, she realized that the enemy was before them. The voices of warriors echoed hollowly as they chanted spells of protection behind their shields.

The Burgunds were close enough so that she could make out the red poppies they had taken as their battle-badge and the contorted beast shapes painted upon their shields. Like the Alamanni, they were drawn up beneath their totems in a broad crescent bulging toward the foe. Mail shirts and golden arm rings glittered upon the chieftains who stood with their *faramen* behind them. Sun gleamed on bare torsos, but beyond the common warriors she saw horsemen in cloaks of dull red with gilded spangenhelms, and a crimson standard on which a serpent shape worked in gold undulated sluggishly in the dying breeze.

"The Gundwurm," said Golla softly, "that the Romans call Dragon. They have borne it in all their battles, many times bloodied, but always renewed. Well, we have magic to slay even a wurm of woe."

Brunahild nodded. She knew that the most important part of a battle was often this moment before the fighting actually began. Now it was that men took the measure of each other's spirits, and will strove with will. The Burgunds appeared to have the larger army, but was the mood of their men as fierce as that of their foe?

"Come," said Golla, and the line opened to let the Walkyriun ride through. They reined in their horses a bare spear's cast from the foe.

"Listen, Burgunds, to this battle-blessing—hearken, heroes, to the Walkyrja's song!" Nine voices surged on a single note shuddering with uncomfortable overtones.

> *"The swords you bear shall never bite,*
> *but sing over skull, and smite your bone!*
> *The spears you shake shall find no foe,*
> *but splinter shafts as soon as thrown!*
> *Nor will shield shelter, shattering,*
> *though sore your need when set upon!*
> *Limbs locked by the battle fetter,*
> *Sapped of strength, will weigh you down,*
> *Weakened, you must wait, unwilling,*
> *For the wight who'll work you woe.*
> *This wyrd Wodan's daughters choose,*
> *This is the doom that you shall know."*

The voices of the singers sharpened to a shriek, and men remembered the hags they'd dreamed.

Higher and higher the note was carried, thinning as each woman reached her limit until it was lost in a whisper of sound that left men thinking it had risen beyond the range of human ears. Before they could recover, Randgrid reined her horse around, and dark cloaks flapping, the Walkyriun galloped back to their vantage point behind the Alamanni lines.

A shiver rippled through the masses of men. *"Clack . . . clack,"* the struck shields thundered. Several Alamanni stepped forward, shaking their spears. The blue cornflowers thrust beneath their cloak pins quivered with each blow.

"What curs in war-gear come with weapons? What thralls think here our hosts to harry?" came a challenge from the Burgunds.

"At eve ye may say, when swine you are feeding, and hungry hounds consume your carcasses, you were laid low by Liudegast's kindred, by sons of Saxwalo and Landbald and Nando. All the men from marsh and mountain by need united defy you here!" the Alamanni spokesman replied.

Beneath shield-crack and shouting another sound was swelling, like the sound a dog makes deep in its throat just before it sets to snarling, or the angry hum that comes from an overturned hive.

"To the Men of the Mists you seem but maidens—bond-maids beating soiled sarks in the stream! Welcome—we shall make you women! To the fortress-fighters you will bear bastards!" A group of men dashed out from the Burgund lines.

"The fortress-folk will father nothing, for gelded you were by Roman god-men!" the Alamann answered. Yells of defiance echoed around him.

"Demons! Spawn of Satan!" came a scream from the Burgunds, breaking the rhythm. "Your devil Wodan abandons you!"

"Clack, clack, clack, clack . . ." Spearshafts crashed on shields, and the ground shook to the stamping. Brunahild felt the hair stir on her scalp. This was far worse than waiting to attack the Alan outlaws. The emotions of so many hundreds, focused by the challenges, battered at her awareness as their noise beat at her brain.

"Why strike our ears with empty insults? Let the hags' horses eat the eagles' food!"

One of the Alamanni chieftains leaped forward, and as if he had been the single stone that starts the whole heap rolling, the wedge of men behind him began to move. A quiver ran through the Burgund army; the Gundwurm uncoiled on a sudden breath of breeze. Horns bellowed, and they rolled forward. The bay mare stamped nervously, and Brunahild reined her in.

Now the men were nearing. The air blurred as the leaders flung their axes. Warriors fell, but they were like the froth splashed aside by a flooding river. Nothing now could have stemmed that momentum. The two armies crashed together, and the world screamed.

An Alamanni warrior jabbed with his last spear at a Burgund; the sharp point pierced the man's leather sark and bored into his belly. The dying man screamed and clutched at the shaft, but his killer laughed. Someone shouted behind him; he jerked the spear free and thrust, but his enemy caught the point in the wood of his shield. The Alamann tried to wrench it free and, groaning, the linden-wood slats began to splinter, but the Burgund brought down his axe and it was the spear that shattered. The axe carved great circles in the air as the Burgund sprang upon his foe. The Alamann tried to stave him off; the axe sheared the truncated spearshaft and whirled onward through the spearman's neck. His head leaped from his shoulders, lips still opening to yell, but the Burgund was already reeling beneath another man's blows.

The Walkyriun rode through the midst of the battle, dark cloaks billowing, ravens who would not wait for day's ending to feed. Where they pointed their spears, men's arms faltered; where they raised their shriek, Burgund warriors fell. A flying axe sliced Raganleob's shoulder, and they bore her from the field; but when men could see the battle-maidens, they gave way before them.

King Gundohar marched into the fray with his comitatus, pro-pelled as much by the pressure of the men behind him as by any eagerness of his own. His head was weighted by the boar-crested spangenhelm the northern smith had made for him, and the king-spear gleamed in his hand. The ground was marshy, at each step seeming to release him regretfully. To Gundohar it seemed as if Earth herself was his enemy.

Above him the Gundwurm snapped and swung as the standard-bearer followed. On his right strode Godomar, laughing. On his left, Hagano struck out with grim efficiency. Pinned between them, the young king jabbed at whatever came at him with the determination of despair. A man-beast half-clad in a wolfskin and bloody from neck to knee rose up before him. He poked at it, saw the flare of Hagano's sword, and gasped as red blood sprayed across his virgin shield. Behind him his men were yelling. Fifty strong warriors had pledged their lives to protect him. But Gundohar no longer cared if he lived or died, so long as his warriors did not know he was afraid.

Galemburgis reined in, staring around her. The battle had disintegrated into struggling knots of warriors, and somehow she had lost the other Walkyriun. Nearby, three men with the cornflower badge of the Alamanni were putting up a good fight against a larger number of Burgunds. Shields shuddered and shafts cracked as they blocked their enemies' blows. Smiling, she rode toward them.

"Alamanni, wield your wound-wands! Sate my steed with food of ravens!" she called, and her tribesmen struck out more furiously against their foes.

A Burgund fell. The others faltered as they saw her. She began to swing her spear toward them, still smiling.

"*Maleficia! Retro me!*" one man shouted, gesturing with his spear as if to sign her with the Gift rune, though it seemed an odd thing to do while cursing. "Begone in God's name, demoness, back to Satanas! May all your devils carry you away!"

Her spear continued its movement as the man rushed toward her, his own weapon gripped two-handed. But hers was the longer. The shock as he hit nearly unseated her. She gripped the shaft with one hand, and with the other clutched at the pony's mane. For a long moment the man stared up at her, impaled upon her spear. Blood sprayed from lips that still mouthed curses. Then the horse threw up its head, snorting, and started to back away, and Galemburgis recovered from her astonishment and jerked the spear free.

"I do not Choose you! Go to Christos or your Satanas as you please!" she spat, wiping his blood from her spearhead. Now only three Burgunds faced the Alamanni. Galemburgis dug her heels into her horse's sides and galloped off in search of more worthy prey.

The wagon of the sun rolled westward. Where in the morning, mist had shrouded the armies, now it was dust that drifted in choking swirls. By noon, the battle had moved a league to the southward. Many had already fallen. The circling birds of prey drifted lower, ready to tear at still-warm bodies as the fighting moved on. The supply of throwing axes was long exhausted. Now the survivors cast rocks at their enemies, and flung broken spears. But most of the fights were hand-to-hand, with sword or club or long axe. They slashed and pounded, sweating and sucking in the dirty air in desperate gasps.

Brunahild swayed in the saddle as her pony came to a halt upon a rise, hot and cold at once, shuddering at the agony that blasted her as another man screamed out his life upon the point of an enemy's spear. Where were the disciplines that she had learned to keep this tide of emotion at bay? It was worse than the attack on the Alans, when the fighting had been over in a hour. Her teachers had never warned her how much energy could be released by the emotions of so many men.

In the distance she glimpsed Galemburgis, brandishing her spear as she swooped down upon another knot of struggling men. Every line of her body expressed her exultation. Dimly Brunahild remembered that riding into that other fight she had been exultant too.

It is because I gave myself to the god without conditions, she understood suddenly. *And his power carried me.* That was the difference. She had not invoked the War Father. She had chanted verses, and curses, to encourage the Alamanni, but so far she had refused to point her spear.

A year ago she had hung upon the tree of testing and known that the god waited within her. But he also spoke from the Tree and the Well, and, she knew now, in the din of the battlefield. *"Dost thou not trust me?"* Even thinking about him opened the channel. *"Remember thy promises!"* The air darkened. Her ears were ringing as the pressure grew. She remembered *all* of her oaths, to the god, and to the Walkyriun. That was why she was afraid.

"Chooser, now the moment of choice is upon thee. Whom wilt thou serve, humankind, or the gods?" The Voice was too great for the confines of her skull. She gripped her spear, but she could no longer feel it. She felt consciousness slipping, and never knew whether she had given way in a moment of weakness or ultimate clarity.

As Sigdrifa, she opened her eyes. Shapes stirred in the swirling dustclouds—spirits still fighting though their bodies had fallen; the wolf-riding hags whose semblance she had worn the night before, loping above the battle. The lifelight of the living pulsed with the red of fury or the grey of despair, but where the pale deathlight played, Wodan's own Walkyriun followed, and when their spears pointed, both Burgund and Alamann fell.

"Lord, you are well served already! What do you want with me?" she whispered. Through the clamor of the battlefield came a burst of bitter laughter.

"I am Ygg, and my face is Terror. I am the Bale-worker who incites strife among the nations. I am on no one's side. War Father, Victory Father, Host Father, the thruster of spears who puts armies to flight. Warriors call me Glad in Battle! By all those names these men have invoked me. And this is the mask they have chosen to see!"

The words trembled in the air like thunder. An icy wind whipped at Brunahild's cloak, and she turned, and *saw.*

Through the dust of the battlefield, two gaunt wolves came loping, red tongues lolling from bloody jaws. Behind them rode warriors, wolf-eyed Sigmund and Helgi, and Hunding whom he slew. At their head a great steed galloped, its eight legs a blur of shadow. She saw the sheen of the grey coat and the gleam of bones beneath it. Eyes of fire glared from within a white skull.

But more terrible than the horse was its rider. The Lord of the Slain rode cloaked in shadow. Above the dark tunic and trousers she saw the glitter of blackened mail. The tarnished plates of his spangenhelm were wrought with reliefs of struggling warriors, and the face-guard was a mask of terror. As he passed her, the stallion slowed. The god's head turned, and Brunahild trembled. Through one eyehole she saw darkness, and through the other, a glitter of light.

"Go, my daughter. . . ." Stillness settled upon her as the words sighed through her soul. *"Give to the warriors that which they have desired. . . ."*

At the edge of the hazel copse stood a weathered longstone, set there to mark some forgotten node of power long before Teuton or Roman had walked the land. A dozen bodies were heaped around it like driftwood after a flood has plunged downstream. Rusty Burgund cloaks lay tangled with the furs worn by the Alamanni; poppies and cornflowers were wilting together on the blood-soaked ground. Upon the bodies the carrion birds were at work already. Wings lifted them into awkward half-flight as suddenly the pile heaved.

The heap stirred again. Beneath it, something was moving. The birds, complaining, fluttered into the willow branches as a figure as bloodstained as any of the bodies struggled free.

His teeth were chattering. He wrenched the pin from his reeking cloak and let it fall. His helm was gone already, and one of his arm rings. He had lost his fine gold-wrought sword. No one now would have taken him for a king. But he was alive.

As he straightened, his long fingers twitching as if he were not quite sure they belonged to him, that awareness filled him with a dull wonder. He had been so sure he was going to die. He could still hear the sounds of battle, but there nothing moved but the birds, returning to their meal.

They would be looking for him—they would *all* be looking for him. He wondered if he feared to be found by the foe or his own men more. The stink of blood and bowels caught in his throat, but he had already retched up everything in his belly. Perhaps men of no imagination could bear this, but had the bards who sang so cheerfully of battle ever been in one?

No more killing . . . He scrubbed his hands against the skirts of his tunic. *No more!*

Where could he run? Blinking, he began to look around him, and then, as if she had materialized from the shadows, he saw the Walkyrja, sitting her horse like an image, watching him. The bay mare's legs were bloody, but the woman who rode her was all darkness. Raven wings framed a vivid, fine-boned face, but the shadowed eyes that met his were cold. He had seen that face in his dreams.

"Brunahild . . ." The word was a whisper, a prayer.

"No. I am Sigdrifa. Bringer of Victory. To the Alamanni."

The air was warm, humid, but he was shivering.

"Have you come for me?"

"Are you a hero? Are you prepared to journey to Wodan's hall?" Her voice was cold too.

The bark of laughter that scraped his throat surprised him. Prepared? For this, what could have prepared him?

"I do not know what I am," he said truthfully. "They call me a king." Too late, it occurred to him he should not have said that. He scarcely knew himself; perhaps she would not have recognized him. But the Walkyrja showed no surprise.

"Do you desire life, or glory?" she asked patiently. Her spear moved as she turned, and he flinched.

"I want to live. . . ." he whispered. Oh gods, to see the sun, to feel the earth, to keep breathing the sweet air!

"This is the field of death. Gundohar son of Gibicho, why are you here?"

Gundohar . . . I am Gundohar. . . . He stared at her, instinct overwhelmed by a flood of memory. His father had begun as one chieftain among many, though the Niflungar were descended from the shrinekings in the old homeland by the misty northern sea. But the best hope for a growing people lay westward, and the Romans liked to deal with sovereigns.

"Not for glory, but my people's need," he said bitterly. It was why, despite his fear, he had agreed to this war.

"I am the Chooser of the Slain," she said then, and the spearpoint inscribed a slow circle in the air. "Are you afraid?"

"Of course I am afraid!" Fascinated, his gaze followed the spear. His brother Godo would have defied her, but to what disasters would *he* lead the Burgunds if he were king? "But I have to survive, for my people and my land!"

"Live, then—" The spear lifted. "Wodan does not want you, but there are foemen coming who will kill you if they can!"

Blinking, he looked past her, and saw a half dozen Alamanni trotting toward him. He thought there were Burgund warriors beyond them, but he could not be sure. Certainty was in the eyes of the men who came baying like hounds as they caught sight of him standing there.

Relief and despair clashed and yammered in his brain, but Brunahild was watching him. The ground here was littered with broken weapons, and one unshattered spear. Without conscious decision he found himself gathering up spearheads and knives and bits of swords. Leaning on the spear, he limped over to the stone. He was dizzy, but what he had to do was suddenly very clear. As the Alamanni neared, he set his back against the menhir and prepared to fling his first missile against his foe.

Brunahild reined her mare away, not wanting to watch Gundohar die. She wondered how long it would take the Alamanni to kill him. She remembered the moment when the cornered animal that had looked out of his eyes had disappeared and she had seen in him, if not a king, a man. Her duty was to Choose him, but the deathlight did not flicker around him. Whatever happened now, he was not destined for Wodan's hall.

Gundohar threw a spearhead, awkward as a boy, and one of the Alamanni yelled and went down. For a moment he stared, and then, laughing, snatched up another one.

"I am a giver of weapons! Come and get them! I am a ring giver, come here for your reward!"

The Alamanni faltered, for that laugh had not sounded quite sane.

The battle-frenzy is taking him! Brunahild thought in wonder, reining her mare round. Behind the Alamanni she could see another Walkyrja, but her attention was on Gundohar. The young king was throwing weapons like a boy casting stones to frighten birds away, snatching up whatever was nearest when his first supply was gone. Then they were on him.

"Come feed the Gundwurm, Alamanni thralls!" screamed Gundohar. He flailed about him with the spear, a lucky swipe taking a man across the face and spinning him away. A maiden new-come to the Walkyriun for her training would have been more graceful, but amazingly, Gundohar's ungainly blows were connecting. Now his foes approached him more cautiously. He saw it, and his pealing laughter rang out once more.

"The Walkyrja brings me victory!" he cried.

Other shouts echoed him. The Burgunds had heard his battle cry and were pounding toward the fray. Gundohar grunted and drove his spear into a man's belly. A sword flashed toward his head; he twisted away, and it slammed into the rock and shattered. And then his men were upon them.

"Gundohar! Gundohar! The Gundwurm wakens!" they cried. In moments all the Alamanni were down. Other men, fleeing, set their fellows moving in panicked flight across the field. The other Walkyrja turned her horse and galloped away.

The wind from the river had freshened. As the spirit-sight left her, Brunahild could see knots of struggling warriors scattered across the plain. Gradually the battle was moving northward. She realized in wonder that the Alamanni were being beaten back.

Someone brought a riderless horse, and they thrust Gundohar up into the saddle. Cheering, the Burgunds began to move toward the nearest fighting. For a moment Gundohar turned in his saddle, gazing back at her. He raised his spear and waved it at her, eyes still glittering with frenzy.

Do not thank me! she thought bitterly. *It was your wyrd, not I, that let you go!*

It was past time for her to be gone. It would have been better still if she had never come this way. Frowning, Brunahild dug her heels into the mare's sweated sides and reined her northward, toward the tatters of the army for which she had sworn to fight that day.

The dying sun stained the dustclouds the same crimson as the Burgund banners. To the features of those who lay still upon the battlefield, it lent a deceptive glow. But the only movement among them was the fluttering of the eagles and the ravens as they tore at the food the Fates had given them, as the blood of the slain fed the earth on which they lay. Presently living men began to move across the battlefield, bearing lost lords and fallen friends away to feed the funeral fires.

The bay mare plodded past Alamanni bodies. Brunahild averted her gaze. She felt sick, and old. *I should have called myself "Bringer of Death," not "Bringer of Victory,"* she thought numbly. Tonight it was the losers of this battle who would feast with the Einherior. She realized then that the only victory Wodan guaranteed was his own. Whichever side won, he would harvest the heroes, and she had done his work well that day. But as she reined her horse toward the rise where the Walkyriun were waiting she knew another thing. The brightness she had seen in the god's eye had been tears.

The smell of cooking gruel came from the campsite. She saw women moving about the fire, and bending over someone stretched motionless on the ground. As she approached, a tethered pony nickered. Someone looked up, and then they were all staring. The mare stopped, and she kicked it to make it go on.

"Brunahild!"

She knew that voice. Galemburgis was hurrying toward her with poised spear.

"It is Brunahild! Seize her! She has betrayed us all!"

Chapter 14 ✳ The Shape of Fear

Land of the Hermunduri, Wurm Fell
Harvest, Full of the Moon, A.D. 418

Sigfrid's pony pricked its ears, and he straightened, listening. Was it a deer? He had already seen sign on the trail. Then he heard the clink of metal from somewhere ahead, and men's laughter—it was a different beast then, less useful, and more dangerous. The land here was mixed forest, rising gently from the open northern plain, and the road ahead was hidden by a green haze of trees. He reined in, waiting for Ragan to catch up to him so they would meet the strangers together. The smith did not seem to have heard. He rode hunched in the saddle, his eyes vague under bent brows. Now that they were on the way, was he wondering whether he really wanted his brother killed after all?

"More men up ahead," Sigfrid said as the smith reached him. They had begun to meet warriors that morning, remnants of the Alamanni army fleeing the great battle in the south in which the Burgunds had defeated them. They straggled along the trail in two's and three's, or in larger bands led by chieftains.

On the whole, Sigfrid would rather deal with the latter, who still kept their men in some kind of order. A war-band could have overwhelmed them, but its leaders knew better than to attack a smith. They might need his services another time. It was masterless men, made wretched by the loss of lord and kin, who might strike out at anything they met to ease their pain.

More slowly, they set their horses in motion again.

"Northerners, from their gear," said Ragan as the little group came into view. "War-arrow flew far this time. 'All the men' indeed!"

Sigfrid nodded, relaxing a little. He counted a half-dozen, better armed than usual, with swords as well as spears. One man had a helm; several others wore pieces of armor. And they were marching in good order. They might have lost the battle, but they had not lost discipline.

"They been in more fights than this one," said Ragan, "but not a comitatus. Wandering swords." He stiffened suddenly, peering under his hand as the sun came out from behind a cloud, and Sigfrid touched the hilt of his sword.

Its weight at his hip was still strange to him. Many days of work had gone into the final grinding and polishing. Now the edge would cut a hank of wool floating on the stream, and he could see a glimmering reflection of his own features in the blade. He had taken time, as well, to make the pommel and hilt and guard secure, and craft a sheath of bullhide with golden fittings from his father's treasure to hold the blade.

His linden-wood shield and hunting spear were tied to the saddle. He wondered if he should free them. Why did Ragan scent trouble from this band, when the others had hailed them or glared at them and passed them by? Now the strangers were close enough to see features. He stared through the watery sunlight at the leader, and suddenly memories replaced the bushy beard beneath the helm with one less streaked with grey. The eyes had not changed, though: cold, pale, and widening now with amazed fury as they met Sigfrid's gaze.

Heming! Fear fluttered in his belly. He had not recognized his old enemy at the fight at Hiloperic's hall, but Heming must have seen him then, and would certainly know Ragan. Once more he was eight years old, helpless in the hold of his enemy. Instinctively his legs tightened, and the pony danced, but something more powerful than panic kept him from loosing the rein.

"Well met, son of Sigmund!" Heming stepped forward as his men spread out to block the road. "It seems this campaign has brought us some luck after all!"

Ragan made a harsh sound deep in his throat, no doubt angered that all his care in raising up a hero should be threatened now.

Behind Heming his men were murmuring. "It is the wolf-child," said one of them, making the sign against evil. Sigfrid felt his lips drawing back from his teeth. *I am no longer the child you tried to kill,* he told himself, *or even the boy who burst like a berserker from Alb's burning hall. I will not fight as a wolf this time. . . .*

"Be easy, foster-father," he said softly, though he could feel his heart drum in his chest. "This had to come one day. Let us learn if I have the skill to be your champion." He moved his pony in front of Ragan's.

"There were too many between us, wolf cub, when I saw you by firelight at Alb's hall," said Heming. "But now I will see if you can do more than snarl!"

Sigfrid swallowed. Then, he had been given only a choice between deaths, and there had been no time for fear. "Sigmund's son smiles to see you, and so does Sigmund's sword!" He pulled the blade free.

"Wodan broke it when your father fought us. Do you think it will serve you now?" Heming was laughing, but Sigfrid had seen him blink as the sun struck silver fire from the sword. *Wodan helped me to reforge it,* he thought, but he would not say that aloud.

"Killer of wild beasts, wolf-kin, it is a man you must face now! Get down and fight me, or we will pull you down."

"Mark space in the road and guard it, so they fight like warriors," said Ragan suddenly.

Sigfrid glanced at him gratefully. He did not know enough of the way men fought to have suggested it, but he was glad not to have to face mobbing by this man-pack. Helmbari had told him a bit about battle, but it was enough to face one man, his first time out with this sword. With a bemused detachment he found himself sliding down from the pony. There was still time to flee. He remembered how the wandering wolf had fled through the forest, leaving a blood-trail on the tawny leaves. Was there ever an end to fear, once you turned your back to your foe?

I am not that whimpering child!

He untied the shield and moved into the square Heming's men had drawn in the dust of the road. They stood at three of the corners, but Ragan had taken the fourth, and Sigfrid was glad to have one friend.

"You have grown, wolf cub," said Heming as he took his place opposite the boy. Sigfrid nodded. When he was a child his only defense had been to run from his enemy. He would not do so again.

Sigfrid settled into the stance that Helmbari had taught him, right foot back and sword arm lifted, left side forward, protected by the shield. Heming's shield was hacked and battered, but it had survived the battle, so its sturdiness could not be discounted. Still, it should not stand against the sword that had shattered a smith's anvil-stone.

"So, it will not be a simple slaughter. Your mother would be proud." Surprise mingled with approval in Heming's grin.

Sigfrid's eyes narrowed. There had been no word from Hiordisa in the year since he had left her. But this man was a northerner. He might know how she fared.

A movement sensed rather than seen was his only warning. He met Heming's first blow awkwardly, and heard wood crack in his shield. Just as well Helmbari had taught him to fight with the boss alone, he thought grimly. At this rate, Heming's shield might outlast his own. Sigfrid tried to pretend this was just more shieldwork, feeling the shock up and down his arm as he blocked the blows, but it was different when you knew the other man was really trying to kill you.

"Fight, curse you!" said Heming suddenly, pulling back. "Do you think you are at play?"

Sigfrid forced a grin. "How do my folk fare, man of the north? What word of my kindred at King Alb's hall?"

Heming's gaze narrowed beneath the browband of his helm. "Do you want me to tell you? You will have to fight for the news!"

Heming's sword smashed down on Sigfrid's disintegrating shield, and the boy blocked and gave ground. He was beginning to understand just how well Helmbari had taught him, for this was a seasoned warrior he was fighting, and so long as the shield held out, Heming could not touch him. Sigfrid began to breathe a little more easily.

"Repeating the same defense can lull yer enemy." The old man's advice echoed in memory. *"But don't get caught in th' pattern—fear an' confidence are both a danger!"* He heard Heming's man stir behind him. Not much room left to retreat, then. Anticipation leaped in his enemy's eyes, and the boy stilled, waiting.

Heming's blade blurred forward. Sigfrid glimpsed the man's neck and shoulder and felt his own balance shifting as Gram flared in his hand. The steel sang as it sheared through mail rings and bit bone. Heming staggered, the sword slipping from his hand. For the first time Sigfrid advanced; splinters flew as he hewed Heming's shield. His enemy reeled backward, and the flat of Sigfrid's sword clanged on the dented boss as Heming went down, rolling.

"Your mother—" he gasped, and Gram paused in its downward swing. Heming had come to rest curled on his left side, breathing hard. Blood was welling freely from his wound. Sigfrid bent over him. He had seen a wounded stag run till blood-loss brought it down, but he did not know how humans died.

"Closer . . ." Heming whispered. "Tell you . . . Hiordisa—" He coughed and twisted. Sigfrid could not see his eyes. The boy dropped to one knee and freed himself from his shield.

"Just after Yule—" Heming gasped, and the boy reached out to him. "She died . . . Alb moved west last spring."

Sigfrid stared down at him. He must have time to understand this. *For almost a year she has been ashes. . . .*

Heming's chest rose with his breathing, and ever so slowly, fell. *Her sweet voice . . . her shining hair . . .*

In the same slow motion, Heming was turning. *All gone. And the hill empty.*

Metal glittered in the silence; a knife in Heming's left hand lifted toward him. But Sigfrid had forever to see it coming—all the moons since Hiordisa had died. *No one will hear the wild geese crying now.*

His hand moved of itself. The fine bones shifted in Heming's wrist as Sigfrid gripped it and slowly began to force the knife back down. *I have no kin . . . I have no home.*

Heming's gaze lifted from the descending blade to Sigfrid as the point paused above his throat. "You are alone. . . ." He grimaced.

And then Sigfrid saw first the hatred, and then all meaning, ebb from his enemy's eyes as resistance ceased suddenly and the knife went in.

Ragan felt a trickle of water ooze down his cheek and pulled the oily wool of his cloak farther forward. Drops were forming at its edge, falling past his face to the neck of the pony, scattering in showers from the branches that grew over the trail, falling steadily from the flat grey of the sky.

Sigfrid's sodden figure bobbed ahead of him, his pony's hoofprints muddying the curling rivulets that were cutting across the path. After the fight with Heming, Ragan had led them off the main road and turned westward by the hidden ways among the hills. And ever since Heming's blood had soaked the ground, it had rained.

It was good the man was dead. He had been a threat, and the fight had given Sigfrid some necessary seasoning. He would not think about how for a moment he had seemed to see his father's body lying there.

"Made a spangenhelm for Helgi, your brother," Ragan said quickly, pitching his voice to carry through the sound of the rain. "First master-work, good as one for Burgund king. Not in Sigmund's hoard, though. Maybe Sigruna put it in Helgi's howe."

Sigfrid's shoulders twitched uncomfortably. Ragan snorted. Was the boy still brooding over his first real man-slaying?

"Fine woman. Hogni's daughter. Folk say she was Walkyrja." He sought more words to fill the silence. The more silent Sigfrid grew, the stronger grew Ragan's need to talk to him of warriors he had known and the weapons he made for them. Of treasure he had seen.

"Made big axe for Dag, her brother. Big as Donar's—" Ragan laughed. "Hogni a rich king. He drank from horns made of gold with figures of gods and men. Old work, not mine—made by a smith of my people for tall folk who came before."

"The Gauls?" asked Sigfrid, as his pony scrambled up a steep part of the path.

The trees were old here, gnarled roots clinging to great outcrops of lichened stone. Ahead, if the clouds had lifted, they would have seen the seven knobbed undulations that were the spine of the earth dragon from which Wurm Fell had taken its name. These were ancient paths indeed, which only the forest hunters followed, kept open just enough to let a pony through. When Ragan was younger he had known them very well. They were the straightest way to the western mines, but these days few seemed to use them. One who knew the way could find the trail, but often he had been glad of Sigfrid's strength to help clear windfalls or hack away branches.

"The Gauls, yes, they make those horns when they were masters here. There been many folk think they own these forests." He laughed sourly. "They come in their wagons, kill warriors and marry women . . . stay a time then move on. My people first of all of them. First ones chased into forests, first to learn earthsong. And still here!" His voice was loud, even in his own ears. Sigfrid had pulled his cloak over his face again.

"You listening?" Ragan demanded suddenly. The boy turned, his yellow eyes opaque, shielding his soul. The smith frowned. His fosterling was hero-born and, since yesterday, a proven fighter, but did he have the passion to face what Fafnar had become?

"The light is fading," said Sigfrid. "We'll need to see to find firewood, and water. We should seek a campsite soon."

"Ahead is river Sig," Ragan answered. "First we cross it. Then we see."

Firelight danced and flickered on leaning logs and the layers of greenery they had laid across them. The rude shelter would not stand up to a storm, but the wind was driving the rainclouds from the west, and in that direction the rock face against which the logs were leaning protected them. Ragan could hear the splatter of rain on the rocks above as another gust of wind harried the clouds. The weather was changing. He sniffed the air, realizing that he had been long enough on the trail so that senses dulled by the smoke of the forge were recovering their precision.

Or perhaps it was because he was on home ground now, in a land whose bones he knew, because they were his own.

"The Gauls, they had lots of treasure," he filled the silence. "Needed lots . . . kept throwing it away."

Sigfrid pulled away the last bit of hide from the carcass of the rabbit he was skinning and looked up, questioning.

Ragan snorted. "They throw it in water," he explained. "Water is blood of the land. Landspirits live in sacred springs. Folk throw in stuff they win in battle to thank gods for victory."

"King Alb's people do that too, I think," said the boy, frowning. Ragan looked at him. Not *my* people. Interesting. Heming's words must have hit home. "We went to make offerings at the marsh when I was small."

Ragan remembered the kingfisher shimmer of wide northern sky on the spreading waters of the marshlands, and then suddenly he was seeing instead the sunlight that flickered through leaves to sparkle on moving water; the crystal fall of a forest stream into the secrecy of a dark pool.

"Andvari's treasure came from the water. . . ." He did not realize he had spoken aloud until he saw Sigfrid's gaze sharpen. "Each new folk make offerings there when they learn ways of land. Leaf-shaped blades of bronze in that treasure," he said slowly, "good still, if you scour the green away, and golden necklets shape of the moon. A silver cauldron with images of gods that southern smiths made, long ago. Twisted Gallic neck rings and bracelets of gold. Power in those things. The Wodan priests knew it. They work spells over the hoard, thinking they could keep it, adding the magic of the Gauls and the other peoples to their own. . . ." Ragan blinked, his vision pulsing with the radiance of the treasure they had heaped upon Ottar's hide.

"What spells?"

Ragan realized he had been silent too long. He shrugged.

"Runespells. Aesir-magic. They put runes on one of the neck rings, I remember, and on a golden rod like a little spear. And for twenty winters now, Fafnar sleeps on that treasure, eating its power."

"Do you want Fafnar's death only, or the hoard?" asked Sigfrid evenly.

Ragan looked at him with sudden suspicion. The boy had never seemed greedy, but the gold-lust could awaken in any man. Fafnar had always loved cold steel better than bright gold—until he saw Andvari's hoard.

"It is my brother's weregild," he growled. "Price of my father's blood. Would you give up Sigmund's hoard?"

Sigfrid shrugged. "The scabbard fittings are pretty, but it was you, old man, who insisted that I claim the rest of it. What use do I have for gold? I asked as a precaution. Fafnar won't tell anybody where to find his hoard once his gut is filled with steel!"

Once more Ragan eyed him. He had seen these moods before, when the boy put on a brutal mask to hide his hurting, mocking all things and himself most of all. He must not give way to anger now, when they were so close to the goal for which he had fostered the boy all these years. When Fafnar lay cold, he would be free at last.

"I can find it," he whispered. "Magic in those things will sing from ground."

"Do you want the gold, or the magic?" Now Sigfrid's tone held simple curiosity. "You told me that your inheritance from your father was smithcraft. What use will such things be to you? Better give them back to the goddess in the sacred pool."

"I am earthblood. All powers must meet in me." Ragan stared into the fire.

"Maybe, but you told me once that gold can breed blood. That hoard has been no good to your kin, Hreidmaro's son. Can any good come of taking gold that was vowed to the gods?"

"Not *my* gods!" hissed Ragan. He jumped as a branch popped and fell, scattering coals like lumps of gold.

"All gods should be respected," said Sigfrid with a severity that came oddly from lips shaded by the uncertain fringing of a young man's first beard. "And if you don't believe in them, why do you want their power?"

"Power of earth is in the gold, and the silver, and the bronze." Ragan touched the cold ground. "Men of many tribes make it into treasure, give it power of their gods. But they put it in Andvari's pool. Offerings to my gods there too. Then Wodan priests take it and add their runes."

"And if you take it what will you become? Better stick to your own craft," said Sigfrid, lifting the rabbit from the spit upon which it had been roasting, and tearing off a strip of smoking meat. "As for me, I won't demand a single piece of gold. I'm quite content with the road I'm on." He slapped the hilt of his sword.

Ragan's eyes narrowed. Perhaps the boy even believed his words. But from both kindreds he was shapestrong, and that sword itself was proof he had mastered Ragan's craft. Who could say what lust for magic might not awaken in his blood when he handled Fafnar's hoard? For the first time he found himself hoping Fafnar would wound the boy before Sigfrid took him down.

"Tomorrow we find out are you any good at it—"

"We're close, then?" Sigfrid straightened, glancing around him as if he expected Fafnar to slither from beneath the trees. Ragan laughed harshly.

"This place the foot of Fafnar's mountain. Up there"—he motioned to the slopes beyond the outcroppings that sheltered them—"is Wurm Fell. He lairs above the spring."

Sigfrid looked upward as if his keen eyes could pierce the wet and windy darkness, but Ragan's gaze returned to the gold that burned in the fire.

Sigfrid dreamed the rain had become a torrent that carried him away. He struggled, but the water was too strong for him. Darkness swirled and sucked him downward. Under water, coarse reeds swayed gently in the current; a green and glimmering light gleamed on odd shapes sunk into the gravel of the river's bed.

Andvari's hoard . . . Some corner of memory still free supplied the words. *I listened too long to Ragan's tales.*

But the vividness of his vision drew him deeper into the dream. He drifted toward the nearest of the objects, a long shape that could have been a sword. As he approached, its form seemed to waver, rearing back and becoming a serpent. Hastily he pulled away. The next thing was larger, and round, perhaps a cauldron. He tried to see, and recoiled as its round mouth opened to expose a gaping maw.

A gilded helmet housed a skull with balefully glowing eyes. Daggers turned to teeth that slashed at his hands; cups contorted; golden coins became a school of snapping fish that swirled around him and disappeared. And yet beyond them all he knew there was something he needed. If he could find it, he could master all the transformations.

And it seemed to him that a voice spoke through the silence of the water. *He who would understand the world must master the rod and the ring.* . . . He saw a leather sack and bent to open it, but at his touch the thing billowed outward, imprisoning him in slick folds. He struggled to get free. . . .

And woke, still tearing at the thing that held him. His heartbeat slowed as he realized it was only the cloak in which he had wrapped himself for sleeping. Carefully he untangled his limbs from the coarse wool. From the other side of the hearth he could hear Ragan snort and whimper, fighting his own nightmares, but outside there was no sound but the pattering of rain.

Rest, he told himself. *It was only a dream.* But he lay sleepless until the pale gold of daybreak gleamed through parting clouds.

"I show you way, then I go back," said Ragan, pointing through a gap in the trees where the light slanted downward like a shower of gold. "Fafnar will sense me. For a lifetime he waits. All his spirits wait to slay me if I come." He felt cold walk down his backbone and looked around swiftly. They were there; he could feel awareness stirring. Memory shied from recollection of what had happened last time he woke those watchers. He stopped where he was, staring up the hill.

"How will I find him then?" asked Sigfrid. Was his voice too controlled? Ragan peered at him. There were shadows beneath the boy's eyes as if he had not slept well.

"He spreads a net of fear, like invisible circle around his lair," said the smith, digging his staff into the wet ground as he climbed. "Maybe last night it touched us, in dreams. You know if you come near it, and he knows too. I think only way is to go under it, in gully below the spring where he gets water."

Sigfrid grunted. At his side hung the aurochs horn and his sword. He had left his cloak behind him, but Ragan frowned as he saw the wolfskin slung across his shoulder.

"Leave that here—" He pointed. "You going to challenge Fafnar to berserker battle? He was master of that kind of fighting before you're born! You don't win with teeth this time, but with sword!" Another memory stirred, and he thrust it away.

Sigfrid shook his head. "It will help me to understand him."

"He will eat you!" said Ragan. "That way, you put yourself in his power." He could see the gully now, and a chill that owed nothing to the water pebbled his skin. The watchers were close; he could feel their hunger.

Oh my brother . . . oh my enemy . . .

"If you want me to kill him, old man," the boy flared suddenly, "then stop trying to make me afraid!"

"That way—" Ragan jabbed the air with his staff. "See—he has worn a trail where he comes down. Wait for him, and you don't need me to learn fear." He turned abruptly, earth-dark eyes clashing with Sigfrid's golden gaze until the boy's unwinking stare forced his down. "Sunset, I come back again."

In the clear morning light he saw the child beneath the overlay of manhood, hands and feet still just a little too large, the telltale rounding of the cheeks beneath the new beard. What was he doing, to pit against this boy the monstrous thing that set his own heart pounding with fear?

Oh my enemy . . . oh my child . . .

Sigfrid hunkered down in the path, listening to Ragan slide and splash back along the trail. *Fafnar could hear him without the aid of spirits.* The thought flitted across the surface of his mind. *I'm safer with him gone.*

Below conscious awareness, other senses were busy, taking in the rich scent of moist earth, the sound of dripping water, the glitter of light on wet leaves. Somewhere nearby a woodpecker was knocking out a new storage hold in a tree; above him the nuthatches were chattering. A flutter of movement focused his attention as a sparrow pounced on a stranded earthworm and bore it triumphantly away.

I would like to be a bird. . . . He blinked as the flicker of wings vanished into the brilliance of the sky. He had no illusions about birds' freedom—he had observed too many squabbles over nesting grounds, but he had always thrilled to the magic moment when a squawking horde of migrating waterfowl became a single symbol arrowing into the sky. And birds saw things from such a different perspective. Sigfrid understood the talk of the wolves, but birds were still a mystery.

And if he had been a bird, he would not have had to worry about drowning in a world that was still melting, even though the rain was done. Carefully he made his way to the edge of the spring. The rivulet that danced down the hillside was brown with runoff, but the spring, trickling from a crack in the rock into a rocky pool, was still clear. Sigfrid bent over it to dip up water and stopped, staring at the face he saw there.

To him it seemed a man's face, the fuzz of his growing beard made darker by the shadowed water, his nose and cheekbones strong, dark-fringed wolf's eyes staring from beneath level brows, all framed by sun-streaked brown hair. Why was he so surprised? In years he was a man as his people reckoned it, of age to take arms—or lie with a woman. Old enough to kill his enemy. But the things in that face that were familiar only made the rest more strange.

He sat up, gazing at the woods around him with the same disorientation. They were like his own forest and yet different, or perhaps they had simply gone strange in the way the land around the Pillars did sometimes, with a darkness about it even at midday, as if there were a shadow across the sun. He stepped across the stream and approached the path. Ragan had spoken of watchers, but Sigfrid sensed one presence only, becoming more palpable the closer he came.

He felt the hair lifting on his neck. This was like the cave of the old bear in the forest at home, or the atmosphere in the forge when Ragan was brooding. If it had been a smell it would have been sour and fetid, like something rotting in a closed place where it could not be cleansed by rain and wind. Whether it was of flesh or spirit, the scent lay heavy on the path. Sigfrid had never encountered anything quite like it before, but he would recognize it again.

I will kill Fafnar, thought Sigfrid, *if only to clear this stench from the world.*

At the limits of his vision something seemed to move. He turned sharply, nostrils flaring, but there was nothing. The branches rippled. Were they tree limbs or serpents uncoiling in the sun? Sigfrid frowned, remembering his dream. Behind him, the wood was waking. A haze of golden light aureoled the trees. Birds scolded; a little wind scattered a last few droplets from the leaves. Before him, shapes moved in the shadows. Trees stirred with an alien life, dripping venom from their wet branches. There were eyes in the stones.

Sigfrid began to wish that he had brought his spear. The sword was for fighting men like Heming; the spear was for boars or bears, creatures from whose teeth and claws the wise hunter stayed far away. But perhaps it was an insult to the beasts to compare them with the spirit he sensed here. Fafnar was, or had been, a man, in whatever form he might appear.

He heard a squawk and looked up. Wings beat as a very large raven flapped heavily downward to join another that was already perched on an oak branch that overhung the spring. The stark contrast between black birds and bright sky made the shifting uncertainty of the shadows before him all the more disturbing. The first bird cooed inquiringly as the second settled beside it, and received a short "caark" in reply.

"Do you wait for me to feed you?" Sigfrid called softly. Ravens were old friends of the wolves. They picked over the pack's kills, and sometimes showed the wolves where to find new prey. But he only understood a few of their calls. "Tell me how I must kill this thing—"

The ravens cocked their heads, black eyes glittering. One of them made a kind of clucking noise, and Sigfrid laughed. Better to take Fafnar by surprise, he thought then. If the distortion of vision was so disturbing here, by the time he reached the troll-man's lair he would likely be smashing his sword on rocks and battering his head into trees. How could he fight his foe when he could not find him? But even a were-wurm had to have water. Maybe Fafnar's illusions would be less overwhelming here, at the edge of his sphere of power.

He would wait for him, then. But he would need someplace to hide. Black wings snapped open, and one of the ravens swept down and past him in a long glide to a rock above the stream. He dipped his bill into the water, then flapped back to his tree, but Sigfrid had seen that beyond the rock there was space for a man to lie hidden, if he dug some of the debris away. He eyed the raven suspiciously.

"I wonder if I should thank you," he muttered, and tugged at a rotten branch. As he lifted it, a salamander, its moist skin gleaming slickly in the sunlight, twitched to life and scuttled frantically away.

Sigfrid had lain hidden in the hollow long enough for damp and cold to set him shivering when he heard a stone roll, and a slow scraping sound. Something was coming down the path. *It is a man so old and lame he cannot lift his feet,* he told himself. But the clattering of the stream had dulled his hearing. The sounds could just as well have been made by the ponderous undulations of a great wurm.

Carefully he raised himself, peering out from beneath the screen of greenery he had pulled across his hiding place. Shadow coiled and curled before him, but within its deceptions, he seemed to see the stooped shape of a man. He lay back, heart pounding.

I was right. It is only a man ... and to slay him from ambush would be a coward's deed!

He rolled a little and fumbled at his side. He had brought the horn to give him courage, but it would carry his challenge now. Awkward in the cramped space, he sucked in moist air and blew.

Sound pulsed and echoed around him. The fellow would think Andvari had come seeking his stolen treasure, as if the horncall were coming from the waters of the stream. Sigfrid heard the last notes die away and held his breath, listening.

For a moment it seemed as if the whole world had gone still.

Then he became aware of an answer, as if the notes of his horn had found a new echo, that distorted its sweet calling as the shadows inside the troll-man's ward distorted the clean light of day.

"Who comes . . . to challenge me?"

If Sigfrid's horncall had seemed to come from the stream, the response vibrated from the bowels of the earth. Darkness flowed toward him.

Snarling, Sigfrid stabbed upward, scattering the branches that had concealed him. He felt the shock as the blade struck something. There was a roar as if the earth had split. He staggered upright, staring around him. The man-shape, if there had been one, was gone. What he saw before him were the darkly glistening coils of the Wurm.

It is just an illusion, he told himself; but when he ran in wolf-shape, was he really a wolf, or a man? He would be a fool not to fight as if it were real. The Wurm reared up, fringed jaws gaping, and trees cracked as its weight came down. Sigfrid leaped aside as the great blind head swung toward him, and slashed again. Once more he heard that outraged groan. Slick coils heaved, and suddenly the thing was using stubby legs to pull it back up the path toward its lair. Wolf instincts sent Sigfrid loping after.

As he closed, the thing seemed suddenly larger. He struck, and the shape split—nine heads now from the trunk came coiling. Again Sigfrid paused; this was too much like his dream! The serpent heads hissed like wind in barren branches. Was it because he was still in man-shape that the thing had power to fool him? He fumbled with the ties, clasped the linked paws of the wolfhide across his chest, pulled the wolfshead over his own.

Abruptly his vision steadied. But what before had been a shadow of horror was now clear in every detail, scaled and segmented, taloned and fanged.

"Now you are in my world, wolf cub—" Nine hideous heads hissed laughter. *"Follow me, if you dare!"* It crashed ahead of him through the trees.

Hackles bristling, Sigfrid trotted after, though the scene kept changing around him. Now the woods were the forest around the forge. The shape ahead of him broadened, bulking out in dark fur, striking out with taloned paws. Sigfrid rose to meet it, and suddenly he had a bear's form too. Blow for blow they traded, roaring, until the black bear grunted and wheeled away.

The scene changed. They were in the marshes of Sigfrid's childhood. A great elk waded through the sedgegrass, weighted by the mature splendor of its antlers. And the pursuer, splashing toward it, became a bull elk also, younger and more supple, though he had not such a rack of armament on his brow. Spray flew from beneath broad hooves as he charged. The other bull turned to meet him. The world went dark as they clashed.

"Who dares to pursue me here?" came the question.

Panic changed to rage as the pursuer realized he did not know.

The world grew white with winter. Two black aurochs battled in the snow. It was autumn, and red stags bellowed as they strove. Eagles screamed in the air, and walruses wallowed on the sand, white tusks growing red. The old beast led the younger through every transformation. And in the end the pursuer knew only that the other was his enemy.

"Who has set you on to kill me?"

How could that question be answered? It was rage itself that drove the attacker, and envy, and fear.

Two dog-wolves snarled, slashing at each other with sharp fangs. There was blood on the old wolf's chest and flanks; bites oozed blood from the younger wolf's shoulder. The old one was on the defensive now, head lowering and ears back. Instinctively the attacker paused, his unwinking yellow glare willing the other to complete his submission.

"Who are you?"

The younger wolf fought to make sense out of the words. *I am the ruler . . . this is my land, my people. . . .* But they stood in a place of mist and shadow. There was no forest here, no other wolves.

"If you do not know who you are, how can you defeat me?"

Whining, the younger wolf took a step backward. The old one lifted his head, but he was swaying. Instinct saw the opening and launched the challenger toward it. His jaws closed in rank fur.

But his teeth scraped slick hide. The thing beneath him heaved, and great coils closed around him. Searing poison burned through wolfhide. The young wolf howled anguish, felt the hide that held him split as the spirit burst free, reclothing itself in glittering scales. Serpent twined serpent in hideous embrace, slashing with venomed jaws. Then even those forms were lost, and there was only a turbulence that eased, finally, to let the warring spirits float free in the dark.

Who am I? What am I? Images of wurm, wolf, elk, bear, moved through awareness. The glimmer of consciousness considered them.

He had been all of them, but were they all he was? Through the wilderness in which the troll-man had trapped him he hunted his identity.

"*Sigfrid . . .*"

The word was a tunnel through the darkness. He fell through it, and found himself crouched above the body of a gaunt man with a wild bush of silver-streaked black hair and Ragan's dark eyes. Behind him piled logs and tumbled stone formed a lair. The blood-trail through the woods showed how they had come here, that, and the splintered trees. Gram stood sheathed in the man's belly; a little blood was pumping sluggishly from the edges of the wound. There were grazes on his throat and brow.

"Sigfrid—" He said it aloud.

"Hreidmaro spoke true. The son of Sigmund the wolf-king and of Lyngheide's daughter . . . has murdered me." Fafnar's words were harsh with suppressed pain, or perhaps it was laughter. "Ragan's fosterling. Should have been mine."

"What do you mean?" Sigfrid found his voice at last. He recognized those names, but they made no sense to him.

"Like me—" He took a careful breath, and Sigfrid heard the rattling. "Learned my magic. Kill me, like killing yourself!"

"No!" Sigfrid drew back, shaking his head. It hurt, and he realized that he had been wounded as well. Fafnar was a monster— He shivered as he began to remember in what shapes he had fought him. *No . . . please, let me be only a man!*

"You are what you are," Fafnar coughed. "Already you have dangerous knowledge, for you walk between worlds of beast and man. Other men sense this in you. Like it or not, you have power."

Sigfrid shivered, remembering how the wolves had sensed the strangeness in the wanderer and driven him away.

"I will not use it. . . ." he whispered.

"Even no choice is choosing, son of Sigmund. You choose not to know who you are? You always let yourself be ruled by others' wills?" His features spasmed, and Sigfrid bent over him again. The leathery skin was clammy, the pulse thready and slow. "Ragan set you on to slay me."

It was true. Sigfrid had let Wyrd and the wills of others move him since the burning of Alb's hall. Even the forging of the sword had been made possible by the help of Helmbari. He eyed the bright blade balefully.

"You take his vengeance because he fears. Where will he get weregild for me?" came the whisper.

Sigfrid stared at him. "Is this your revenge, to set me against the man who raised me? Tell me where you have hidden your hoard!"

There was a sound that might have been pain, or laughter.

"Do you . . . desire it? No good to you. Andvari cursed it. Now I understand . . . doom that Dwalin's daughters give. Go now, or bright gold be your bane. . . ."

"All that lives dies someday." Sigfrid forced himself to speak boldly. "And goes down into the dark." Fafnar's weathered skin was growing gray.

"Strong . . . son of Sigmund. Stronger than me. Could have taught you . . . much. . . ." He gasped, and bright blood ran out beside the blade. "Sky-steel burns in my belly. Pull out sword."

"You will die."

Fafnar's lips writhed back from stained teeth in a dreadful grin. "You . . . too . . ." The grizzled head moved a little against the leaves. "Earthblood seeks earth. . . ." he whispered, and then, almost in surprise: "No . . . time."

His eyes closed. Sigfrid leaned forward to touch the pulse-point, thinking him gone, but there was still a flicker of life beneath his hand. *Don't die,* he thought. *Don't leave me alone!*

"Blood of Hreidmaro," Fafnar's head rolled. "Don't trust . . ."

The boy bent close to listen, but there was no more. One of the ravens cried as a gust of wind set all the leaves to shivering, and Sigfrid bent, gripped Gram's hilt, and jerked the blade free.

Chapter 15 ✳ Kindred

Ragan ground his forehead against the oak tree's rough bark, as if the pain without could deaden the turmoil within. In another moment he would have been screaming, and he had only touched the edges of Fafnar's power. Would Sigfrid be able to endure it? The boy had been raised free of the shapechanger's magic. Surely he would come to the deed with his own warrior instincts to guide him, and without the fear.

Fear is my brother . . . Ragan thought grimly, waiting for the roiling in his belly to ease. Even in the long ago days of his childhood, Ottar had been the one who laughed with him, and Fafnar the one who made him afraid. And with the thought, memory took him captive, and he was a child, and the world was bright once more.

He laughs, waving the stick above his head, while the great otter darts playfully back and forth, trying to snatch it away. And then he casts it outward in a wheeling arc above the river, and Ottar's shape blurs as he slides down the well-worn track in the bank and into the stream. In a moment his sleek head breaks the surface. He is holding the stick in his jaws. He ripples through the water and propels himself up the bank so that Ragan can take the stick back again.

Grinning, the child waves the wood high, and shrieks as a shadow looms over him and it is plucked from his hand. Fafnar is laughing, but there is no humor in the sound. He looks at his prize, breaks it over his knee, and stalks away. Ragan stares after him and rubs his eyes so that his brother will not see the tears.

Ragan came back to awareness, shaking. So long ago that had been, it seemed the morning of the world. He had been afraid of everything when he was a child, but his big brother, with his great strength and uncertain moods, he had feared most of all. Even when they grew to manhood and Ragan learned the smith's craft, it had not been much different, for Fafnar had been a warrior by then, the valued servant of kings. Thinking of those days thrust Ragan once more into the stream of memory.

In Hreidmaro's hall the fire is blazing. Smoke swirls up through the thatch; firelight gleams on flushed faces, on golden neck rings and the hilts of swords. Hreidmaro sits upon his high seat with King Ralf beside him, drinking golden mead from silver-mounted horns. Fafnar sprawls at their feet, gnawing on the champion's portion of the bull.

The king's bard stands forth to praise the deeds of his heroes. He calls Fafnar the War-serpent and numbers his slain, though some men mutter behind their hands. And Hreidmaro raises his horn and proclaims Fafnar the best of his sons. Ottar sits near the doorway, smiling as he dreams of his sunlit stream, but Ragan frowns. As he rises to leave, one of the king's men shows him a dagger hilt that needs mending, and offers him Roman coins. He knocks the man down and runs from the hall. Behind him he hears laughter, and does not know if they are mocking him or the other man.

But even that was so long ago that King Ralf was a legend. Only Fafnar and he still walked Middle Earth of those who had feasted in Hreidmaro's hall. Better remember times less distant—He lifted his head and shuddered. They must be fighting now. . . .

At the thought, Ragan's awareness opened like a gateway thrown wide to an invading army. He felt Fafnar's outrage and Sigfrid's desperate fury, and then a surge of pure animal rage that could have come from either. He had sent warriors to challenge Fafnar before, and they had died. But none like Sigfrid. Perhaps they would kill each other.

Ragan's fingers dug into the damp earth, and he groaned, tortured by the knowledge that their combat had led them where he would never follow. Even the echoes of that battle sent him spiraling into a nightmare in which he relived the day he had challenged Fafnar to the battle Sigfrid was fighting now.

He staggers back as the great Wurm rises before him. And then suddenly it is a sword, with the marks of his hammer still upon the blade, that turns on him, keening. He runs, and the forest floor sprouts knives; the trees rain spears.

"Mastersmith, you flee your own weapons?" Fafnar's mocking laughter follows him. "Fool, be gone, and be glad I feel friendly! Send no more swords against me. Blade that kills me, be your bane!"

"No!" Ragan's shout reverberated from rock to rock. "I will be master!" He stilled, waiting for the blast of fury that would reply. But there was nothing. He lifted his head, looking around them. There was an emptiness in the world, like the silence after thunder, as if one of his senses had gone.

Was the battle over? He got to his feet, holding to the tree trunk like an old man. The force that had troubled his spirit since the moment they set foot upon the mountain was there no longer. Knowledge came to him then. *Fafnar is dead.*

No hurry, he told himself. *It's finished. Now hoard is yours.* He tried to think about the glory of gold that waited. Works of craft never forgotten, though he had only seen them once, long ago. But with every step, the knowledge beat in his brain. *My brother lies dead beneath the trees. . . .*

Sigfrid gazed down at the man who had been the great wurm of battle. He seemed smaller than Ragan, consumed by his magic. With no heartbeat to pump it, the great wound in his belly had ceased to bleed. The wood seemed very quiet, the only sound the flutter of wings as a flock of nuthatches, neatly clad in grey with black caps and white bellies, darted from branch to branch of the beech tree.

He felt as if the world had stilled so that he could appreciate its beauty. The young sun blazed through the dying gold of the beech leaves, and the moisture left by last night's rain glittered like silver. *With wealth like this in the world,* thought the boy, *what need have I for Fafnar's hoard?*

A branch cracked beneath a heavy, hesitant tread. *Ragan . . .* Even if he had not recognized his step, Sigfrid would have known the wave of emotion that came with him, like Fafnar's, but less powerful, and with more pain. He sighed, and gathered up a clump of dry grass to wipe his sword.

"He's dead, then," came Ragan's rumble behind him. "You fight well, hero-child. No braver warrior walks Middle-Earth. I knew even when you were little, playing by forge, you were born for this deed."

"I was brave enough for this battle, anyway." The boy shuddered, remembering how, in the end, he had *been* his enemy. Remembering the wurm, he shuddered once more. And he had killed him. What had he become? "I don't know about others." He fought back his emotion. "The houseguards boasted of their courage in my grandfather's hall, but now I wonder if any man really knows if he is brave until he faces his foe."

Ragan walked around him to look down at the body. The strengthening sun shone from behind him, and for a moment Sigfrid saw only Ragan's shadow lying there.

"Boast, yes—you have reason, now you wipe my brother's blood from your blade."

Sigfrid cast away the bloodstained wisp of grass. He had not meant to sound triumphant—had Ragan even been listening?

"I boast too," the smith went on. "I brought here the hero whose sword did the slaying." He did not sound very happy, but then, when had Ragan ever shown joy?

"You were not here when I wielded it," said Sigfrid bitterly. "Do you think this deed was glorious? Grass cleans the sword, but how do I clear my memory? Heming was my foe, but I had no reason to wish this man dead—he had done no harm to me!"

Ragan shrugged. "Men kill for glory, or for gain. Where is the hoard?"

"How should I know?" snapped Sigfrid. He waved the blade toward the shattered trees. "We were fighting!" He turned away, slamming the sword back into its sheath, and felt Ragan's gaze boring between his shoulder blades. He had spoken truth, but Ragan was right to wonder what Fafnar had told him. He only wished he could forget his words. He would be happy, he thought, to leave the shapeshifter and his wealth behind.

"Do you grow crafty, now you are hero?" muttered the smith. "Never mind. I know how to win wisdom . . . Gather wood," he said aloud.

"To burn the body?" asked Sigfrid. "Why not drag it back to his lair and let the earth take it? Maybe we will find the hoard there—"

"A small fire—a cookfire," Ragan replied. "All things my brother had are mine. His wealth . . . his power. This is old way of my people. I eat my brother's heart, then I know everything."

Sigfrid gaped as the smith pulled at the tattered furs Fafnar wore. The sword wound was a red mouth gaping in the pallid skin of the slain man's belly. Ragan jabbed his dagger into the end of the wound and tore upward beneath the rib cage. More blood trickled out, and the smith bent to lick at the edges.

The boy shuddered. Wolves fed thus, tearing at the flesh of their kills; why did it seem so monstrous when it was a man? He began to gather up sticks with a frenzied urgency, trying to ignore the sounds. When he turned back with his arms full of branches, Ragan had reached in beneath the ribs and torn out his brother's heart. Arm red to the elbow, he held it high.

Shaking his head, Sigfrid scraped moist leaves away from the earth and built the branches into a cone. Pith and tender inner bark made kindling, and two forked sticks would hold a spit above the blaze. It took several blows of his fire striker before a spark leaped from the flint into the little pile of moss, so he could blow it into flame.

Ragan smiled dreadfully and held out the bloody mass. Sigfrid took it, shuddering. It was still warm. *May the fire set you free,* thought the boy, as he jabbed the stick through it. *You belonged to a brave man.*

Ragan sat back as the first drops of blood fell sizzling into the flame, staring at the red on his hand. His eyes were dilating already. Sigfrid looked at him anxiously. If the taste of Fafnar's blood had affected him so strongly, what would eating the whole heart do? Suddenly the smith let his hand fall and looked around him.

"Tired . . ." he said thickly, licking his lips. "Must rest. You watch fire. Turn spit until heart is done."

It would serve him right if I just left him here, thought Sigfrid, watching the smith collapse, as if by stages, on the ground. *Fafnar's heart can burn to a crisp for all I care.* For a moment Ragan lay curled on his side, then he rolled onto his back, legs splayed and mouth open, his bloody hand curled as if he were appealing to the sky. *And why is he so weary?* he thought then. *I'm the one who fought the battle!* But a long habit of obedience kept him still.

Ragan slept, but Fafnar's blood burned in his brain. Once more he saw Sigfrid standing over the body with the bloody blade in his hand. But in a moment the vision changed. Now the red sword was raised in battle. The boy charged at the head of a horde of shrieking warriors, and the madness of the berserker blazed in his eyes. The scene changed. Sigfrid sat feasting in hall with the warriors, gold glittering on his neck and arms. Ragan whimpered as he recognized ornaments whose beauty he had never forgotten. They belonged to him! They came from the hoard!

The feasters were shouting Sigfrid's name, hailing him with horns held high. A fair woman came forward with a flagon of mead, and Ragan moaned again, for she looked like a woman he had lain with long ago. His anguish grew, and the air darkened. Now there was menace in men's shouting. He blinked at the flash of spears. Sigfrid reared up among them with a cry, and Ragan flinched away. The form was Sigfrid's, but the face was Fafnar's.

The figure staggered toward him, red with blood. *"Vengeance!"* it cried. *"Who will avenge me? My blood cries out against my murderer!"* The cry of fury thinned to a shriek of laughter. Fire flared between them, and in its flames he saw the gleam of Andvari's gold.

Ragan covered his eyes, for now the face beneath the bloody mask was Hreidmaro's. He felt the blade pierce him, and did not know if it were his father's death he was feeling, or Fafnar's, or his own.

Somehow the silence of the forest had filled with birdsong. Sigfrid looked up, wondering when that had happened. Birds fluttered on the branches as if to replace the leaves that had fallen, chirping and trilling, cocking their heads to watch him, flitting from twig to twig. Surely all those birds had not been there while he was fighting. Perhaps they were migrating? He counted the chaffinches, dappled russet and white and brown, and the masked sparrows who belonged in the forest, and his old friends the nuthatches. Only the ravens seemed black blots upon the brightness of the morning, sitting in uncharacteristic silence as the other birds sang.

"Give me a song of laughter, little ones—" He looked up at them. "I need the cheer!"

He poked at the fire, and the roasting heart sizzled. His nostrils flared involuntarily at the savor. Strange that man-flesh should smell like any other meat once it was kissed by the fire. Perhaps he should turn it again. He grasped the end of the spit, but as he started to rotate it, he saw the heart slipping. Instinctively he reached out with his other hand to steady it and gasped as the hot juices foamed out where the spit pierced it and seared his left thumb.

He sucked on his thumb to cool it. The agony in his flesh faded, but Fafnar's blood burned in his brain. The pain took him so swiftly he could not even cry out, and then he was beyond such simple sensory definitions. He was aware of himself, Sigfrid, sitting by the fire and nursing his burned thumb. But suddenly he was also sensing the world through perceptions grown subtle with experience, every breath of wind or blade of grass telling its own tale. Sigfrid gazed in amazement at the forest's beauty, but to that Other within him it was a place of patterned power. He looked around him, and knew the nature of everything he saw as if he were a part of it, and knew, as if he himself had hidden it, the location of the hoard.

And in that moment, when identity trembled like a leaf that the next wind would pluck from the tree, Fafnar's laughter boomed suddenly within his soul.

Sigfrid's eyes opened. On the other side of the cookfire, Ragan was pushing himself upright. Their eyes met, and Fafnar's soul looked out of both brown eyes and gold.

"Traitor!" Ragan got to his feet, his big hands clenching and unclosing like a bear groping for prey. "You steal my power!"

"There smokes your brother's heart!" cried Sigfrid, "roasted and ready. If I wanted, when you slept I could have eaten it all!"

Ragan grabbed for the spit, bit into the sizzling meat, tongue burning, thumb burning, world spinning round. Fafnar's gaze mocked them both; from each other's throats they heard his laughter.

"You know where gold is!"

"*We* know. . . ."

"*In Fafnar's lair lies lustrous gold,*" sang the titmouse.

"*The heaped hoard to the hero should belong!*" the nuthatch replied.

The two men turned from the birds to each other, and Ragan's eyes blazed. "Even birds know you betray me—"

Sigfrid blinked. "I don't want it. I told you. Let me go now, and you can find another place to hide the gold."

"No—no—" Ragan was trembling. "I don't mean that. You fought Fafnar. You have right to see." He turned, took two staggering steps to a long stone wedged between the roots of a beech tree. "Help me—" Fafnar's lust for the gold flared in them both. It had been many winters since the shapeshifter had had the strength to shift the stone and look at his hoard.

Ragan squatted, got strong smith's fingers around one end of the slab. Sigfrid knelt and set his supple strength against the other. Grunting, they worked the rock back and forth; moist earth clung to it, but men's need was stronger. Presently something gave way. Lips curled back over teeth in a snarl as they heaved the stone onto the grass.

From the cleft in the earth that it had covered came a blaze of gold.

"*Bright in earth's belly blazes the gold,*" sang the nuthatch. "*How will the victor and victim divide it?*"

Ragan knelt beside the opening and lifted a golden beaker onto the grass. "This I remember," he said softly. "I stand by my father as Wodan priests lay the treasure upon the skin of Ottar to pay for his killing. Piece by piece, the bronze and silver and gold."

Sigfrid watched as the smith brought the beautiful things out into the daylight, and laid them out in the shape of a skin. Even in Sigmund's hoard there had been nothing to match them. He gaped as the face of a goddess gleamed from a silver cauldron.

"Every hair of his hide they cover, all but his whiskers, and Fafnar stepped forward with his axe, snarling. Then the tall priest takes something from his robe."

Ragan reached farther into the cavity, fumbled around, and pulled out a bundle of soft leather. He opened the flaps. A golden rod gleamed from the leather, perhaps as long as Sigfrid's forearm, with the head of a bird. Beside it was a neck ring of solid gold with hooked ends. Both were carved all over with runes.

"These things—" He nodded. "And now Ottar's hide was all covered. But the man of my people who was with them laughed.

"'The weregild is paid,' he says. 'We wish you well of it. It comes from the pool below Andvari's falls!'

"My father looks angry then. 'Well for you I did not know that,' he answers. 'Your blood would be better payment than Earth Mother's gold!'

"'And what's my share?' asks Fafnar, fingering this rune rod as if he did not hear.

" 'Nothing—' says my father. 'Better I take the bane on myself, and you be free. . . .'

"'Take it then!' Fafnar jumps up, and his axe smashes into my father's side. 'And I will take the hoard!' He stood over the gold, roaring at all who came near him, already becoming the wurm, berserk in rage.

"My sister runs to Hreidmaro, weeping, and he whispers will she avenge him? 'Though father be felled,' says Lyngheide, 'few sisters would seek brother's blood!'

"'Then your son or your daughter's son I doom to do it—Hreidmaro's blood, Hreidmaro's blood avenging—' and his eyes go empty. But Fafnar roared in fury and chased us out of the hall."

Ragan shook himself as if to get rid of the memories, and looked up at Sigfrid. *"Beware Hreidmaro's blood . . ."* Fafnar's words echoed between them.

"And now you have avenged him—" said Sigfrid, leaning against the oak tree with folding arms, "and won the hoard."

"His blood," answered Ragan craftily, seeming to return to the present abruptly, "stained *your* sword."

"Do you think to avoid the blood-guilt by laying it on me? If it was my deed, then the hoard should be mine!" He laughed as Ragan interposed his massive body defensively between the boy and the gold, but he did not like the crazy look he saw in the older man's eyes.

"You killed my brother. . . ." the smith said slowly, looking down the hill to where Fafnar's body lay. "You spill his blood on ground."

"There sits Ragan, wretched in winning, bound to seek vengeance upon the avenger," the chaffinch sang then.

"Be still!" Ragan cried aloud, holding his head in his hands, and Sigfrid covered his eyes, sharing the pain.

"Safer for Sigfrid to strike the smith, winning the wealth for himself alone!" his mate replied.

"I don't want the gold!" the boy shouted. "Or the blood-guilt that goes with it. You set me on to it, Ragan. You were the wielder—I was only the sword in your hand!"

"Not me . . ." whispered Ragan. "Not my doing. His blood burns, and who pays now?" The smith looked up, and suddenly his gaze was terrible. "You were doomed to do it!"

Sigfrid stared back at him, and a chill lifted the hairs along his spine. What was happening? Was this Fafnar's revenge on them, or had Ragan finally gone mad?

"All my plans—all my craft—nothing! Ragan is only hammer of wyrd that shapes you for deed! Now I understand!"

A shadow of Fafnar's spirit coiled between them, and Sigfrid shuddered. Once more he heard the shapeshifter's mockery.

"What do you mean?" Like an echo came the question.

Ragan swayed back and forth, laughing. "You do not know . . . who you are!" Those words too were Fafnar's, or nearly. "I knew," he went on. "I did not think what it means, till now!"

Sigfrid leaped forward, and Ragan heaved to his feet to meet him, breathing in harsh gasps. "Lyngheide was Hiordisa's mother. You are daughter's son of Hreidmaro's daughter! Doomed!"

"Fafnar knew . . ." said Sigfrid softly, still not quite believing. "That's why he laughed at me." His head throbbed, and he did not know if he felt his own or Ragan's pain.

"The blood burns!" Ragan was whispering. "Only more blood can cool it." He reached out clumsily as if to snatch a weapon from the air.

"There stands Ragan and plans he lays to betray the youth who trusts in him. Lying words with wiles will he speak, the smith of bale will avenge his brother—" sang the birds.

Ragan looked up at Sigfrid from under bent brows, and the boy saw that he was weeping. "Now you see why I must kill you?" he asked.

"No," Sigfrid answered, his voice shaking. "We will put this cursed gold back into the ground, and then we will both go home."

"Like loving kindred?" A gnarled finger jabbed toward the boy's heart. "With Hreidmaro's blood, your mother's blood, red on your hands. Kin-slayer!" He looked at his own reddened hand, and his voice cracked with loathing.

"Stop it!" Sigfrid yelled at him. "Don't say that. It isn't true!" His head was ringing like an anvil stone.

"Is truth!" Ragan snarled. He tugged the hammer from his belt and looped it drunkenly through the air, and the birds lifted, screeching, from the tree. "Kin-slayer, can you kill me?"

Fafnar's fury uncoiled in Sigfrid's awareness, a cold rage more deadly than Ragan's fire. *I can't do this, he raised me*—he argued, but unbidden, his body was already flowing through the sequence of movements Helmbari had taught him, drawing his sword. *I will not!*

Ragan's hammer hummed through the air. Sigfrid leaped aside, turning, Gram's momentum bringing the blade around as if it had a will of its own.

"You are . . . the sword . . . in my hand!" Ragan cried, rising into the blow, and then the edge bit, and his head, its lips still writhing, spun away. Time stilled as it arced outward and rolled, ever so slowly, to rest beside Fafnar's body. And it seemed to Sigfrid that the two faces, so similar in feature, bore an identical mocking smile.

When he had finished retching up the last of Fafnar's blood, Sigfrid made his way back to the hoard. Fatal gold indeed. He did not want it. He shuddered at the cold caress of the metal as he fitted the pieces back into their earthen grave. Let them lie here, he thought, where they could curse no others.

Only the rod and the neck ring made him hesitate. He was no king, nor did he seek mastery, and so he set the rune rod with the other things. But the glitter of light on the ring made him think of sunsparks on water, or the silken ripple of bending grain. In the ring, surely, there was only beauty. His fingers lingered on its smoothness, then he wrapped it in the piece of leather and slid it into the journey pouch at his side.

Even his young strength strained at the task that had been easy for two, but he dragged the stone into place once more. It was past noon by the time he had finished. It seemed to him an age of the world since the dawning, and before the sun could set another age must pass.

He looked down at the bodies of the two brothers. His kills. Fafnar had been right to bid him be wary of the blood of Hreidmaro, but the veins in which it flowed were his own.

It is a kinsman's right to bury his relations, he thought grimly, *or a kin-*

slayer's responsibility. But there is no one to whom I can report this killing. The reward and revenge-right for this day's work both belong with me.

He carried first Fafnar, and then Ragan, to the lair that the shape-shifter had gnawed into the mountain. He laid the bodies together and covered them with Fafnar's sleeping furs, and then, giving rein to his grief with a roar that frightened the birds once more from their perches, he pulled down the tree trunks that made its walls and the stones that had supported them.

"Farewell, you sons of Hreidmaro," he said when the rumble of falling rock had faded, "fare you well to the land where the green hemlock grows. Sit at feast once more with your father and Ottar. Let the children of earth sleep in the earth together, linked in peace by death as in life your hatred severed you."

There was no one within the prescribed degree of kinship but himself to complain of the killings, and no one from whom he could ask forgiveness; no one who could do what he had done for Ragan and wash away the blood of the men he had murdered with his own. He understood, with some detached part of his awareness, that this death was the last best gift he could have given to his foster-father—his great-uncle. But that knowledge did not ease the pain.

Heming had spoken more truly than he knew. Now, indeed, Sigfrid was alone.

Exhausted, he leaned against a linden tree. In its branches the birds were still chirping as if there had never been any death in the world. He did not want to hear them. Heartless creatures—their advice had been part of his madness. If the power of Fafnar's blood was still in him, he would rather listen to the linden tree.

The tree was ancient. Before Fafnar arrived it had been growing, and would continue to flourish as he became a memory. *Do your roots reach down to earth's heart, grandmother?* he wondered. *Do they twine with the roots of the Worldtree? If only I could find the center, then I could rest.* And it seemed to him that as the wind sighed in the branches an answer came to him:

"Every tree is part of Yggdrasil, the center-pole that supports the worlds. Become one with me—"

Sigfrid turned, embracing the smooth trunk with both arms and laying his cheek against it. As awareness reached earthward with the tree roots, a tingling ran through his body, like the prickling he felt sometimes on a day of high wind. Its source was deep in the ground, but the tree was drawing it skyward. The tension in his body grew as the earthpower rushed up through the tree trunk; he groaned, grinding his body against it, and cried out in release as it fountained out through the crown of his head and the spreading branches of the tree.

When he could stand once more, he realized that his body had released more than tension. But the fountain of energy had washed away the worst of the anguish that had imprisoned him. The pain was still there, but now a swift river seemed to be flowing between him and his memories.

"Hai! Sigfrid has overcome all of his foes," chirped the titmouse from the top of the linden tree. "Holds he the hoard and the sword, of all ties he is free!"

"Waits now the world for the hero whose courage burns bright—" the chaffinch continued. "Wondrous the woman who waits for the man without fear!"

"Hai, Sigfrid, hear! From the height of the hill see thy way!" The nuthatch flitted toward a rowan tree a little ways up the hill.

Sigfrid looked up at the birds and laughed. "I think I must be still a little mad, but at least your song is more cheerful now."

An hour past, he had wanted only to be away from here, but vantage points were rare in this land of trees. Even if it was only his fancy, there was something in the bird's song. He was nearly to the top of the mountain already; he might as well go high enough to see of the countryside.

The path to the summit was faint, but clear. Fafnar had come this way, but not often in recent years. *He was growing old*, Sigfrid realized then. *He was waiting for me.* He had seen the same thing among the wolves, when they culled a stag or bull elk past his prime. The old warrior would fight to the last, but at the end, death was accepted.

Sigfrid tripped over a tree root and paused, reminding himself to pay attention. Such thoughts might hold some comfort, but they skirted too close to the grief that had downed him before. Better to concentrate on the world around him and let the dead rest.

The bones of the earth showed more clearly as he got higher. Some ancient battle of the gods had shoved the great rocks edgewise. He marveled at the overlaid slabs of grey, water-smoothed stone. Young trees had rooted in the crevices, softening their starkness. Beech trees and rowan, oak and hazel, fought for a share of the thin soil. Here on the summit cold winds had advanced the season. Green grass still clung around the roots, but the leaves that remained were gold and bronze. Rowan berries made a bright scatter of color against bare branches, and the somber green of a few fir trees showed up all the more strongly as winter began to sweep the other foliage away.

Now the path twisted steeply upward, but Sigfrid's muscles were loosened by the exercise, and he leaped up the trail like a young deer. Before him, a core of grey stone burst free of the earth that clothed it. Sigfrid grasped a knob of rock and pulled himself up, got his feet under him and, four-limbed, ran up the rim. Rock curved away before him; he straightened, and suddenly he stood at the summit of the world.

The land fell gradually away in folds of forest behind him, but to the south the drop was a sheer cliff, easing off a bit to the west, but still precipitous. And beyond it—space, light, an immensity defined by blue-veiled hills toward which the sun was sinking. Below him crawled the mightiest of all serpents, its glittering surface a blaze of living gold.

Sigfrid had been born where the great bowl of the northern sky curved over marshland that dissolved into the sea. He had grown to manhood embraced by the woodlands, but always his world had been circumscribed by a close horizon, the scope of his keen gaze limited by reeds or trees. For the first time in his life, he was able to see. His mind told him that the shining wonder below him was the Rhenus. But his heart knew otherwise. All rivers were living beings, but the scale of this one was beyond his imagining. It had carved this great valley to live in; it had shaped the land; it gave meaning to the confusion of the world.

Sigfrid drank deeply of the clean air, and his senses reeled as if it had been mead. *From the height of the hill see thy way!* the bird had told him, and from here he could see everything. But where should he go? The Albings had made it clear there was no place for him among them, even when his mother still lived. He did not suppose that he would be any more welcome in Ulpia Traiana. But he could not return to the forge.

Northward the river disappeared into a mist that seemed to have dissolved the land, though he knew that it flowed through flat fields and marshes toward the sea. But southward the Rhenus curved between round hills like a great gateway. What lay beyond?

Something stirred in the branches below him. He looked down and saw the two ravens who had been watching him all morning sitting there. As if his attention had been a signal, they spread their wings and launched themselves upon the clear air. Three times they circled the summit, then they flapped slowly off southward.

"I need no wurm's blood to understand your meaning," whispered Sigfrid, staring after them. "To the river Wyrd calls me. There lies my way."

Chapter 16 ✳ Judgment of Fire

Taunus Mountains
Harvest, Waning Moon, A.D. 418

Dark, humped woman-shapes gathered around the girl in the center of the circle like ravens trying to decide if a body still lived before beginning to feed. *Ravens eat the dead beside the Longstone . . .* thought Galemburgis, glaring out from beneath her hawk-wing headdress. *Alamanni dead! But they will eat the Burgunds too!*

Once more the judgment seats of the Walkyriun had been set up on the High One's Hill. But there were three fewer than had been there a moon ago. Randgrid was dead and Raganleob wounded, and Brunahild sat with bound hands and feet upon the bare ground. A little wind sprang up and fluttered the golden leaves that still clung to the branches of the birch trees. Galemburgis looked at the lonely figure in the center of the circle and shivered, although the day had been unseasonably warm, and until now, still.

How could you betray us? her heart cried. *We trusted you!*

"Our sister Sigdrifa sits before us," said Hlutgard formally. "Who accuses, and what is the charge that has been brought against her?"

"Oath-breaking is the charge, and I, the accuser." Galemburgis took a deep breath and stood up in her place. "She broke the vows she swore to us and betrayed the Alamanni whom we had agreed to defend."

"That is a heavy accusation," said Hlutgard.

"I do not believe it. She rode with us upon the spirit wind," said Thrudrun. "Her voice joined ours when we laid the curse upon the Burgund army."

Galemburgis nodded. She had not wanted to believe it either. But she could not forget what she had seen and heard. The plain below where the armies had battled was hidden now by autumn haze, but she remembered. Women were wailing in the Alamanni lands, and children would starve because the men who should have provided for them were gone.

"All those things we did together—" The Walkyriun would be hard to convince, but Galemburgis had had long hours to consider every possible objection. "Brunahild had no choice but to go along. But how do we know that even then she was not betraying us, for surely our curses did little harm."

"You are young in craft indeed if you rate our spells so high," old Huld said dryly. "If our magic was infallible, the Rome-folk would never have come into this land. You were eight to one. Nothing that a single one of you could do would have been enough if the gods had willed an Alamanni victory."

Galemburgis stared at her. Was the old woman so partial to her fosterling that she would rather blame the gods?

"We took the omens," Golla whispered harshly. "The signs favored the Alamanni. We could not have been wrong!" The warmistress sat sunk in upon herself as if she had taken the death-wound that had killed Randgrid. Only now did Galemburgis understand how great a love had been between them. Randgrid had died in Golla's arms.

The Alamanni grieve and we grieve, thought Galemburgis. *And it is all your doing, Brunahild, all yours!*

Brunahild sat without speaking, curled in upon herself like a frightened child. She had screamed and railed at them when they had taken her, but since then she had been still. Did fear or fury lie concealed in that silence? Galemburgis shivered a little, watching her, despite the warmth of the day.

"In the two weeks since the battle I have spoken with many of the Alamanni chieftains," said Hlutgard slowly. "The omens were with them. They say they were winning, until the Burgunds rallied around their king."

"I have seen many battles." Huld's voice was biting. "And after the first few blows, they are always a muddle. If the Alamanni think they can pin down the moment they began to lose, they have been listening to too many songs! The bard uses words to make sense of the chaos, but let us not confuse that with reality."

"But all things must have causes!" Golla lifted her head. "Or the etins will eat the world!" As if to echo her words, wind swept the hilltop, plucking berries from the rowan branches and scattering them across the stones.

"Will you listen to the men who fought or an old woman who was not even at the battle?" cried Galemburgis. "All know the Burgund king was untried as a warrior, but somehow he put heart into his men. And he did it after Brunahild spared him. I saw how she faced him, how they talked together!"

"But you watched from a distance," Huld objected. "How could you know what passed between them? Perhaps she was cursing him—"

"Perhaps, but we do know what the Burgund king said, for there were many who heard him," said Thrudrun reluctantly. "He cried that the Walkyrja had spared him, that she had brought him the victory."

In the west, the sun was lighting its own funeral pyre. The day was dying and the year was dying, and the flower of the Alamanni warriors had burned on the Longstone field.

"It does not matter what they said. The man was alone and unarmed. She could have spitted him, and it would have been over. Are we not the Choosers of the Slain? Were we not clearly instructed? Brunahild did not even point the spear!" Galemburgis's voice thinned on the last words. *And then the Burgunds attacked the Alamanni, and my brother. . . .*

"You accuse her of disobedience?" asked Hlutgard.

"I accuse her of treachery!" exclaimed Galemburgis. "We know that she is a friend to the Burgunds. When Gudrun came to plead with us, Brunahild took her off where no one could hear what they had to say. I say it was then that the Burgunds bought her. She and Gudrun plotted how to betray the Alamanni army that day!"

They stared at her in appalled silence. There was doom in those words. Wind rattled the bare branches like bones.

"Brunahild, you must speak to us," said Hlutgard. "Your sisters do not wish to condemn you unheard."

A quiver ran through the folds of the blue cloak, but Brunahild made no sound. *Does she admit it?* thought Galemburgis, amazed, despite her fury, to find that the thought gave her pain. Perspiration trickled down her back, soaking into her gown.

"Sigdrifa, you stubborn child, hiding from this will not make it go away!" said Huld tartly. "If you did not break your vows, then say so. If you did, then do us the courtesy to say why!" She sounded irritated, but perhaps the odd warmth was making them all a little mad.

"Which oaths?" The answer came muffled, as if from underground.

The accused straightened then and shook the tangles of dark hair back from her face, and Galemburgis took a step back, as if she had seen a troll-woman sitting there. "I swore to obey the gods, the voice of my soul, and the will of the Walkyriun, but you never told me what to do if they did not agree. So I kept the oath I swore to the god!"

"You lie!" exclaimed Galemburgis. "The gods favored the Alamanni!"

"I did not see the deathlight," she said dully. "In all else I obeyed, but I would not send one to the Hero Hall whom Wodan did not want there! You serve the gods; how dare you accuse me?"

"How do we *dare?*" said Hlutgard, frowning. "Some of us have served the gods for more winters than you have been living. Do you think that in all that time we have not learned to know their will? And shall we now distrust the skills on which we have based our lives because of one green girl?"

Exultation surged in Galemburgis's breast as she realized that the leader of the Walkyriun was angry.

"Such gifts, such gifts," said Golla softly. "But even if she meant no wrong, how can we trust her?"

"Do you defend her?" Galemburgis said furiously. "It is because of her that Randgrid died!" *And my brother* . . . the thought went on. *My little brother, who was like a babe to me.*

"She cannot remain one of us," said Thrudrun regretfully.

"She must be punished, or the tribes will no longer trust us," said Hrodlind.

"She must pay the blood-price!" cried Galemburgis. "The spirits of the slain cry out for revenge!" She saw her brother's dead face, as she had seen it in nightmares, beardless chin cleft by a Burgund blade.

"No!" Huld stood up suddenly. "This is not justice, but your own fears speaking. We are the Walkyriun! Will you let the chieftains make our policy? Are we so uncertain that we can bear no difference of opinion? So weak that we fear the strength of one girl?"

"She must be cast out," said Hlutgard rigidly. "She has disobeyed."

"Disciplined, perhaps," Huld began, "but what is this talk—"

"But not killed," said Thrudrun. "The Huns may have cast off their daughter, but such an act even they could not ignore. . . ."

"Let her go," said Golla. "We were wrong to accept her." Her words were followed by a murmur of agreement.

"This is unworthy of our sisterhood!" Huld exclaimed. "I warn you, if Brunahild is cast out you will also lose me!"

"Go, then!" exclaimed Hrodlind. "This is your fault, Huld. We let you go your own way, and now your fosterling thinks she can defy us."

"I do defy you!" Brunahild found her voice at last. "You think my curses are powerful? Perhaps I'll curse you all!" Her breath came out in a harsh *"carrk,"* like a raven, and Hrodlind's fingers flickered in the warding sign. Brunahild gulped air and made the sound again.

With horror, Galemburgis realized that it was laughter. "Don't you see she is dangerous?" she cried. "It is not enough to send her away. She must be stripped of her powers!"

"Why do you hate me?" shrieked Brunahild. "I did Wodan's will!"

"I see that you believe that—" said Golla sadly. "But if we ordered you to accept his will as we hear it instead of as you do, would you obey?"

Brunahild stared at the warmistress. The struggle was clear in her green gaze, but she did not answer. *She cannot!* thought Galemburgis in triumph. *She is too proud to give in, and so she is doomed!*

"My child, even if you swore to obey I fear we could not believe you," Golla went on. "You will always do what your heart says. You must see now why we cannot trust you. We will let you go, but when captured warriors are set free it is without their weapons. So you will also understand that we must take back all that we gave. . . ."

Galemburgis took a long look around her, willing the pounding of her heart to ease. On every side the land fell away from the hilltop, ridges hazed with distance on one side, on the other, the hidden plain. What was done here would be forever. This place was the center of the world.

Hlutgard stood up, trembling, and wrenched the blue cloak from the prisoner's back. "You say you did Wodan's will. Well, if you know his will better than your elders, then let the god show us as he did before! You are Brunahild, only Brunahild—Sigdrifa dies here. Thus do we sever you from our sisterhood. Your blood will be washed from the harrow. No more will you work magic. If Wodan loves you, let him prove it now!"

She turned her back, the folds of her dark cloak settling to stillness once more. Swiftly Hrodlind did the same, and then, one by one, Thrudrun and Hadugera, Swanborg, and Golla, and finally Galemburgis, with a triumphant swirl of blue wool. Only Huld remained seated, her cloak drawn over her face in mourning. But Galemburgis could hear the hiss of breath from the one who was Sigdrifa no longer, and like an echo, the moaning of that strange, warm wind around the High One's Hill.

"Brunahild . . ." The voice was gentle with mockery.

"I am Sigdrifa!" She turned her face against the hard ground, wincing, for they had left her only a coarse shift to shield her from the stones.

"Doom-driver, rather, for doom is what you bring, to yourself as well as others. Would you not rather be Brunahild?"

"You were always bitter as an oak gall, Galemburgis," she said hoarsely, and winced as a heel thudded into her ribs.

"None of that, Galemburgis," came Golla's voice behind her. "Or you will be sent back to Fox Dance. This is justice, not some child's revenge."

Do you want me to thank you? thought the prisoner. *At least I can hate Galemburgis, and understand why she hates me.* The ground was gritty with chips from the outcrop of quartz-veined granite that pushed through the skin of soil. She had seen the place once, from below, shining in the sun above the remains of the old Roman wall. It was known as a place of power, but the Walkyriun did not use it for their workings. *Until now. But why here?* she wondered dully, and then, *why me?*

"Father . . ." she whispered into the empty darkness. "They do not believe the word you gave me. It is you they have rejected—help me, show your power!"

She heard the click of flints and then the crackle of kindling and a breath of heat against her back. Such a simple, familiar thing—but it filled her with fear. All the familiar things were turning against her now.

"Bring her—"

She thought that was Hlutgard speaking, but sounds came muffled. Hard hands jerked her to her feet; she was pulled forward. And then, finally, they untied the blindfold. She blinked and turned her head away from the sudden light, recoiling as she saw the blank face of the woman who held her.

The Walkyriun were masked. She grimaced. Did they think she would not know them? But perhaps they were right—the fight went out of her suddenly—for if they could do this to her, then truly she did not know them anymore.

"Sigdrifa is dead. . . ." Hlutgard's voice rang like bronze. "With her we must kill all that held her power—"

"Hlutgard—" the girl cried, seeing the folds of dark blue wool in the Walkyrja's arms. "How can you do this? You brought me here! You yourself said it was Wodan who chose me!"

The only answer was a flash of metal and a tearing sound that rasped her soul. They were tearing up the cloak—long strips of wool flapped in the red light of the fire. And then, one by one, they cast the pieces on the flames.

"This we do for the good of the Walkyriun." Was that supposed to be an answer? Abruptly Brunahild understood. Hlutgard was like a mother bear who sees her cubs threatened.

"But I loved you—I would never hurt you—" she whispered. If she did not fight them, perhaps they would believe and forgive her, even now.

"Liar," responded Galemburgis. "You already have."

The bonfire was burning strongly. Wind whipped the flames into fiery fingers that reached for their prey. She coughed at the stink of burning wool, but she could not look away.

She remembers the cloak wrapped warm about her as she feasted with the others after her initiation. All that night they sang and drank the heady mead, laughing at each other's jokes in perfect understanding. They had all been equals then, sharing the same joy, and she had belonged among them. Would she ever belong anywhere again?

Another masked figure came forward with the white linen gown on whose weaving she had labored so long. She thought she recognized Hadugerda, who had helped her to build her loom. She thought of the dreams that had gone into the gown's making . . . her dreams were burning . . . they were taking away her memories.

She remembers how she warped the threads, sorting through the tangles, measuring them out and tying the stones to their ends so that they would hang straight and true. And each one had a name—courage and endurance, skill, understanding. . . . Where will she find a warp on which to weave her life anew?

And then it was the turn of the raven headdress. Black feathers were plucked out by Swanborg's skillful fingers, crisping into blacker ash as they touched the fire, or whirled away by the wind that whipped the flames.

Brunahild turned to her. "Swanborg, it was you who taught me the ways of birds. You saw how the ravens came to me. How can you take that from me?" But the other woman did not reply.

She remembers how the ravens circled the cave where she sought shelter from the snowstorm. She remembers how they watched from the fir trees when she took her oath to the Walkyriun. Would the ravens still follow her now?

The night was moonless, and the wind was rising, lifting the hair that clung to her damp brow. *Fly home to the heavens!* she thought despairingly as those feathers of ash floated upward. *Be my messengers! Father of Ravens, where are you? You said you would come to me!*

She stiffened as Thrudrun held out the linen bag in which she kept her rune staves.

"These runes we gave to our sister," she said harshly. "Now they are taken away. . . ." She drew out a stave, and Sigdrifa moaned as she saw the shape of *Naudhiz*, carved into the wood and reddened with her own blood. *Thrudrun, Thrudrun, you taught me how to carve and stain those runes. Were you afraid I would outstrip you in skill?*

Frowning, Thrudrun tossed the stave into the fire. *Berkano* and *Mannaz*, *Eiwaz* and *Sowilo* and *Laguz*, one by one the others followed. The yew sticks burned readily, sparking and glowing and falling at last into bars of white ash. But Brunahild had no skill to read their pattern. The runes had been destroyed without the patterning of chance or of design.

She remembers how she read the runes for a young woman, the time Huld took her out among the steadings where the folk scratched a living from plots cleared among the trees. She had seen fortune, a good man, and children. The girl had given her fresh milk and oatcakes warm from the baking slab, and Huld had praised her.

The god had said that the runes would remain with her, but would those strange signs scratched into wood or stone still have meaning now?

They broke her wand and cast it into the flames. Golla threw in her shield and sword and spear. The fire was not hot enough to melt the metal, but sword and spearhead sagged and twisted, losing edge and temper until their shape was gone.

I will never ride armed like a warrior again, seeing in men's eyes that flicker of admiration and fear. That is what they are doing to me, she thought then. *My body remains, but all that made me myself they will destroy. And if I am not Sigdrifa, am I still Wodan's daughter? Is that why he has not come?*

And still the flames were fed. Hrodlind threw in the mortar and pestle with which she had prepared her herbs, and they cracked in the fire. Did the herbmistress hate her because she had learned more from Huld?

"When the arrow seeks a prey the hunter did not target, it must be broken," said Golla, breaking Brunahild's bow and the arrows she had taught the girl to fashion and tossing them into the fire. The rising wind fanned the flames.

She had loved the other priestesses as her sisters, but as they continued their destruction she found herself thinking of all the reasons they might have to dislike her. Though they had said they loved her, all except Huld were now her enemies. She had thought they cared for Huld too, but they had imprisoned her. Was everything she had believed a lie?

The things that had been her life for eight years burned like the gravegoods men lay on the pyre. But if she had been dead, their essence, and her spirit, would have gone free. They burned, and hope burned with them, and faith, and love.

"I am Sigdrifa!" she whispered desperately.

"You are no one and nothing," came Galemburgis's voice at her ear. Brunahild saw the glitter of eyes behind the mask.

"You are making me a spirit, unblessed and unburied. But such beings have power to haunt the living. Perhaps, Galemburgis, I will haunt you!"

She hiccoughed, and felt herself shaken once more by laughter. Madness gibbered very close now, and why should she resist it? Once, she had known spells that could blast the body and sear the soul. Now they had left her only despair.

"Even a doomed spirit can be bound," said Hrodlind. She turned, a knife gleaming in her hand.

"Stab me!" cried Brunahild. "Burn me! I will become Goldmad and arise from the flames!" She was burning already, with fever or the fire.

"Nothing so easy—" said the Walkyrja. She grasped a handful of Brunahild's tangled hair and began to hack at it with the blade.

Brunahild screamed. The fire blazed up in a sudden gust of hot wind. She struggled, gasping at the pain, then Galemburgis's fist slammed into her temple, the dark strands parted, and she fell. Hrodlind grunted and cast the handful into the fire. Dazed, Brunahild tried to roll away, but the others held her while the woman sawed at each handful and fed it to the flames.

There was a great deal of it. Brunahild's hair had been glossy as a raven's wing, as long as a mare's tail. It burned with a stink worse than the wool, the long strands curling like serpents as they took the flame.

"Why?" whimpered Brunahild when it was over. "You have cast me out already. Why this shame?"

She rolled her head against the earth. It felt light, as if it would float away. *Soon I will leave this body,* she thought hazily, *and be free.*

"Only a free woman can use power," the words came like an echo. "So we cut your hair like a thrall's. Your tools and weapons have been broken. Now your body must be bound."

She began to struggle again as they lifted her. Someone lifted a torch, and she saw iron staples set into the stone. They thrust her down upon the hard surface. The bonds on her feet gave way as someone cut them, but before she could kick, new ropes tightened around each ankle. She felt them pulled taut, the tension as they were tied to the rings. Then her arms were wrenched apart and tied as well.

"Why not kill me quickly," she gasped. "Why leave me for the wolves?"

"You will not die—" said Hlutgard softly. "Each day someone will feed you. But bound you will be until some man finds you. You will be his then, to warm his bed and bear his children. And that servitude will cut you off forever from your powers."

"But what if no one comes?" asked Hrodlind.

"They'll come—" hissed Galemburgis. "We'll put the word about in the hunting camps and on the river that a woman lies here for the taking. If he is wise, her new master will use her before he even unties her bonds!"

She could feel them looking down at her. She blinked, but the world was whirling around her. In the silence, the voice of the wind grew louder, the hot breath of Muspelheim rattling drying leaves.

"Do you still believe the god spoke to you?" asked Hlutgard then. "He has allowed us to strip and shame you. Do you still believe you know his will better than we?"

That is why they are punishing me, she thought, her head still ringing from the blow. *Not because of the Alamanni, but because I challenged them.* . . . She had tried to obey. Had her vision on the battlefield been all a delusion? Why had Wodan made no sign to save her, if his commands had been real?

Had the god abandoned her too?

"I loved you," she whispered. "But you have killed love. I am what you made me . . . and what you are making me now! If Wodan will not curse you, then listen to me. May all that you have made me suffer come upon you—your sisterhood be severed, your tools and weapons burned. May you too be shamed and cast out to wander, and your names forgotten by the world!"

How hot it was—she must be fevered, and soon death would set her free. As if from a great distance she heard women arguing, and then other voices, shrieking war-cries upon the wind. She knew that she was moaning, but she did not try to stop. What need had she for courage, or even reason, now? Fragments of old songs chased each other through her awareness and were lost in the shadows that were gathering around her.

She knew, as if in a dream, when the Walkyriun left the hilltop.

Nine by nine the Choosers ride. . . .

She slid into the dark.

* * *

Huld started up from her seat by the dead hearth. Had she heard the Walkyriun coming? The door was up, for the night was still warm— too warm, thought Huld. The muspel-wind was blowing, and it brought madness. Through the dark opening she saw the darker shape of the man they had left to guard her, but nothing moved beyond him but the wind in the trees.

I was mad to speak my mind to them, she thought grimly. *I should have seen they were in no state to hear reason.* She would have been free to help Brunahild now if she had pretended to go along. She understood all too well what had happened. She had even suspected that this confrontation must come. But not so soon!

We proclaim Wodan's will as if our runes were a ring in the nose of a bull, but as well hope to bind the wind. He has his own purposes, and you cannot buy his favor . . . and Brunahild is his child. . . .

She sighed, wondering how much tonight's ritual would leave of the girl she loved. There had been a terrible thoroughness in the way they had gone through Brunahild's belongings. They had taken everything that might be used for magic—

No, Huld thought suddenly, not quite everything. They had not known about the arrow that had carried Brunahild's message, that time she was lost in the blizzard. It had been found later, and the girl had given it to her teacher.

Smiling grimly, the Walkyrja went to her bed-place and felt in the otter-skin bag in which she kept the tools of her magic until she found the arrow. Its fletching was tattered, the sinew that held the point coming unbound, but it vibrated with Brunahild's essence.

"High One," she whispered, "you listen to me!" She waited, and in the close stillness it seemed to her that she sensed something waiting, at once angry and a little amused. She grunted. In a long life, she had learned well how to argue with the god. "Laugh at me if you will, but it is your fault that child is suffering. At least give her some comfort. Find her a new life, since we in our foolishness have destroyed her world. I know the Walkyrja's warding spells. Listen, and I will sing a way through their circle for you to go to her."

Huld sat down then, turning the arrow between her stiff fingers, and began to sing.

Brunahild's spirit swung between troubled sleep and bitter waking, bound to her body by a tie more tenuous than the ropes that held her to the rock. The crystalline stone beneath her amplified every emotion.

Even if she had been in any normal state, by then it might have been hard to know what was real.

When discomfort drove her toward awareness of her body, grief beyond bearing would drive her spirit out again. She spun beyond time or direction, wailing like a lost child.

Once more she galloped through the encampment of the Alan outlaws, and where she rode men died. Words echoed in memory. *"Go back to the west, little one. Let Wodan use you there."*

"He has used me—" she cried. "Am I a broken blade to be cast aside when the battle is done?" And very faintly, in a voice that sounded like Huld's, came an answer: *"Even the broken blade may be reforged. . . ."* An image came to her of a hammer breaking metal, and the pieces sparking and twisting, as her possessions had burned in the fire. But she could see only the destruction, not the weapon that would come out of that flame.

Awareness whirled once more. She was a tiny child. A huge man with a black beard was tossing her up into the air and catching her with a roar of laughter. *"See, she does not cry. She never cries, my battle-maid!"* he said to the warriors around him. And then he put her into the arms of a woman and went away. But when the doorflap had fallen closed behind him, she stood and wept bitter tears.

Brunahild groaned aloud, reliving that desolation.

"Father, where are you?" she cried, as she had cried when she was bound upon the tree. The world whirled around her. And once more the answer came to her. *"Where I have always been . . ."*

A door opened, she felt his presence and lay sobbing, aware at once of the pain in her flesh and an ecstasy that expanded until human consciousness could no longer contain it. Suddenly she was standing on the rock, looking down at the form pinioned to the stone.

"Am I dead?"

"The silver cord still binds you—"

Stark against the stars she saw the cloaked shape of a man with a broad-brimmed hat, leaning on a spear. Brunahild flinched away, then stopped, facing him as she had faced him among the stones.

"The ashes of my life float upon the wind. Where were you when they mocked me? Men call you betrayer, but I never believed them. Masked One, why did you betray me?"

"Why did you betray the Walkyriun?" It was a word spoken by the darkness, illuminating everything.

Shock stilled her spirit. "I did what you wanted—"

"What I wanted was what must be. . . ." came his reply. "Only

Fricca knows all fates. I watch her at her weaving, and I see Change; I see possibilities. To the man on the ground, the flare of lightning in the forest is random, but I know why Donar throws his hammer, and I see where the tree will fall."

"I am not a tree!" she exclaimed. "Could you not have protected me?"

"Indeed." He nodded. "A tree does not make choices. The threads Fricca weaves are twined by the choices of men upon a warp spun by Wyrd. You swore to serve me. . . ." The cloaked figure turned, and she cowered against the stone.

"You said that you would love me—"

"I told you—" Now she heard the pain. "To those I love, I am most cruel of all. . . ."

"Death and danger I will face laughing, but will your purpose be served by shaming your daughter? Will I be able to serve you, slaving for some thrall?"

She saw the gleam of an eye beneath his hat's shadow, and heard thunder, though there was still no moisture in the air. A memory came to her then, of a story she had heard, and suddenly she saw how something splendid might come out of this destruction.

"If you cannot free me, then give me to a hero! Ward this rock so that only a warrior like Helgi can approach it, and I will be his Walkyrja, and hold up my head once more!"

There was a great silence. The god turned, gazing westward, and it seemed to her that he sighed.

"A warrior like Helgi . . ." he echoed her.

"Do it," she gasped, "for if I am taken by a man unworthy, I will cut my own throat and go to Hella, and never seek your hall!"

"Child"—the voice of the god was suddenly gentle—"do you think to threaten Me? I may heed only the prayers that serve my purpose. If I give you a hero, you will be the instrument of his destiny. I have been your father, but you will forget me in a lover's arms. Chooser, is this what you choose?"

"I do!"

"You do not ask me for content or comfort?" he said with bitter laughter. "That is well, for all I have to give is ecstasy!"

He turned to her, and she trembled, seeing for the first time his face unshadowed. His right eye glittered feverishly, but his left swallowed light. She flinched from the one, but the other was more terrible, for if she looked into it she would fall into the dark well of his wisdom and be lost.

"You are light in the darkness!" she cried, feeling a strange heat building within. "You are fire in the mind! Strike, and I will endure your flame!"

His face blazed. "It is in the fire that you will find me, my beloved. . . ." His kiss burned her brow.

She was whirling back into her body, falling into a friendly darkness that cradled her in strong arms. Resting in that powerful embrace, she found peace.

Then she felt a cool weight, as if a cloak had been drawn over her. Sound receded, but it seemed to her that she heard a whisper. *"Sleep, my child, and dream of glory. . . ."* and then, *"No one who fears my spear shall pass this fire. . . ."* If there was more, it was lost in the sudden rush of the wind.

Brunahild dreamed.

The wind swirled the remains of the bonfire, and an eye of fire opened among the embers. Again wind gusted. From the ashes of Brunahild's life leaped a spear of light. The wind swept it skyward in a shower of sparks that arched over the nearest trees to lodge in the tangled boughs of a fallen fir. The dry needles sparked, brightness ran down the branch, and suddenly it was blazing. Heat fed on heat, dry wind driving it down the hillside. The bronze leaves of an oak tree caught fire, and it began to burn steadily, but the evergreens were like torches, primed with pitch and dry from a summer of little rain, exploding and seeding sparks everywhere.

The fever wind gained strength from the heat the fire was releasing. Fitful, it sent a spear of flame backward, and a clump of thorn began to burn on the other side of the hill. Then it was blowing down the slope, driving the smoke and the worst of the heat away from the rocks at its summit and the human who lay bound there.

I am the fire. . . . Laughing, Brunahild rode the wind down the mountain, striking tree after tree until the hilltop was surrounded by a ring of fire.

Somebody was shouting. Huld came out of her trance, smelled smoke, and coughed.

"But there is a whole valley between us. The fire cannot come this far—" said someone outside.

"The forest is dry, and the muspel-wind changes direction like a mad thing," a closer voice replied. "No telling where it will drive the flames. I think we should be ready to flee."

Huld came to the door of the hall and peered northward, frowning at the red glow in the sky above the Feldberg. Suddenly a jagged flicker of brightness rimmed the top of a hill.

"This is Brunahild's doing!" That voice was Hrodlind's. "We should have gagged her before she could curse us—"

"No such thing!" snapped Hlutgard. "Thrudrun and Randgrid were lax in putting out the fire!"

Bale-worker, thought Huld, *is this the way you chose to set your daughter free? Ring her with fire, but do not let her burn, lord—or us, either!* she added, as more shouting called the rest of the women to awaken, to pack their belongings on the ponies, to flee.

Smiling sourly, she turned back into the house to gather up her things.

As the fire blazed through the Taunus, Brunahild's spirit soared. She saw the slopes between her and Fox Dance burning, and the figures of the Walkyriun hurrying down the path toward the plain. Awareness sped farther, drawn by the dark gleam of the river. On its bank, she saw the glitter of a campfire, and beside it, sitting with a bright blade laid across his knees, a boy with wolf's eyes.

Chapter 17 ❄ Awakening

Taunus Mountains
Blood Moon, A.D. 418

The breeze still carried the stink of the burning. Sigfrid squinted upward, but this was not the strange hot wind that had kept his nerves on edge the day before the fire, and the plume of smoke that had darkened the sun that morning was thinning to a grey veil. *"The sons of Surt ride from the south,"* he had heard a harper sing once in Alb's hall, but if Muspel's fiery army had touched the earth, it had passed on.

The ponies picked their way between cliffs of brown-red stone and the strongly flowing grey-green waters of the Rhenus, scorched leaves and bits of charcoal crunching beneath their hooves. The fire had centered in the heights to the south and east, but high winds had carried live embers for miles, hurling them through the heavens like bits of burning star. Throughout the night he had sat watching the red light grow, all his senses prickling with unease. Beside the river he had been in no danger. Perhaps it was some aftereffect of Fafnar's blood that made him so aware of the anger, and the anguish, in that wind. He did not want to feel it. He had enough sorrow of his own.

Ahead, the cliffs curved away, and he glimpsed thatched roofs through the trees. Settlements clustered wherever the streams that came rushing down from the Taunus had carved out a bit of level ground. Some of them maintained outposts on the low islands that thrust themselves up through the waters where the river was shallowest, and levied a toll on the boats that tried to run the shifting channels there. But whether it was because Sigfrid seemed to have nothing worth stealing, or perhaps because they saw his sword, no one had troubled him. One of the Roman coins he had found in Ragan's pouch should buy him a supply of food and fodder for the horses. There had not been much time for hunting, and grass was scanty on the rocky riverbank.

"See the fire?" said the man they told him to ask. "Burned all night, sent everything up there running. Big stag came crashing through here like his tail's on fire, whang into my old woman's washing!" He shook with what was meant to be laughter.

"Didn't she just swear when she saw the clothes all muddy," said a girl who was bringing a bucket of water up from the stream. "But they was all over soot from the fire already. She'd have to wash them again anyhow."

"That's not all came running," said one of the other women. "They say the Walkyriun—" She paused as a big man appeared in the doorway to the sleeping hall, yawning. His torso was bare, but he wore an arm ring of gilded bronze and there was an old scar on his shoulder, and Sigfrid stiffened like a strange wolf when the pack leader appears.

"Hardomann, son of Hardobert, welcomes you—" The chieftain looked Sigfrid up and down without expression, trying to reconcile his ragged breeches and leather vest with his richly mounted baldric and sword.

"Wulf Wurmsbane," Sigfrid replied, though "Wolfshead" might have been more accurate. He was not very proud of his own name just now.

"Are you heading into the hills to seek the woman, then?"

"A wondrous woman waits. . . ." a bird sang in memory. Sigfrid's gaze sharpened.

"They say the Walkyriun have staked out that girl who betrayed us to the Burgunds," Hardomann continued thoughtfully. "Left her on a rock for any man to find. Some of my thralls tried the road this morning, said the fire was still burning. But a man like you might be able to get through."

"It was a big fire," said Sigfrid slowly. "Could anything live?"

The chieftain shrugged. "That's your only road south, anyway, unless you want to swim. The cliffs come right down into the water just beyond that bend."

Sigfrid nodded. If the girl was dead, he would bury her bones. But in the oak tree behind the hall he saw two ravens waiting, and his heart began to beat with the same anticipation he had felt on the peak above Wurm Fell.

*   *   *

Sigfrid rode through a wasteland, coughing as the dawn wind reawakened the acrid stink of the fire. It was a world from which all color had been stolen, a land of scorched rock and seared bushes and the blackened skeletons of trees. Nothing seemed to move but the swirling ashes, but the stillness was deceptive. There were still hot spots beneath the charred branches, and sometimes a particularly strong gust would stir them to flame.

Sigfrid used to dream sometimes, when he and Ragan had labored too long at the forge, that he walked among the glowing hills and valleys he saw in its coals. The night before, he had camped at the edge of Muspelheim. He rode through it now, but the flame that had swept through the world was burnt out, as his old life had been burned away.

The pony snorted, and Sigfrid looked up, blinking as he realized that the treetops that were catching the first rays of the sun ahead of him still had leaves. Had they crossed the fire zone already? Then he saw that the devastation curved around the hill, a lake of grey ashes lapping an isle of green trees and upthrust stone. The waterskins tied to his saddle sloshed as he turned the pony uphill, and the beast shook its head nervously as wind whistled suddenly through the trees.

An outcropping of granite jutted ahead of him, shadowing the path. The pony's ears pricked; Sigfrid saw someone emerging from the darkness and reined in. The day before he had met several other men coming back down the mountain, discouraged by the desolation or frightened by the flames. He wondered why this one waited here. The wind picked up, and Sigfrid's nostrils flared at the sudden overwhelming smell of fire.

"Who comes . . . to challenge me?" The voice seemed to resound from the very earth. The hair lifted on Sigfrid's scalp. Those were Fafnar's words.

"Fafnar's bane." The answer came unbidden. "Do you return from Hella's hall to accuse me?"

The horses sidled nervously, and Sigfrid slid a leg over the beast's side and dropped to the ground. Was this Fafnar's spirit, or someone with the same powers? If only he could *see*.

"Go home, warrior. A foe too great for your strength waits here."

"This sword has already killed some who thought so," said Sigfrid stoutly, and Gram's hilt settled into his hand. It seemed to him that the rising wind hissed with laughter in reply.

"I have a spear that can break that sword. . . ."

Sigfrid stared, the prickling in his scalp spreading to his skin. Wodan had broken Sigmund's sword, but surely it was the god who had taught him how to forge it again. Had he helped only so that Sigfrid could get rid of Fafnar? Did he too desire the hoard?

"What do you want of me?" the boy cried. There was a long silence.

"To warn you—" The voice was gentle now. "The enemy that awaits will pierce your heart with a blade sharper than your sword, and burn you more fiercely than this fire. Will you choose that danger willingly?"

"I choose," snarled Sigfrid, his fury exploding at those who had manipulated him into becoming a murderer, "not to be threatened by you or anyone! I am going up that hill, and woe to whatever stands in my way!" Gram hissed from its sheath, and he started forward.

Wind roared and a spear of light lanced toward him. Instinctively he swung up the sword. Radiance glanced from its blade and flared around him, igniting anything that remained unburned. Heat seared his skin as the fire roared skyward. He tried to shield his eyes with his arm. If this was illusion, it could not harm him. But if the flames were real and the girl was still alive up there, they could kill.

Holding his breath, Sigfrid plunged through the fire.

Brilliance blinded him, but suddenly the heat was gone. He stopped, blinking, and felt his cheeks cooled by a great rush of wind. When it had passed, he could see again. The fire, and whatever had caused it, were gone. The light he saw gleamed from the veins of white that banded the grey rock above him. Fir trees surrounded it, still unscorched by the flames. Swiftly he clambered upward.

The lower part of the rock was still shrouded in the deep shade of the trees. It took him a moment to realize that the patch of darker shadow upon it was a crumpled length of wool. He felt his way downward across the rough stone, lips thinning as he saw the shape beneath the cloth, and pale hands tied by thick ropes to iron staples sunk into the stone. But Gram made short work of such bonds. He sheathed the sword and knelt to draw the cloak away.

For a moment he thought the rumors had been wrong, and it was a boy, a thrall with cropped hair, who lay there. Then he noted the delicate curve of cheek and chin and the faint swell of a breast beneath the coarse shift she wore. But she had been ill-treated. Her skin, pale as old ivory, was mottled by dirt and bruising, and she was woefully thin.

The girl seemed deeply asleep. Frowning, he watched the slow rise and fall of her chest, touched her brow, and found it hot. After such an ordeal dryness was to be expected, and probably fever. Carefully Sigfrid tucked the cloak back around her, then ran back down the hill to catch the horses, bring up food and the waterskins, and build a small fire in the ashes where an old campfire had been. The water in his bronze kettle had just begun to steam when he heard a sigh.

In a moment he was beside her, carrying one of the waterskins. Holding his breath, he dribbled a little between her lips, and after a moment he saw the tip of a pink tongue licking at the moisture. He smiled, remembering a fox kit he had raised once, and gave her some more. Light flowed down the rock as the sun rose. The girl moved a little, whimpering, and at that moment the sun lifted above the trees and lit the top of the hill.

"Easy . . . easy . . ." Sigfrid whispered as she moaned. "You are safe now. It is only the day!"

She was trying to sit up. He got his arm beneath her thin shoulders and lifted. She started to struggle, eyelids flickering, and then, with a suddenness that startled him, she focused on his face and, blindingly, smiled.

Brunahild blinked, dazzled as she saw the radiance of the god who had kissed her to sleep reflected in the face of the boy who had awakened her. She had seen him in her dream of glory, and now she saw the light of a new day blaze in his eyes. Words the Walkyriun thought they had stripped from her welled through her—

"Hail to thee, Day!" She wondered if she were dreaming still. "Hail to thee, Day's sons! Hail, Night, and daughter of Night. With blithe eyes look on both of us, and grant to us victory." Her rescuer frowned as if he thought her sufferings had driven her crazy, but she laughed. He would learn, when she began to teach him her magic. She had gone through madness to awaken to this glorious day!

"Hail, holy gods—" "Hail, goddesses! Hail, Mother Earth, who givest to all—" She set her palm against the cold stone and felt a quiver of power in reply. "Goodly spells and speech bespeak we from you, and healing hands in this life!"

The ecstasy the god had promised rushed through her, then she sagged back, gasping as each abused joint and muscle began to yammer in pain.

"Lie down now, please—" the boy began. "No, the stone's cold. Let me get you down by the fire!"

Brunahild bit her lip as he lifted her, distracted a little from her
pain by the strangeness of being held. She could feel the movement
of muscle in his body like the sliding strength beneath a horse's skin.
He carried her without apparent effort, which was just as well. She
would have fallen in a heap if she had tried to move.

Then she saw the circle of ash and embers where the Walkyriun
had burned her life away.

"Not there . . . not there . . ." Strengthless fingers scratched at
his arm; she turned her face into his chest so as not to see.

"Are you afraid of the fire?" came his voice in her ear. "I'll make
a bed for you on the fallen needles beneath the trees. No need to
fear." Awkwardly he patted her shoulder, and her trembling began to
ease.

He held her one-armed while he spread the cloak, then laid her
down. Brunahild's head spun. In another moment, it seemed, he was
back with two more cloaks to cover her. A shiver ran through her—
odd, since she had been so filled with light a moment before. He
tucked the cloth around her, and very gradually, warmth began to
return to her limbs.

"I'm making broth," he said softly. She tried to nod, but exhaustion
was already reclaiming her. She swallowed automatically when he held
the cup to her lips, and then slid down into unconsciousness once
more.

For three days and nights Sigfrid fought for the girl's life as once
he had fought to defend his own. Dimly he felt that giving life back
to this battered creature might wash away some of the blood that
stained his hands. She shook alternately with chills and fever, or slept
so deeply it frightened him. When she burned he sponged her skin
with a wet cloth, and when she shivered he held her; when she slept
he ranged the woods beyond the fire line in search of healing herbs.
Neither he nor Ragan had known much illness, but he had nursed
ailing animals, and sometimes in their forest walks the smith would
toss him some bit of the earthfolk's lore.

In her fever the girl babbled. Disjointed fragments from her nightmares told him something of what she had suffered. He knew now
why she had feared the dead campfire, and more than he would have
wished of the cruelty with which even women could treat those who
broke the law of the tribe. He cleansed her of the stains of that torture,
and again when she soiled herself. And all through the darkest night,

when her lifelight dimmed like a dying ember, he held her cradled close in his arms.

When Sigfrid awoke on the fourth morning she was watching him, her eyes deep and clear as forest pools. Instinctively he touched her forehead, and found it cool. She twitched and he jerked his hand away. Now that she was in her right mind, she might not like him touching her.

"Who are you?" she whispered. For the first time, the question did not anger him.

"I am Sigfrid . . . Fafnarsbane," he added with a touch of bitterness. Astonishingly, she smiled.

"I should have known that. Huld told me about the boy she had seen in the north, with the wolf's eyes. Sigfrid Sigmundson the heir of the Wolsungs." She nodded with a curious satisfaction. "And Ragan has raised you to be a hero! Huld cast the runes at your birth, did you know that?"

Sigfrid blinked, a little dizzied by all these revelations. Weak in body she might still be, but it was becoming clear that the head beneath that crow's nest of cropped hair would test his own. But perhaps he could startle her.

"And you are Sigdrifa—" He grinned as she stared at him. "In your fever, you shouted it," he explained, "as if they were trying to take your name away."

"They did, but I won't let them." Her dark gaze turned toward the ashes of the fire. "I was—I *am*—a Walkyrja! And Wodan promised me a hero!"

Sigfrid stiffened. "Suppose I don't want to be a hero?" he asked. "All my life, I've had to fight or flee because of what people wanted me to be. To get free I had to kill—" He bit his lip, forcing back the memory. "I'm not about to run my head into the same trap twice like some foolish hare!"

Her eyes widened, and he forced himself to relax. No point in scaring the girl out of her wits once more.

"Surely not a hare," she said slowly. "You look more like a wolf when you snarl." Once more he found himself off-balance. Weak she was, and possibly crazy, but it would take more than his bad temper to frighten her. Sigfrid found his pity tempered by curiosity.

"What do you need a hero for anyway?"

"You heard some of it, when I was raving," she said bitterly. "The Walkyriun tried to destroy everything that I am—it would have been kinder to kill me. But there is another way to be a Walkyrja—Sigruna's way. If I rode with you, we could do deeds that would make the bards sing till the end of the age!"

Her bright eyes met his, and he felt suddenly dizzied. Abruptly he got to his feet.

"Will you be all right until dark? We need meat, and I might get a deer when they come down to the meadows at sunset."

"Of course." She sounded angry. "When I am stronger, I will come with you."

"You hunt?" None of the women in Hiloperic's clan had done so, but he knew so little of the world.

"I was trained to hunt and to fight as well as any man," she said fiercely. "And I will do so again!"

Brunahild sat up when Sigfrid had gone, willing the dizziness to go away. She had to get her strength back. She would never get that stupid boy to understand the wyrd the Norns had so clearly woven if she tottered about like a newborn foal.

Why, she wondered, did she not fear him? She was a female, and in his power. But perhaps in those long days of illness, her body had learned to trust him. Sigfrid had told her he had little sisters. That must be how he thought of her, though she was a winter or two older than he. But Brunahild had never had the ripe curves the other girls said men loved, and now she was a scarecrow. He was no more likely to feel lust for her than he would for some fledgling fallen from its nest that he was trying to teach how to fly.

At the edge of the clearing there was dry grass growing. Stopping often to rest, Brunahild gathered it. How could she make Sigfrid understand? As she laid out bundles of grass to make a mattress for his bedding, she considered what she had to work with. Certainly he had the strength to be a hero, and he must have reasonable skill with that sword, but so had many a man she had marked for death on the Longstone field. What strength of the spirit had enabled him to kill Fafnar, who from all she had heard was a master of magic? What had brought him through Wodan's fire?

He had been patient enough to nurse her through the fever, or perhaps he was just too stubborn to let her die. As far as she could see, the only thing Sigfrid did fear was the idea of being a hero. Some pain haunted him—in his voice she could hear it. She had to learn what it was.

Brunahild finished his mattress and started on her own. She was sweating from the unaccustomed activity, but already she felt a little stronger. By the time Sigfrid returned with a fat doe, she had mint tea boiling over the little fire.

"Are you sure you can hold this?" asked Sigfrid as the girl lifted the forked end of the pole. The fine weather had broken, and clouds were gathering. They had moved their camp farther down the mountain where there was more protection from the wind, but Sigdrifa was not yet ready to travel, and they needed shelter.

"I'm stronger than I look." She grinned at him. "And this will go much faster with two pairs of hands."

He nodded, for it had been awkward setting the other endpost alone. Together they carried the log to the hole that he had dug for it and tipped it in. She did look much better. Once the fever had broken she had recovered quickly, and there was a wiry strength in those skinny arms that he had not suspected.

She helped him to raise the ridgepole, though she was not tall enough to lift it all the way. But it was she who dragged the smaller side poles over so that he could bind them to the ridge with strips of deerskin. Together they tied branches crossways, thatched the slanting roof with greenery, and made walls for the two ends with mud-chinked poles so that the whole looked rather like a Roman tent built out of branches and leaves. It was a kind of house Sigfrid and Ragan had made sometimes when they went out to burn charcoal, good even against snow.

But Sigfrid could not help thinking how different the building had been with this girl. He and Ragan had rarely laughed as they labored. Sigdrifa seemed to know what he wanted without his needing to tell her. It was like play to work with her. She did not challenge him, as another boy would have done, nor did she complain. By the time the first drops of rain began to fall, their house was finished. Laughing, they dragged their things inside.

"You see, I am good for something—" she said from the shadows as Sigfrid fussed with the fire.

"Quite a few things, I should imagine," he answered, poking a dry branch into the infant flame. "Can you weave and spin as well as handle a shield and spear?"

"Yes . . ." Her face flared briefly into vision as it blazed up. "The robe I wove was one of the things they burned."

"I'm sorry—"

She shrugged. "I have my wounds, and you have yours. But to me, it seems you are the lucky one. You have always questioned, but

I never doubted my future, until the Walkyriun took it away from me. Why are you so afraid of being pushed into something you don't want to do?"

Sigfrid's throat tightened, but the ease with which they had worked together allowed him to get out the words. "It's myself I'm afraid of," he whispered. "When I am pushed to the point of killing, I am worse than a wild beast. Even the wolves only fight in self-defense, or to protect the pack, or for food. I killed Ragan, who raised me, though I did not want to. I am a berserker, and when my little sisters looked at me they were afraid!"

"I am not afraid of you." She touched his shoulder.

"Are you afraid of anything?" The flames blurred and ran as he blinked back tears. There was a long silence.

"I am afraid of being tied to garth and hearth . . . of being unable to choose my path," she said finally. "That's what it is to be a hero—the choosing. I would never try to trick you into something you did not want. The Walkyrja shows her hero what his choices are."

"I thought the Choosers told men their doom," Sigfrid said then.

"The Norns spin our threads, but we weave them into the pattern." She rolled the loose threads at the hem of the tunic he had given her into a single strand, then unraveled them. "Wyrd is always becoming. When we understand, we will what must be."

Sigfrid turned to her. "Can you help me?"

"I don't know—" Her eyes were pools of darkness. "The Walkyriun tried to destroy my magic. Alone, I am nothing. But if you will trust me, perhaps my wisdom will wake once more."

Brunahild stared into the clear waters of the spring below her hilltop, tranced by the play of morning light and shadow as the wind stirred the trees. When the branches were still, the surface disappeared, and she could see fingerlings flitting through the brown shadows. When they lifted, sunlight blazed from the water and blinded her. But sometimes there was a moment between, when she saw a sharp-angled face with haunted eyes gazing back at her from the pool. Which, she wondered, was the truth? The glimmering depths, the brilliant surface, or the elfin image that appeared between?

She supposed the face must be her own. The picture broke up as she dipped water and smoothed it across her hair, but as it re-formed she saw that the short strands were still standing up in damp spikes like a fledgling's feathers. Tears blurred the image again as she remembered how the Walkyriun had chopped off her long, glossy locks—

her only real beauty. But that did not matter. What she had to know was whether the shearing had cut off her power.

The image dislimned as she shifted position, letting her vision sink into the glimmering depths of the spring. She willed herself to remember her earliest training, to count each breath, to let the tension in her muscles ease so that the fluttering pulse in her throat would slow. Stillness . . . silence . . . Forms moved in those shadows, but she could not allow them to disturb her. For a moment she thought she saw the lean shape and powerful, underslung jaw of a great pike lying still in the bed of the stream. She forced the image away; she must become empty, unresisting as the water's flow.

And then, when all thought had dissolved but one, Brunahild allowed herself one image—never forgotten since first she saw it—the Eye within the dark well.

Was that a point of brightness? She felt her heartbeat speed and fought for control as the light expanded. Features shaped themselves around it: the jut of a nose, the glint of silver in hair and beard. This time a broad hat hid his right eye. It was the left that stared into her own, the one he had sacrificed to the Well of Mimir, and she knew then that this vision was true.

"Father, help me," she whispered. "You have sent me a hero. Give me the power to protect him, make him believe in me!"

"The power is in the earth and the water," the answer came.

"They have not taken away my knowledge of herbs, or the flowing spring," she agreed, "but what of the runes to empower them? May I use them still?"

"Remember . . ." the voice stirred in her soul, *"the tree of testing. You yourself are the only one who can wall that knowledge away."*

Brunahild frowned. Did the wisewomen's power over her depend on her need for them and her willing acceptance of that bond? The face in the water contorted as she struggled with the complexities. In her world there was no greater ill than to be without tribe or family. Did all authority depend on consent, and was the kindred wiser than any one of its members alone? They had all agreed to her punishment. Did that make their crime forgivable, or worse than her own rebellion? *How could she be sure?*

Her heart wept still for loss of the joy she had known when the Walkyriun rode all together, and she wondered if it was worth trying to go on without them. But she would not be alone, Brunahild told herself then, if she rode with Sigfrid.

"Father," she whispered, "what do you want me to do?"

"Dare . . . desire . . . learn. . . ."

Wind ruffled the surface of the water, and sunlight swept across the surface of the stream like a shower of gold. Brunahild sat back, blinking. Was that the answer?

As her eyes recovered, she saw mugwort growing on the damp ground above the spring. The god had said the earthpower was waiting to help her. The correct charm came to her lips unbidden as she reached to pluck the pungent, toothed leaves from the stiff stem.

Sigfrid paused at the edge of the clearing, his nostrils twitching at the odd odor coming from the pot that swung above the fire. Two raw fox pelts were slung over his shoulder. It was beginning to look as if they would stay here for a while, and they both needed warmer clothing. He wanted to make Sigdrifa a cape of the rich furs.

"Dinner?" He hooked the skins onto an oak branch. The girl looked up at him, her face flushed from the heat of the fire.

"You challenged me to prove I still have magic—" she said, frowning. "If you have the courage, I will show you now!"

Sigfrid lifted one eyebrow. He had not been aware that he was making a challenge, but he was certainly not going to let her think him afraid.

"So long as I don't have to drink that," he said, grinning. He could smell goose grease and the mixed pungencies of a variety of herbs.

"It is an oil I am making . . . of protection. . . ." Her voice faltered a little, and he carefully quenched his smile. "A Walkyrja's first duty to her warrior is to guard him. This is not the best season for hunting herbs, but I have found enough of them to make the oil, and the runes know no seasons. All day I have been gathering the herbs, hallowing them, seething them in this cauldron. If you are willing, I will work a spell to enchant your hide against every harm."

Sigfrid blinked. He would rather trust to his own courage than any witch's spell, but clearly doing this for him would help her own healing. He peered into the pot, where odd bits of greenery floated in the dark-colored fat, and grimaced as the sharp scent swirled upward.

"What's in it?" he asked.

"No wolfsbane, if that's what you're fearing," she snapped back at him. Then she turned to the cauldron again, chanting:

"By masterwort and betony,
Shall soul and body shielded be;

> *Mugwort gives might to endure,*
> *Comfrey cures the traveler;*
> *Mullein wards wild beasts away,*
> *Celandine will set you free;"*

She paused to add a little more wood to the fire, watching the brew intently. Then, more softly, she continued her song:

> *"Wormwood from venom of the wurm.*
> *Goat-weed guards from lightning's harm;*
> *Vervain makes friends out of foes,*
> *Garlic's power will ward off blows;*
> *With woodruff you're invincible—*
> *Now with sweet sedge I seal the spell!"*

"That sounds useful," said Sigfrid, sneezing. At least there was nothing in the list he knew for poison.

"Those are only the herbs," she went on sternly. "I have also put in leaves from the hallowed trees. The ash will ward you against danger by water or the venom of serpents. Berries from Holda's tree reverse hexes; long life comes from the linden tree." Her voice retained the resonance of her chanting.

"What is the black stuff in the little bowl?"

"Leaves of the foxglove. That is the ink with which I will draw the runes of power."

She bent over the pot once more, whispering into the steam, and suddenly he began to believe her. He had tried to wall away the awareness that had come with Fafnar's blood, but now his skin was prickling. He remembered old Huld, whom Sigdrifa said had been her teacher. Why should he be surprised that the girl had power?

"Very well," he said more gently. "What must I do?"

"Go to the spring and cleanse yourself. When you return, we will begin."

When Sigfrid came back, his body tingling from the icy water, she had built up the cookfire and laid his bedding in front of the hut. Runes were scratched into the earth around it. The oil had been decanted into a wooden bowl. But she was standing with her cloak wrapped around her and her back to the blaze.

"What is it?" He set his hand on her shoulders and felt them shaking with unvoiced sobs.

"How can I do this?" she whispered. "Without my cape and my

cap, my necklaces and my white gown? I should have used my spirit knife to cut the herbs, and my mortar and pestle to grind them, not a rock and a smooth stone. This is not how I was taught to work— I'm sorry—" She broke off as his grip tightened on her arms.

"Do you mean I froze my toes in that stream for nothing? I don't believe it—" He gave her a little shake. "Anything that smells that bad must be magic! Besides, when you were stirring that brew, I felt the power." She gave a shaky laugh and turned to him.

"Did you really?"

Sigfrid nodded. Her lips curved briefly in response, and he stared, confused by the bird-wing flicker of beauty in her smile.

"Then you can take off your sark and breeches," she told him. "Did you think I was going to anoint you through your clothes?"

He nodded, but his hands were clumsy on the laces, and suddenly he would much rather have tackled Fafnar in his lair. He knew it was foolish. She had trusted him to tend her, and she had much more to fear. What could she do to him, after all? It was only, he thought, that he had so little experience of touching. No one had tended him, really, since his mother sent him away. With extra care he folded his things, and then, hoping that the heat he felt beneath his skin would look like the glow of the fire, he lay down.

"Good—" Her impersonal survey of his body reminded Sigfrid of the way Ragan used to look when he was deciding just where to begin hammering at a particularly unpromising piece of iron. Any fears he had that his body's involuntary response to her touch might embarrass him fled.

She knelt beside him and set her palms to the earth, lips moving in prayer. "I start with your hands and arms," she said softly. "In battle they are the most vulnerable. Rest in safety—you need do nothing more."

She lifted his right hand and began to massage the oil into it. Her touch was strong and sure. Tensions of which he had been unaware fled from his fingers; they lay loosely curled as she drew the first rune in the center of his palm.

"*Fehu* I give you, that all to which you set your hand may prosper!"

Her knowing fingers began to work their way up his arm and Sigfrid sighed, feeling it grow heavy as their pressure drove out the hidden strains. "*Tiwaz*"—she drew what felt like an arrow along his arm—"that you may strike with the might of the god of war."

Now she was kneading the top of his shoulder, moving along the strong slabs of muscle that ran into the chest. He thought it was the

Torch rune that she gave him then, but though his skin tingled where she had touched it, the rest of his body was relaxing. With each moment Sigfrid slid more deeply into a state in which he was aware of nothing at all.

"*Learn*—" the god had told her. As Brunahild spread the protecting oil across Sigfrid's chest and drew the rune of Strength over the muscles there, it occurred to her that she had never before had such an opportunity to examine a male body. And Sigfrid's seemed to be an excellent example. He came of warrior stock, and the forest had fed him well. But it was the forgework that had given him such a remarkable torso—the right arm corded with muscle from swinging the hammer and the left from pulling the bellows. She worked down the shield arm, marking Donar's rune on his shoulder, and on his left palm the rune of Giving.

Fine brown hairs grew down the center of Sigfrid's chest toward his belly. The skin was peppered by a few white scars where slag from the forge had stung him, but was remarkably fine in texture. The muscle beneath it was hard, perfectly delineated beneath the fair skin. Over his heart she drew the Joy rune, and above his solar plexus the rune of Victory, and felt his breathing deepen and the flesh grow warmer as the sun-strength radiated from that glowing center of power.

In wonder, she traced the veins that fed those muscles. The skin was so smooth, the flow of life in him so strong! She could feel the pulse of energy when she moved her hands above his body. Where the oil glistened, his skin seemed to glow. She inscribed the Water rune upon his belly, then her gaze moved upward once more.

He appeared to be asleep. Brunahild marked the strong column of the throat with the rune of Wodan, worked the oil along the line of his jaw below the young beard. From the soft curves of the boy's face she could see the angles of the man's features emerging. At his temples she traced the runes of Necessity and of the Turning Seasons; the rune of Mastery on the crown of his head, of Transformation on his ears.

From one eyelid to the other she drew the rune of Dawning, crossing its lines on the point of perception between his brows. They did not quiver. Surely he must be deeply tranced or sleeping. Her touch erased marks of tension she had not suspected were there until she saw his face for once unguarded. His lips were a little open, beautifully shaped; they would have been soft if she had touched them. They had always been tight before, as if repressing pain.

He has given himself to me like a child to its mother, she thought, smoothing the oil into the skin of his brow with a tender hand. The trust in those closed eyes and gentle mouth astonished her.

Brunahild found her eyes stinging and sat back suddenly. In another moment she would have put her arms around him and wept for this boy who had endured her bitter moods with such uncomplaining kindness, so deprived had his life been of any gentleness at all.

His body is perfect, but inside he is wounded, she thought then. *And that pain is what I have to heal.*

She took a steadying breath, then moved down to his feet, massaging upward, becoming ever more conscious of the texture of his skin and the sensuous slide of the oil on her hands. His thigh muscles were hard and sinewy. Smiling, she drew the Horse rune upon the legs with which he had run with the wolves.

Brunahild stopped then, staring at the thing she had been avoiding. She was amazed to find that she was trembling. She could tell him to turn over now. He would never know—but she would betray herself as well as Sigfrid if she did not extend her warding to the core of his power.

"To the holy seed I give my blessing," she whispered, and with a feather touch traced the rune of *Ingvio* upon the tender, textured skin, so fragile a protection for a man's future. As she touched his seed-sack she saw the member that had lain flaccid beside it stir. "And to the channel through which it flows!" Swiftly she drew an upended Well rune along it.

In a single moment she remembered the softness of a foal's nose, or the fuzz on a leaf, or the petal of a flower, and knew that Sigfrid's skin—there—was softer. And in the same instant she felt his manhood harden and swell with power.

It was the lightning that divides light from darkness, the awakening of the god.

As if from a great distance she heard Sigfrid's breathing, gone ragged as if he had been running.

"You may turn over now." Somehow she managed to keep her own voice steady. She realized that she was sitting bolt upright, her fists clenched in the folds of the tunic *he* had given her. Her hands twitched with longing to caress the thing they had wakened.

Finish it—she told herself, *his feet, his back—finish it quickly, while you can!*

She kneaded the hard muscles of Sigfrid's calves with a frenetic vigor, forbidding her fingers to linger, and drew on his feet the rune of Home and Heritage. She moved up the backs of his thighs and felt her face grow hot and all her own skin tingle; stroked his buttocks, shivering, and marked the rune of the Rider there.

The bowl of warding oil was almost empty. Brunahild spread it as far as she could, regretting only that when it was gone she had no more reason to probe the strong muscles that ran toward the spine beneath their pelt of fine brown hair. Of all his body, Sigfrid's back was probably the least vulnerable, for he would never flee from an enemy.

Still, she could give him the rest of the rune blessing—the Birch rune at the base of his spine, the Icicle in the middle, and the Yew where it met the skull, and then, wrenched between pain and relief that it was ending, the Elk rune of protection over all.

Brunahild lifted her hands from Sigfrid's body, drew the cloak up, and tucked it around him.

"Rest," she whispered. "Let the spell sink in. Rest and heal. . . ." She heard him sigh. The cloak stirred a little as if he were trying to turn over. Then exhaustion claimed him, and he stilled.

Carefully Brunahild got her feet under her, surprised she could still stand. The night was windless. Beyond the circle of treetops the stars stared down at her with unwinking eyes. *Bright sisters*, her spirit cried, *do not betray me! Do not let him know what I feel!*

By morning, surely, this overwhelming awareness would have faded. If she could maintain her calm, surely Sigfrid would assume that anything he had noticed was his imagination. The self she had reconstructed from the ashes of the Walkyrja's fire was such a fragile thing. If she allowed herself to desire this child-man who had saved her, she would be lost.

Brunahild had assumed the rite of protection must be done without passion. It had not occurred to her how completely one must be willing to know the person one was warding. And what in her life could have told her that such knowledge would inevitably bring understanding, and with it, love? *Oh my father*, her heart cried, *was this what you wanted me to learn?*

Chapter 18 ❄ Winter Storm

Taunus Mountains
Frost Moon, A.D. 418

Teh wandersong of the wild geese came drifting down the wind. Sigfrid looked up to see them, the arrow-shaft he had been carving forgotten in his hand. The sky was a clear, pale blue, but that morning, frost had glittered on the fallen leaves. The geese knew it was time to make for winter quarters. The bears would be thinking about snug caves, and creatures that roamed the forest through the winter were storing up fat to get them through the cold.

"Do you want to follow them?"

Sigfrid turned and saw Sigdrifa looking at him. Now that he thought about it, she had been watching him all morning. He shrugged and began to scrape at the stick again.

"Where would I go? Still, winter is coming, and it's hard traveling in the snow. You have your strength back. We should think about starting for your homeland soon."

"If I still have a home . . . I have no mind to let my sister see me until my hair has grown." Her winged brows bent as she worked a piece of sinew through a hole in the bridle strap she was mending, then her glance flicked back to his face once more.

Was she trying to see if her magic had worked? The stuff she had rubbed on him certainly smelled strong enough to scare a troll away. He had washed it off that morning, preferring not to announce his presence to every animal in the forest. But it had felt good when she rubbed it on. In fact, he felt more at ease than he had since he had set out for Fafnar's lair, or even since he had left Alb's hall.

"Someplace to winter, anyhow." He reached for one of the bone points he had fashioned to take small game. The feeling of protection Sigdrifa's magic had given him made him remember his mother, and inevitably he wondered if he would ever again have a home and kin. He thrust the thought away and began to work the base of the point into the notch he had cut in one end of the shaft.

"You don't have to stay here because of me," she said then. "As you say, I am strong now, and I grew up in these hills. I can survive."

"Not alone," Sigfrid said starkly. "Not without having spent a summer gathering stores. Ragan and I had some lean times, and we had the food people traded for his work at the forge. Even the wolves know enough to run in packs when the snow begins to fall."

A wave of color reddened the girl's sun-browned skin. "But this year it will be easy to hunt. All the beasts that fled the fire are here." She knotted the sinew and yanked at the leather to see if it would hold.

Sigfrid dabbed some gluey stuff he had boiled down from deer hooves around the point and the shaft. "Will you be using all of that sinew?"

"No. The mend is finished now." She rose awkwardly to her feet. It was not stiffness, but tension, he decided as she came toward him, as if she had taken all the strain she had massaged from his muscles into her own.

"Thanks—" He reached out to take the sinew and she dropped it into his lap, jerking her hand away.

"What's wrong with you? Did you get chilled last night, tending me?"

"I'm fine!" she snapped, and then: "You slept so sound I'm amazed you noticed anything at all!"

Sigfrid got to his feet, suddenly angry.

"What was I supposed to feel?" His hand closed on her wrist and he pulled her closer. "Try this arrow if you want to know whether the magic worked, and see if it does me any harm!"

For a moment he held her. He could feel her warmth, the race of the pulse beneath the skin. He took a deep breath as the warming air brought her scent to him. Her eyes met his, darkening as he held her gaze.

"If I were to shoot at you, it would be with mistletoe," Sigdrifa whispered then, and jerked free.

Sigfrid stood where she had left him, frowning. She had said she was well, but something was different. It was her scent— He frowned,

trying to think when in his limited experience of women he had encountered it before.

Suddenly he remembered. One of the thrall-women had tried to
persuade him into her bed when he was at Alb's hall, and when she
had placed his hand between her thighs, she had smelled the same.
Did Sigdrifa want him? He gazed after her, eyes narrowing in speculation. When a queen-wolf came into season, at first she herself did
not seem to know what was going on. It was the males who could
smell the change, and who encouraged it by courting her until she
was ready to accept one of them.

Until now, Sigfrid had been concerned with survival, but this
altered everything. He felt his own body stir even thinking about it.
Sigdrifa bent to hang the bridle inside the door to the hut, and as the
tunic molded itself to her body he remembered the warmth of her
hands upon his skin and the wiry strength in her slender limbs. She
knew his flesh— He stiffened as he remembered how she had touched
him. And he knew hers, though only now was it beginning to stir him
with desire.

Sometime during the past moons he had ceased to be a boy. Was
it when he killed Heming, or when he walked through the fire? It
would be better, Sigfrid thought, to prove his manhood by loving a
woman than by killing any more men.

Brunahild's breath caught as Sigfrid, reaching around her to untie
his pony, pressed his body against hers. In a moment they were apart
again, but everywhere they had touched, her flesh burned. She licked
her lips, feeling once again the hunger that assaulted her whenever
they came in contact, which seemed to be happening surprisingly
often, until she wondered if it was he who had become so unaccount-
ably clumsy, or she.

She had only meant to ward his body, but she felt as if she had
extended not only her protection, but her essence, around him. She
wondered if she had forgotten some step that should have separated
them when the rite was over. Certainly her teachers had not mentioned
this effect when they described the ritual.

Her own pony whickered and pulled at the rein, and she made
herself grasp its coarse mane and pull herself up. The horses had grazed
down all the grass near their camp, and it was easier to ride them to
more distant pastures than cut fodder and bring it in. In the direction
of Fox Dance, the land was still seared and waste. But except for the
slopes immediately surrounding the rock on which they had bound

her, the hinterland was untouched, the forest spotted with grassy clearings still deep in good grass.

Sigfrid was already well ahead of her. Brunahild kicked her pony into motion. It was more used to bearing loads of charcoal than a rider, but after carrying Ragan, the creature seemed to welcome her, and it was good to have a horse moving beneath her again. She curved her slim legs around the round barrel, enjoying the slide of muscle between her thighs as the pony strove to catch up with its companion—

—and abruptly felt heat flame through her again as she wondered what it would be like to feel Sigfrid there.

I don't want to run back to my sister like a kicked cur, she thought then, *but how can I survive a winter with him alone?*

"Give in," said a seductive voice within. "*He will not resist you.*"

But that way lay disaster. The Walkyriun had expected the man who found her to rape her and destroy what integrity she retained. But she would have fought a man who abused her body, and in the battle become stronger. She faced now another and more terrible danger. If she succumbed to this inflammation of the senses, she would be betrayed from within, for where would her will be, and where her wisdom, if all she could think of was the hard strength of Sigfrid's arms and the smoothness of his skin?

From somewhere ahead she heard a clack and a clatter as if someone were practicing with wooden swords. Sigfrid had reined in and was listening, so intent she could almost see his ears pricking to locate the sound.

"Stags," he whispered when she reached him. "Down in the glade. I saw the old king there this morning, watching over his does."

He pointed, and through the trees she glimpsed something moving. For a moment then she saw clearly the noble head and the branching seven-tined antler crown. Then there was a bellow, and the other stag charged him. The forest echoed with the crack as their antlers clashed.

"So far he has defeated all his challengers," Sigfrid said as the two beasts strained together, their hides gleaming red-brown in the sun.

"But why do they do it? Have the does no choice at all?"

Sigfrid's gaze searched her face, and Brunahild began to tremble once more.

"The does choose that the strongest shall father their fawns," he said quietly. "You of all women should understand, who made a god promise that only a hero should come to you through the fire!" He took her hand, his fingers hard and warm, and this time she had not the will to pull away.

"Are you a king stag?" Brunahild's gaze devoured the sun-streaked brown hair, drowned in his yellow stare.

"I am a wolf, and you are my queen." Sigfrid leaned forward.

Her vision blurred at the warmth of his breath; his lips brushed hers. . . . Panicking, Brunahild struck out and felt her fist graze flesh, then her pony shied and skidded away.

"What are you doing?" she shouted, trying to calm her horse and herself at the same time. Curse him, he was laughing!

"Courting you. But don't worry, I can wait until you're ready for me."

With an effort Brunahild forced her mouth to close. She had been so certain he did not know!

"I can't," she whispered. "I won't—"

"Why not? I know that you want me." It was a simple statement of fact, not even complacency. "Why should there be a problem? When the queen-wolf is ready, she mates, and so will you."

"We are not animals!" Her shout shook the forest, and for a moment the sounds of battle from the glade below ceased.

"No." Sigfrid frowned. "From what I can see, the beasts handle these things a good deal more sensibly. You think too much, that is all."

Speechless, she whipped the reins across the pony's neck, and the startled creature plunged past him. By the time he had caught up with her, Brunahild had got back a measure of control.

"Very well. Suppose I do want you," she said to him. "As your Walkyrja, I must love you. But a wife and a Walkyrja cannot be the same. If I ride by your side, we two can make a story the bards will sing about, but not if I lie in your arms."

"Why do you make this so complicated? Do you think you will lose your fighting skill? I never observed it so among the wolves!" He looked genuinely confused.

"I was taught . . ." she said slowly, "that the spirits that Wodan sends to harvest the battlefield are only one kind of Walkyrja. They can act through women who are trained in battle-magic. But there is another kind. Everyone has a spirit that protects him. It appears as a woman, or a flicker of light, or an animal. When a human Walkyrja bonds to a hero, her spirit becomes part of his."

"Is that what you did to me?" His pony flattened its ears at the sudden sharpness of his tone.

"That's what I did to myself," she answered bitterly. "Don't look so frightened. I thought that I was simply warding you, and now you have all my protection as well as your own. Sigfrid, son of Sigmund, I will teach you mind-runes and heal-runes and battle-runes—everything I know. Spirit to spirit, I can foresee your danger and be your wisdom. Is that not a greater gift than my body?"

"Is it?" He looked at her, and his gaze was like a physical touch on her skin. His lips tightened and relaxed again, and she licked her own, trying to ignore the ache between her thighs.

"If I lie with you," she whispered, "all I will be able to see is the light of your eyes. . . ." The blood roared in her ears. "Until you die."

"Death comes to all, both wolf and man. Do you think I fear it? You are all around me, but I cannot touch you, Sigdrifa. Let me reach the life in you, and I will dare whatever else Wyrd may weave for me!"

The horses had come to a halt before the hut. In silence they dismounted, tethered the beasts, and built up the fire. Need was like a bowstring drawn tight between them. Brunahild had thought it could not be worse, but now she bore the weight of his desire as well as her own.

That night she lay wakeful, and the carefully regular breathing from the other side of the hut told her that Sigfrid was finding sleep distant too. Sometime before dawn she fell into an uneasy drowse filled with images of blood and fire. It seemed to her that she was Sigruna, and Helgi was running toward her across the sand. He laughed for joy as he caught her in his arms, and her fingers clenched in his dark hair, but when he bent to kiss her, she saw that he had Sigfrid's eyes. She tried to push him away then, but his kiss was a fire that turned her to flame.

Sigfrid pulled the deerhide, still dripping from the bath of ash and water in which it had been soaking, across the rough wood of the graining block, swearing as liquid slopped onto his shoes. A handful of hair came away, and he had to scrape it from the block before repeating the process, coughing as the alkaline stink of the soak caught in his lungs. His head ached already from lack of sleep, and suddenly the prospect of a morning spent wrestling with the wet hide seemed unendurable. Next to the storage shed Sigdrifa was scraping the last of the flesh from a stretched skin.

He straightened, looking up at the sky. It was not just his spirit that was restless. A high haze veiled the sun, and a rising wind had begun to pluck at the last of the leaves. *Storm coming in, maybe even snow.*

He could feel tension growing around him as the world waited for it.
As I wait, he thought then, *for Sigdrifa to come to me.*

As if the thought had summoned her, she looked up. For a moment
their eyes met, then she turned to her task again, drawing the blade
across the hide with vicious strokes as if she were trying to kill the
animal all over again.

To Sigfrid's eyes she seemed to crackle with energy, like a young
mare prancing across a meadow, all awkward grace and undirected
power. Sigdrifa's beauty was in motion. He felt himself hardening as
he thought about moving with her, but that ache had never entirely
receded since he first became aware of her. He ought to be used to it
by now. He wished he could solve the problem by simply grabbing
her, but he had seen wolves that miscalculated a female's receptivity
mauled.

Sigfrid's hand slipped, and the hide slithered into an uncooperative
heap on the ground. He swore, and heard the girl's laughter.

"Be quiet," he said, "unless you want to wear it the way it is!"

Suddenly he knew that he would go mad if he had to spend a
whole morning struggling with the hides.

"I'm going hunting!" he said abruptly. Sigdrifa set down the
scraper, and he realized that she needed the release of action as much
as he.

As they started down the trail to get the horses, he heard a raven's
call from somewhere to the north of them, and wolfsong answering.
Sigdrifa paused, listening.

"She calls to tell her friends where the game is. Let us see if I can
find a deer for you!"

For the first time that morning Sigfrid felt the release of honest
laughter. She could not match his woodcraft, but she did know these
hills. Still laughing, he fell back and let her lead the way, anticipating
the moments when the skirt of her tunic, flipping back from her leg-
gings, gave him a glimpse of bare thigh.

Wolf and raven, they coursed the forest together. By the time
they found a fresh trail it was past noon, and the sun was a pale glow
in the greying sky. The tracks were of a big buck, but not a herd-
king, for he was alone. Perhaps he had been defeated in the mating
battles, thought Sigfrid, peering down at the wedge-shaped marks in
the sand, for he seemed to be favoring his right foreleg.

"He'll have gone to lie up in the hazel copse until evening—" He
pointed to a tangle of branches on the side of the hill. "We'll tie the

ponies back there. You flush him out, and I'll wait downwind where I can get a clear cast with the spear."

It seemed very silent after Sigdrifa started her stalk up the hillside. She might not move like a wolf in the woods, but she had melted into the brush more silently than most men.

Grey clouds were settling across the hilltops; a few chill droplets brushed his brow. Sigfrid cast an experienced glance across the slope, calculating where a startled beast might seek a path. Below the hazels the ground fell away sharply. The stag would come out flying, aiming to land on the grassy stretch beyond. From the ridge he heard a raven calling, and for a moment thought it was real. He settled into position, spear ready, as motionless as the trees behind him.

Suddenly the branches rattled. Bare twigs lifted—no, it was a crown of antlers, and now the hunter could see the shape of the beast below them, growing out of the trees. For a moment it hesitated, velvet ears flicking nervously. Then the rising wind brought the human scent more strongly. The stag shouldered free of the branches. Sigfrid's thigh muscles shook with strain.

Come to me, he cried silently. *Your wyrd awaits you.* He must choose his moment exactly, for he would have only one chance at a clean kill, and he had no wish to follow a blood-trail halfway to Hunland with a storm coming in.

Uphill, a branch cracked.

The stag leaped and Sigfrid threw, all the strength of his body uncoiling behind his arm. The red-brown body blurred huge above him; the beast seemed to hang in the air. But it was the haft of the spear, whipping around as the stag plunged past, that cracked against Sigfrid's head and brought him down.

"Sigfrid!" A little breathless, for when the stag broke cover she had half run, half slid down the hill, Brunahild ducked under a branch and straightened, staring around her. "Sigfrid, did you see?"

The stag was still struggling with the spear in its side. Blood spots on the frost-seared grass showed where its leap had ended. Beyond them she saw Sigfrid, lying still upon the ground. Her sight darkened. Somehow she got down the hill without falling and cast herself down beside him, gripping his shoulders, reaching out to the life that burned within.

"My warding was supposed to protect you!" she exclaimed.

He was not dead. If Sigfrid's spirit had gone she would have known. Drops of blood were beading where something had grazed his temple—the left temple, on which she had drawn the rune of Necessity. Now Need drove her, and all her fears were swallowed up in the greater terror that he would not wake again. Trembling, Brunahild kissed the wound. At the taste of his blood, awareness of his being filled the separation that had been between them. She sank down upon his body with arms and legs wrapped around him.

"My blood and my breath for you," she whispered. His eyes were closed, his lips a little parted. Hungrily her mouth closed on his, her spirit arrowed into the emptiness that had claimed him, and all other awareness fled.

Darkness engulfed her, then Sigfrid's spirit surged up from the depths in a golden flood that swept her back into her own body again.

His mouth moved on hers, tasting, exploring; or was it she who was feeding on him? He kissed down the side of her neck, and she gasped for breath. Heat ran along her veins as his hands moved over her body. With each touch, a new sense seemed to awaken. She clutched at him as for a moment he pulled away from her, then his hand slid up between her thighs, and her flesh melted in liquid fire.

Gasping, she strained toward him. A sound came from deep in Sigfrid's throat, half moan, half snarl. His body thrust hard against hers, but Brunahild felt flesh and spirit expanding to encompass him, and the emptiness at her core at last was filled.

When they became aware of the world once more, the stag lay still, its hide already lightly powdered by falling snow. While they made love, the deer had been dying. Brunahild stared down at it, understanding the balance in what had happened, but unable to put it into words. Blood trickled from the beast's side as Sigfrid pulled his spear free, like the blood on her thighs.

"Life and death . . ." Words came to her at last. She touched her finger to the wound and drew a circle of blood first upon Sigfrid's brow and then on herself with fingers that did not seem to be her own.

Brunahild felt the kiss of the snow, but it did not seem cold to her. Galemburgis had sworn that the man who took her maidenhood would take her magic, but instead, she had become a new being with expanded senses and unimaginable powers. Did she still walk the waking world? She met Sigfrid's eyes, and saw the same confused exaltation there.

"I should gut the stag now, before it stiffens." With an effort, he pulled himself together. "Will you bring the horses here?"

By the time they reached their camp, the snow was falling fast. They hurried to settle the ponies and haul the carcass of the deer into a tree out of reach of the wolves. Moving carefully, like a cub whose eyes have just opened and still must learn to see, Brunahild pulled their sleeping furs together into a single bed while Sigfrid carried wood to the hearth in the hut and made up a fire. They no longer seemed to need words to work together, but they touched often, and each swift clasp of hand on hand was a promise that what had just happened had not been a dream.

Night fell, and the white blur of the snow greyed to shadow. Inside the hut a flicker of firelight danced across the slanting roof as the flame took hold, and white smoke eddied along the ridgepole and out through the openings beneath the eaves. Slowly the chill air began to warm. They hung damp clothing from the roofpoles and dove beneath the blankets of pieced furs, recoiling at the shock of cold skin, then came together again, holding tight until their shivering began to ease.

The urgency that had tormented her through the past days was gone. Now there was a pleasure in anticipation. Brunahild gasped as he brushed the bud of her breast and it hardened under his hand. As the air warmed, Sigfrid pushed away the blanket, and she glimpsed the long curve of her own body, its purity of line containing the strength beneath the smooth skin. She lay back with a sigh, allowing the hands that had killed the deer to go where they willed, and his discovery of her body was her own.

"Sigdrifa . . ." Sigfrid brushed the strong-springing black hair back from her temple. He kissed her brow and her eyelids, stroked gently down the smooth stem of her throat until the banked coals within her began to kindle once more. "You are a golden lily that opens at the edge of the snow!"

It was true. She could feel herself opening, melting, and reached out to him with sudden hunger. His flesh warmed as her hands moved across his body, defining the hard muscles of his arms and shoulders, kneading down the long muscles along his spine.

"And you are an oak tree!" she breathed in his ear.

"Now my heart begins to heal from the killing of Fafnar," Sigfrid said softly, "since his blood let me understand the birds who showed me the way to you!"

"Now I could even forgive the Walkyriun," she answered. "They served the god, though they did not know it. I think he meant me for you all along, and you for me!" She turned a little, sliding one smooth thigh between his. He stroked down her side and across her hip, cupping the soft flesh and pulling her closer.

"Was it he who challenged me when I came through the fire?" Sigfrid asked.

"You saw him? Tell me!" She straightened. She had control over her limbs once more, but the flesh with which she caressed him was that of a goddess now.

"If Wodan can walk in the body of a mortal man, then I have seen him several times. He taught me how to forge my sword." As Sigfrid told her about Helmbari he traced the winged line of her eyebrow, the curve of her cheek, kissed the corner of her mouth until she laughed and clasped him hard against her.

"When you hold me like this I can even believe that there might be a purpose in all that has happened to me," he said. His breathing was becoming unsteady, and she could feel his desire growing once more to match her own.

"I thought that his will for me was to become the greatest of the Walkyriun," Brunahild whispered, torn between her need to feel him within her and her need to understand. "But Wodan goes his own way always. You have his sword. You are his warrior. All my training was only a preparation, so that I could ride with you."

Sigfrid moved a little, and her hand brushed his manhood; she recoiled, then reached out again, fearing no longer to wake the god. He stilled, trembling.

"But why?" he asked in a stifled voice. "What does he need us for?"

"The world is changing, and he is changing with it. You and I are beyond all boundaries. Alone, I am only an outcast Walkyrja—"

"And I a kin-slayer . . ." His breath stopped as her grip tightened.

"—but we make a whole being when we are together. In our exile is our freedom. We can go anywhere, and Wodan will go with us, experiencing all we know—"

"Let him feel this, then," Sigfrid said hoarsely. "Hold me! Raven, enfold me with your wings!" His arms closed around her. All Brunahild's awareness was focusing into a single, glowing core.

"Fill me," she whispered, and shifted position to guide him. "Be my center." She was melting; she felt body and spirit surround him as he sheathed himself within her flesh once more. *What god invented this?* she wondered dazedly. *Was it Wodan, or did Froja teach him this magic?*

For a moment it was enough simply to be held safe within the circle of Sigfrid's love, to be so utterly accepted, no longer alone.

"I am Sigdrifa," she breathed, "and you are my hero. I will bring you victory!" Her fingers dug into his back, her lips brushed across his cheek, seeking his. She had thought herself home, but as he pressed against her, she found herself opening even further, and knew they had a journey yet to go.

Brunahild felt her body arching upward unbidden and clutched at Sigfrid's shoulders. This was not like the first time, when his release had overwhelmed her own. With all their strength they strained together, but it was not enough. Spirit and body expanded until she no longer knew where her flesh stopped and his began. Though they moved together, she was floating higher with each moment that passed.

She could not bear it, and yet it continued. Once more the flames of the god blazed up around her. *If this is death, it is welcome....* she thought then. A deeper knowledge answered, *"My child, it is not death, but ecstasy,"* as consciousness exploded in a ring of fire.

Throughout the night the winter storm raged around the hut in the forest, but its white wings only fanned the blaze within. Near dawn the wind dropped, and the lovers slept exhausted in each other's arms. When they woke at last, a diffuse radiance was glimmering through the smokeholes. Sigfrid unpegged the doorflap, and they peered beneath it into a world grown strange and new.

Over a foot of snow had fallen, weighting the branches of the trees and covering the ground with a white blanket through which only the tips of the grasses still showed. Snow mounded the roof of the storage shed and made the hut into a miniature mountain. Crisp air made his nose tingle, and he let the flap drop once more, blinking in the sudden dark. Then Sigdrifa blew on the coals of their hearthfire, and he saw an answering flicker in her eyes.

He reached out to her, and she nestled back against him, a part of himself that he had never known was missing until now. He pulled the covers back over them and kissed the dark silk of her hair.

"Do we have to get up?" she murmured into his chest. He sighed as one of the horses whickered from the pen down the hill. This cocoon of warmth where they lay was the center of the world, and he wanted to leave it no more than she.

"The ponies will be hungry—"

"You too, I should think." Her hand moved down his body, and she giggled. "You'll need your strength again soon."

Sigfrid laughed and smacked her bottom, and then, before his resolve could falter, slid out from beneath the covers and grabbed for his clothes.

But despite the crisp air, he scarcely felt the cold. By the time he returned, whistling, Sigdrifa had made up the cookfire. Meat was sizzling on the spit, and the cauldron steamed above the flames.

She stood up to greet him with the assured grace of some wild thing and he blinked, wondering whether it was the snow's reflected brightness or some inner light that made her seem to shimmer. The world had been transformed, and surely neither he nor she were the same people they had been yesterday. She smiled, and poured steaming liquid into a drinking horn.

"It should be ale, but you will have to be content with yarrow and camomile." She drew a rune over the mouth of the horn and held it out to him.

> *"This drink I bring you, oak of battle.*
> *With strength is it blended, and brightest honor,*
> *with magic I mixed it, and mighty songs,*
> *with goodly spells and wish-speeding runes!"*

He drank, and tasted the power in it, or perhaps the night's madness still fired his veins. Sigdrifa's gaze was a little unfocused, as if she had looked too long into the light.

"The paths are knee-deep in snow already," he said when he had finished drinking. "If we had wanted to winter in garth or guard we should have left yesterday." He looked at her speculatively.

She turned to him, her face alight.

"I have been thinking. When spring comes I will go to my people to wait while you get the arms and gear we will need. But first there is so much I must teach you. I was wrong, Sigfrid, my shining one— so long as we are together, I have not lost my magic. But it lives in you, now, and I must show you how to use it. Cannot we stay here?"

"The wolf lies in the wilderness all winter, and so does the raven," he answered, feeling elation sing through his veins. "We are as much outliers as they. We can live if we hunt together. I will teach you the woodcraft that Ragan taught to me."

"Do you think we are without protection?" she exclaimed, staring around her. "A circle of light wards us here—do you not feel it? This is hallowed ground. Here we are safe from the world."

"A circle of light . . ." he repeated, and remembered how the sunlight had glittered on the gold of the hoard. Suddenly he could look back on all the suffering that had brought him to this place, as a man who has crossed a great river looks back at the farther shore. He would not mind being a hero, so long as he did not have to be one alone. Leaving her staring, he ducked into the hut and brought out the pouch that was hanging there.

"Sigdrifa"—flushing, he sought for the right words— "I have no feast for you, no family to swear the oaths or witness our joining. But let this be your morning-gift. It is the only thing I was willing to take from Fafnar's hoard."

Gold flared blindingly as he pulled the neck ring from the pouch and held it out to her. Sigdrifa's eyes widened as she traced the runes.

"Do you know what this is?"

"It is the ring of the goddess, and you are the goddess to me," he said steadily.

"I am your Walkyrja," she whispered. Sigfrid unhooked the neck ring's curved ends, and twisted the flexible gold. As he fastened it around her slim neck he could feel her trembling. "To death and beyond it I claim you, as you have claimed me!"

"To death and beyond—" he echoed. Sigdrifa's dark beauty blazed against the white snow. Blindly he reached for her, and as they touched he felt the cool curve of the ring pressed between them.

They stayed thus, unmoving, for one moment, or perhaps it was an age of the world. As the sun lifted above the trees, light flowered from the gold and danced upon the snow, and the raven that had been watching from the fir tree opened its wings and soared away.

Background & Sources

Any attempt to summarize the historical origins of the Germanic peoples must of necessity oversimplify and some points are still disputed by the scholars, but in brief, Indo-European peoples appear to have moved northward through Europe and spread into the Baltic and Scandinavian region by the beginning of the first millennium B.C.E. A period of isolation there would have allowed the diversification of languages to become complete, resulting in the earliest forms of the Germanic languages. A worsening of the climate several hundred years later may have started some of them moving slowly southward again, expelling or assimilating the Celts who still occupied the mid-European lands. By the second century C.E. Germanic tribes were living along the coast of the North Sea and between the Baltic and the Danube, still moving south and westward. From Caesar's time onward, they began to come into conflict with Rome. The history of the empire in the west was a cycle of incursion, conflict, and transformation of barbarian tribes into citizens of Rome. In the late fourth century, however, the advance of the Huns began to push the German tribes westward in numbers that could no longer be assimilated by the disintegrating Roman Empire.

HISTORY

At the beginning of the fifth century, the Burgunds (Burgundians) occupied the highlands east of the upper Rhine. By this time the Huns had incorporated most of the Ostrogoths into their own empire, while the rest were in the service of Rome. The Vandals and Visigoths had already fled before them into Gaul. Now the Huns moved westward once more, and the Burgunds sought new land in the valley of the Rhine as allies of Rome. Their kings were the Niflungar (the Nibelungs).

The advancing tribes moved into lands that had known many earlier inhabitants, from the pre–Indo-European peoples who by this time survived mainly as forest-dwellers, to the Celts, whose first recorded cultures were in these lands, Roman settlers in the west, and earlier Germanic tribes. When a tribe migrated, some of its people, the more prosperous or perhaps the more conservative, remained on their original lands, to be conquered or absorbed when new folk moved in. Some of the later "tribes," like the Alamanni and the Bavarians, were actually confederated survivors of earlier peoples.

Although there are certain structural and ceremonial commonalities in the religions of all the Indo-European peoples, there was never a universal creed or theology. Each linguistic group, and indeed, each tribe and family, had its own ways of worshipping. Spiritual activity was centered on the kin and the land. Rituals were performed in sacred sites at springs and in the forest, in the fields, and in the home, and the deities, though they might resemble similar figures elsewhere, had local names.

Although traces of Georges Dumézil's tripartite division of divine powers can certainly be found in the religion of the migrating tribes, such neat analyses are most attractive to those for whom the gods are no longer living realities. In practice, the people gave names and offerings to the powers they perceived in the world around them, the spirits who dwelt in the living world outside their walls and the ancestral spirits and deities who helped them to survive. Their gods, therefore, were concerned with the fertility of the flocks and fields, the magic that protected them from the beings of the Otherworld, and the warrior skills that defended them from the inhabitants of this one. It was not the personifications of elemental powers, but those who helped humans to deal with them, who became the gods of recorded mythologies.

When a tribe migrated, it was uprooted not only from its land, but from its local gods, and tribal cults were assimilated and simplified. Nonetheless, a people who had no tradition of philosophical abstraction continued to experience their gods as persons, with the rewards, and sometimes the stresses, attendant upon any personal relationship. They felt the presence of these powers in the calls of birds, the wind in the trees, or in the prickling of the skin, spoke with them in vision or sometimes in the persons of other men.

The essential characteristic of the world in which this story takes place was mobility. It was a time in which the world was on the threshold of change—in language, culture, religion, and above all, in homeland and identity. To the Roman, the world consisted of lines and surfaces that could be described and catalogued. To the Teuton, it was an environment of overlapping levels of reality, in which it was just as possible to travel vertically between states of consciousness as it is to move horizontally through Midgard—the world we know.

A nomadic lifestyle forced the tribes to develop a more disciplined political organization than the loose regional clan federations of their homelands. This military democracy apparently evolved into a true monarchy in response to the Roman need to have someone who could swear oaths and sign treaties for the tribes (a situation somewhat analogous to that of the American Indian tribes during the European conquest). As the tribes changed, their god added to his shamanic functions the role of lord of Asgard.

Nonetheless, the cult of Wodan was not nearly so dominant as the events in this book might make it appear. Wodan appears so prominently here because he is the god of the migrations, and the god of magic. A story that focused on farmers or even warriors would give more prominence to other deities.

In a world of transformations, Wodan, the god whose powers transcend tribe or territory, had the power to guide men between the worlds. He is above all a god of knowledge, of Consciousness that knows itself through the different modes of human experience. He points the way to a freedom based on the ability to live with paradox and danger. It is an ecstatic path, not for those who require certainty. Its symbol in the story is the rune wand from the dragon's treasure (referred to only in a single verse of the *Nibelungenlied*) that gives the one who understands its use power over all things.

Some of the uprooted peoples who populate this story were able to follow his way; others sought to reclaim the old earth religion, the cult of the Goddess, which survived among those who tilled the soil and linked the folk to the land. In the story its symbol is the neck ring from the hoard (an arm ring in the *Volsungasaga* and a finger ring in the *Nibelungenlied* and Wagner) that gives the owner wealth and fertility.

The third spiritual force in the situation was Christianity, adopted by the princes to gain Roman support and as a tool for transforming a military democracy into centralized monarchy. In a time of transition it was also a comfort to those who needed simple certainties.

The interaction of these three forces forms the spiritual environment of the story.

The story of Siegfried appears to have had a more northerly and archaic origin among the Franks or Scandinavian tribes than that of the Nibelungs. Under various names, he was the victorious one, the descendent of Wodan who killed a dragon and gained its treasure, then awakened a Valkyrie from her enchanted sleep upon a mountain surrounded by fire.

For me, Sigfrid's kinship with the wolves is the key to his character. The farther back one goes in Germanic history, the more apparent the totemic and shamanic elements in the culture become. Figures on Migrations Period helmet plaques show warriors dressed in the skins of wolves or bears, and the berserker is a stock figure in legend. There are stories of skin-changers who take the forms of a variety of birds and animals in the sagas, and specific creatures are associated with each of the gods.

In Old Norse, *hamr*, the term for one's shape or "skin," is the root for a number of words having to do with shapechanging for military or magical purposes. Such talents seemed to run in certain families, one of the most notable being the Volsungs. But despite their usefulness, in Germanic culture as in many others, the "skinstrong" were viewed with mixed emotions. The wolfskin, in particular, not only identified the berserker, but the outlaw, the "outlier" who had put himself beyond the boundaries of ordinary society. Sigfrid is not stupid, but his upbringing "alienates" him from ordinary human society in a way that neither he nor those with whom he comes in contact really understand.

The character of Brunahild, on the other hand, has traditionally been defined by her identity as a Valkyrie. To understand her, we must transcend the image of the Wagnerian soprano with brass bra and winged helmet. Ancient images were harsher—keening hags who rode wolves with snakes for reins, or their human counterparts, armed women who supported the warriors with their spells. In this as in other kinds of magic, women, believed by the Germanic peoples to have a special aptitude for magic, played a significant role.

Although the Valkyrie training school portrayed in this book is an invention, the gatherings of witches, which according to Grimm took place on various holy mountains in medieval legend, may recall an earlier period in which the Sacred Women of the tribes journeyed there to train their priestesses. The skills that Brunahild learns there are those ascribed to such spiritual practitioners in Tacitus, in the sagas, or by later folklorists such as Grimm. The rune-names used are the Old High Germanic forms of the twenty-four-rune Elder Futhark. A simplified summary of their meanings is given at the end of this essay. Much of the herb lore comes from the leech-books of the Anglo-Saxons. Analysis of the few surviving pagan German spells demonstrates a close enough relationship to justify using the Old English material as models for the spell-craft in this story.

The Walkyriun, like all spiritual specialists, enjoy a mixed reputation in the communities they serve (in Scandinavian folklore, even Lutheran pastors are credited with arcane powers). Like many another religious body, they depend on group cohesion for protection. In such a situation, individual inspiration can only be tolerated when it serves the whole. Brunahild's acceptance among them, already weakened by her origin as a princess of the Huns (a traditional part of the legend), cannot survive what they perceive as her disobedience. One encounters similar conflicts between individual heroism and military discipline in the mythology.

BIBLIOGRAPHY

I find it even more difficult than usual to decide which volumes from the several boxes full of books surrounding my desk should be cited as sources. Perhaps the best solution is simply to list those works that would be most useful to someone who wished to learn more about the various areas touched on in the story.

For general information on Germanic folklore, the most accessible source is Grimm's four-volume *Teutonic Mythology*, published by Dover in trade paperback some years ago. Another excellent and relatively available book is *Gods and Myths of Northern Europe*, by H. R. Ellis-Davidson, published in paperback by Penguin and often reprinted. The history of the Burgundians is covered by Otto Perrin's book *Les Burgondes* (Baconniere). Herwig Wolfram's *History of the Goths* (University of California Press, 1988), although it focuses on a different tribe, has a great deal of ethnographic material that is applicable to the tribes in general.

For herb lore, I drew mainly on *Anglo-Saxon Magic*, a translation and analysis of all the Old English magical material by Dr. G. Storms, most recently published in a Folcroft Library edition in 1975. This book is unfortunately almost impossible to find, although some of its material appeared in *The Old English Herbals,* by Eleanour Sinclair Rohde (Dover, 1971). The most useful history of the runes is given in Edred Thorsson's *Runelore* (Samuel Weiser, Inc., 1987). The British Museum rune book by R. I. Page is also of interest. The best book on smithcraft I have found is *The Complete Bladesmith,* by Jim Hrisoulas (Boulder, Colo.: Paladin Press, 1987).

Among the original sources, Tacitus' book *Germania,* available in a number of translations, the *Volsungasaga,* and *The Elder Edda,* most commonly available in the translation of Lee Hollander published by the University of Texas (1962), are of great interest.

CALENDAR

The month names used here, derived from among those listed by Bede for the Anglo-Saxons and those used by the Norse in Iceland, can be equated with the modern calendar as follows:

Winter Nights festival, first full moon after Autumn Equinox
Oct./Nov.	Blood Moon
Nov./Dec.	Frost Moon
Dec./Jan.	Yule Moon
(The Outmonths)	
Jan./Feb.	Offering Moon
Feb./Mar.	Hretha's Moon
Mar./Apr.	Eostara's Moon

Summerday, first full moon after Spring Equinox
Apr./May	Milk Moon
May/Jun.	Eggtide Moon
Jun./July	Litha Moon
July/Aug.	Haying Moon
Aug./Sept.	Harvest Moon
Sept./Oct.	Winter Moon

THE RUNES

FREYR'S AETT:

RUNE	NAME	SOUND/ LETTER	MEANING
ᚠ.	FEHU	"F"	CATTLE, property, fertility, luck. Rune of Freyr/ Freyja (Fro)

RUNE	NAME	SOUND/ LETTER	MEANING
ᚢ	URUZ	"U"	OX, vitality, physical resources, manifestation of energy
ᚦ	THURISAZ	"Th"	GIANT/THORN, elemental creative energy, defense. Rune of Thor (Donar)
ᚨ	ANSUZ	"A"	GOD-MOUTH, words, inspiration, mental activity. Wodan
ᚱ	RAIDHO	"R"	RIDE, moving and being moved, progress, travel, right action
ᚲ	KAUNAZ	"K"	TORCH, fire, illumination, craftsmanship, purification
ᚷ	GEBO	"G"	GIFT, giving, interaction, exchange of energy
ᚹ	WUNJO	"W"	JOY, weal, happiness, success, joining and fellowship

HAIL'S AETT:

RUNE	NAME	SOUND/ LETTER	MEANING
ᚺ	HAGALAZ	"H"	HAIL, ice-seed, primal matter, harm that may help
ᚾ	NAUDHIZ	"N"	NEED, lack, constraint, necessity, drive to act, destiny
ᛃ	JERA	"Yuh"	YEAR, seasonal cycle, harvest, summer, reward for labor
ᛁ	ISA	"I"	ICE, absolute cold, inertia, stillness, integrity, constraint
ᛇ	EIHWAZ	"Ei"	YEW, Worldtree, paradox, connections, change of state

| | | SOUND/ | |
RUNE	NAME	LETTER	MEANING
ꛕ	*PERTHRO*	"P"	DICECUP or WELL, chance, fate, luck, uncertainty, play
Ψ	*ELHAZ*	"Z"	ELK, protection especially by using natural forces, animals
Ͷ	*SOWILO*	"S"	SUN, solar wheel, guidance, clarification, progress

TYR'S AETT:

↑	*TIWAZ*	"T"	TYR, justice, duty, moral strength, will, control of violence (Tiwaz)
ᛒ	*BERKANO*	"B"	BIRCH, birth, roots, nourishment, feminine, life-passages
M	*EHWAZ*	"E"	HORSE, movement, change, partnership, increase of power
ᛗ	*MANNAZ*	"M"	MAN, mastery, humanity, human inheritance and potential
ᚱ	*LAGUZ*	"L"	LAKE, water, womb, the unconscious, feminine, creativity, flexibility
⋈	*INGWAZ*	"—ng"	YNGVI, fertility, masculine creativity, transformation, transition
ᛞ	*DAGAZ*	"D"	DAY, light, awakening, enlightenment, increase, good
ᛟ	*ODHALAZ*	"O"	ODAL, inheritance, homeland, kindred, relationship

Family Trees

THE WOLSUNGS

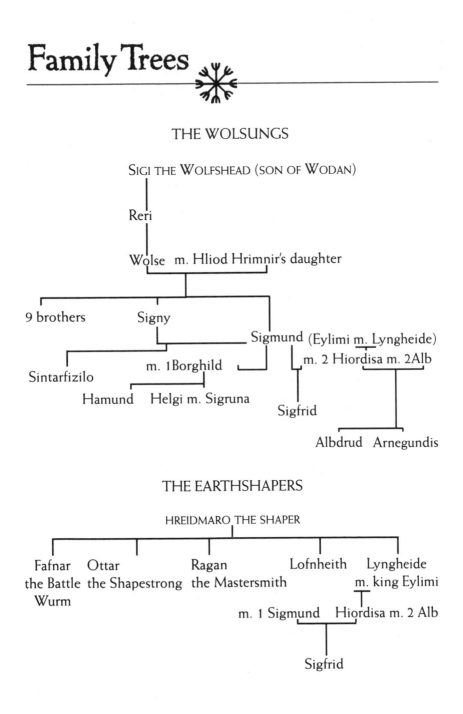

SIGI THE WOLFSHEAD (SON OF WODAN)

Reri

Wolse m. Hliod Hrimnir's daughter

9 brothers   Signy   Sigmund (Eylimi m. Lyngheide)

m. 1Borghild   m. 2 Hiordisa m. 2Alb

Sintarfizilo

Hamund   Helgi m. Sigruna

Sigfrid

Albdrud   Arnegundis

THE EARTHSHAPERS

HREIDMARO THE SHAPER

Fafnar   Ottar   Ragan   Lofnheith   Lyngheide
the Battle   the Shapestrong   the Mastersmith   m. king Eylimi
Wurm

m. 1 Sigmund   Hiordisa m. 2 Alb

Sigfrid

Glossary of Names

TRIBES AND KINDREDS

Aesir—a group of Indo-European function gods
Alamanni—a federation of tribal fragments, especially Swabians, located north of the Main River and east of the Rhine
Alans—a steppe tribe, formerly allied with the Huns, most of which migrated into Gaul in 407 C.E.
Albings—a clan of the Franks living near the North Sea
Angles—a tribe being pushed out of southern Denmark by the Jutes
Burgunds—the Burgundians, an East Germanic tribe living in the area between the Neckar, the Main, and the Rhine
Cherusci—a West German tribe of the first century C.E.
Cimbri—Celto-Germanic tribe which attacked Roman Gaul in 105 B.C.E.
Earthfolk—remnants of pre–Indo-European people dwelling in the forests
Galli, Gauls—Celtic tribes
Gepids—East Germanic tribe allied with the Huns
Greuthingi—Ostrogoths/East Goths
Herminones (Hermunduri)—Thuringians, living in central Germany
Heruli—a tribe living at that time along the North Sea, great seafarers
Hundings—the sons of Hunding, enemies of the Volsungs
Huns (the Hsiong-nu?)—a probably Turkic people from the East,

occupying what is now Hungary, Austria, and the northern plain of
the Danube at the time of this story

Ingaevones (Ingvingar), **Saxons**—descendents of Ingvi son of Mannus
son of Tvisco/Tiu), a tribe living on the coasts of northern Germany

Istaevones, Franks—a strong tribe living in the northwest of Germany
and Holland, divided into the Salic (saltwater) and Ripuarian (riverbank) clans

Jutes—a warlike people, strengthening their hold on Denmark (Jut-
land)

Marcomanni—East Germanic tribe living north of the Danube

Niflungar—"People of the Mists," the Nibelungs, ruling family of the
Burgunds

Romani—the Romans, Rome-folk

Tall Folk—Earthfolk name for Indo-Europeans

Tervingi—Visigoths/West Goths

Teutones—Germano-Celtic tribe that attacked Roman Gaul in B. C. E.

Vanir, Wanes—clan of agricultural, fertility deities allied with the Aesir

Walkyriun—(Valkyries), a college of priestesses living in the Taunus

Wolsungs (Volsungs), descendents of Wolse and Sigi, a line of heroes

PEOPLE

(CAPITALS indicate living characters who take an active part in the
story; a * indicates a historical figure; = indicates the form of the
name most familiar in legend)

*****Flavius AETIUS**, a Roman, former Hun hostage and ally of Attila

Adelburga, a student of the Walkyriun, one of Brunahild's "Nine"

Adolfus, a king of the Visigoths

*****Airmanareik** (Ermanaric, third-century king of the Goths, defeated
by the invading Huns)

*****Alaric** (king of the Visigoths)

ALB (= Alf), oldest son of king Hiloperic, later king of the Albings,
second husband of Hiordisa and Sigfrid's stepfather

ALBALD, Alb's brother, Sigfrid's enemy

ALBDRUD and **ARNEGUNDIS**, daughters of Hiordisa and Alb, Sigfrid's half-sisters

Albodisa, assumed ancestress of the Albings

Andvari, an earth elemental who in pike shape guarded the Niblung
treasure

*****ATTILA** "little father," son of Mundzuk, warleader of his clan

Baldur (= Baldr), the Beautiful, son of Wodan and Fricca

*Balimber son of Uldin, Hun chieftain who defeated Airmanareik

BERTRIUD (= Beckhild/Bertrut) Bladarda's older daughter, fosterer of Brunahild

Brettad, a Marcomanni chieftain

BRUNAHILD, Bladarda's younger daughter, who becomes a Walkyrja

*Bladarda (= Budli), son of Mundzuk, prince of the Acatiri Huns

Dag, Hogni's son, killer of Helgi Sigmundson and brother of Sigruna

Domfrada, a student of the Walkyriun

Donar (= Thor), the thunderer, god of storms and strength

Donarhild, a student of the Walkyriun, one of Brunahild's "Nine"

Drostagnos, headman of the Gallic village of Halle

Dwalin, ancestor of dwarfs; his daughters are the Norns who decide the wyrd of the Earthfolk

Eberwald, a man of Alb's houseguard

Eormanna, a student of the Walkyriun in Brunahild's "Nine"

Erda, Earth goddess

Eylimi, father of Hiordisa, grandfather of Sigfrid

Eyolf, a son of Hunding, killed by Sigfrid

FAFNAR (= Fafnir), son of Hreidmaro, the battle-wurm, a berserker and shaman who killed his father for Andvari's treasure

Farmamann, a trader whose body is used by Wodan

Fricca (= Frigg), the weaver of fate, wife of Wodan

Fridigund, a student of the Walkyriun in Brunahild's "Nine"

Fro (= Freyr), god of luck and fertility, brother/lover of Froja

Frodi, a demigod, considered an aspect of Fro

Froja (= Freyja), dis of the Vanir, goddess of love and fertility

FROJAVIGIS, Burgund student of the Walkyriun, one of Brunahild's "Nine"

GALEMBURGIS of the Alamanni, a student of the Walkyriun, one of Brunahild's "Nine," her enemy

Gefion, "the Giver," goddess who receives the souls of maidens

GEIRROD, son of an Albing clan chief, Sigfrid's youthful enemy

*GIBICHO (= Gjiuki/Gibich), chieftain of the Niflungar, *hendinos* (high king) of the Burgunds

Goldmad (= Gullveig), usually considered an aspect of Froja

*GODOMAR, "Godo," Burgund prince, Gundohar's brother

GOLLA, a warmistress of the Walkyriun, Randgrid's lover

*GISLAHAR (= Giselher), Gundohar's youngest brother

GRIMAHILD (= Grimhild, Kriemhild the elder), Burgund queen, mother of Gundohar, Godomar, Gudrun, and Gislahar

*GUNDOHAR (= Gunther/Gunnar), oldest son of Kipicho, later, king of the Burgunds

GUDRUN (= Gutrune/Kriemhild), daughter of Gibicho, Gundohar's sister

Hadugera, a senior Walkyrja

HAGANO (= Hogni/Hagen), Grimahild's son by a man of the earthfolk

Hardomann, son of Hardobert, an Alamanni chieftain living on the Rhine

HEIMAR (= Heimir), a Marcomanni chieftain, husband of Bertriud and foster-father to Brunahild

Helgi, Sigmund's son by Borghild, lover of the Walkyrja Sigruna, killed before Sigfrid's birth by the Hundings

Hella, Loki's daughter, queen of the Underworld

HELMBARI, an old warrior whose body is used by Wodan

HEMING, a follower of Hlodomar, son of Hunding, and Sigfrid's enemy

HERIBARD, a Burgund chieftain and counselor

HERIMOD, a man of Alb's houseguard

*Hermundurus (Arminius, first-century leader of Cherusci and Hermunduri against the Romans)

HIORDISA (= Hjordis), daughter of Eylimi and Lyngheide, widow of Sigmund the Wolsung and mother of Sigfrid

Hiorvard, father of Helgi in his first incarnation

HILOPERIC (= Hjalprek), king of the Albings, foster-grandfather to Sigfrid

HLODOMAR, younger brother of Hiloperic, a leader of mercenaries

Hludana, goddess of the hearth

HLUTGARD, leader of the Walkyriun

Holda, a goddess of women's crafts, especially spinning

*Honorius, emperor of the West, 395–423

Hreidmaro the Shaper (= Hreidmar the dwarf), a shaman of the Earthfolk, father of Fafnar, Ottar, and Ragan

HRODLIND, herbmistress of the Walkyriun

HULD, a wisewoman of the Walkyriun

Hunding, a king in the north, killed by Helgi

Ingvio (= Ingvi), aspect of Fro, ancestor of the Ingviones (Franks)

Iscio, ancestor of the Iscaevones

Irmino, ancestor of the Herminones

*Jovin, attempted to usurp the Empire of West, 412

*Julian, Roman emperor, 361–363, who tried to restore paganism
*Kharaton, overking of the Huns
Landbald, an Alamanni leader
LIUDEGAR and LIUDEGAST, Alamanni chieftains
Liudwif, a student of the Walkyriun, one of Brunahild's "Nine"
Loki, the trickster, a *Jotun* (usually) allied with the gods
Lyngheide, daughter of Hreidmaro, wife of Eylimi, and mother of
    Hiordisa
Lyngvi, a son of Hunding who killed Sigmund
*Marcus Aurelius, emperor 161–180, Stoic philosopher
*Mundzuk (= Mundjouk), a prince of the Huns, brother of Oktar,
    father of Bladarda
Muspel's sons (fire elementals)
Nando, an Alamanni leader
Nanduhild, a student of the Walkyriun
*Octa, called Hengest, an Anglian *"wrecce,"* follower of Hlodomar, a
    survivor of the battle at Finnesburg who later goes to Britain
*Oktar, king of the western Huns
Ordwini, Dragobald's son (= Ortwin of Metz), a Burgund chieftain
Orgelmir (= Ymir), primal being from whose body the world was
    made
Ostrofrid, lawspeaker (*sinista*) of the Burgunds
Ottar, son of Hreidmaro, shapestrong as an otter, killed by the priests
    of Wodan; his weregild is Andvari's treasure
PERCHTA, servant of Hiordisa
Father Priscus, a Catholic priest in Gundohar's household
RAGAN (= Regin), son of Hreidmaro, mastersmith of the Earthfolk,
    Sigfrid's fosterer
RAGANLEOB, a Walkyrja, a few years ahead of Brunahild
RAGNARIS, son of Kursik, a Hun/Goth warrior, one of Attila's cap-
    tains
RANDGRID, warmistress of the Walkyriun
Reri the Great, son of Sigi, an ancestor of Sigfrid
Ricihild, a student of the Walkyriun, one of Brunahild's "Nine"
*Ruga, (= Rugilo), king of the eastern Huns
Ruodpercht, a man of Alb's household
Saxwalo, an Alamanni leader
Father Severin, an Arian priest in Gundohar's household
SIGDRIFA, Brunahild's magical name as a Walkyrja
Siggeir, the king who married Signy and murdered her family
SIGFRID, son of Sigmund and Hiordisa

Sigi the Wolfshead, son of Wodan, ancestor of Sigfrid

Sigmund son of Wolse, the Skinwalker, Sigfrid's father, killed by the sons of Hunding

Signy, daughter of Wolse, wife of Siggeir

Sigruna, daughter of Hogni, a Valkyrie, wife of Helgi Sigmundson

Sindald (= Sindold), a Burgund chieftain

Singereck, a king of the Visigoths

Sintarfizilo (= Sinfjotli), son of Sigmund by his sister, Signy

Sleipnir, Wodan's eight-legged horse

*Stilicho, Roman general of Gothic origin who drove back the Vandals, executed 408

Sueva (= Svava), a Valkyrie, lover of Helgi in his first incarnation

Surt, a Jotun, ruler of Muspelheim

SVALA, the swallow, a Burgund student of the Walkyriun, Brunahild's friend

Swanborg, a senior Walkyrja

Tiw (= Tyr), god of war and justice

THRUDRUN, runemistress of the Walkyriun

*Turgun, a servant of Attila

*Uldin, first known king of Huns

Unald (= Hunold), a Burgund chieftain

Unna, a young student of the Walkyriun

Uote, ancestress of the Niflungar

Walburga, another name for the earth goddess, worshipped on May Eve

*Wallia, king of the Vandals

Werinhar, a man of Alb's houseguard

WIELDRUD, the midwife of the Walkyriun

Wodan (= Odin/Wotan), lord of the Aesir, worldwalker, god of wordcraft and warcraft and magic, also called High One, War Father, Victory Father, Host Father, Bale-worker, appears as Farmamann and Helmbari

Wolse, a god of fertility in the eastern lands

Wolse (= Volsung) the fruitful, son of Reri, father of Sigmund

Wolund (= Volund, Wayland Smith), patron of smithcraft

Ygg (Norse), the Terrible One, a wrathful aspect of Wodan

PLACES AND NATURAL FEATURES

Waters:

Albis—Elbe river

Danu, Danuvius—the Danube
Maeotis—Sea of Azov
Moenus—the Main river
Nicer—the Neckar
Rhenus—the Rhine
Scythian Sea—the Black or Euxine Sea
Sig—Sieg river
Visurgis—the Weser river

Mountains and Forests:
the **Taunus**—Hochtaunus, above Frankfurt
    High One's Hill—Altkönig, near Königstein
    Brunahild's Rock—Brunhildestein, near the Grosser Feldberg, Taunus
Broken Mountain—the Brocken, Harz Mountains
Holy Hill—Heidelberg
Forest of the Teutones—Teutobergerwald
    Ragan's Forge—in the Teutobergerwald near Horn
    Pillar Stones—Externsteine, in the Teutobergerwald, near Horn
Wurm Fell—the Drachenfels, above Königswinter on the Rhine
Yggdrasil—(Norse) "The steed of Ygg," the Worldtree

Towns and Dwellings:
Borbetomagus—Worms
Colonia Agrippina—Köln/Cologne
Constantinopolis, Mundberg—Istanbul
Halle—Schwäbisch Hall
Hiloperic's Hold—isle in the marshes near Oldenburg
Mogontiacum—Mainz
Rome—capital of the empire
Walhall—Hall of the Slain, Wodan's hold in Asgard
Ulpia Traiana—Xanten

Geographical Divisions:
Asgard—home of the gods
Belgica Secunda—approximately the Low Countries
Britannia—Great Britain
Germania Prima—lands just west of Rhine, approximately Koblenz to Basel
Germania Secunda—lands just west of Rhine, North Sea to Koblenz
Iberia—Spain

Hel—the Underworld
Midgard, Middle Earth—the world of men
Muspelheim—the world of elemental fire
Noricum—Roman lands south of Danube, Germany
Pannonia—Roman lands west of the Danube in Hungary
Scandzia—southern Scandinavia
Ultima Thule—anything north of Scotland

TERMS

alf, alfar/elves—(Germanic) male ancestral spirits worshipped as demigods
aurochs—great wild ox of northern Europe, now extinct
bard—professional poet and singer of tales
beck—(Germanic)—creek, small stream
bilwisse (German)—a wild man of the woods
Brisingamen—Froja's necklace
comitatus (Latin)—chieftain's personal bodyguard of sworn men
dis, disir/idisi (Germanic)—female ancestral spirits, guardians of families
Draupnir—a magic ring that produced nine rings like itself every ninth
  night
duergar (Germanic)—dwarfs
Einherior (Germanic)—the heroes who dwell in Wodan's hall
etins (Anglian)—"giants," mighty elemental powers
fara, faraman (Burgund)—warriors who owe battle-service to their lord
  (= the Anglo-Saxon *fyrd*)
feoderati (Latin)—barbarian tribes who have sworn oaths of alliance
  with Rome in exchange for lands within the Empire
fibula (Latin)—a long brooch like a decorated safety pin
ger (Hun)—a round dwelling like a yurt
Gundwurm (Burgund)—"battle-worm," dragon standard
Gungnir—Wodan's spear
hendinos (Burgund)—high king, hegemon
jotun, jotnar (pl.) (Germanic)—"giants," mighty elemental powers
kam (Hun)—shaman
khan (Hun)—noble lord, prince
khatun (Hun)—noble lady, princess; "*tänri khatun*" = heavenly lady
lager (Germanic)—circle of wagons
limes—"limits," borders of Roman Empire in Germany
lochagos (Greek/Hun)—a "notable man" among the Huns

muspel-wind—the *fön*, a hot wind from the south that brings madness, like the "Santa Ana"

nixie (Germanic)—waterspirit

Norns—spirit women who fortell the fates of the newborn; "the Norns," guardians of the Well of Wyrd

sagum (Latin)—rectangular cloak of heavy wool

sinista (Burgund)—lawspeaker, chief counselor

spangenhelm—Iron-age round helm with a nasal and jointed side and back pieces

spatha—(Latin) long Roman cavalry sword

su tzur (Hun)—captain of troops

thrall—a born slave or bondslave

thurs—an elemental being of giant-kin, often monstrous

troll, troll-wife—one of the wild powers, can appear fair or foul

Walkyrja—(Germanic) "Chooser of the Slain," an initiate of the Walkyriun

warg (Anglian *wearg*)—"wolf," outlaw, lawless wolves

Well of Wyrd—Norns' well at roots of Worldtree

Well of Mimir—at roots of Worldtree, holds Wodan's left eye

weregild (Germanic)—the fine or settlement paid to the kin of a victim of murder, or for other crimes

wisent—European forest bison

wrecce—(Anglian) a wandering warrior, a lordless man, roughly equivalent to the Japanese *"ronin"*

wurm—European earth dragon

wyrd—(Germanic) "weird," fate or destiny that flows from the inner compulsions of origins and character